GARY THOMPSON
ALL-AMERICAN

By Chuck Offenburger

"What every man wishes he'd been,
what every boy wanted to be."

—John Crawford, Iowa State teammate of Gary Thompson

Foreword

Gary Thompson's longtime broadcast partner, network TV play-by-play man Jay Randolph, says Thompson's story "is an inspiration to anyone who truly loves the game."

St. Louis, Missouri

IT WAS March 1, 2005, a beautiful day as I landed in Des Moines, Iowa. I noted the continuing improvements in the airport and the roads as I headed toward Ames.

This was a journey I had made many times in the 1970s and '80s. Gary Thompson and I had teamed up to broadcast Big Eight Conference basketball for 19 seasons on TV throughout a vast region that started along the Mississippi River in Missouri and went west to Colorado and stretched from Iowa and Nebraska south to Oklahoma.

This trip would be different because it was Gary's last game. The Iowa State legend known as the "Roland Rocket" had called me during the winter to tell me the Missouri-Iowa State game at Hilton Coliseum would be his last telecast.

I could tell from the sound of his voice it had been a tough decision, but he had made up his mind to go up in the stands and watch the games with his wonderful wife Jan and his children and grandchildren. Bob Helmers, a longtime TV executive and former Big Eight basketball TV crew member, phoned me in early February asking if I would like to be reunited with Gary for his final game. Our friend Dave Armstrong, the number one announcer on what was, now, the Big Twelve Conference TV package, had made the suggestion. I said, "Yes, yes, yes."

As I drove toward Ames on Interstate Highway 35, so many warm memories flooded my mind. I recalled when talented Merle Harmon was asked to leave the Big Eight to do the Big Ten. I was tapped to replace Harmon on the Big Eight and work with Thompson.

John Crowe from Houston was our wonderful producer and director. The chemistry between the three of us was magical. John would referee the continuing argument between us—Gary always maintained that as the play-by-play man, I was more important to the broadcast, and I would contend that the audience really was more interested in what he had to say as a former All-

American player and now a game analyst.

I remember well the season when Crowe and I brought our sons with us for a game in Ames. It snowed big time, and the Crowe boys had never seen snow. What a time they had. There was a pizza party by the motel's indoor pool, and my son Brian entertained with a magic show.

There were so many memorable nights with sports information directors and coaches and athletic directors and crew members.

Over the years there would be special restaurants where we would gather. The Flagstaff House Restaurant, at 6,000 feet above Boulder, where we created the "Brandy Randolph"…the Haunted House, in Oklahoma City, once the hangout of Bonnie and Clyde…Misty's, in Lincoln…the Steak Deburgo at Palmas, in Ames…Keck's, about 30 miles outside Manhattan on a back road to Topeka, for great steaks…the Celestial, in Stillwater.

It was special that Norm Stewart was also in Ames for Gary's last broadcast. The former Missouri coach was doing color commentary on the Tiger telecast. He joined us at a coffee group the morning of the game. His stories were priceless. Like so many of the coaches we worked with, Stewart had been a genuine friend.

After nearly 15 years, working with Gary again was a joy. There was a wonderful tribute at halftime, and Iowa State won the game.

Later, there was a celebration as friends and family looked out on Ames from a new club in a high-rise building. Imagine that, a high-rise in Ames.

In my 50 years of sports broadcasting, working with Gary Thompson on Big Eight basketball was a special career highlight. His story is an inspiration to anyone who truly loves the game: The undersized crew-cut kid who shot his way to All-American honors, with dedication to detail later as a coach and TV analyst.

Gary Thompson has touched so many people over the years with his work ethic and with his keen awareness and understanding.

The opportunity to be at his side for so many TV basketball games has only reinforced what I have always known—the analyst is the star.

—*Jay Randolph*

Author: Chuck Offenburger
Cover Designer: Mark Marturello
Layout/Designer: Maribeth Fleischmann
Copy Editor: Roy Reiman
Production Coordinator: Brian Sienko
Print Coordinator: Dale Miller

Detailed credits in the back of the book.

©2008 Hexagon Grandhaven Group, 115 S. 84th St., Milwaukee WI 53214

International Standard Book Number: 978-0-615-23038-2
Library of Congress Control Number: 2008939401
All Rights Reserved. Printed in U.S.A.

For additional copies of this book, write:
Our Iowa, 2501 North Loop Drive, Ames IA 50010
Price: $19.95 (plus $3.95 shipping & handling; or just $4.95 total s&h for two or more copies). Make checks payable to *Our Iowa*.

FAST BREAK PREVIEW
Full details on these photos and more in pages ahead.

GROWING UP in Roland.

BEGINNING a career as a Roland Rocket.

ALREADY FLINGING in from all angles.

MAKING TEAM as a freshman (far right).

BECOMING a hometown hero later in life.

APPEARING on Ed Sullivan Show...

INTERVIEWING coaches...

GETTING KEYS for first good car from Ames dealer...

GETTING MARRIED to his high school sweetheart...

PLAYING against Wilt (left) and named to All-American first team (above).

ACHIEVING All-American in baseball…

MEETING lots of great friends…

GETTING STARTED broadcasting…

EARNING RESPECT of coaches…

BEING head coach of Phillips 66ers (upper left) and handling color commentary on TV for 34 years.

RECIPIENTS of many awards over the years.

SHOWING license plate loyalty.

RECOGNITION of long support for Iowa State University.

PROUD FAMILY—two sons and a daughter.

CYCLONE FANS say thanks in a big way on a special night at Hilton Coliseum.

Table of Contents

Foreword, by Jay Randolph 2
1. "Ga-ry Thomp-son! Ga-ry Thomp-son!" 10
2. Roland Kept Right on Rolling 23
3. Roots in Roland – and in Sports 29
4. Roland Rockets Rise to Basketball Fame 44
5. Growing Into That Baseball Uniform 87
6. Roland Experiences Had Lifetime Effect 92
7. This High School Romance Worked 97
8. Life's Different at Iowa State 107
9. New Era for Iowa State Basketball 120
10. Sweetest Time to Be a Cyclone! 140
11. Helping Cyclones to Baseball Glory 160
12. Stay Amateur? Or Go Pro? 168
13. Golden Era for Phillips and 66ers 172
14. Playing Days Over, Back to Iowa 188
15. Coach Thompson and the Phillips 66ers 196
16. An All-American Turned Entrepreneur 210
17. Thompson Oil Grows and Diversifies 225
18. Getting His Start in Broadcasting 232
19. Hit Bigtime in Network TV 238
20. In the Eye of Some Iowa State Storms 256
21. Neat Way to Bow Out of Broadcasting 285
22. Life Today for Gary and Janet 298
23. The Extended Thompson Family Today 305
24. A Favorite ISU Alum Stays Involved 313
25. Gary's a Real "Grinder" at Golf 324
26. Gary and Janet Look Back at Their Lives 332
27. What Others Say About Gary Thompson 338

Epilogue, by Gary Thompson 342

Chapter 1

"Ga-ry Thomp-son! Ga-ry Thomp-son!"

"GOT a basketball I can use for a few minutes?"

It was not a question that State Gym equipment cage manager Jerry Rupert often gets from 70-year-old men, like the one who was suddenly standing in front of him at Iowa State University. It was early afternoon on a cold December day in 2005, and it was unusually quiet in the historic old gym, which has served basketball players, other athletes and fitness enthusiasts since 1913.

"Sure," said Rupert, his face lighting up. He grabbed a ball from an adjacent bin, squeezed it once to test the air pressure, bounced it once, then handed it across the counter. "That one ought to work."

"Do I need to sign something?" the visitor asked.

"Oh, no," said Rupert. "I know who *you* are!"

Indeed. Half a century after he was a great Cyclone player, nearly everybody at Iowa State—and for that matter, most people around the whole state of Iowa—still know who Gary Thompson is.

Back up the stairs the two of us went, and out into the classic old basketball arena itself. Steel rafters are overhead, arched windows grace the brick walls. A running track is hung at balcony-level along the sidewalls. Somebody ought to make a movie here, I say.

Thompson and I were the only people on the gleaming wood floor. A female jogger up on the track, wearing earphones, never gave us a second look.

Silly as it seems, I had told him, I want to see you on a basketball floor. I had seen old black-and-white film clips of him in action. I had read hundreds of old newspaper and magazine stories describing his play. But, I told him, I want to see you dribble down the floor like you once did.

A walk is fine, no running needed. I want to see you stop dribbling at about the same spot where you would have pulled up back then. I want to hear you tell me what you would have done with the ball, and see how far out from the basket you were when you would take a shot. Even if it's in slow-motion compared to how you once played, I said, I want to see it.

We were standing then at the free throw line on the west end of the floor.

"Well, O.K.," he said, with a chuckle. "Let me get rid of my coat here." He discarded his leather winter jacket over near the gym door, came walking back to me wearing a yellow sweater, red plaid sport shirt, khakis and street shoes.

"You know, I haven't really played any since 1995," he said. "I haven't even shot recently. I've never been one to push that on my kids or grandkids—to get out and play basketball together. I've always let them ask me, if they want me to shoot around with them. My own kids used to ask some, but the grandkids now must not think that Grandpa could play very well, because they don't ask me much anymore."

He chuckled again.

Then it was time for the demonstration. Even though it had been a long time since he'd done anything like this, Gary Thompson was going to take it seriously. He has always taken his basketball seriously.

He spit on both hands, "to get a better grip on the ball," he explained. Then he rubbed them together, bounced the ball forcefully once and said, "Let's say I'd get the pass in-bounds, and I'd start up the floor, like this." He dribbled east on an imaginary line, just to the right of the middle of the floor. He even did a little skip as he dribbled, crossing the half-court line, looking left and right, then pulling up about two feet outside the top of the free throw circle.

"I might have already made a pass to somebody else by the time I got here," he said. "Or if not, then I'd take another look inside from here, then probably pass to somebody over on the wing," and he threw me the ball. "Then I might have gotten a quick pass back." I took the cue and threw him the ball.

And?

"I'd probably put up a jump shot, from about right here," he said, taking a quick step right, then launching a 19-footer.

It was more of a shot-jump than a jump-shot but, hey, give the guy a break for his age. Plus, he was wearing street clothes and street shoes.

And?

He buried it! His first shot in ages, and it was nothing but net! Swish!

"Like that!" he said when the net popped, and he laughed out loud.

This *was* like a movie.

I swear the head of that female jogger with the earphones snapped around to look our way.

What followed was 20 minutes of Basketball 101 with Gary Thompson, who knows as much about the game as anyone on Earth. He showed me the shot he used in high school in Roland, Iowa, "the knee-up one-hander." He told me he "was a good hooker," and then proved it by tossing in two consecutive hook shots 8 to 10 feet from the basket. He talked about the importance of learning to pivot, using both forward and reverse pivots. He'd use those while faking a pass in one direction, thus opening up a passing lane to a teammate cutting in the opposite direction.

Other times he would fake a drive to set up a jump shot, or fake a shot to set up a drive to the basket. "Faking is really important on offense," he said, "and it's just as important on defense. I always tried to use defensive fakes to help me guide the offensive player in the direction I wanted him to go. I wanted him to react to my fakes rather than me waiting to react to his play. I felt that gave me a definite advantage playing defense."

Since he played college ball at about 5 ft. 10 in., "I had to learn to use a lot of fakes and deception when I would attack the basket inside against the bigger players," he said. "You learn to go up in the air for a lay-up, show the ball, then hang and reverse the ball off the other side of the board with some spin." He dribbled in under the basket and did just that, even if he didn't really hang in the air this time.

How about shooting from outside? That was his specialty, after all.

"First, I always tried to get 'squared up' to the basket," he said. "And then it was relying on what you were taught and practiced every day—keep the elbow in, keep your eyes on the front of the rim, you release the ball, keep your eyes on that rim and not on the arc of the shot, following through with the flip of the wrist. You're visualizing from the time you set yourself up for the shot until the final follow-through."

"Gary had become an Iowa legend before he was old enough to drive…"

But what I was visualizing there in State Gym was something more than a nice jump shot, or one of those old-fashioned "knee-up one-handers."

I was seeing one very happy older man there—dribbling, pivoting, faking, spinning, shooting. Time not only stopped for 20 minutes, it ran backward for five decades.

It was wonderful to see and sense that.

THE GARY THOMPSON STORY is much more than one man's sports reverie.

It is a story shaped by a spartan boyhood during World War II. It bloomed in the 1950s, a very nostalgic time for small towns and small high schools in rural Iowa. It was enhanced in the affluence that has stretched from the 1960s to our modern day, a time when America has gone nuts over basketball and television—and Gary Thompson has been a prime player in both. Along the way, he got into the oil business when it was booming. And he has lived a love story and family life as solid as it is idyllic.

Hundreds of people are directly involved in this one man's story, tens of thousands more indirectly.

One of the latter is Robert James Waller, who knows a few things about what makes a good story, and he says the Thompson story indeed is one.

That's because Waller, author of the best-selling novel "Bridges of Madison County," also knows about basketball and small Iowa towns. Waller was a star in the late 1950s and early '60s for the Rockford Rohawks in north central Iowa. He began his college career with the University of Iowa Hawkeyes, but transferred to then-Iowa State Teachers College in Cedar Falls and became a star for the Panthers. He followed a similar path to what Thompson had blazed four years earlier with the Roland Rockets and then the Cyclones at Iowa State.

"Gary Thompson," Waller said, after I told him I was doing this book, "he of the crewcut, a slayer of giants. What a hero he was. I'm glad to hear his life has been a good one."

Yes, life has treated Thompson well, as this overview will tell you.

Thompson knows how blessed he has been. The fact that he has almost always understood that—and that he has been genuine in his gratitude for all he got—makes him all the more enjoyable to be around.

"When I look around at all this stuff," he said, as we walked into his memorabilia-filled office in the basement of the Thompson home in northwest Ames, "I'm kind of embarrassed. I really wasn't interested in having all this up, but Janet and the kids said we should.

"You know what the most important thing to me about it is? The people. It's the people that I've gotten to know because of sports and then the broadcasting and business, too. I've been so fortunate that way. There have been a lot of times when I've been sitting, visiting with somebody who's really interesting, or I'm getting to go some great place, when it hits me—'I'm just a kid from Roland, Iowa. What am I doing here?' "

That's one of his most endearing qualities.

He and his brother DeLon, seven years younger than Gary and also an excellent athlete, were raised to keep things in perspective. Well, actually, their mother Abbie Thompson made it even plainer than that.

"I think the first mention I ever got in an out-of-town newspaper for something I did in sports was when I was a freshman in high school and we played a second-team game in our county seat town of Nevada," Gary said. "A few days later, the Nevada Evening Journal had a sports item that called me 'a little kid you want to watch in the future.' I was kind of excited about that, but when my mother saw it, the first thing she said to me was, 'Don't you even think about getting the big head!' "

So he didn't.

But he sure could have.

In March, 1951, the Roland Rockets from the small central Iowa farm town knocked off mighty Waterloo West 43-40 in a quarterfinals game in the Iowa boys' high school state basketball tournament, which was played then in the mammoth fieldhouse at the University of Iowa in Iowa City. Of the hundreds of basketball games Gary Thompson played during his whole extended career, "that game against Waterloo West may have been the most important," he says now. "Almost all the opportunities that came my way later in life happened because of what got started in that one game."

It was a shocking upset. *Des Moines Register* sportswriter Bert McGrane wrote that "a majority of 14,000 throats set up a sustained roar that fairly rattled the fieldhouse rafters." In a "tingling thriller," McGrane continued, the Roland Rockets had become "the new Cinderella team of Iowa high school basketball."

There was a reason, he noted, why Waterloo West had led 18-10 in the first quarter, but only scored nine points in the third and fourth quarters combined.

"Little Gary Thompson, a 15-year-old sophomore who measures just 5 ft. 6 in. in height, was fairly taking the breath of the onlookers with his exploits," McGrane reported. "He hounded the opposition. He stole the ball from dribblers and captured rebounds in spite of his lack of height. And he pitched in baskets from anywhere."

And talk about being prophetic, check this line from McGrane: "*Thompson, a lad seemingly destined for stardom, caught the fancy of the crowd, and the crowd got on the Roland bandwagon.*"

Heck, stardom was confirmed before that weekend was over.

In the semifinals, Thompson's playmaking helped Roland to another stunning upset, 46-37, over Des Moines East, the tallest team in the tournament.

That set up a championship game on Saturday night between little Roland and mighty Davenport High School. Consider the contrast:

Roland had 73 students in high school, 40 of them boys, and the Rockets were playing in their first state tournament. Davenport High, then the only public high school in that eastern Iowa city, had 2,710 students—1,335 of them boys—and the Blue Devils were playing in their 15th state tournament.

Despite the apparent mismatch, Thompson fired the Rockets to an amazing 35-31 lead after three quarters. Sportswriter McGrane reported that nearly all of the 16,127 in the fieldhouse were screaming, "Let's go Roland! Let's go Roland!" And, "Beat Davenpo-ORT! Beat Davenpo-ORT!"

The Rockets responded.

"Roland, the storybook team from the small school in Story County, fought Davenport's Blue Devils off their feet for 29 of the 32 minutes," McGrane wrote.

But then Davenport "came on with a ruthless sweep that piled up nine points in 90 seconds of that last crucial three-minute period" for a 50-40 victory.

Despite the loss in the championship game, Roland's Gary Thompson had become a genuine Iowa sports legend—before he was old enough to drive.

"He's going to be a great one," his coach Overton M. "Buck" Cheadle told the sportswriters.

And when the boys got back to Roland, Thompson discovered he'd been receiving 25 or more letters per day from all over Iowa.

The state's fans stayed on the Roland bandwagon for his junior and senior years, too, which included return trips to the state tournaments in both basketball and baseball.

In the four seasons of Thompson's 1949-'53 high school basketball career, he and his talented Rocket teammates rang up records of 29-2, 35-1, 31-3 and 32-2. Five of those eight losses happened in the one-class state tournaments. In baseball, during his sophomore, junior and senior years, the team was 51-7.

He says now that one of the things he enjoys most, looking back on all that, "is how much fun Roland people had with it."

Here were all those Norwegian Lutherans, often chanting *"Me-ska-vinna!"* in the language of their motherland, translating it for those who asked as, "We shall win!" Meanwhile, their leader Coach Cheadle, a Chickasaw Indian originally from Oklahoma, would jubilantly use a tribal "war whoop" in the dressing room after particularly big victories: *"Eeeeyi, yee, yee, yee!"*

Thompson was a three-year All-State first team selection in basketball, in which he set the career and single season state scoring records and in which he averaged 25 points per game as a senior. There was no All-State baseball team picked then, but he would have been on one, because he pitched six no-hitters and had a career batting average of .450. For crying out loud, he was even a two-time state champion in horseshoes at the Iowa State Fair—"but just in the junior division," he now protests.

"He was also the two-time state champion in horseshoes!"

THE BEST WAS YET TO COME, when Thompson enrolled at Iowa State College, as it was known then.

Playing from 1953-'57, he led the Cyclones out of the basketball wilderness to rankings in the nation's Top Ten. It was a time when he and other players moved from using one-handed set shots to flying jump shots, and Thompson was as much a deadeye with the new shot as he'd been with the old.

There was an even more profound change happening in the college game. Iowa State and other Big Seven schools for the first time began recruiting African American basketball players. And the white kid from little Roland was one of the players quickest to step up in defense of his black teammate John Crawford, who'd come from the Bronx in New York City, when Crawford was subjected to occasional taunting or other discrimination around the college games.

Thompson was recruited by Cyclone coach Clayton "Chick" Sutherland, but he says he remembers "almost no real recruiting, like we think about today. I never really gave much thought to going anywhere but Iowa State."

His ties there were strong. His father Maurice Thompson was already working as a carpenter at the college. His steady girlfriend since high school, Janet Sydnes, who had grown up in nearby Huxley, was working on the campus as a secretary for the Iowa State Extension Service at Morrill Hall. Basketball coach Sutherland spent summers managing the semi-pro baseball team at Mason City, and when Gary played for him there after his senior year at Roland, the manager clinched an Iowa State basketball commitment from the young guy.

"We all knew about Gary Thompson from everything he'd done in the high school state tournaments," said Howard Johnson, now retired in Shenandoah, Iowa, a senior on the Cyclone team in 1953-'54 when Gary began his freshman year. "I was sorry I was never going to get to play on the same team with him, since freshmen weren't eligible for varsity back then.

"But I think my mother was even sorrier about that," Johnson continued. "She *adored* Gary Thompson. I remember my folks coming to Ames to see me play one game, and there was a reception for all the players and their parents. We were in there, and when I saw Gary walk in with his parents, I said, 'Mom, there's Gary Thompson right over there.' She let out kind of a shriek and went running right over to meet him. It was one of the most exciting moments of her life. I'll tell you, she was much more excited about meeting Gary Thompson than she was about watching me play another basketball game."

Sutherland gave up the Cyclone basketball job that spring and was succeeded as coach by Bill Strannigan, at the same time Gary started his varsity career. He became an immediate starter in a line-up with four seniors, Stan Frahm, Larry Wetter, Don DeKoster and Chuck Duncan. Others who became key players were Arnie Gaarde, Gerald Sandbulte, Chuck Vogt, Don Medsker, Lyle Frahm and Crawford.

During Thompson's three years on the varsity, the teams went 11-10, 18-5 and 16-7. It was an amazing turn-around for a program that had struggled through six consecutive losing seasons prior to Strannigan taking over.

What is most remembered about that generation of Cyclones are their epic battles with perennial power Kansas.

"We were 5-4 against Kansas during my career," Thompson now says proudly.

During the 1955-'56 season, a win over Kansas propelled the Cyclones to the Big Seven Conference Pre-Season Tournament championship in Kansas

City, between Christmas and New Year's. That led to what today is still one of Thompson's most prized pieces of memorabilia—a personal letter from the great Kansas coach Forrest C. "Phog" Allen. That name is as golden in basketball's history as that of the game's founder James Naismith and the legends Adolph Rupp of Kentucky and John Wooden of UCLA.

Early in January, the Cyclones had to play on the Jayhawks' home floor in Lawrence. Kansas won that one, and Allen referred to it in beginning his January 26, 1956, letter:

> Dear Gary,
>
> Ever since our basketball game here in Lawrence, I have wanted to sit down and write you to tell you how very much we appreciated your sportsmanship in coming up and shaking hands after the tough battle we had here at the fieldhouse. I also remember your doing it after we were fortunate in defeating you at Ames last year.
>
> There are not many fellows who, as players, do this thing after a heated battle, and I want to commend you on your fine attitude in being able to take yourself in hand and extend the hand of congratulations during a trying incident.
>
> I have always been most favorably impressed with your great skill on the basketball court. Coach Chick Sutherland told me what a wonderful player you were as a freshman. He said, "He is one of the best I have ever seen." And I heartily concur in Chick's estimate of you. I thought your play in Kansas City bordered on the phenomenal, and I wanted to be as gracious in defeat in K.C. as you have always been.
>
> I trust that after you get out of college, you are as highly successful on the fields of friendly strife off the basketball court as you have been thereon.
>
> With continued good wishes to you, I am,
>
> Sincerely,
> Forrest C. Allen

Allen also once told a reporter that "inch for inch, Gary Thompson is probably as good a player as the Big Seven has ever seen—and it's seen some fine ones."

So there were good feelings underlying that great rivalry. Allen retired that spring of '56, and was succeeded in the 1956-'57 season by Dick Harp. The big news on the Kansas team that year—actually it was *very big* news—was that 7 ft. Wilt "The Stilt" Chamberlain was eligible for varsity competition.

The sophomore from Philadelphia was already showing that he would become the greatest basketball player of his time. The first month of the season, he averaged 31.8 points, 20 rebounds and eight blocked shots per game. The Jayhawks won the Big Seven Pre-Season Tournament, but their victory over Iowa State was a squeaker, 58 to 57, on a buzzer-beater shot by KU's Gene Elstun. Chamberlain was held to 12 points.

That set up what many still today regard as the biggest game in Iowa State men's basketball history.

On Monday, January 14, 1957, the 12-0 and No. 1-ranked Kansas Jayhawks found their way through a raging snowstorm to get to Ames for a battle against a 9-2 Cyclone team that was ranked No. 9 in the nation. All 7,800 seats in the Armory, the noisy military science building with a gymnasium where Iowa State played its home games, were filled. WOI-TV and seven radio stations broadcasted the game to fans across the state.

Iowa State played a slow-down game, hoping to frustrate Chamberlain, and the strategy worked almost to perfection. Tied 37-37 in the last minutes, Don Medsker's 20-foot shot at the buzzer gave the Cyclones a huge victory.

Afterward, United Press International's story reported: "Gary Thompson of the Cyclones stole the show from the gangling Chamberlain, piloting their slow-down strategy by frequently holding the ball in mid-court while his mates jockeyed for position, and also taking game scoring honors with 18 points."

Chamberlain was congenial in defeat, visiting the Cyclone dressing room to shake hands with his opponents and saying to the reporters about Thompson: "He's great."

Max Falkenstein, who for 60 years was the voice of the Kansas Jayhawks in basketball and football, remembers broadcasting that game in Ames.

"What I remember, of course, is that there was a whole lot more passing and dribbling than there was scoring," Falkenstein said in an interview. "Iowa State built a web around Chamberlain, and he really could not move. To the Cyclones' credit, what they figured out and demonstrated in that game was that if a team could get Wilt slowed down, he would lose interest in the game."

The third time the teams faced each other that season, in Lawrence, the Jayhawks won 75-64 in front of 17,000. Thompson scored 21 points—and got seven rebounds—while Chamberlain scored 19 points.

At season's end, Thompson was showered with honors.

Highest of all was that he was named first team All-American by the Associated Press, along with Chamberlain, Lennie Rosenbluth of North Carolina, Chet Forte of Columbia and Rod "Hot Rod" Hundley of West Virginia.

Fans in the Midwest, especially, knew they had seen something special in the Iowa State star. They knew Thompson was much more that a dead-eye shooter and a game-controlling playmaker of a guard.

He often startled opponents and fans with the way he would take the ball inside, out-maneuver much taller opponents and score with everything from hanging jump shots to classic hook shots. And he was a constant pest on defense.

Maurice King, an all-conference guard for Kansas in that era, often was assigned to guard Thompson. "He was probably the toughest defensive player I had to go against in college," Gary said. "I really had to work hard but with the help of teammates setting 'picks,' I always scored well against Kansas. Maurice was a first class guy, and I had a lot of respect for him as a player and a person. I think he brought out the best in me."

King, who died in 2007 after retiring from a career as an executive with Hallmark in Kansas City, had described Thompson to me as "a dynamite, smart, cagey basketball player. He wasn't very tall, but he played big. He was one of those players who always seemed to be in the right position, and he could score from anywhere. He was also a very annoying defender, but a great leader for his team. They seemed to rally around him."

> *"Keep the elbow in, your eyes on the front of the rim…"*

Another old opponent with real respect for Thompson is Fred "Tex" Winter, who coached the Kansas State Wildcats to eight conference championships from 1953 to '68.

"He was a tough customer, one of the best basketball players in the country," Winter said in 2005 when he was 83 years old and retired in Salem, Oregon. "He gave us a lot of misery, I can tell you that.

"Gary was always a real competitor, but yet, a good young guy—certainly one of my favorite opposing players in all the years I coached. You know, I look back on those years, and there was a lot more camaraderie between players and between the coaches than there's been in more modern times."

After the '57 season, Iowa State sports information director Harry Burrell wrote this statistical snapshot of Thompson's individual records: "Over the years, Gary has scored more points in one game, 40, more in one season, 475, and more in his career, 1,253, than any other Cyclone cager. And in between those major marks, he holds records for the most points by guards, the most baskets, the most free throws, the most this, the most that—in fact, you name it and Gary Thompson has the most of it."

His No. 20 that he'd worn for the Cyclones was retired, just as his No. 24 had been at Roland High School.

Thompson also helped Coach L.C. "Cap" Timm's 1957 Cyclone baseball team become the first from any Iowa school to qualify for the College World Series, in which they were eliminated by the eventual champions from the University of California at Berkeley. Oh, by the way, he was named All-American in that sport, too.

One bit of good fortune, as I was pulling together the Gary Thompson story, is that in October, 2004, I had a long conversation with Burrell, the former ISU sports information director. He died in January, 2005.

Burrell was 93 when we talked, his health was obviously slipping but his eyes were full of his trademark twinkle as he told story after favorite story about Thompson.

The Roland years? "Everything you could think of about that was like a fairy tale," said Burrell, who had done radio commentary during Gary's long-ago high school state tournament games. "It was the biggest thing ever to happen in Roland."

When Thompson decided to attend Iowa State? "A great celebration," Burrell said. "We knew what we were getting. All of Ames made a grand push to get him."

His own relationship with Thompson in those years? "One of the fondest moments of my career was when I got to tell Gary after the 1957 basketball season that he had been named first team All-American," he said. "I showed him a telegram, he read it and then he said something like, 'Gosh, I can't believe it. I've dreamed all my life of this moment.' I'll never forget that.

"Gary was never a swell-head," Burrell continued. "He was a nice kid who happened to have a real mean streak as a basketball player. Oh, nothing dirty, but he was going to do anything he could to beat you."

It reminded me of something Burrell had written about him back in '57.

"It was not just the playing ability that made Thompson the greatest of Iowa born and bred basketball players," he wrote then. "It was his attitude of devotion to the game, to its highest ideals, his fighting heart, his determination that he was going to try to be a better player every day than he was the day before. It was those things, combined with an unbelievable modesty, that won him a permanent place in Iowa State's history."

In his Iowa State student years, he was already one of the most widely-recognized and admired persons in the whole state. "Few Iowa athletes have so completely captured the fancy of the public as has this clean-cut young man," wrote Bill Bryson, of the old Des Moines Tribune.

"He out-scored Wilt Chamberlain 21-19..."

And when Gary and his high school sweetheart Janet got married between his sophomore and junior years at Iowa State, it made statewide news.

He did not realize until years later that at least three baby boys in the state were named after him, so enthralled were their parents with the Thompson story. You'll learn more about them later.

AFTER IOWA STATE, Thompson played in the college all-star games and was named the MVP in one of them, he played 5 years for the Phillips 66ers in AAU basketball, which at the time was much more popular than the pro game in the National Basketball Association. Playing for Phillips offered more economic security, too, since the players were also full-time employees of the oil company with normal 8-to-5 jobs, generally in management training.

Thompson missed what seemed to be an almost certain spot on the U.S. Olympic team in 1960 because of an injury. He says it was the only serious disappointment in his sports career.

Still, basketball allowed him to see a lot of the world, and his association with the Phillips 66ers eventually paved the way for his later career. He played internationally on AAU All-Star teams that toured the Soviet Union and the Middle East; he was on the U.S. team that played in the Pan-Am Games in Chicago, and he played on the U.S. team in the World Games in Manila in the Philippines.

He continued his 66ers playing career through the 1962 season, which ended with the team winning the national AAU championship and Thompson being named MVP of the tournament. He then worked 2 years as a Phillips 66 district distributor in Cedar Rapids, Iowa, before being summoned back to Oklahoma in 1964 to become head coach of the 66ers. He also got to coach the U.S. team in the World Games held in Santiago, Chile. He continued as coach of the 66ers until the company ended its basketball program after the 1968 season.

That's when he and his young family settled back in Ames, where he became highly successful in the petroleum products and convenience store business. At his Gary Thompson Oil Co., he has worked with his wife, Janet, daughter, Kim, two sons, Rick and Scott, later his son-in-law Tom Wierson and occasionally the grandchildren.

In 1971, he began what became a 34-year career as a color commentator on telecasts of college basketball games. That included 19 years with play-by-play broadcaster Jay Randolph of NBC-TV on the Big Eight Conference "Game of the Week," as well as doing NCAA tournament games.

On March 2, 2005, as the Cyclone men's basketball team was winding down the 2004-'05 season, Thompson worked his last college basketball game as a TV analyst after deciding to retire from broadcasting. The Cyclone Television Network brought back Randolph from Saint Louis, Missouri, to do the play-by-play, just for old times' sake.

The telecast opened with a shot of Thompson's No. 20 hanging in its spot of honor in the rafters at Hilton Coliseum. When the starting line-ups were introduced before the game, the Cyclone players each ran across the floor, shook Gary's hand and gave him a hug before they went to mid-court to meet their counterparts from the Missouri Tigers.

At halftime, ISU officials surprised the Thompsons by calling both of them to center court, where Gary was honored for his long broadcasting career by ISU President Gregory Geoffrey, then-Athletic Director Bruce Van De

Velde, Ames Mayor Ted Tedesco and Cyclone TV Network Producer/Director Bob Helmers. They unfurled a long banner saying "Forever a Cyclone" and presented Gary a plaque, while the ISU students chanted "Ga-ry Thomp-son! Ga-ry Thomp-son!" It choked him up.

The game resumed, and it was with 4 minutes left when Randolph mentioned to Thompson and the audience that it had been a very special night.

"I was floored by the halftime ceremony," Thompson responded. "Jay, I'll repeat what I said here 48 years ago when they retired my number. What I said then, I say again now—Iowa State has always given me more than I've been able to give back. But I'm going to keep trying, and see if I can catch up!"

A few weeks later, *Des Moines Register* writer Ken Fuson recalled that tender moment in a column.

"Why doesn't the state of Iowa just declare Gary and Janet Thompson the classiest couple who ever lived here and be done with it?" Fuson wrote. "Every time I turned on a ball game this year, Thompson was receiving recognition for his many years of broadcasting. I'm opposed to this. Nobody should be allowed to retire who looks like he can still drop 20 points on Kansas."

> *"His first shot in ages... and he buried it!"*

Yes, even now in his 70s, Gary Thompson still has the shot, that's for sure. I saw it that day in State Gym in December 2005.

Spits on his hands, dribbles up the floor, stops, makes a pass right, gets one back and drains a 19-footer. "Like that!" he says.

Life's been good, very good, for Gary Thompson.

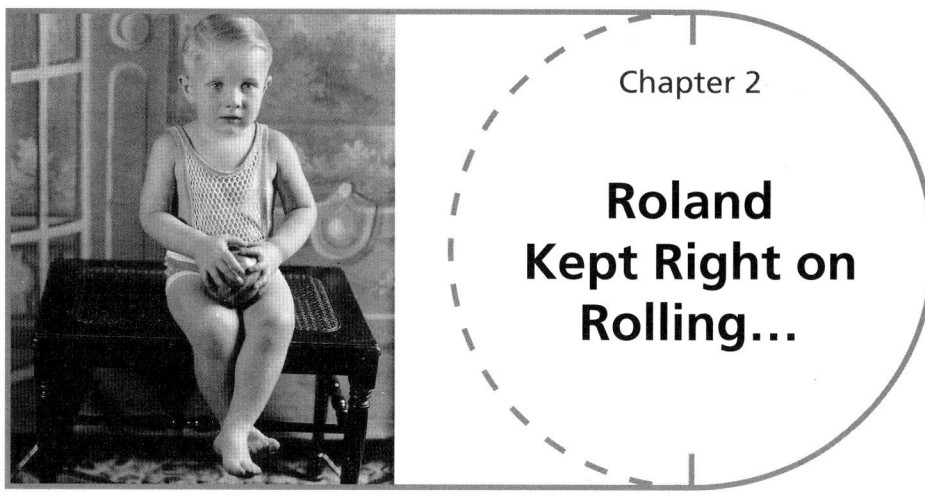

Chapter 2

Roland Kept Right on Rolling...

TODAY the town of Roland, Iowa, is a much different place from when Gary Thompson grew up there in the 1940s and early '50s.

A lot of small towns in rural Iowa have withered up over the last half century. Not Roland. It's twice as big.

The population in the 1950 Census when Thompson was in high school was 687. By the 2000 Census, it had reached 1,324—the biggest Roland has ever been—and the town appears to have grown substantially since then, too.

"It was a farm town, a town unto itself," said Jerry Twedt, Thompson's high school classmate, recalling the Roland of their youth. Most people who lived in or around Roland also worked in the town or on the farms in the area. Twedt wrote about that era in a delightful 1994 book, "Growing Up in the 40s."

He has watched Roland evolve on his many visits back home over the years from Florida, where he spent most of his career as a producer, director and stage manager for television news and other shows. "Now it's basically a bedroom community," he said, noting that much of Roland's workforce commutes the 15 miles to jobs in Ames.

Up and down Main Street, there's only one business—Boyd Accounting—that's still in the same location and same family ownership. Bill Boyd is third generation in that firm, which was founded in 1905.

Gone are the town's major employers of 50 years ago, like Ames In-Cross Chickens (home of "America's No. 1 Business Hen") and Marshall Canning Co., which processed, canned and shipped vegetables that were grown on contract by local farmers.

But replacing those companies as local economic engines are the Heart of Iowa Cooperative, a huge grain elevator operation that employs 70 at eight locations from its Roland headquarters; the JA Max Machine Co., Inc., high-tech machinists and manufacturers; Innovative Lighting, Inc., employing 80 in the development and manufacturing of lighting technology and products; NGE, Inc., makers of gym and athletic equipment, and a few other companies in a still-growing "industrial park" on the west edge of town. One of the streets there is aptly named "Progressive Avenue."

Old Roland High School, home of the Rockets, is gone. In 1969, the schools in Roland and Story City, a larger town 5 miles to the northwest, were consolidated. The high school is located in Story City and the middle school in Roland.

The old brick building that had been Roland High was demolished in 1988, and was replaced by a new building for the middle school. However, the gymnasium Gary Thompson played in, which was built in 1941, has been well cared for and is still in use by young athletes. In 2007, the Roland-Story Schools did a major renovation of the old gym while adding on another whole gym to the south, complete with new locker rooms, new wrestling room, new bathrooms and other improvements.

But there are no more Roland Rockets. Instead, the teams are the Roland-Story Norsemen. There have been some very noticeable changes in the leadership of Roland, too.

When Thompson and Twedt were in high school, Roland's mayor was M.O. Rod, a man then in his 60s who had been editor and publisher of the respected weekly newspaper, the *Roland Record*, and later was in insurance and real estate.

Elected mayor in 2005 was Sam Juhl—then an *18-year-old senior* at Roland-Story High School! He was the only person who filed nomination papers to get on the ballot. He received 112 votes and won easily over 12 write-in candidates; the runner-up among them was the fire chief, with 53 votes.

> *"Roland High School, home of the Rockets, is gone..."*

Juhl, an Eagle Scout, singer, football player and heavyweight wrestler, told reporters he had long been interested in history and politics, and decided to run when he saw no one else stepping up. With his election came a tidal wave of outside media attention.

In fact, while it had taken more than a half-century, Roland finally had a high school kid make even bigger news than Gary Thompson did. Stories about young Juhl's election ran worldwide. "I couldn't believe it," the mayor said. "I even got interviewed by a radio station from Colombia in South America!"

Juhl apparently served well—he was re-elected in 2007. He attended Des Moines Area Community College in Boone, then went on in 2008 to become a history major at Iowa State University.

Roland today is also not the homogenous place it was earlier. "We not only all knew each other, but most of us were related one way or another," Jerry

Twedt said. "I figured out once that if I'd go back three or four generations in my family, I was related to just about everybody in the whole bloomin' school."

"The whole town, too," said Jerry's older brother Harris "Pete" Twedt Jr., who now lives in Story City.

One day over lunch in Roland, at the deli in the rear of Anderson's Meat & Grocery, I asked several of the regulars about the changes they've observed in the town through the decades.

"When I was in school back in the 1940s," said Argyll Amenson, "all there were here were Norwegians." Loren Britson, a 1941 Roland High School graduate, agreed but added, "Now there are not so many." But they did note that at Anderson's deli, they still serve an old Norwegian favorite *kumla* for lunch on Wednesdays.

Britson, who died in 2007, had served 15 years as Roland City Clerk and helped with the development of four new housing subdivisions. When we visited over lunch, he said, as the town's population had grown over the years, there was much more diversity in the ethnic and religious heritages of the community.

Even so, there are still only two churches in town, Salem Lutheran and Bergen Lutheran, located one block from each other. Both are in the Evangelical Lutheran Church in America denomination.

What's the difference in the Salem and Bergen churches? I asked a dozen different people—most of them members of one or the other—and never got the same explanation twice. I began to think it's one of those things you have to be Norwegian or Lutheran to understand, and that may be true.

"You've got to go all the way back to Norway to understand that," said Jerry Twedt. "The Bergen church traces to what was the 'state church' in Norway. The Salem church came out of what was the 'reform movement.' There were differences in whether the ministers wore robes or not, and differences in the hymnals. There were people when we were kids who wouldn't step foot in the other church, although that was more among the older people and not our generation."

Gary Thompson's family belonged to Salem Lutheran. His brother DeLon Thompson, who now lives in Tucson, Arizona, chuckles and recalls, "Salem was always considered the blue collar church, and Bergen was considered the more upper crust church—if we actually ever had an upper crust in Roland."

All who knew Roland in the 1940s and '50s seem to agree on one thing, though: The most powerful people in the community back then were the pastors of the two churches. Rev. Olaf Holen served Salem Lutheran from 1926 to 1957. And Rev. Allen E. Nelson served Bergen Lutheran at the mid-century.

"Nothing was done without first considering whether or not the two churches would approve," Jerry Twedt wrote in his book. "There was seldom any trouble since the town's secular leaders were also the moving forces in the churches…

"The church's power was embodied in its pastor. He was the central figure in a community's spiritual, social and political life. His advice was sought on many diverse questions, and he was often called upon to arbitrate family and business disagreements. If the pastor was a strong willed individual, he could acquire almost baronial control of a town..."

It was a strict environment. There were never any dances in Roland, community or school. Students in the public school in Roland took Lutheran religion classes during the school day, taught by a teacher hired by the two churches in a classroom that the churches rented right there in the public school building.

> *"Roland's town sign says, 'Home of Gary Thompson'..."*

Twedt concluded that the two Roland pastors, in that era, "were well aware of the multifaceted role of their calling. They also felt keenly the power of their offices. But, to my knowledge, neither ever used his position for self-serving purposes. To their credit, Rev. Nelson and Rev. Holen conducted themselves as shepherds rather than overseers. Both served their God, community and congregations well."

And both were avid fans of the Roland High School Rockets. In fact, Rev. Nelson's son Roald, who stood 6 ft. 4 in. and weighed 215 pounds, was a star basketball player from 1947-'50. "Roald was *the* role model in our school and community until Gary Thompson came along," said Bob Birkeland, who in his 80s is still one of Roland's biggest sports fans.

When the community celebrated "Gary Thompson Day" after his college career had ended, Rev. Holen wrote one of the testimonials in a special edition of the *Roland Record* on July 14, 1957.

"Your name is known throughout the state, and even beyond its borders, chiefly because of your ability as an athlete," Rev. Holen wrote. "You have been hailed by the multitudes for your outstanding accomplishments on the basketball court and on the baseball diamond, and I have joined the chorus in singing your praises."

He also observed this: "As you grew up, you never forgot your Sunday School, Luther League and Church. It has made me happy that you have remained faithful to your Church through the years. In this respect also, you have been an inspiration to the young people of your home community and elsewhere."

It would have been unimaginable to people back then that 50-plus years later, the pastors of both the Bergen and Salem Lutheran churches would be women. In 2008, Rev. Rachael Hanson was serving Bergen, and Rev. Joelle Colville-Hanson was serving Salem.

"I'm the first woman pastor at Salem, and I'm pretty sure Rachael is the first at Bergen," said Colville-Hanson, a California native with 20 years of ministerial experience. "Who'd a-thunk, huh? Changing times, for sure."

She noted that "most women my age in the ministry, when we've gone to new calls, have been the first female pastors in those churches. But now, when younger female pastors get calls, there have often been other women serving there earlier. So the younger ones kind of get the benefit of the earlier experience some of us have had.

"But, you know, when I was getting out of seminary in California, it was actually much easier for women to find churches out here in Iowa and the Midwest than in a lot of other places. I think the reason was that these Iowa farmers fully understood that women are real partners in all the work. The women here get right out there on the tractors and work in the fields. They actually run a lot of the churches and other organizations.

"There's just not much room for 'trophy wives' and shrinking violets in Iowa life. Women here work, always have and they also have a lot of power. So, in a way, it might have been easier to become a female pastor here. Oh, there's still a little thread of resistance you see every once in a while, but generally, our people now accept the idea that women can be good pastors."

Colville-Hanson said the hold that both the Salem and Bergen churches have on the souls, minds and hearts of the people in the Roland area is not as strong as it was in the 1940s and '50s.

"People will travel more today, for church and everything else," she said. "They have a lot more choices. If you don't really want to be a Lutheran in Roland, it's pretty easy to drive to Story City or other places for church. And nobody notices as much if you decide to sleep in some Sunday."

But both churches still have full, active programs, and they work together a whole lot more than they did 50 years ago. (Incidentally, in the interim before Colville-Hanson arrived at Salem, the church's sign out front, instead of indicating they were without a minister, listed the pastor as "Rev. Bjorn Again." A little Norwegian Lutheran humor there.)

> *"We not only knew each other, most of us were related..."*

But Roland is a town that has indeed been born again. It's no longer as much the farm town, or a town unto itself. It's more the growing bedroom town—"and there's no reason to think we won't keep growing as long as Ames keeps growing," boasts young Mayor Juhl.

The people are no longer all Norwegians and Lutherans. But they're still proud enough of that heritage for the attractive signs on the edge of town to say "*Velkommen til Roland.*"

And they're still proud of their most famous native son. In 1999, Roland saluted him by placing a sign on the edge of town saying, "Hometown of Gary Thompson." It was the work of sports fan Gail Glasnapp, a retiree who long served as the "Norski" mascot for the Roland-Story Norsemen teams.

"My wife Judy and I thought that up," Gail Glasnapp said about the sign. He rounded up help from Kelly Popp, and Mark and Justin Hanson, and they ordered and erected the sign. "It was just time to recognize Gary, not only for his sports but for how loyal he still is to Roland," Glasnapp said.

The gesture meant a lot to Thompson, who was half-choked up when I took his photo next to the sign a few years later.

It's just like the banners up and down Main Street said in the summer of 2006: "Welcome to Roland—Honoring the Past, Embracing the Future." And they do seem to enjoy it when strangers meander in, as they still do, to ask what it was like "when the magic happened".

Chapter 3

Roots in Roland—and in Sports

GARY THOMPSON'S roots in the Roland area go back to 1871, when his great-grandfather Torres Robin Thompson and great-grandmother Serri Orland Thompson settled in the community that had been started by other Norwegian immigrants.

Torres and Serri had come from the area around Stavanger, Norway, where both were born in 1835. By the time they immigrated, they already had four young children. Two more were born after they settled in Iowa.

The family stories hold that Torres and Serri and their children came to the U.S. via a 6-week-long ocean voyage. The journey to the Midwest was accomplished by riverboat, railroad and finally a covered wagon.

The first of the Norwegians began arriving in northern Story County in 1855. Then they began spreading east and south, buying up land that was being sold by the U.S. government in the 10-year-old state of Iowa for $1.25 per acre.

Torres, Serri and their children at first lived with relatives who had preceded them to the new country, according to Helen Thompson, of Nevada, Iowa, a granddaughter-in-law who has studied the family's history. Then for a time the family lived in a sod house in the north part of the county. Torres and others were involved in digging ditches to drain the ample marshlands around what is today Roland and McCallsburg.

The youngest of their four children who came from Norway was also named Torres Robin Thompson, and he was born in 1869. This son, Torres, came to be known as Thomas Thompson when he grew up around Roland. Later generations of Thompson athletes can probably trace their athletic inclination and ability to him.

When he was 92 years old in 1961, Thomas Thompson was asked by a Story County reporter, Karen Haugsted, if he had taken time for sports in his earlier years. To answer, he "displayed several discolored and misshaped fingers," she wrote, and began talking of his life-long love of baseball.

He was nearly as old as the game itself, and the early equipment was primitive. "Everything was handmade," she wrote, recounting his description of it. "The baseball was started from a core of old rags. Then by tightly winding twine around the core a hard, compact baseball was developed. Today's expensive gloves were unheard of, and as a result, the players suffered constantly from broken fingers and burst blood vessels."

Thomas married Josephine Brekke, of LaCrosse, Wisconsin, and they bought a farm 3 miles southwest of McCallsburg, the town 6 miles straight east of Roland. They became the parents of 10 children—six boys and four girls. That generation of Thompsons for years made up a good part of the school and town teams in McCallsburg.

> *"He never walked any place—he always bounced..."*

"All the Thompsons were good in any sport you put them in," said Stan Thompson, of Murrieta, California, a first cousin and contemporary of Gary Thompson. "Sports were their thing. Four of the boys played on one town baseball team—my dad Sanford and his brothers Julius, Maurice and Earl. Nobody could beat them."

Baseball, basketball, billiards, skating, horseshoes, and later golf, track and water skiing—Thompsons have been good at it for at least three generations.

Maurice Thompson was the third of the 10 children of Thomas and Josephine Thompson. He was born in 1905.

In the late 1920s, young Maurice married Abbie Hemnes, a native of Roland, and they settled there. On June 4, 1935, they had their first child—Gary Lee Thompson. Seven years later, their son DeLon Ray Thompson was born.

Gary said he's never forgotten DeLon's birth. "I was always asking Mom and Dad if I could ride my bicycle out to Uncle Leonard Christian's farm, which was a mile east of Roland and then south, to visit Leonard and Esther, and my folks always said no, they didn't think I was old enough to do that," Gary said.

"But then this one day, my parents asked me, 'Gary, would you like to ride your bike out to Leonard's and Esther's?' I was so surprised—that was a big deal. I said, 'Yeah!' So I left right away, rode my bike out to their farm, stayed most of the day and then rode back. When I got home, I had a baby brother!

"I had never even realized my mother was pregnant," he continued. "I didn't know what that was. Parents didn't talk about those things with kids back then. If you asked where you came from, the answer would be, 'You came from Norway.'"

Gary's earliest school teachers all remembered him as a bundle of energy. "He never just walked any place—he always bounced," said Mabel Burger Dial, his first grade teacher, in a conversation before her death in 2005.

Mavis Cunningham Kingsbury, who taught Gary in second grade in 1942-'43, recalls the same thing. "He didn't walk," Kingsbury said. "He did this kind of a half-skip with every step. And he was always throwing an imaginary ball while he scooted along—overhand, underhand, sidearm. He'd have that arm in motion. And he was always an outdoor kid. As soon as school was over, out he'd go, and he'd be organizing some kind of game in one sport or another."

She can still visualize him "in striped bibbed overalls and with a butch haircut. He was such a likable little guy. He was a good average student, not the best in the class by any means, but good. He was strong in math, and he's told me as an adult he can still remember the flash cards we used in class to learn addition and subtraction."

She paused, then said she is always amazed that Gary Thompson still thinks about any of that, or for that matter, that he thinks about her. "How many people remember their second grade teacher?" she said. Actually, Thompson got together with both those former teachers—Dial and Kingsbury—several times over the years and would take them to lunch.

That time period in 1942 and '43 was a memorable one for everybody in Roland and, for that matter, all across America. It was when the full impact of World War II was becoming known.

"After Pearl Harbor, in December of 1941, it took some time to penetrate what this was all going to mean," said Kingsbury. "It really started hitting home for us when the men started leaving for service. The big question on everybody's mind was, 'How long?' And we all started to do a lot of map work, keeping up with where the soldiers whom we knew were being sent for training, and then wondering where they were being sent in the war."

School classes everywhere launched "scrap metal drives," to bring in extra steel and iron that could be reprocessed into armaments in the war effort. The kids also collected milkweed pods that were used in making parachutes, and hemp that was made into rope.

An old photo shows 7-year-old Gary with classmates Jerry Twedt, Wallace Frandsen and Everett Sather sitting in front of a huge pile of scrap metal. "The kids just kept bringing it," Kingsbury said. "I borrowed a scale from my landlord, and we had to weigh all of it. First they filled one box, then another, then many others. The country kids would bring in pieces off old farm implements. It was a way that let even little children feel like they were helping. There was a common feeling that our country had been harmed, and we were determined to defend it."

As the war went on, young Gary Thompson and his pals learned in first-hand ways that their little town of Roland was just a small part of a very big world, populated with all kinds of different people.

With so many local men away in the military, additional help was needed at planting and harvest times, both in the private farm fields and in the vegetable fields that were contracted by the Marshall Canning Co. Some of the labor was provided by German Prisoners Of War who were brought to the community, as well as by migrant Jamaican workers. And a band of Gypsies would come through Roland most years in horse-drawn wagons, moving to stay in favorable weather.

"I remember as a boy going over to the park and we'd play ball with the Jamaicans when they were off work," Gary said. "And they'd play cricket, too—it was the first time I ever saw that game. They were good athletes, I remember that."

He also recalls the extreme sadness which gripped Roland when three young soldiers were killed in the war, two of them brothers in the Willie Quam family and Virgil Twedt. "It wasn't like kids then were really scared about the war," Thompson says today, "but it was always on people's minds. Everybody knew somebody who was gone to the war."

In a town so small, where everyone knew one another, all concerns, serious illnesses and deaths were felt community-wide. Thompson says he remembers that when one of the church bells would begin ringing at a time other than for services, "we all knew it meant someone had died, and the bell would toll the number of years the person had lived."

But, still, the early 1940s allowed for the normal fun activities of childhood. Parents generally let their kids have the run of the whole town, knowing that other adults would be keeping an eye on them.

"One of the things I remember from back then is that the town whistle would blow at 12 noon and 6 p.m.," Gary said. "As a young kid, if you heard that, you better head for home real quick."

On one outing, he recalls losing a tooth, at age 5 or 6, "when we were 'playing fish.' Someone would be the 'fish' and put a chord in your mouth, and somebody else would try to be the fisherman and land you, by yanking the chord. You tried not to have the chord pulled out of your mouth and not to be dragged in, either. I was the fish, and I wasn't about to let a neighbor kid Clark Twedt, who was a year older, land me. But Clark yanked so hard, he pulled a tooth right out of my mouth."

When Gary was 6, he learned to ice skate. "We had an ice storm that lasted about 2 days, and one of the girls, Patty Gorton, whose dad was the school superintendent then, came around wanting to sell her shoe skates," he recalled. "They were girl's skates, but that didn't bother me any. I kept begging until my parents finally said O.K. and we bought them for $3.

"I put those skates on, and skated up and down the street, back and forth. Other times they'd flood the tennis court at the school, too, and we'd skate there. When it was starting to melt a little, I'd come in from recess completely soaked from playing 'Crack the Whip' on skates."

There were "war games" and "cowboys and Indians," with the preferred weapons being "rubber band guns"—blocks of wood carved like guns which you could use to "shoot" rings of rubber that were cut from the tubes for tires.

There were also bike rides out to the farm home north of town of another

Twedt family, including Gary's classmate Jerry Twedt, whom you met in Chapter 2, his two brothers and two sisters. The oldest brother, Harris Jr., or "Pete" as he became known, was 5 years older than Jerry and Gary Thompson, and though Pete would play with them, "he thought we were kids getting in his way a lot of the time," Jerry said.

Jerry Twedt had "Tony," a pony that was a favorite of Roland kids for years. "Tony was already 12 years old when I got him for my 6th birthday," Jerry said. "He was pretty tame—until you first tried to ride him. Then he'd try to throw you. I think Gary rode him before I ever could."

Gary remembers Tony "would barely move when you were riding out away from Twedts' place, but then as soon as you turned him around to head home, he'd go like crazy and would try to brush you off on the corner post heading up the lane. He could be an ornery one. Another classmate Dave Twedt would ride 'Beauty' from a half mile away and join us for the day."

There were also some sneak trips, by bicycle, to the farm where another of their friends, Dave Peterson, lived. "When no one was there, we'd try to ride their calves, pretending that we were playing rodeo," Gary said.

There was sledding on "Sheldahl Hill" in the southwest part of Roland, and movies that were shown on the walls inside the Legion Hall downtown. There were also certain "initiations" all young kids went through.

"You'd be with some older kids or adults, doing something, just glad to get to hang out with them, and they'd send you up to the hardware store to get 'a board stretcher' or 'a sky hook,' some dumb thing like that," Gary said. "Years later, you'd find yourself doing that same thing to some other young kid."

Gary's father Maurice Thompson for years was the player-manager for the Roland town baseball team, the "Independents." He stayed in the line-up until he was 40 years old, playing first base or pitching, and was always a good line drive hitter. Young Gary became the batboy.

"I grew up carrying around a gunny sack of balls and bats for Dad," Gary said. "I'd help tack up the broken bats and wrap them with tape."

He had another duty with the team, too.

"We had a '37 Chevy that Dad would use to drag the infield on the ball diamond," Gary said. "The 'drag' was two or three big wood planks that Dad had wired together, and he'd pull them behind the car. I'd ride back there, sitting on the drag, to help hold it down. I'd wind up covered with dirt, but I loved it."

He was also one of the most competitive chasers of foul balls during the Independents' games, racing other Roland kids to find the balls, sometimes diving to get them first, or crawling around under cars to retrieve them, all for the nickel reward that would come for turning in a foul ball. "Mom would look at my jeans, with grass stains all over them, and she'd say, 'You're ruining a $3 pair of pants for a nickel foul ball!' " he said.

The town team would always play Sunday afternoon games. "Mom's credo was always if you can play ball on Sundays, then you can go to church first," Gary said. "And we always did."

And you couldn't cheat on church. Abbie Thompson seemed to have radar, or spies, to prevent that.

"Mother would give me a nickel for a collection at Sunday School, and one day I kept it," Gary recalled. "I walked over to the gas station across from church and bought myself a candy bar. I was sure no one saw me. But when we got home, she said, 'Where'd you get the candy bar? Did you spend your Sunday School money?' I at least had enough sense to tell the truth and admit it. She said, 'That won't happen anymore!' And it didn't."

Besides Gary's experience as a batboy for town team games, he also was a regular sitting on the scoreboard during Roland High School baseball games, putting up placards with big numbers on them to show the score by innings.

That gave him a prime seat for a moment of glory for the Rockets in the spring of 1944. First Des Moines North and then Des Moines Dowling—two of the largest schools in the state—brought their teams to Roland for games in the district and sub-state tournaments, and Roland beat them both.

"We were a terrific baseball town, and that was one of the big moments," said Tommy Thompson, who was a junior on that Roland team and is not related to Gary. "Dowling came with sparkling white uniforms, and it seemed like about 50 bats. We came with our old Roland uniforms, and we only had about six bats—and most of them were taped up because they'd been cracked."

Tommy Thompson had the winning hit for the Rockets in a 7-6 win over Dowling, with 8-year-old Gary watching from the scoreboard. The two Thompsons both went on to make names for themselves in sports, Tommy becoming a noted sports broadcaster and later producer in both radio and TV in Des Moines. Tommy Thompson, incidentally, remembers that winning hit of his "as a sharp line drive, but I've had other people remember it as a looping fly ball, too."

Gary Thompson's family lived in the town of Roland for most of his early boyhood. "Yeah, I was a town kid—a city slicker from Roland," Gary says with a laugh.

He was born in a two-story white frame house that still stands at 217 Park Street on the east side of town, across the street from Erickson Park. When he was about 6, the family moved a couple of blocks on west to 114 Erickson, a two-story cottage-looking home that also still stands.

"My folks bought that house by paying cash, something right close to $1,100 from what they told me later," Gary said. "They always told us that when you were getting ready to make some big purchase, 'You save your money until you can buy it.' They were death on borrowing money."

The house on Erickson was the Thompsons' real home until 1963. By then, Gary was beyond both high school and college, and DeLon was a student at Iowa State. That's when Maurice and Abbie built a new home at 109 Martha

Street. However, in the 20-plus years they owned the house on Erickson, they twice rented it to others while the family moved for different jobs.

The first of those was a move far away, to the southwestern corner of Washington state at the height of World War II. It was a time when most of America was on the move. Some in Roland surely must have wondered if the Thompsons would ever return. But they did, after a year, as the war was ending.

The second move came 4 years later when a New York banker, who was managing farm property in the Roland area, hired Maurice Thompson to build and renovate hog houses, corn cribs and other buildings on the farms, and allowed the family to live free in one of the farmhouses. They did for just over 2 years, when Gary was an eighth grader, freshman and sophomore in high school.

The big move to the town of Vancouver, Washington, across the Columbia River from Portland, Oregon, was in the fall of 1944 as Gary was starting fourth grade. Maurice, Abbie and Maurice's cousin Bertha Brekke Brazier, whose husband was in the war, all got jobs as welders in the Kaiser Shipyard in Vancouver, helping build new warships. The

> *"I was a batboy for Dad's team..."*

move and the new job especially appealed to Maurice, who had more of an adventurous streak than most people around Roland did.

"Dad was always kind of a flyer," Gary said. "Mother would say Dad was always trying to hit something big. She was more conservative. She'd always say, 'I'd rather have a little than nothing at all.'"

The Thompsons, with 9-year-old Gary and 2-year-old DeLon, and Bertha were a crowd in the '37 Chevrolet, with their essential belongings packed in a luggage carrier on top of the car. It was one long car trip.

"I remember we were around Cheyenne, Wyoming, when the car started making some odd noise," Gary said. "Dad checked it and found that we were carrying so much weight, three lug nuts had broken off one of the wheels. We had to stay overnight somewhere while we got it fixed, and Dad was really worried about how much all that was going to cost us."

In Vancouver, they lived in a housing complex with other war workers. "We were out there a year," Gary said. "I knew I'd miss my friends in Roland, but at my age then there wasn't any arguing with your parents about moving like that—you just went wherever they did." He said his Roland fourth grade teacher, a Mrs. Christopherson, and classmates back home all wrote him letters while he was in the Northwest.

Looking back on it, he says the opportunity to live somewhere else for a time was good for him. "I learned a lot that year we were gone," Gary said. "For one thing, since all the adults were working, there were daycare programs for the kids. In Roland, there was no daycare because nearly all the mothers stayed at home.

"But out there, we'd go to daycare when school was out, and at the daycare center I went to, at least half the kids were black. It was the first time in my life I'd been around black people, and one of the black kids—I remember his name 'Leotis'—became one of my best friends. I've often wondered what ever happened to him."

There was a big amusement park named Jantzen Beach nearby, and Gary recalls family trips to snow-covered Mount Hood where "we thought it was great because we could throw snowballs up there." But he said the weather was generally "frustrating" to a sports-crazy boy like himself, because "it was always warm enough to play ball, but there always seemed to be a mist, too."

When the family returned to Roland in the fall of 1945, Maurice and Abbie had saved enough money to buy an apartment house as a rental property. They moved back into their own home on Erickson Street, which Maurice had leased to an employee of the company that operated the Great Lakes Pipeline Co. control station just east of Roland. Maurice himself worked there at times over the years.

The end of World War II was marked with an exclamation point in the community. Reuben Weltha, a native son who was a pilot in the Army Air Corps, was ferrying a huge B-24 bomber across the Midwest when he buzzed his hometown at very low level.

"I can remember standing on the corner where Clark Twedt lived when that happened," Gary said. "First we heard the plane, and then we saw it. It was so low the tree tops were just swaying! It scared the heck out of me!"

Later, Weltha told the homefolks that from the plane, "they could see cows so scared they were running in all directions, with their tails sticking up in the air, and chickens flying straight up," Gary recalled. "Meanwhile, the crew was up there in the plane laughing!"

Roland people were glad to see the Thompsons back in town, and not just because they'd missed them. "I remember our school superintendent C.P. Thompson (no relation to Gary) telling us when they were coming back that 'we have a good little basketball player coming up' and naming Gary," said Bob Birkeland, a 1939 graduate who was just heading into service then.

Birkeland's girlfriend Mazel Hoversten, a 1941 Roland graduate, was back home teaching fifth grade, and became Gary's teacher that fall. Bob and Mazel Birkeland married in 1947, farmed for 30 years and are retired in Roland. They've been friends of Gary Thompson since they first met him as a young boy. "I always said Gary would've been an All-American even if he'd never played any ball at all," said Mazel.

But as his teacher, she did have to call him down on one transgression. "The kids were always supposed to go to the bathroom before they'd go outdoors for recess," Mazel said. "Gary was in such a hurry to get out there, and get started in some game, that he didn't have time for the bathroom. When he had to 'go' outdoors, he'd water the bushes. The older kids told on him, and I had to talk to him about it."

Decades later, after she'd sent him a note of congratulations on some new accomplishment, she got a thank-you back from him and in it, he wrote, "Mazel, I was out watering the bushes again today—with a hose this time!"

Gary's teacher for seventh grade in 1947-'48 was Helen Harrison, a native of nearby Maxwell, who was straight out of Iowa State Teachers College. She eventually also became his aunt, after she married Francis Thompson, the youngest brother of Gary's father, and she is the family historian referred to earlier in this chapter.

"I call those times 'the golden days of teaching,' particularly in Roland," Helen Thompson says now. "The relationship between home and church and school was so strong. And the Roland kids were so wholesome."

She remembers Gary Thompson "would always pull up a wooden chair in class, and he'd sit in the aisle leading up to my desk. He was always wadding up a piece of paper, and shooting it at the waste basket like it was a basketball. I tried to explain to him that he couldn't be doing that, but he would anyway, so then I'd have to keep him in for recess.

"I kidded him later that I helped make him an All-American in basketball with all that 'shooting' he did in my class. He'd always come back with, 'But you don't know how good I might have been if you'd let me go outside and really practice instead of making me stay inside for recess!' "

There was occasionally some devilment away from school, too, the typical derring-do of small town life. Gary and Clark Twedt would spend occasional idle times "throwing walnuts at cars going through town," Gary said, and often had to run for their lives, even "running into Clark's house and hiding under his bed" when one angry motorist figured out which house might be harboring the walnut throwers.

And once, while he and Ralph Johnson, who eventually would be a key teammate in high school, were watching the town baseball team practice, Gary decided to try smoking a cigarette. "I was 11 or 12 years old, and Ralph would have been an early teenager then," Gary said. "There was a bunch of picnic tables kind of stacked up that we thought would hide us. So we got in between them, and lit up cigarettes.

"What we didn't know was that Dad could see us from over on the ball field. He didn't say anything, but when we got home, Mom right away said, 'Have you been smoking? That stuff will kill you!' I couldn't believe she knew! She said, 'Get inside here and we'll wash your mouth out with soap.' " She did, and that was the end of Gary Thompson's smoking experience.

Any chance a kid had to make a little money, he'd jump at it. "I'd go out and walk a whole country section, meaning a 4-mile walk, hunting for pop bottles and beer bottles with a gunny sack, to turn them in at the store or tavern for the deposit," Gary said. "Some of the pop bottles didn't smell like pop, and that's when I learned what 'spiked' was."

When he'd redeem the bottles in town, "I didn't mind taking the pop bottles into the grocery store," Gary said, "but I didn't want to take the beer bottles into Schneider's tavern. I didn't want anybody seeing me there because Mom always warned me about staying away from the taverns. So I'd sneak up the alley behind Schneider's, knock on the back door and say, 'Here's four bottles! Give me 8 cents—quick!' " He also worked setting up "duck pins" for a form of bowling that people did.

In the post-war era, Maurice Thompson operated a Phillips 66 service station for a year, and Gary got his first taste of the gas and oil business, which would eventually become his career. It was at the main intersection in Roland, on the same spot where a Casey's General Store is located today.

That old Phillips 66 station had a special pump for "Ethyl" premium gas, where the attendant would hand-pump the gas up into a visible globe that would show the number of gallons, and then it would flow by gravity into the car's tank.

Gary Thompson remembers pumping "regular" gas for customers there for 20 cents per gallon. The station became quite the hang-out for Gary and his pals.

"There was a grass lot behind the station, and that became our field for touch football," Gary said. "And Dad put a horseshoes court in beside the station," and that drew men and boys.

One "game" there at the station got Gary into trouble. "We'd go to the fair over in Story City, and we loved the carnivals," he said. "The carnies there had this one game where you'd throw a ball and try to knock over milk bottles. Well, once after we came back from the fair, I thought I was going to be a carny myself.

> *"There was a basket in every driveway in Roland..."*

"So down at Dad's station, where I was supposed to be watching things, I set up Coke bottles and was charging my friends to throw balls at them. I wasn't smart enough to 'load' the bottles so they wouldn't go down so easy, so everybody was knocking them over, and I was in Dad's till, paying off the 'winners.' "

As you hear the old stories, you begin to realize that Roland, from the mid 1940s and on into the 1950s, was an environment in which people—including the kids—entertained themselves and were very active.

The Thompsons, for example, were also a musical family—except for Gary.

"My parents were both real musicians," he said. "Dad could play anything with strings, Mom could sing and when my brother DeLon came along, he could sing, too. Really, our big entertainment as a family was always to go visit our cousins, maybe have dinner or supper together, and then we'd all sit around and sing. I especially remember everybody singing 'Old Red River Valley' and 'You Are My Sunshine.' It was fun, but you know, I couldn't carry a tune in a bucket."

No one sat home watching TV then. The first ones didn't appear in Roland until the early 1950s, and not until the late '50s did most families have one.

There was plenty to do. It seemed like there was always some kind of game to play or go watch.

Gary's introduction to real competition came in pick-up baseball and basketball games on the yards and driveways of his friends' homes around the town.

"My memory is that there was a basket and bang board in every driveway in Roland," he said. "I think one of the reasons we started having good teams was that, growing up in a small town like that, there was never enough kids so that you could just play with your own age group. You had to play with the older kids, too."

He went through being a tag-a-long in those games, as did his younger brother DeLon. They'd often "call up our cousins over at McCallsburg and get them to ride their bicycles six miles over to Roland and play with us, too," Gary said.

Stan Thompson, a neighbor 4 years older than Gary (and try not to confuse him with Gary's McCallsburg cousin of the same name, Stan Thompson!), remembers "when I was a senior, I'd go by Gary's house, and he'd be out there all alone, shooting baskets. Shooting and shooting. It seemed like he played basketball, or baseball, year 'round, sun-up to sundown.

"We'd get back-yard basketball games, and most all of us were older than Gary was," Stan Thompson continued, in a phone interview from his home in San Benito, Texas. "He was so little then, but right from the start, you knew he was going to be good because he had such desire."

There were also boxing matches with Loren Jacobson, another neighbor boy across the alley, a year older than Gary and much bigger. "We'd tie ropes around trees to make our boxing ring, put on real boxing gloves and have at it," Gary said. "I was a lot smaller than Loren was, but I was quicker. I'd start hitting him, and he'd get mad, throw off his gloves and chase after me. If he could catch me, he'd pull me down and sit on me."

There were games of "Bunt & Run" in baseball with the older kids in the neighborhood—Stan Thompson, Dick Erickson—and their friend from the country Pete Twedt. There were other baseball games with the Erickson brothers, too—Dick and the younger Ericksons, Al and Owen.

"We'd play games of 'work-up' in baseball," Gary said. "You'd play all the positions around the diamond, eventually working your way up to be one of the batters. I hit a long ball, got excited and threw my bat. It hit Willard Erickson in the head, and he started bleeding. I got scared that he was really hurt, but I still took time to run all the way around the bases—and then ran home."

When no one else was around to play ball, Gary would play by himself. He had fashioned a square—the size of the strike zone in baseball—on a garage door. "I'd take tennis balls out there and pitch at that square, pretending I was a Chicago Cubs pitcher," he said.

He'd seen the Cubs play at Wrigley Field in Chicago during family vacations to a dairy farm in Millington, Illinois, where Abbie Thompson's uncle and aunt lived. They'd make day trips into Chicago for ball games, or an amusement park, and sometimes Maurice Thompson would go watch the trotting horses. "I started watching the Cubs then, and I've been a Cubs fan ever since," Gary said.

Back home in Roland, especially during Gary's high school years, there was also spirited competition in horseshoes. Maurice Thompson had built another horseshoe court in their yard on Erickson Street, one that Gary remembers as nearly professional-caliber, with clay pits around each stake that Maurice meticulously watered and groomed. The regulars in the games then included Gary, DeLon, Maurice and an eccentric old bachelor Chris Halvorson who lived next door to the Thompsons.

Halvorson, who rarely left home, had an outhouse and woodshed out behind his house, and as far as the Thompsons knew, lived on welfare checks from the county government. In his later years, he had a heart attack, and when he needed medical care, he directed Maurice Thompson to the woodshed where he had between $4,000 and $5,000 stashed in Prince Albert tobacco cans.

Gary Thompson remembers he and DeLon often irked Halvorson by teasing him. "We knew Chris would be watching us out his window, so we'd go over to his tomato plants and act like we were going to pull them," Gary said. "He'd come running out, point at us and say, 'You dirty little rascals, you!'"

The first time Gary's talent was noticed by an actual coach was when he was in the sixth grade. He stood 4 ft. 4 in. tall and weighed 82 pounds.

"We had a new high school coach then, Kenneth Lepley, and somehow he picked me out and brought me up to play with the seventh and eighth graders on the junior high team," Gary said. "I remember him telling me, 'Gary, during the noon hours at school, I want you to go out on the basketball floor and dribble up and down that floor, and never look at the basketball. You look at the wall.'

"So I did that, and eventually, he'd put cones out on the floor, and I'd have to dribble around them, without looking down. He got me started working on those fundamentals.

"But here I was, a sixth grader, and really, I'm 4 ft. nothin' tall and scared to death of going up and playing with those junior high kids," he continued. "I was supposed to get out of class early to go to my first game, but it got to be 3:30 in the afternoon, and I was just too scared to ask the teacher. So I sat there, and I wound up being late getting to the game.

"Our uniforms for junior high back then were the old high school jerseys and pants, and I was so little that the arm holes on the jersey drooped clear down into my shorts. The shorts were so big, I knew I was going to have to get somebody to help me. So I was peeking around the corner of the gym, trying to get someone's attention to come and help, because the team was already on the floor. Finally someone came and got safety pins to hold up my pants—for my first organized game!"

He was a good junior high basketball player, as a seventh and eighth grader, but was still so small he was hardly a dominating player. But varsity coach Lepley kept his eye on Thompson, and kept pushing him to master the ball handling techniques and to learn all he could about the game.

Meanwhile, Lepley was building real basketball excitement in the community. His 1947-'48 Roland Rockets varsity boys' team went 28-2, followed by the '48-'49 team going 29-2.

He must have wondered if the real glory years of Roland basketball might well be just ahead, with Gary Thompson ready to start high school in the fall of '49. He also must have wondered if Thompson would ever grow, and if it would make sense to stay on as teacher and coach in Roland. It was not unusual for good young educators, especially coaches, to put in 2 or 3 years in small schools like Roland and then move on to bigger schools or better career opportunities. And that was what Lepley decided to do then—leave education for a management job with the Ames In-Cross Chickens industry there in Roland.

About the same time, the Thompson family made their move to the farm, not quite 2 miles southwest of Roland, on what today is 600th Avenue South. Part of the deal for their rent-free living in one of the New York banker's farmhouses was that Gary, then an eighth grader, would do the chores. That included feeding some hogs and cattle, hand-milking a jersey cow "Bessie" while sitting on a one-legged milking stool and occasionally helping slaughter chickens.

"It's funny now thinking about some of that stuff, how it was such a part of life back then, and how today very few people know anything about doing chores like that," Gary said on a recent visit to the farm site, where now there is no house or farm buildings, just an open field. "I'm sure my kids have never seen a chicken flop after its head is cut off."

He said he still feels a little guilty about killing a baby pig at his Uncle Leonard Christian's farm. "Leonard and Esther had part of their barnyard set off for little pigs and cattle," Gary said. "I was out there, and I was going to help Leonard while he was bringing in bales of hay for the cattle. He went off with a tractor and trailer, to pick up the hay, and while he was gone, I started throwing dirt clods at the little pigs. I hit this one, and I was shocked when it fell right over and died. It had blood coming out of its mouth.

"About that time, Leonard came back with a load of hay. He told me to get behind the trailer in the barnyard, and keep the little pigs out of the way while he was backing up. So I got back there, and I'm yelling, 'Come back! Come back! STOP! STOP! Oh-oh! You hit one of the pigs!' All he said was, 'Gary, that's what I put you back there for, to scare away the little pigs.' He was mad because that meant a loss of money. I didn't tell him until 10 or 15 years later that the little pig he supposedly ran over was one I killed by hitting it with a clod!"

It was a fine country neighborhood where the Thompsons lived, close enough to town that Gary could ride his bicycle in for Saturday morning confirmation classes at Salem Lutheran Church. There were good friends close by, with two of Gary's high school classmates, Dave Fausch and Wally Frandsen, living on neighboring farms.

Maurice Thompson set up a rough basketball court, nailing up hoops and bang boards on telephone poles. "We thought it was great—a full-court," said Gary. "It wasn't long and we had all the grass worn off. In the wintertime, we'd shovel it off as soon as it snowed, and we'd play in five-buckle overshoes."

The farm is also where Gary's horseshoes pitching became competition-ready. "Dad started me out on a horseshoes court he built here," he said. "I was throwing end-over-end 'flops,' and he taught me to throw 'flats' that would turn 1¼ turns on their way to the stake. Otherwise, they might bounce away. Dad said later it wasn't long before I could beat him, but it seems to me like he always gave me a battle."

Joe Hill, another farmer in the Roland area, won the "Farmers Division" horseshoes pitching championship at the Iowa State Fair in the late 1940s. Then he started coaching his own sons Jake and Junior, as well as their friends Loren and James Olson. They all wound up as top finishers in the State Fair's "Junior Division" competition in the early 1950s. One year when Gary was the champion, he won over 11 other youngsters—and claimed the top prize of $12. In the consecutive years that he won the "Junior Division" competition at the State Fair, he didn't lose a match.

The farm years, Gary acknowledges now with some embarrassment, were when he also became a typical adolescent challenge for his parents. He recalled so angering his mother a time or two that that she came after him.

"She was going to cuff me on the side of the head, but I was quick enough that I could fake her off, and jump out of the way," he said. "Of course, that made her all the madder. She'd yell, 'You better come back here, or it's just going to be worse!' Dad would take over after that."

There was quite a blow-up with his father over their meandering collie-shepherd dog named "Watch". "Fausches called one day and said our dog had been chasing their sheep," Gary said. "Dad told them if that ever happened again, 'Just let us know' and he'd 'take care of Watch.' Before long, they called again and said Watch was back over there. Dad grabbed his shotgun, jumped in the '37 Chevy and went roaring over there. Well, when Watch saw Dad coming in that car, he came running across the field with his tail between his legs. So then Dad came roaring back home in the car, jumped out, grabbed Watch by the collar and started whipping the dog's rear end.

"I was an eighth grader, and the emotion of the moment was just too much for me, I guess. I yelled, 'Damn you, Dad!' Believe me, we didn't use that kind of language at home. It was like everything stopped for a second.

"Then Dad dropped the dog, grabbed me and I became the dog! He swung to give me a big blow, and he suddenly grabbed his chest and yelled, 'Oh!' I was afraid for a second that he was having a heart attack, but what happened was that he swung so hard, a carpenter's pencil that he had in his bibbed overalls jabbed into his chest and cracked a rib or two. The pain just stopped him!"

Despite those little fusses, he looks across the farmland now and remembers his time living there as a good time with both parents and little brother DeLon. If they weren't playing basketball outdoors, it was indoor basketball, shooting tennis balls through hoops they fashioned from clothes hangers and pieces of cloth for nets. In warm weather, it was baseball and football. There was always a game.

And there was good news from down the road.

Wally Frandsen's father Bill was president of the Roland Board of Education. Bill came home in a blizzard on Maundy Thursday night in 1949, and said that while he'd had to miss the service at Bergen Lutheran Church, he and Superintendent C.P. Thompson had managed to hire a replacement for Ken Lepley as basketball and baseball coach. Overton M. Cheadle had been teaching and coaching in Norwalk, south of Des Moines.

Cheadle arrived an hour late for the interview, because of the storm—he had to stop in Ames enroute to have chains put on his car's wheels. The board president and superintendent sat in the Roland school office waiting for him, and once he arrived, they managed to pull a quorum of the board out of their respective church services.

> *"When the church bell rang, we knew someone had died..."*

A half-hour into the interview, one board member said "Overton" didn't sound much like a coach's first name, and asked if Cheadle had a nickname. He'd already told them he was a Chickasaw Indian, originally from Oklahoma, who'd married an Iowa girl while serving in the U.S. Navy. He was the first Native American most of the Norwegian Lutherans had ever met.

Thinking fast, he decided not to tell them his old high school nickname, "Cheadle Bug." Instead, he invented one. "You know, we Indian guys are always proud of our heritage," he said. "My nickname is 'Buck.'"

Truth was, he'd never used "Buck" until that moment. But they believed him.

"At the end of the interview, they sent me down the hall for 20 minutes while they talked about it," Cheadle recalled. "Then they called me back into the room. Bill Frandsen said, 'If you're crazy enough to drive up here in a blizzard for an interview, we're crazy enough to hire you.'"

Two days later the *Des Moines Register* carried a small story with this headline: "Roland Hires Buck Cheadle"

The town, the school and a whole lot of lives were about to be changed forever.

Chapter 4
Roland Rockets Rise to Basketball Fame

AS Gary Thompson has said repeatedly over the years, Roland High School boys' basketball "was good long before me."

He's right. Check the Rockets' season records for the 5 years before he started high school, beginning with the 1944-'45 season: 20-6, 18-2, 12-7, 28-2 and 29-2.

He can remember as a young boy "that on game days, people would be lining up to get into the gym about the time school was getting out, and for the big games, those lines would get to be 2 blocks long before the gym doors opened."

But the Roland teams never could make it to the state tournament. They seemed to be especially cursed when they'd run into teams from small Catholic high schools in the sub-state tournament.

In Thompson's freshman year, 1949-'50, when he was not playing a lot but was indeed on the varsity squad, the team finished another 29-2 season. But they lost in the sub-state finals to Holy Family of Mason City, 41-27, in a game played in Ames.

New coach Buck Cheadle was sitting in the front passenger seat of the school bus carrying the Rockets back home to Roland, not feeling half bad about the season. But suddenly sliding into the seat beside him was the team's captain, Roald Nelson, the 6 ft. 4 in. 215-pound Lutheran pastor's son who had just seen his brilliant high school basketball career end. They talked about the whole team's disappointment, particularly in continually getting stopped a game or two shy of the state tournament.

And then, as Cheadle recalled it, his star player said, "Coach, we're superstitious. We can't beat parochial schools." Cheadle said he looked at Nelson, knew he was serious and said, "Well, Roald, we're going to get over that."

The coach didn't really have a clue right then what he might do to overcome such a superstition among his players. But he knew that he was going to be completely rebuilding his team anyway, because he was losing Nelson and three other graduating starters—Wayne Strum, Dave Swenson and Vern Egland. He figured he could probably find some way to address the parochial school psyche-out, too.

Cheadle had already started introducing some innovations that quickly distinguished the Rockets from their opponents in the North and South divisions of the Story County Conference.

He'd been a high school and college basketball player himself in his native Oklahoma. One of his coaches there, Merle Rousey, had been the first All-American player for Henry Iba, the legendary coach at Oklahoma A&M, which was later re-named Oklahoma State University.

As coaches, both Rousey and Cheadle used some of the same approaches that "Mr. Iba" was known for—having his players wear rolled up towels around their necks when they began their pre-game warm-ups; generally not allowing them drinking water during the games and "just a little at halftime," and when he'd talk to players during time-outs in the games, he'd have them lie on their stomachs on the floor "just to get them off their feet for a minute or two," he explained.

He also taught them the "sergeant jump" he had learned as an athletic specialist in the U.S. Navy during World War II—timing your lift-off from the basketball floor so you could grab a rebound at the very high-point of your jump. They all wore the Converse Chuck Taylor All Stars sneakers, the best basketball shoe available at the time, $6.75 per pair.

But Cheadle knew what could really help his players reach the next levels of success in basketball was if they were in better physical condition than their competition.

So he strictly enforced training rules—absolutely no soda pop or candy during the season, non-negotiable curfews with phone calls from the coach to the players' parents to verify compliance, a rule that all had to wear caps or hats when they were outdoors in the wintertime, and lots of running. The rules were equally strict for the Roland girls' team, which Cheadle was also coaching.

"Buck was a very strict disciplinarian, as far as getting our sleep and what we ate," said Ralph Johnson, now of Dayton, Iowa, who was the only starter returning from the 1949-'50 Roland team. "As an example, I remember one of the players on the girls' team talked a student manager on the boys' team into buying her a candy bar at lunch at school. Buck found out about it, and both the player and the manager had to run a exorbitant number of laps at practice that day.

"I think the community picked up on it, too," said Johnson, who was later a teacher, coach and school administrator. "We had hours when we were supposed to be home, and if we were out late, people in the community would call him. As a result, he had hundreds of sets of eyes watching all of us. He was tough himself, and tough on us. But the team bought into it—oh yeah—100 percent. No one got upset and quit."

The result?

The Roland Rockets of 1950-'51 were able to overcome the heavy losses to graduation and win like never before. It didn't happen just because of their talent—they had plenty of it, especially for a small school—but because of their superior physical conditioning, self-confidence, higher expectations and teamwork.

They went on a 35-game winning streak that took them to the state tournament for the first time and then to that epic championship game against Davenport. There were return trips to the state tournament the 2 years after that, with season records of 31-3 in 1951-'52 and 32-2 in 1952-'53.

Roland Rockets basketball had been elevated from good to great. Gary Thompson, setting single-season and career state scoring records, became the most talked-about high school athlete in Iowa. And the community of Roland was in absolute nirvana.

"It was one of those things that happens every once in a great while in a small town," said Loren Britson, a former city clerk, looking back on the Thompson era during a 2005 conversation over lunch in the deli of Anderson's Grocery in Roland. Britson died in 2007.

"It was the thrill of a lifetime," said former teacher Mazel Birkeland, still a super fan in Roland.

Dave Swenson, one of those seniors when Thompson was a freshman, said he still gets out his Roland scrapbooks and enjoys the memories at his home in Arrington, Tennessee, near Nashville.

"Absolutely no soda pop or candy"

"It seems almost like a dream," Swenson said. "We won all those games—and got so much attention. We all thought the next groups wouldn't be able to continue it, but they did. You'd cheer on the kids coming along behind you."

He said he sometimes wonders whether people not from Roland can ever understand what it was like. "If you didn't live it, maybe you can never realize how that basketball team gripped the heart of that town," Swenson said. "It seems almost surreal, like another life and another time."

Gary Thompson has been known ever since then as "the Roland Rocket," a nickname he has never tired hearing. "I like that, I really do," he said. "Some guys say, 'You still like being called that?' And I do, because I like the way it ties me back to my hometown."

Many people remember the story as being even better than it was.

"It was like the movie 'Hoosiers,' except for one thing—we never won it,"

Thompson said. "A lot of people come up to me today and say they remember watching us win the state championship, and I have to tell them it didn't quite happen that way—but we were close!"

The story can be told in some amazing vignettes:

—Roland's boys did not lose a home basketball game from 1946 to 1958, which includes all four seasons when Gary Thompson was in high school.

—Poor McCallsburg! That was the archrival school, the next town east of Roland. In Thompson's 4 years on the Rockets varsity, Roland was 13-0 against "Burg," as it was known. The McCallsburg gym was so tiny, and the Roland gym could hold 1,000 or more, that McCallsburg school officials decided to play all the games at Roland to accommodate the crowds, sell more tickets and divide the revenue. But in Gary's sophomore year, the McCallsburg fans were grumbling that if they could just play Roland in their own small gym again, they were pretty sure their boys could knock off the Rockets. So they moved the next game back to McCallsburg, and Roland won 48-34. Gary called it "one of the most satisfying wins of my high school career, because it put an end to McCallsburg saying they could beat Roland 'if we played them in 'Burg.' " Helen Thompson, Gary's aunt and former teacher, remembers that "sometimes McCallsburg even had better teams with more power in those years, but Roland had the magic."

—Most opponents realized they were facing a special player in Thompson. "I always told Gary I was one of the guys who made him All-State, because he'd score 43 points against me and sit out the whole second half," said Alan Hoskins, who was a guard for the Lynx of neighboring Zearing in Lincoln Township. He went on to become a sportswriter and college publicist in Kansas City, Kansas. "I can't imagine there's ever been an Iowa high school athlete who was more idolized than Gary Thompson," Hoskins said. "Heck, back in Zearing when we'd play pick-up games, we'd pretend to be Gary Thompson!"

—To reach the state tournament back then, teams had to win a lot more ball games, since there were more than 950 high schools in Iowa, and only 16 teams would make the all-in-one-class state tourney in Iowa City. In the 1951, '52 and '53 tournaments, Rockets had to win seven games to make state— three in the old "sectional" tournaments, two in the district tournaments and two more in the substate. And then if you were going to win the state championship, you'd have to win four more games during the week in Iowa City. In the 2007-'08 school year, there are 392 high schools in Iowa with boys basketball teams that will compete in four classes at tournament time. Hence, some teams will make state by winning only two games! So, now think back to the 1951 tournament, when Roland carried a 32-0 record to Iowa City—and the Rockets would play four more games there. Think of the pressure. Think of the travel—and there were no Interstate highways yet. Think of the expense. And think of the fun. Can you imagine all that today? The Roland fans lived it. And loved it. "It'd be a ghost town when the team was on the road," Loren Britson, the former city clerk, recalled for me. "And it didn't matter whether there was snow or ice. Everybody went to the games." Added Bob Birkeland: "The town was crazy, just crazy!"

—To give you an idea of just how dazzling a player Gary Thompson could be, listen to Bernie Saggau describe one of the moves he saw Thompson make when Saggau was officiating one of Roland's state tournament games. "One thing I've never forgotten is seeing Gary coming down the middle of the floor and jumping at about the free throw line as he came toward the basket," said Saggau, who in 1967 became executive director of the Iowa High School Athletic Association. "He came off the dribble with the ball in his right hand, he brought the ball behind his back, touched it with his left hand back there, brought it back around with his right hand, then laid it in the basket before his feet hit the floor again. I'd never seen anybody do a move like that in a game."

—Fans back then practiced a higher level of sportsmanship, right? Hah! Twice during Thompson's high school career, he was slapped by girls from the opposing school before he could get off the court. In the 1952 state tournament in Iowa City, after Roland had taken a dramatic 49-46 victory from Readlyn, he was suddenly confronted by a girl who slapped him, yelled "Oh, you!" and then stomped her foot and ran away. The second time it happened was in his senior year, about mid-way through the 1952-'53 season, in a game at Randall. "Just as I was leaving the floor at halftime, this girl came out of nowhere and slapped me," Thompson recalled. "The funny thing about it was that I was having a bad game, and people kidded me later that maybe she was actually a Roland fan!"

For all the travel that was involved in Roland's tournament runs, the Rockets seldom had to leave the rural neighborhood during the regular season. Playing in the North Story County Conference with them, the McCallsburg Eagles and the Zearing Lynx were the teams from Fernald, Gilbert and Milford Township. Playing in the South Story County Conference were Slater, Huxley, Shipley, Collins, Maxwell and Colo.

The high schools in Ames, Story City and Nevada were larger and played in other conferences. If you are counting, that indeed means there were 15 high schools in Story County in the early 1950s.

One longer road trip, though, was to play in Diagonal when Thompson was a freshman and a reserve on the varsity. Diagonal, located in Ringgold County in south central Iowa, had been a small-school basketball powerhouse since 1938, when the Maroons won the state championship, and '39, when they were runners-up. When Roland started making a name for itself, a home-and-home series was arranged with Diagonal for a 4-year period.

"That was a long enough trip for us that we stayed overnight at the Iowana

Hotel in Creston the night before our game, and it was the first time I'd ever stayed in a hotel," Thompson recalled. "Don Holland was a sophomore, and he and I were two real rookies on the squad, so we roomed together. Ralph Johnson and Frank Egland, who were juniors, were in the room next door to us.

"They called us on the phone, and said, 'Hey, look out your room's window!' So we rushed to the window, leaned out and immediately got hit with a wastebasket full of water by Ralph and Frank! Ralph waited a few minutes, then told us to call the guys in the next room on the phone, and tell them to look out their window. So we leaned out our window, with our waste baskets full of water ready to soak them, and when we did, Ralph hit us with another wastebasket of water! We were rookies, all right!"

The Rockets' 53-47 win at Diagonal on that trip proved to be a sign of good things to come. The only game they lost in that '49-'50 season—before the sub-state finals—was the next to last game of the regular season, a 45-38 loss at Clemons, located in northwest Marshall County, "in a gym that was the size of a volleyball court," Buck Cheadle remembers. Clemons was led by Tuck Rhodes.

Cheadle said an incident that very night, after the loss to Clemons, made him realize that his team's success had created some very high expectations in the community.

"Late that night, Don Holland's dad Overt Holland showed up at my house with two cans of beer in his pockets and said, 'Let's go down in your basement and talk about the team,'" Cheadle said. "He said he just felt so bad for us, after our first loss of the year after winning 19 in a row, especially after we'd beat Clemons 51-25 earlier when we played them at Roland. I said, 'Overt, let me tell you something—I'm *glad* we lost that ball game tonight because it'll take the pressure off of being undefeated. It'll relax us going into the tournament.'

"Dad's down there drinking beer!"

"I think he was shocked that I wasn't upset. But I knew how serious he was when he brought those beers along, because that didn't happen much around Roland then. In fact, one of my own little boys came down in the basement, saw us and ran up yelling to my wife, 'Dad's down there drinking beer!'"

That team then went on a nine-game run winning the Story County tournament, then the sectional and district tournaments, before losing to Mason City Holy Family in the sub-state finals, with Phil Vega as Holy Family's team leader.

For the following season, 1950-'51, Ralph Johnson was the only starter returning. So fans and opponents all knew that Coach Cheadle was rebuilding, and expectations for the Rockets were not high.

Seniors Frank Egland and Jake Hill joined Johnson in the starting line-up, as did sophomore Gary Thompson, who grew 4 inches since his freshman year and stood at 5 ft. 6 in. Don Holland and Dave Peterson alternated in the other starting spot. Johnson, at 6 ft. 2 in., was the only player taller than 6 feet.

It was unimaginable, as the season began, that this team would win 35 in a row, become the first Roland team to make the state tournament and then play for the state championship. Looking back, some think the key was the explosion on the Iowa basketball scene by Thompson, who was the team's leading scorer with 463 points for the season, a 13-points-per-game average. Not so, he says today.

"The real key is that those three seniors would accept me in the starting line-up," Thompson says.

As he has said many times—all the successes he went on to have in college and AAU basketball, in coaching, in broadcasting and in business—can be traced back to what happened to the Rockets and him in his sophomore season. So in 1991, when the great Rocket team was getting together for a 40-year reunion, he wrote a heartfelt letter to those three '51 seniors Johnson, Egland and Hill. Here it is:

April 30, 1991

Dear Ralph, Frank & Jake,

I do not really know how or where to begin with this letter, and I know that I do not have the ability to "use words" to express the true feelings that are inside me. I do know that this is written with great feeling and sincerity. Here it goes!

Basketball has provided me with wonderful experiences and great opportunities throughout my entire life and, at age 55, I am still closely involved with basketball because of my television work. It was a fun high school career, a college career with a free education, an opportunity for a business career with Phillips, a chance to see the world and the opportunity to return home with our own business.

My "ride" started in 1950 when a part-Indian named Buck Cheadle began coaching at Roland and established a policy that it did not matter who your parents happened to be, how big you stood or even what church you attended. It was the 1951 Roland Rocket team and *you three seniors* were responsible for everything!

I remember the first write-up I received in the paper and Mom saying to me, "Don't get any ideas about getting a 'big head' or thinking you're pretty 'big stuff.' You do that and the older players will freeze you out of the game and won't pass the ball to you."

Pretty good advice from a parent, and I always tried to wear the same hat size. Yes, I have always known that I received more publicity and credit than I deserved, and it was simply because I stood 5 ft. 6 in. tall and was a sophomore. The media loves that combination and they still do to this day. I got far more and you received far less because of it, which was *not fair*.

Going through life, I have seen and heard of similar type situations and how jealousies and self-serving attitudes have destroyed good teams. I was too young to understand at the time, because all I knew was that we should all play hard together and try to WIN! Growing older, I have often thought back to 1951 and wondered how could a situation like that be anything but TROUBLE? The only answer is that you three guys were the seniors, and you sacrificed so that in my opinion, the 1951 Roland Rocket team could become the school's GREATEST TEAM!

I do want you to know that over the years when people talk about the 1951 Roland Rockets, I have always tried to give CREDIT to the TEAM and I would explain that I just got more "ink" because I was 5 ft. 6 in. and a sophomore.

What I am really trying to say is that basketball has provided me a lot of wonderful experiences and opportunities, and they may have never existed if it had not been for the success of the 1951 team. You were the guys that were the backbone of the team, and you did not let the unfairness of the "hype" surrounding the team interfere with the team's success. I will always have a "special feeling" for you guys and the way you handled that situation, but most of all, for our continued friendship.

I had planned to present these thoughts at our reunion, and was worried about my ability to handle it emotionally. I have had troubles with my emotions just writing this letter. See you at the reunion.

A teammate,
Gary

Ralph Johnson said, looking back on it, they all knew each other so well from growing up together that Gary's sudden stardom was not a problem. "I don't remember even thinking about that kind of thing," Johnson said. "We were a team, all working together, with no feelings about who should play, when you should play, or any of that. If the coach put you in, you gave it everything you had for as long as you could. Gary was always a real scrapper, and he played just as hard as all of the rest of us."

Egland, retired in Battle Creek, Michigan, after a career with the U.S. Army Corps of Engineers and later the Federal Emergency Management Agency, agrees that there was genuine harmony on that team. "When you're from a small school in a small town, you know who is coming up and who is looking good," Egland said. "We all knew Gary was going to be good, and we looked forward to him being on the team with us. The chemistry was there. He got a lot of attention, but it never went to his head. His focus was the team."

Hill, who settled on a small farm outside Loveland, Colorado, where he owns a produce stand, says Gary Thompson "has had a fabulous life, but he has always worked for it. In basketball, he always tried so hard. He gave 110 percent all the time, and that's what made him successful. And he was a team player. He scored by far the most points of all of us, but there was no conflict among us—we really played as a team."

The season opened with a 47-11 victory over Ellsworth, and the Rockets roared through the rest of it, with only McCallsburg, Nevada and Collins coming within 10 points of them. Two rugged teams from a distance, Diagonal and Rinard, came to Roland but were beaten by 14 and 20 respectively.

The early stages of the tournament were waltzes, too, but then as Roland was getting ready for a sub-state first-round game against Mingo, a serious accident threatened to ground the undefeated and high-flying Rockets.

A major snowstorm blew into the area on the Sunday before the Monday game. School was canceled on Monday, and by early that afternoon, Coach Cheadle and the Rockets were awaiting word whether the game would be postponed. Ralph Johnson and some other pals had gathered at Anderson Garage, a car repair business that was a hangout for some of them.

"A friend's car had gone in a ditch in the snowstorm, it stayed there for a while and then he got it pulled out and brought it into Anderson's," Johnson said. "The motor was covered with snow—it had blown in all around it—so we were cleaning it off. I was using a blowtorch to melt some of the snow down around the motor. My friend tried to start the car, while I was using the torch, and the flames got sucked into the engine where the breather cap was, and then it exploded."

That breather cap hit Johnson in the forehead while flames blasted across his face and eyes.

"I thought I was blind because I couldn't see a thing at first," he said. "Then after a few seconds or minutes, I still couldn't see anything out of my left eye, but I started to be able to see out of my right eye, but not much."

The friends rushed Johnson to one doctor, who said he couldn't treat the injury. Then they hurried him to Dr. J. A. Snyder, the Roland doctor who'd presided at the birth of nearly everybody in the area the previous 30 years.

"Dr. Snyder mixed up some solution, held my eyes open and started washing them out, over and over," Johnson remembers. "As I think back on it, I don't think it entered my mind at first that I'd miss basketball. I was wondering whether I'd be able to see at all. Then I remember Dr. Snyder saying, 'I think you're going to be O.K.' That's when I started thinking about whether I'd be able to play basketball and how soon."

He left the doctor's office with patches on his eyes and his whole face bandaged.

Luckily, the snowstorm had forced postponement of the sub-state tournament game that night, and then again on Tuesday night, when the storm lingered. The game was re-scheduled for Wednesday evening. Just hours before tip-off, the bandages were removed from Johnson's eyes, and he not only played, he played well. Roland beat Mingo 57-44, with Johnson scoring 14 points and "his rebounding was all that any coach could desire," Cheadle told the sportswriters afterward.

That set up a Saturday night sub-state finals game in the Iowa State Armory in Ames, with Roland in another match-up with Rinard. That tiny school in Calhoun County had only 33 students in high school, making it less than half the size of Roland. They had a rookie coach in Lewis "Buzz" Levick, who was in his first year out of college and later would go on to coach two state championship teams at Newton and then coach for 28 years at Wartburg College.

Rinard also had a senior superstar, Larry Wetter, a sharpshooter guard who was averaging 21 points per game (and who later was a teammate of Gary Thompson at Iowa State). "There were nine of us in my Rinard graduating class in 1951," said Wetter, now retired from a career as a business executive in Oregon. "Years later, when I was encouraging our children in school, they asked me, 'Well, how were your grades in high school?' I said I was the salutatorian. They said, 'You weren't even in the top 10 percent of your class!' "

The Roland-Rinard re-match was much anticipated. "There had been a lot of hype when we played them over in Roland earlier that year, about it being a big game between the state's two small-school powers," Wetter said. "I remember going into the locker room in Roland, and there was my photo plastered on a locker with a sign that said, 'This is the guy you have to stop!' "

Roland won the sub-state championship game 48-39 in front of huge crowd in the Armory. All was not lost for Wetter, though. "I think that game in the Armory was when Chick Sutherland, the Iowa State coach saw me play, and that's when he decided to recruit me," he said.

Meanwhile, the Rockets began preparing to travel to Iowa City for the school's first appearance in the state tournament, which ran Tuesday through Saturday, March 27-31, in the University of Iowa Fieldhouse.

On that Monday, there was another winter storm, this time ice. School was canceled for the day, and Ralph Johnson was back hanging out at Anderson Garage. "Orvis Anderson had to go to Story City to get some auto parts, and one of our teachers Robert Wilder and I decided to ride along with him," Johnson said. "We got 2 ½ miles west of town on the icy pavement, lost control and rolled the car. Luckily, we were going slow enough that none of us got hurt."

That second close call for Johnson resulted in a brief story on page one of the *Roland Record* weekly newspaper. A headline said, "Ralph Tries It Again," and the brief story reported the roll-over accident, then closed with this observation: "For the sake of the basketball team, as well as the good of his own health, we hope Ralph will stay away from the garage—at least on Mondays."

Either of those accidents—the explosion while he was thawing the motor one week or the car roll-over the next week—could have easily sidelined Johnson, who was the Rockets' only "big man," as well as the second-leading scorer and the leading rebounder. Without him in the sub-state, Roland probably could not have beaten Rinard. Without him in the state tournament, Roland would undoubtedly have made a quick exit.

But the undefeated team did make it to state, and Johnson said he'll never forget when they walked into the U of I Fieldhouse.

"You take a bunch of little Roland kids who probably hadn't much more than been out of Story County a time or two," Johnson said. "Put us in that atmosphere at the Armory at Iowa State, and that had been overwhelming to us. Then we got to Iowa City, and I don't think any of us had ever been in the Fieldhouse before.

"I remember walking into that place, and it was huge! We were—in today's language—blown away! We walked up into the upper deck, and looked down on that floor and really couldn't believe we were there. Buck Cheadle just kept reminding us, 'Boys, that basket is the same height as back home in Roland.'"

They checked into the Hotel Jefferson in downtown Iowa City. "We were taking taxis back and forth from the hotel to the Fieldhouse," said Johnson, "and that was a big thing for us."

The Rockets did not have warm-up pants to wear over their uniforms, only warm-up jackets. Cheadle thought that looked pretty country, so he borrowed the black warm-up pants from neighboring Story City's team. "Both schools had colors of red and black, so that worked out fine," he said.

> *"It was the first time I'd ever stayed in a hotel..."*

Each team was allowed a 1-hour practice on the Fieldhouse floor as the tournament was starting up. Roland's first-round game, set for late Wednesday afternoon, was to be against Hull, another Class B team, from northwest Iowa, but a significantly taller team.

Roland was starting its workout "when I looked up and saw this other team arrive and start watching us," Cheadle recalls. "The coach had a clipboard, was making notes and I saw these big kids wearing letter jackets with the letter 'H' on them. I knew it had to be Hull. So I called my team together on the floor.

"I said, 'Guys, we're going to do something a little different here—we're going to play a zone defense.' We never played zone. We *always* played man-to-man. In fact, when I said we were going to play a zone, Ralph Johnson said, 'Coach, where do we stand on the floor?' None of them had any idea.

"So I quickly talked through how a zone defense works, and we practiced it while the Hull team was watching. Then when they left, we went right back to man-to-man. It worked. In the game, they kept trying to play a zone offense against our man-to-man defense, and we beat them, 65-46." Thompson led Roland scoring with 16 points.

After the game, Cheadle explained some of his strategy to the sportswriters. "I'm from Oklahoma, and I've always stressed ball control and a sliding man-to-man defense, like Mr. Iba's teams," he said. "But I knew we were going to be small this year, so I got all the books I could find and studied up on the fast break and pressing defense. The boys have done fine with that."

When they would set up an offense on their end of the floor, it was what Cheadle called "a guard-around offense" or "a guard-inside" offense, with Thompson normally the guard who was directing the flow of play. "Generally, we'd freelance," Cheadle said. "Those kids were good enough that they'd keep moving, and then somebody would hit the open man with a pass, and we'd get a pretty good shot."

The Rockets had looked good, nearly everybody thought, but how could they ever handle tournament-favorite Waterloo West in the next round on Thursday night? It seemed like such a physical mismatch. Roland's starting line-up averaged 5 ft. 10 in. in height. Waterloo West averaged 6 ft. 2 ½ in.

Roaming the inside for the Wahawks were 6 ft. 7 in. Bob Miller and 6 ft. 4 in. Jim Lutgen. Dick Roeder, at 6 ft. 1 ½ in., was another forward, while the guards were 6-footers Mike Jackman and Dick Berray. They were 31-1, and had beaten Des Moines East, another team in the state field, twice during the regular season.

The Wahawks were coached by the legendary Glen "Shrimp" Strobridge, whose teams won 680 games in his 42-year career, which still today ranks him second all-time among boys basketball coaches in Iowa.

"We'd beaten Lost Nation by 30 or 40 points in our first-round game in the state tournament, and they were supposed to be good, maybe the best of the small schools," said Jackman, now a retired basketball coach in Claremont, California. "So we expected that same kind of outcome with Roland. We didn't give them the respect they deserved, that's for sure. And Gary Thompson? We weren't aware of him as the leader of that team. Coach Strobridge didn't single him out ahead of time as someone we needed to be overly concerned about."

Berray, now a retired pharmacist in Blackduck, Minnesota, recalled "we didn't know anything about Roland. In fact, I hadn't really ever heard of Roland."

Meanwhile, Coach Cheadle remembers telling his Rockets "we know Waterloo West is good, and we know this is the first time we've played a big school like them, but, guys, they put their pants on just like we do." He said he also recalls adding, "and they comb their hair just like we do, too."

No one was left at home in Roland, Cheadle said. "I think everybody in town was in Iowa City that night," the coach said. "The Story City firemen came over to Roland just to keep an eye on things."

Waterloo West went up by 10 points early in the game and led 31-24 at halftime, and 14,000 fans were sensing that the Wahawks had the game under control.

"But Roland was a very poised team," said Jackman. "They didn't get flustered at all during that first half. Then in the third quarter, they started to shoot the lights out. Gary Thompson, particularly. He just didn't miss. Dick Roeder was one of our guys who was trying to corner Gary—he was waving his arms at him, yelling at him—but it didn't make any difference. Gary just kept burying the shots."

Meanwhile, Waterloo West went ice cold. Roland took a 36-35 lead after three quarters. Then with 6:27 left in the fourth quarter, young Thompson, playing too aggressively, fouled out with the score tied at 38. He had totaled 15 points.

"He came to the bench crying," Coach Cheadle recalled, "and I was about to cry myself. But I put in Dave Peterson, who was like a sixth starter for us—I always tried to have six—and that's when we quit playing Waterloo West and started playing against the clock. I told the boys, 'We're going to put the ball in the deep freeze,' and we really did."

As the Rockets stalled, Don Holland and Ralph Johnson did most of the ball control. Each of them also slipped inside for a basket, Holland picked up a free throw and Roland held on for a 43-40 upset that sent shock waves across the whole state.

"It was heartbreaking for us and for Coach Strobridge—he was in tears," said Roeder, who is retired in LaQuinta, California. "That was one of the toughest losses in the history of Waterloo West athletics, I'm sure. But I've been in touch with Gary through the years, and I always tell him we were the guys who made him famous."

Brad Wilson reported in the *Des Moines Register* that "in the Waterloo dressing room, you could have heard a pin drop. There was only dead, gloomy silence."

The Roland victory, he wrote, made the big crowd "slightly daffy in excitement." The Rocket fans were chanting their Norwegian cheer "*Me-ska-vinna!*" And Wilson reported that young Thompson yelled out of the dressing room to a Roland fan, "What'd I tell you?"

Dick Lashier, a retired school superintendent in Clear Lake, was one of the referees who worked the game. "It was a wild and exciting one, with the crowd really noisy and pulling for the little school against the big school," he remembered. "It was one of those that everything Roland did, went well, and everything that Waterloo West did, went wrong. It was the first time I'd been aware of Gary Thompson. I noticed he was pretty little, but he was a good shooter and could really handle the ball."

While the Thursday games went on, another major snowstorm hit eastern Iowa.

"It was a blizzard, and a lot of our folks couldn't get home," said Roland fan Bob Birkeland. He, his wife Mazel Birkeland and the coach's wife Ruth Cheadle, who was riding with the Birkelands, managed to get out of Iowa City a little quicker than many of the Roland people.

"It was horrible from Iowa City to Tama, and a lot of people wound up getting stranded on the road in that stretch," Bob said. "We'd started just soon enough that we were able to make it to Tama, and then it wasn't as bad from there on to Roland." He said many Roland farmers who'd attended the game felt a special urgency to get home because "in those days, a lot of them were milking cows." Some of them got home just in time to do the Friday morning milking and then head back to Iowa City. Some who got stranded in the storm had to rely on neighbors doing the milking.

Next up for Roland, in the semi-finals of the tournament, was Des Moines East. The Scarlets were the tallest team in the field, with John Englund listed at 6 ft. 8 in., Bob Witt at 6 ft. 3 in., Ray Kaiser and Dick Koskovich both at 6 ft. 2 in. and Fritz Kasner playing point guard.

There were 14,600 fans in the Fieldhouse for the game, and there wasn't much doubt who they were backing "They were hanging from the rafters, and when we ran out on the floor, all of them were booing except for maybe the 100 people who were cheering for us," said Dick Tuller, an East reserve then who went on to a career in school administration in Des Moines. "I think my ears finally cleared up from all that sometime the next week. I'd never heard such booing!"

Kaiser, who had a long career teaching and is now retired in St. Paul Park, Minnesota, said their East coach Wendell Webb "was one of the first to use the 1-3-1 zone defense, and that usually worked real well with all our height."

But Cheadle told his Roland boys their game plan would be to try to get an early lead on East, go into a stall game and force East to abandon its zone and play man-to-man against the smaller, quicker Rockets. It worked to perfection, with Roland taking the lead 11-7 after the first quarter, 24-16 at the half and 36-27 after three quarters.

"Roland's little invincibles did it again here Friday night, subduing East of Des Moines 46-37..." wrote sportswriter Bert McGrane in the *Des Moines Register*. "The restless, relentless little outfit from a Story County high school of 73 students, spotted the Des Moines team a height advantage of 5 inches a man, and out-shot the big Scarlet array to rack up victory No. 35 in an undefeated season."

Later in the story, McGrane noted that "Roland stalled throughout much of the last period, constantly faking the slower East lads out of position."

Meanwhile, Ralph Johnson played his best offensive game of the year for the Rockets, ringing up 19 points. Gary Thompson "contented himself for the most part with a smart passing game," McGrane wrote, "but he still found time to score 9 points."

East High's Kaiser remembers that "we did not shoot well at all. Our defense was pretty good—we held them under 50 points—but as big as we were, Roland should have been a snap for us. We realized you can get beat any time, but we didn't expect them to beat us."

And Tuller came off the bench late in the game "to guard Gary Thompson, or I should say to try to guard him. He was extremely quick. He played outside, but then he'd go into the post, too. He had that flattop haircut and that grin. The crowd was all for him."

That set up the Saturday night championship game against the mighty Davenport Blue Devils, the defending state champions. It was a classic David vs. Goliath match-up that had the state enthralled.

Cheadle said of the "200 telegrams and letters" the team received during the week of the state tournament, one of his favorites was the telegram from Roland farmer and fan Aaron Braathun:

Rockets go up! Devils go down! Let's keep it that way! Beat Davenport!

Alas, it was not to be. Here is how the sportswriter McGrane began his account of what happened in the *Des Moines Sunday Register*:

> IOWA CITY, Ia.—Those game little guys from Roland finally lost a basketball game here Saturday night, but 16,127 onlookers will attest they fought like fiends before yielding, 50-40, to a Davenport team that was truly a champion...
>
> Sometimes little Gary Thompson, the 5 ft. 6 in. kid who is only 15 years old, would have to spin his high one-handers from afar when his mates couldn't get in for shorter shots. He did that eight times for baskets that just about took the breath of the onlookers...
>
> Davenport was fast, accurate and tall. Roland was only fast and accurate...
>
> Both teams were loaded with grit and a 10-man show of courage never waned until the game was over. As a result, one of the finest championship games this observer has witnessed was fought out before a crowd whose sympathies were with the smaller Roland entry, no doubt, but was quick to accredit a real championship winner in Davenport.

Roland's coach Cheadle said afterward "We made a mistake trying to run with Davenport in the last few minutes." But the real problem may have been well beyond Roland's power to do anything about, as sportswriter Tony Cordaro noted in the *Sunday Register*. "You could tell the grueling grind of three straight games against Class AA schools took its toll physically on the Story County boys," he wrote.

On two consecutive Roland possessions, Davenport's Merle Jensen stole the ball and got lay-ups, giving the Blue Devils a 35-35 tie with the Rockets. Then a reserve Ed DePooter hit two baskets and two free throws in the final 4 minutes to seal the deal.

DePooter, retired in Bettendorf after a long career with John Deere in the Quad Cities, recalled that he "was a skinny, 6-foot-tall senior that year, and I never was a starter. In fact, I hadn't played much in the state tournament at all until the semi-finals. I came off the bench and had a pretty good game that night, so Coach (Paul) Moon played me a little more in the championship. I think I wound up scoring 9 points in the fourth quarter of that game. Merle Jensen was stealing the ball and feeding me, and I got hot."

Four of the starters on that Davenport team all recalled in separate interviews that Roland had given them a very stiff challenge.

"Gary Thompson kept launching that one-handed push shot of his, and he was killing us with it," said Jensen, the team's captain, now retired in Atlanta, Georgia, after a career with IBM. "They were a remarkable team from such a small town. They had such great heart. I'll never forget that after the game, when it came time to make the awards, they called up the Roland team first for their awards. All of us Davenport players stood up and applauded for them. They deserved that. They'd had such a great run."

Carl Widseth, the 6 ft. 5 in. junior center who played on three state championship teams during his high school years in Davenport and then became an All-American at the University of Tennessee, recalled before his death in late 2007 that "we knew Roland was highly-touted, but we were able to keep them under control. That Gary, though, was quite a player. I saw him a few years later playing for the Phillips 66ers when they had a game in Nashville, and he was even better then." Widseth, who also had a career with IBM, had lived in retirement in Minneapolis.

"We got hit with a wastebasket full of water!"

Frank "Ott" Sebolt, then a sophomore guard for Davenport, said he "was impressed with Gary Thompson—he had an excellent shot—but what impressed me even more was the way their team played together. They were helping each other out on defense, sagging in on Carl Widseth, and they managed to handle him pretty well—and Carl was just a great high school player.

"We were able to stay close to them, using our zone defense, and then in the fourth quarter when we started fast-breaking, they tried to run with us and that was a big mistake for them. You couldn't run with a Paul Moon Davenport team back in that era. No one could." Sebolt went on to play at the University of Iowa, then had a career in insurance and now splits time between residences in Florida, Connecticut and Maine.

Frank Schwengel, who was a senior forward for Davenport, said his memory "is that Gary Thompson could score from everywhere on the floor, and he could play defense like you couldn't believe. He'd steal the ball, beat us all down the floor and score. He was a Bob Cousy-type of player—not necessarily very fast but very quick with the ball. That's how Roland stayed ahead of us for so long in that game.

"Plus, they were such crowd favorites. But finally we wore them down because we could bring a lot of fresh players in off the bench." Schwengel, whose father was U.S. Congressman Fred Schwengel, went on to play football and run track at the University of Iowa, then had a career in finance and banking in Santa Monica, California.

After the game, Coach Moon came into the Roland dressing room, shook hands with each of the Rockets and told Thompson, "Little man, you had a busy week!" He joked that he understood a group of Davenport High School basketball boosters "are rounding up money to buy Maurice Thompson a farm somewhere in the Davenport School District, if he'll agree to move his family."

Moon not only would joke like that, with players and coaches on opposing teams, but he went beyond that in his sportsmanship. Two weeks after the state tournament, young Thompson received a personal letter from the Davenport coach, congratulating him on being named first-team All-State.

"Dear Gary, congratulations!" Moon wrote in the letter. "That's quite a load for a sophomore to carry. I certainly hope you don't let it spoil your play from now on. Buck (Cheadle) writes you are all taking things right 'in your stride,' which is what every coach would hope. Best of luck in your baseball season... Would be nice if we were closer and could meet in baseball. Hope we can arrange a game in basketball next season."

And indeed Moon did invite Cheadle to bring the Rockets to the Davenport High gym, which could hold 3,500 people, to start the 1951-'52 season, "but we just couldn't afford to make the trip," Cheadle remembers.

Of course, immediately after the '51 championship game was completed, there were a few long faces among the Rockets—until Cheadle reminded them what they had accomplished. A few minutes later, they were swept up in the arms of their cheering families and friends. And then on Sunday morning, the fun really started.

"We left Iowa City Sunday morning, and we're seeing a lot of cars along the road, and I was thinking they must've been left out there in the snowstorms," Cheadle said. "But then we realized that people were lining up on the roads to see us, then following us. And when we started driving through other towns, there were people outside waving at us. We stopped in State Center and had dinner at a restaurant, and the people there all clapped and cheered for us when we came in."

Jake Hill, one of the seniors, remembers that "on the ride home, you'd have thought we won the tournament. At almost every bridge, people would be standing there waving at us. A lot of towns turned out for us."

Once the caravan reached Story County, there were brief receptions for the team in Colo, Nevada, Ames and Story City. Then it was on to Roland where 1,200 people had jammed the school gym to await the Rockets' return about 5:30 p.m.

The team came in dutifully wearing their overboots, winter coats, gloves and hats as ordered by Coach Cheadle. But they were also wearing their Sunday-best clothes. One sportswriter reported that Gary Thompson had on "a bright pink necktie and matching socks." (Thompson now explains, "Charcoal and pink were the popular colors back then. I even had a pink and charcoal belt.")

Among the dignitaries who showed up to congratulate the team were Iowa State College basketball coach Chick Sutherland; Iowa State's sports information director Harry Burrell; WOI radio's Dale Williams, who'd done the play-by-play on radio broadcasts of the state tournament games; Brad Wilson of the *Des Moines Register*, and others. The ceremony, which was like a pep rally, included enthusiastic welcomes from community and school officials. And Cheadle told the crowd, "I wish I could tell you how I have appreciated working with this team—your boys and my boys!"

The celebration went on into the night. That same evening, Thompson was given some shocking and sad news by his parents. On the Tuesday the state tournament had started, his uncle Sanford Thompson, of McCallsburg, died of a ruptured appendix at the age of 47.

"Gary's parents, uncles and aunts were shocked—and afraid that the news of the death would rattle him," Gus Schrader reported after the tournament in the *Cedar Rapids Gazette*. "So Gary played…in the most tremendous games in Roland's basketball history without knowing of his uncle's passing."

The funeral was held Saturday afternoon—the same day of the championship game. The first Gary knew of the ordeal his family had been through was on Sunday evening.

Sanford Thompson's widow Emma was left with seven children, ages 16 to 3. Gary had been closest with the three oldest, twins Marilyn and Marcia, who were a year older than Gary, and Stan, who was a year younger. Marilyn was an outstanding basketball player herself, for McCallsburg High and later for an Amateur Athletic Union team in Marshalltown. Stan Thompson, a leading scorer for McCallsburg, and his cousin Gary usually wound up guarding each other when their teams played.

"We'd never get mad at each other during the games, and our families would all get together after the games for ice cream," Stan said from his home in Murrieta, California. "Then on the weekends, our families would visit each other, and we'd all get out and play ball together on our outdoor courts. We had a lot of fun together. It was kind of like that with our teams, too—we all knew each other. Oh, we in McCallsburg got tired of losing to Roland, but we never got mad about it."

When he got the news of his uncle's death, Gary Thompson was suddenly as spent emotionally as he was physically, and yet, youngster that he was, he was able to bounce back very quickly. For him and the Rockets, a long run of celebrations and sports glory were just beginning. And they were ready to work even harder for it, too.

Cheadle, now in his late 80s and retired in Oklahoma, said he'll never forget how exhausted he was after the tournament and grand homecoming.

"By that Monday evening, I was so tired that after supper, I could barely keep my eyes open," he told me. "But I glanced out from my house and I could see the lights were on over at the outdoor basketball court behind the school. So I walked over there, and here was my whole team, scrimmaging! They had shoveled the snow off the court and were out there playing. They were the most coachable kids I ever had."

In the coming days and weeks, the Rockets were honored again in Story City and Ames. Cheadle was in demand as a speaker at other schools' basketball banquets. And the post-season banquet in Roland was bigger than ever before.

Those banquets were always for both the boys' and girls' basketball teams, and Cheadle was coaching the girls to almost as much success as the boys were having. His first year at the school, the Roland girls went 10-8, and their combined records the next two seasons was 40-6. In the same '51 season when the boys went 35-1, the girls had been beaten in the finals of the district tournament, or they would have been in their own state tournament.

"They were the most coachable kids I ever had..."

So there was plenty of cause for celebration at the Roland basketball banquet. More than 300 people attended. There was a big meal, there were songs by the 18-member Roland Men's Chorus, then skits involving chorus members and more music.

Bob Birkeland was a chorus member and remembers insurance agent Don Boyd was their director and Loren Rosheim was accompanist. "We were just a bunch of so-sos at singing, really," Birkeland said, "but Don and Loren were so good they could make a bunch of fence posts sing!"

Boyd, hatchery manager Orris Osheim and banker/farmer Pete Twedt acted as "the singing announcers," performing hilarious musical introductions of the special guests and honorees. WHO radio broadcaster Jim Zabel came from Des Moines to be guest speaker, and of course Cheadle made special remarks about the teams and individual players.

"Zabel had called me and said he wanted to come speak at our banquet for free," Cheadle recalled. "He brought along a six-pack of beer, too. So afterward, he came over to our house, and he and I drank some beer while we talked. I told him he had to take the empty beer cans back to Des Moines with him, because people in Roland thought I was O.K., that I didn't drink, and I couldn't be setting the empties out with the trash."

Meanwhile, the accolades kept piling up for Gary Thompson. One of the nicest salutes probably came in a column by Gus Schrader, of the *Cedar Rapids Gazette*.

"The most terrific sophomore in 20 years of state tournament basketball —that's what they're calling Gary Thompson, Roland's rapid runt," Schrader wrote. "The kid helped Roland throw the tourney dope book out the window, and he did it by overcoming incredible shortcomings of height, age, experience and big-time competition."

A half-century later, Thompson looked back on that '51 season and tournament, which as he says launched him toward the career and life he has enjoyed ever since, and is still a little awed by it all.

"Naturally we were disappointed in not winning," he said, "but it was so unbelievable for a school our size doing what we'd done—phenomenal really."

Frank Egland, one of those three seniors who'd been such steady players on the team, says now, after all these years, "I think the biggest disappointment in my life was that we got beat that night. I've always said, 'If that was a three-quarters game, we were state champs!' But what we did that basketball season has carried through the years for me and helped me in my career. I could always think back to that experience in Roland and say, 'Well, if you do the right thing, things will pretty well come out right.' "

The 1951-'52 season, when Gary was a junior, was about to begin in November when the whole Gary Thompson story nearly ended—in a car accident on a dark gravel road between Ames and Roland late one Sunday night.

"Three buddies and I had been to a movie in Ames that night, and we were sitting around Frango's restaurant talking after we had something to eat there," Thompson recalled. "The other three guys were seniors—LaVerne Anderson, Loren Jacobson and Hollis Fosse. Hollis and I were on the basketball team, and our Sunday night team curfew was 11 o'clock. All of a sudden, I looked at a clock and it was 20 'til 11. I can't remember whether it was LaVerne or Loren who said, 'Geemanee! We've got to get you home!' "

They knew Buck Cheadle would be checking on Thompson and Fosse. They all ran to the nearly new Oldsmobile that Anderson was driving, with Thompson in the front passenger seat.

"Hollis and I wanted to go the normal route, up Highway 69 and then east to Roland, but the other guys wanted to go the back roads because he thought it'd be quicker," Thompson said. "So we took off on Dayton Avenue, which was a gravel road then, and LaVerne was gunning it—60, 65, 70 miles an hour.

"We were coming down a long sloping road, and then right in front of us was a 'T' intersection that we didn't know was there. I yelled, 'LaVerne! Turn! Turn!' He managed to get the car turned about 90 degrees, but it started sliding and went sideways into the bank. If we'd hit that bank head-on, I know I would have gone right through the windshield because I was sitting in the 'suicide seat,' which is what we called the front passenger seat."

The car rolled upside down after hitting the bank. It was totaled. Thompson had blood all over his face, and his ribs were screaming. Driver Anderson wound up cramped up under the steering wheel, and later found out he had a broken leg. Fosse broke his ribs. Jacobson, the least injured, was the first to shake off the wooziness and climb out of the car. Thompson and Fosse then climbed out. Anderson was still pinned.

The three boys could see a farmhouse's light about a half-mile away, and were about to start walking there, but then they heard another car's door open, and saw the car parked along the lonely country road. "It was an older gal from Roland and her date who were parked out there," Thompson said. "They gave us a ride to that farmhouse, and the farm people called for help for us."

Iowa Highway Patrolmen rushed to the scene, and officers Chuck Elliott and Melvin Hove, both based in Ames, were among those who got the four boys to the hospital in Ames for treatment. "I told the troopers the first thing I had to do was call Coach Cheadle," Thompson said, "but they were calling our parents and told us our folks would take care of calling the coach."

The cut on Thompson's head required 12 stitches to close. He missed one early season basketball game, but then was quickly back to top form on the court. "All four of us knew how lucky we'd been," Thompson said.

Years later, a woman approached Thompson in the Ames Post Office and told him he had helped introduce her to the man who became her husband. Thompson didn't know what she was talking about, but then she explained she had been a nurse working at the Ames hospital the night Patrolmen Elliott and Hove brought Thompson and the three other Roland boys in after the car accident.

"I was just out of nurse's training and was the R.N. on duty that night," Myrna Wilhelm Elliott recently recalled. "I was so busy, trying to get vitals on the boys and getting them ready for the doctor to see them, that while I did notice the two Highway Patrolmen there, I didn't pay much attention to them. But apparently Chuck Elliott was paying a little more attention to me, because two nights later he called me up and asked me out on a date."

In September, 1952, they married and they stayed in Ames. Chuck Elliott died in late 2007. Myrna Elliott also recalled something unusual that happened when she was taking care of the Roland boys on that long ago night.

"I knew who Gary Thompson was, because I'd read all about him in the newspapers for his basketball," she said, "but I didn't know the other three boys. I do remember that one of the others, when I was checking on him, was more worried about Gary than he was about himself. He was saying, 'Is Gary still going to be able to play basketball? Is this going to end his career?' I said, 'No, it isn't going to end his career—Gary's going to be just fine—don't you worry.' "

The '51-'52 Rockets had to rebuild, after losing the three senior starters from the previous year. Thompson, who had grown to 5 ft. 8 in., and seniors Don Holland and Dave Peterson were returning starters, and four newcomers stepped up to play key roles—seniors Kenny Lein and Clark Twedt, and juniors Stan Tjernagel and Dave Twedt.

Coach Cheadle said that Lein and Clark Twedt represented quite a story. "When I took the job at Roland in 1949, there were 73 in high school and 41 of them were boys," the coach said. "When basketball started, 34 of the boys came out for the team. I was shocked—and overwhelmed. I had to divide them up some way, so I could work with them like I needed to.

"So I picked an 'A' squad and a 'B' squad. Then I told the other kids that I really didn't want to cut them, but there was no way I was going to be able to coach them every day. Several of them said, 'No, that's fine—we'll go outdoors and practice on the outdoor court—we just want to play.' So we made them the 'C' squad, and I'd check on them as much as I could. Well, two of those 'C' team guys were Kenny Lein and Clark Twedt, and we eventually had them in the starting line-up!"

The Rockets won five in a row to open the season, then were beaten by a good Storm Lake team, 48-37, in a "basketball clinic" game played at Grinnell. "Storm Lake played a zone trap against us, something we'd never seen," said Thompson. "We were down by almost 20 points at halftime, but then we came back pretty well on them."

Roland wouldn't lose again until they got to Iowa City for the '52 state tournament. But they were pushed hard in two notable games in the sub-state tournament against small-school powers. In the first round, they beat a talented LuVerne team, the Wrens, 61-42. Then they faced the Boxholm Swedes, who had been aching for a match-up with Roland, in the sub-state finals in the Armory at Iowa State.

Bob Looft, coach of the Swedes, "figured we had a way of stopping Gary Thompson. We'd get a hand in front of his face all the time and chase him all over the floor. We were staying close to them, but then that stinker hit about a 30-foot jump shot that turned the tide. But I didn't stay mad at him. I was so tickled with what they did in the '51 tournament, and Buck Cheadle always did such a good job with the talent he had. It was fun to watch them."

Roland won it 47-43, and the *Nevada Evening Journal's* account of the game is a classic: "The mighty Gods of the Northland decreed last night that the intrepid Norwegians of Roland would represent Scandinavia in the contests of the greats at Iowa City. The powerful Lords of Mortal Warriors & Conquerors did first cast their lots to one side and then to the other. Nor would they choose until the clock did end the game and behold the strength of the Rockets had prevailed."

Just like that *Evening Journal* sportswriter, the Roland fans were having all kinds of fun with their ethnic heritage. It was almost expected of them, after the state's media "discovered" it during the '51 state tournament run.

The Roland team often was referred to in print as "the Nervy Norwegians." And the "Norwegian Yell" the cheerleaders would use contained at least two lines from the old country that the crowd would roar, "*Du-maw-vinna!*" ("We must win!") and "*Lot os gaw*" (presumably "Let's go!"). Here's how it went, according to one old transcription the newspapers reported:

"The team was in the huddle, The coach had said his word! We over heard the conversation, And this is what we heard:
Du-maw-vinna, Du-maw-vinna! (clap) *Lot os gaw!*
Du-maw-vinna, Du-maw-vinna! (clap) *Lot os gaw!*
Come nu Roland,
Lot os gaw!"

If some crowd was chanting that today, other fans might be howling about English being "the official language." But in 1952, it was all in good fun.

Brothers Pete and Jerry Twedt recalled another cheer that was a favorite of the Roland crowd, reserved for when the Rockets were ahead by 20 or more with about two minutes left in a game. Everybody would chant:

Du-maw-vinna, Du-maw-vinna! Tu-sa-ta, ha!
We're gonna beat you,
Ha-ha-ha!

"That's why the other schools hated us," Jerry Twedt said with a laugh.

Gary Thompson, who was carrying a 21.3 points per game scoring average in his junior year, was increasingly sought out for interviews, as the Rockets got ready for the state tournament. It seemed like every publication wanted to have a Thompson story.

The Iowa Temperance League even featured him in a testimonial ad in their magazine "The Margin," which circulated statewide. It identified him as the 16-year-old Roland star and quoted him this way:

"I think alcohol is one rotten thing that lowers the standard of living a lot. It's hazardous to other people who do not drink it, and who have to drive the highways with drinkers on it. I think if we got rid of all the taverns, this country, and the whole world, would be a better place to live. I even hate the smell of drink, and hate to associate with a person who drinks alcoholic beverages."

Roland, coming into the state tournament, was "the big thunder among the B's," Brad Wilson of the *Des Moines Register* wrote, referring to the Class B schools that had made the Sweet 16 with the larger schools. He noted that Thompson was even "playing some center" when the Rockets would face a man-to-man defense, presumably because Thompson could fake his way open and get to the basket. He "is blessed with every shot in the book," Wilson wrote, who also referred to him as "the Midget Mikan," as in George Mikan, the 6 ft. 10 in. superstar of professional basketball in that era.

Jack North, writing in the Des Moines Tribune, previewed the '52 state tourney field, including this: "Gary Thompson, an All-Stater as a sophomore last year, is again the playmaker of the Rockets, and his brilliant work has been responsible for another great season for Coach Buck Cheadle's squad. He has occasionally been playing the post on offense, and when bottled up under the basket, Gary moved out in front where he hit with his one-handed shots. He's been given a lot of splendid cooperation from Don Holland, Clark and Dave Twedt, Dave Peterson, Stan Tjernagel and Ken Lein in helping the school complete at 29-1 record this year."

The tournament games in the Fieldhouse at the University of Iowa were as packed as always. Fans from Glenwood, in far southwest Iowa, were so excited when their team qualified for the tournament that they chartered a DC-3 transport airplane to carry people to Iowa City and back.

Roland had a close call in its opening game at state, scrambling to beat another small school Readlyn 49-46. And it was immediately after that game when a girl, a furious fan of the Readlyn team, confronted him on the floor and slapped him.

In the second round, Roland dominated Spencer, 46-33, shutting down the Tigers' Bob Carpenter, who had scored 32 points in a first-round game but could get only 10 against the Rockets. (Dan Neville was a guard on that Spencer team, and 30 years later, as principal at Ballard High School serving Huxley and Slater, he gave Gary and Janet Thompson's daughter Kim Wierson her first teaching job. Another 20 years later, Neville's son Joe coached the Thompsons' grandson Brandon in basketball.)

In the '52 semi-finals, Roland could not handle the Keokuk Chiefs and its 6 ft. 5 in. center, Bill Logan. Keokuk won, 55-43, with Logan scoring 30 points and Thompson getting 10.

Logan, now semi-retired as chairman of his family's State Central Bank headquartered in Keokuk, recalls that "we knew that Buck Cheadle had put together a heck of a program in that little town. Three straight years in a one-class state tournament, from a town of 750? That's really something, isn't it? His kids had played together since they were little boys, and it showed.

"They all knew everything each other was going to do. They were all pretty good shooters and pretty fair rebounders, but they didn't match-up very well with somebody my size, so I pretty well controlled the rebounding. When we were preparing to play against them, we knew we had to slow down Gary Thompson. My classmate Bobby Williams was about 6 ft. 2 in. and our best defensive player, so he was assigned to guard Gary. Bobby stayed on him really good—and that's what really won the game for us."

Logan went on to be a starter on the "Fabulous Five" team at the University of Iowa that was in consecutive NCAA Final Fours, and finished runner-up in 1956 to the University of San Francisco team starring Bill Russell and K.C. Jones.

Even after all the fine arenas and big games he played in, Logan says the atmosphere at the Iowa boys' state tournament "was something I've never forgotten. The Fieldhouse seemed like it was packed all the time. Teams would come down and stay all week long, so there were lots of people at every game. Davenport would come out on the floor, with what seemed like about 5,000 fans cheering for them, then the rest of the fans would start booing! It was great!

"The maintenance man at the Fieldhouse back then was 'Windy' Brown—maybe the nickname was because he always had a lot to say—and he'd run that temperature up to about 78 degrees in there. Kids would get on those old steel bleachers, be stomping their feet in unison, and the noise was just deafening!"

After the loss to Keokuk, Roland played in the Saturday consolation game against a good team from little Dinsdale, and the Rockets lost 48-46 in overtime. That ended another great season, with a 31-3 record.

Two days after that '52 state tournament was over, Coach Cheadle dropped a bomb on Roland, announcing he'd be leaving at the end of the school year to become head basketball coach at Burlington. "The people here have been wonderful," Cheadle told reporters. "However, like all young coaches, I feel that I've gone about as far as I can at Roland, and now is the time to move up to a bigger school."

He'd had a three-year record of 95-6 with the Roland boys and led them to second and fourth place finishes in consecutive state tournaments. His Roland baseball teams, in 2 years, had a 44-8 record, with one more spring season to go. He'd been paid $3,500 his first year at the school, including his coaching pay. He got a $100 raise for his second year, and a $300 raise for his third year.

"I got a better raise, going to Burlington," he said, "and they had a local pilot fly me back and forth for the interviewing. They took me around to all the civic clubs while I was visiting. Burlington had always been a great football town—they'd won the mythical state football championship 2 years in a row—but it had the reputation of being a basketball graveyard. They said they were ready to build the basketball program, and I told their school board if we didn't make it to the state tournament within 5 years, I'd resign. My first year there, we got some breaks and went 16-9, and the community started getting interested in basketball. About the third year I was there, we made it to state."

Cheadle spent 8 years in Burlington, then went on to Rockford High School in Illinois for 7 years. He returned to Iowa to coach 7 years at Pekin of Packwood in southeast Iowa, then in 1974 returned to his native Oklahoma.

He directed the Indian Education Program in Putnam City there for two years, then for 8 years was a counselor for Indian students at East Central State University in Ada. He retired in 1984, but still worked in the adult education program for the Chickasaw Nation while continuing to live near the tribal headquarters in Ada.

"My time in Roland was the best 3 years of my coaching life," Cheadle said during an interview in Oklahoma. "I still think about Roland all the time. In fact, the other day I was thinking about it and I got tears in my eyes. You know, I'm still mad at myself for leaving before Gary Thompson's senior year. I had good years after Roland, but I still wish somebody there would have kicked my rear and said, 'You at least want to stay here one more year!' "

Thompson remembers being "disappointed when Buck left, of course, but we all understood why he did. It was a good opportunity at a larger school. It was rough at first on him there at Burlington, because it had never been a basketball school, but he had them playing for state championships within 5 years. And we stayed in touch with each other. We communicated all through that next year, and actually have stayed in contact ever since."

To show you what high regard fans across the state had for Buck Cheadle, he was invited to be the guest speaker when the Boxholm Swedes had their annual basketball banquet in that early spring of 1952. Remember, Cheadle's Rockets had beaten Coach Bob Looft's Swedes in the sub-state finals game.

"There was a really funny introduction of Buck," Looft said. "I can't remember who did it, but the fellow was telling all that Buck's teams had done at Roland, and then he said, 'And now I'd like you to meet Gary Thompson's little helper—Buck Cheadle!' "

Cheadle played right along with that introduction, and mentioned how young Thompson had helped the coach get a big new job. But within a few days, another job change was announced—Boxholm's Looft would move to Roland and become head coach of boys' basketball and baseball.

"I became 'Gary Thompson's little helper' myself quite a few times in the next year," Looft now says with a laugh.

He was a native of Armstrong in north central Iowa who, after graduating from high school in the World War II years, went immediately into the U.S. Navy. He took officer training at DePauw University in Indiana, went to military duty and then returned after the war to finish his college degree work in science at DePauw. He came back to Iowa State College in the summer of 1947 to get his certification as a teacher, and landed his first teaching and coaching job at Boxholm in the fall of '47. He was at Roland from the fall of 1952 to the summer of 1956.

"I don't think I really knew who Duke Ellington was..."

"We had a whole lot of talent in Roland, not only with Gary, but with a lot of young kids coming up through the grades," Looft said. "It's interesting how when you get a good program like that going, you see the results for years to come."

He directed the Rockets back to the state tournament in 1953; they lost in the sub-state finals in 1954, and went back to state in 1955 and lost to eventual champion Ames, in the first-round of the first state tournament played at the new Veterans Memorial Auditorium in Des Moines. When he left Roland in '56, "we had a good bunch starting high school then, and 2 years later, in 1958, Roland won a Class B state championship after the tournament had been changed to two classes," Looft said.

He had completed his master's degree at Iowa State in 1955, so when he moved on from Roland he began his administrative career. He served as superintendent of schools in Volga in northeast Iowa for a year, then Ruthven in northwest Iowa for 4 years and then Clarinda in southwest Iowa for 5 years. In 1966, after he had earned his doctorate at Iowa State, Looft became the founding president of Iowa Western Community College in Council Bluffs. He served 21 years in that position and is now retired in that city.

But now back to Roland in 1952. "My wife Marilyn and I were both small town people, and we really enjoyed our life there in Roland," Looft said. "She had grown up in Gilbert, attended church in Story City and her mother was living in Story City, so we'd been nearby and had already had a lot of contact with Roland. When we moved in there, it was very easy to get to know the banker, the grocery, everybody. We quickly felt right at home there.

"Of course, everybody knew that Roland had a lot of basketball players and that Gary Thompson was very talented," Looft continued. "But it was nice to see that in Roland, the people didn't treat him as a star. He was one of the kids. His parents were very nice people, very down to earth, very supportive." Did the new coach feel extra pressure to produce?

"I didn't feel there was too much pressure," Looft said. "It was more like the community had healthy expectations of the kids. But people were willing to leave the coaching to me. I had one parent who did come to me privately and say he was concerned that his son was not getting to play enough. So I invited the parent to attend practice, and you know what? He agreed with me, that his son needed to work harder!"

So the Rockets began the 1952-'53 season with a new coach, a new line-up and somewhat of a new attitude from opponents.

"My sophomore year, we kind of sneaked up on everybody," Gary Thompson said. "My junior year, everybody seemed to be waiting for us. By my senior year, most of the towns around us were kind of tired of us winning all the time, which isn't hard to understand, and they were against us."

Thompson, who had grown to 5 ft. 9 ½ in., was joined in the starting line-up by four of these other five Rockets—seniors Stan Tjernagel at 6 ft. 1 in., Dave Twedt at 5 ft. 10 in., LaVerne Hovde at 6 ft. 3 in., junior Harlan Hall at 6 ft. 3 in. and sophomore Alan Erickson at 6 ft.

They were an amazing team, really. They went on a 19-0 run through the regular season, and the closest any team came to them was Randall in the 47-41 game—the one in which a girl slapped Gary at halftime.

"Gary had an excellent season," said Looft, and the statistics support that evaluation. He averaged 24.6 points per game, four rebounds and four assists per game for all games, including their tournament run.

"He was very innovative," Looft continued. "With the kind of talent we had, you didn't really use set plays. I'd just let the kids play their game. I'll never forget that tight game we had at Randall. It went right down to the wire. Gary came in on the left side, stopped 8 or 10 feet from the basket and took a shot that banked into the basket to win it—a shot that I'd never seen him take before. I think he kind of made it up in mid-air.

"He would do whatever had to be done to get a victory. Another time, toward the end of the season, a team was double-teaming and triple-teaming him. So in a time out, I said, 'Gary, we're going to get you the ball out at mid-court, and everybody else will clear out, and I want to see if you can get through whoever they put on you.' So we did that, and three of the opposing players came out to guard him out there at mid-court. That stinker went through all three of them and scored. It was really fun to see him do it."

Perhaps that was the last regular season game, at Nevada, a fairly tight game Roland won 61-52. One of the officials in that game may have been Lloyd Dresser, a former coach and school administrator who did a lot of refereeing in addition to selling textbooks to schools. Dresser, in his late 90s in 2006, recalled in his Ames home how he had officiated a Roland game against Nevada in Thompson's senior year.

"It was kind of a slow humdrum game starting out, except that Nevada had a real burn going because they hadn't beaten Roland for so long," Dresser recalled. "In the first quarter, Gary wasn't hitting his shots very well, and he wasn't hitting free throws, either. He really was mumbling to himself. And Roland fell behind. At the half, Nevada was still ahead and their fans were getting excited.

"After three quarters, Nevada was still leading and their crowd was aroused! But then Gary got hot, and started hitting from all over the floor. He'd shoot over the man guarding him, or drive around him, or drive to the corner and hit a potshot from there. My memory is that he scored 18 points in that fourth quarter, and Roland won it. The crowd was irate at the end."

There was a neutral fan at that game who had a different view of what happened. He subsequently wrote a letter to young Thompson, blistering him for the way he had played. Interestingly, among a very few letters that Thompson has saved over the decades—like the ones from Coach Paul Moon at Davenport High School and from Coach Forrest "Phog" Allen at the University of Kansas—is that one from the angry fan. It is dated January 26, 1953, and was signed by a David C. Mathis of Des Moines. He clearly wanted to deliver a message to the rising young superstar.

Mathis began by explaining that he had seen Thompson play at Nevada, and then wrote:

> ...I had heard quite a bit about you, and read more. I came prepared to see a smooth technician in action, an almost flawless high school

performer. I did see that. But, to my disgust and disappointment, I saw more. By your obvious "show-off" antics on the floor, you relegated yourself back to just another publicity-struck youngster. In my following of, and participation in, sports, I have seen literally hundreds like you who are on the way to becoming something, there is a brief moment of stardom, and then—oblivion!

On the other hand, the truly great athlete need not shout his prowess to the world.

Whaddya think, Gary, do you want to become known as a two-bit exhibitionist, or four-flusher, a phony when by the Gods, you could be terrific? If you plan to go on to college, kid, get that show-off attitude out of your way of thinking. Believe me, you'll be a sad sack if you don't. And, of course, the Army is not too far ahead of you. Nuff said.

This is written in genuine appreciation of your talent, and not intended to sound off, because I realize you are still immature, and perhaps you may not think you are making rather an ass of yourself.

Bests wishes, I remain,

David C. Mathis
Des Moines, Iowa

All these years later, I could not find Mathis to talk to him about his letter. But if he is still out there somewhere, he can know that his point was well-taken by Thompson. After all, Gary has kept the letter. It's been another good reminder for him, just like his mother's long-ago warning, "Don't you even think about getting the big head!"

Of course, the Roland Rockets tried to set-up Thompson with good shots as often as possible. "Gary and I were the guards most of the season," Dave Twedt recalled in an interview in Newton, Iowa, where he is retired after a 35-year career in the payroll department at Maytag Corporation headquarters. "My job was to get the ball outside, set screens and start what we called a 'three-man roll' or a 'five-man roll' that would try to get Gary loose for a shot. I didn't care to shoot myself. I knew if we could get the ball to Gary, our team had a better chance of winning."

And Lloyd Dresser, the old referee, said he "never thought Gary was hogging the ball in high school. He was really a good team player. But when he'd get hot, his teammates would naturally keep going to him."

They cruised through the county tournament, and won all three sectional tournament games by more than 30 points. In the district, Roland beat Jordan by 19 and then had a close game with Slater before winning 46-39. In the sub-state, they beat Coach Looft's former school Boxholm by 11 in the first-round. And

(Continued on page 81)

The Roland Years

LAUNCHING THE ROCKET. The central Iowa town of Roland has a population of more than 1,300 today, but it was only 687 when Gary Thompson grew up there. He helped lead the Rockets from old Roland High School to statewide acclaim before he graduated in 1953. Below are his parents Abbie and Maurice Thompson, now deceased, and to the right of them is a recent photo of Gary (right) and his brother DeLon Thompson, now a professional country singer in Tucson, Arizona

GIVE HIM THE BALL. A formal photo of the infant Gary Thompson, already with a ball in his hand. At the left, Thompson stands outside the Roland home of his high school years.

ON THE WAY UP. Above, Gary Thompson (left) and his classmate Darrel Egemo had lunchroom jobs pouring milk and washing dishes, for "free noon meals for us, plus 50 cents per hour, plus all the ice cream we could eat." At the left, Gary played in the era when players moved from the old "set shot" to the jump shot. The 1949-'50 team photo below shows 5 ft. 2 in. freshman Gary (back row, next to Coach Buck Cheadle) as a member of the traveling squad.

1950 Roland Rockets

Front row: Vernon Eggland, Dave Swenson, Roald Nelson, Ralph Johnson, Wayne Strum
Back row: Loren Jacobson, Don Hplland, Loren Twedt, Stan Tjernagel, Jake Hill, Dave Peterson, Frank Eggland, Gary Thompson & "Buck" Cheadle

TWO-SPORT SENSATION. Gary Thompson helped the Roland Rockets reach state tournaments in both baseball and basketball. Above, he's shown at a state baseball tournament game at Mason City. Below, Thompson was probably best known for his basketball play. He reached 5 ft. 6 in. as a sophomore, then 5 ft. 9 ½ in. as a senior, and he became Iowa's all-time career scoring leader and was named first team All-State three consecutive years. In the recent photo, Thompson stands in the old Roland High School gym, where the Rockets did not lose from 1946 to 1958, including Thompson's four years as a player. The gym is now used by middle school students in the Roland-Story Schools after a long-ago consolidation between Roland and Story City.

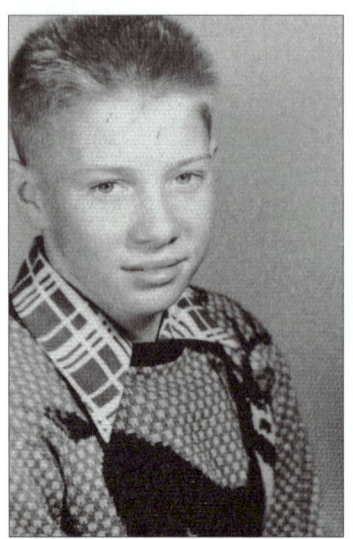

MAKING MAGIC. Left above, Gary Thompson is shown in his freshman year at Roland High School. At the right, Ralph Johnson, now a retired educator in Dayton, Iowa, was one of three seniors in the Roland Rockets' basketball starting line-up in 1950-'51 when sophomore Gary joined them. Roland fans had thought it would be a rebuilding season. But the Rockets finished a magical 35-1 season, with their only loss coming to mighty Davenport in the state championship game. Below, Coach Buck Cheadle would have his team sprawl on their stomachs during timeouts "to get them off their feet for a minute or two," as he said.

OLD PALS. Alan Hoskins, now of Kansas City, Kansas, grew up in Roland's neighboring town of Zearing and was a high school opponent but admirer of Gary Thompson. "I always told Gary I was one of the guys who made him All-State, because he'd score 43 points against me and sit out the whole second half," said Hoskins. At right, young Gary about the time Roland fans began noticing his athletic potential.

THE HANGOUT. In the early 1950s, the hottest hanging-out spot for teenagers from across central Iowa — but mostly the small towns — was the new Skateland roller rink on the south side of Ames. It's where Gary Thompson first met Janet Sydnes, of Huxley, starting a romance that has endured more than 50 years. They skated four nights a week in their high school years. Skateland owner Floyd Penkhus, now retired in Ames, remembers the atmosphere: "I don't know how we ever got it done, but the girls had to wear dresses or skirts, the boys had to wear slacks, and some would even wear coats and neckties. We wouldn't let a kid in with a T-shirt."

Personalities . .

On the basis of personality, citizenship, scholarship and participation in extracurricular activities, the student body nominated Charlene Hall and Gary Thompson as representative girl and boy of the class of '53.

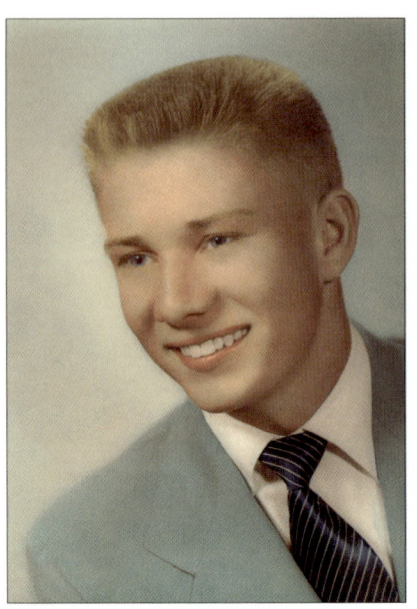

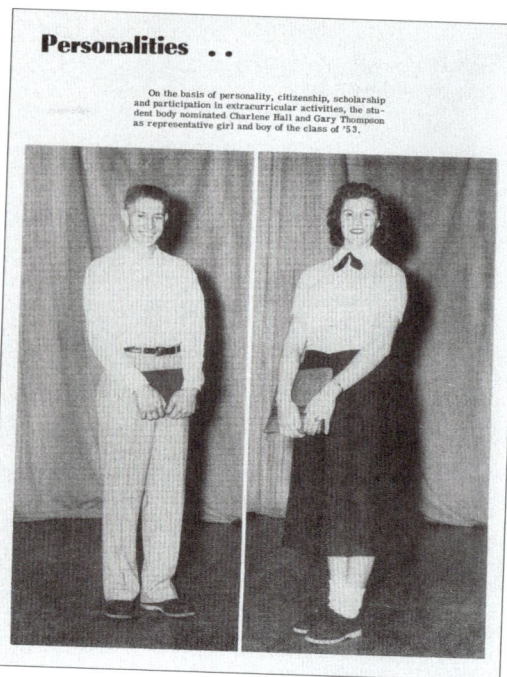

BIG REWARDS. Gary Thompson, above at left, in his high school graduation photo. He and Charlene Hall, a star on the girls' basketball team, were "representative boy and girl" of the Class of 1953 in the *Rocket* yearbook. Below, sophomore Thompson leaves '51 state tourney game against Waterloo West. "Almost all the opportunities that came my way later in life happened because of what got started in that one game," he says.

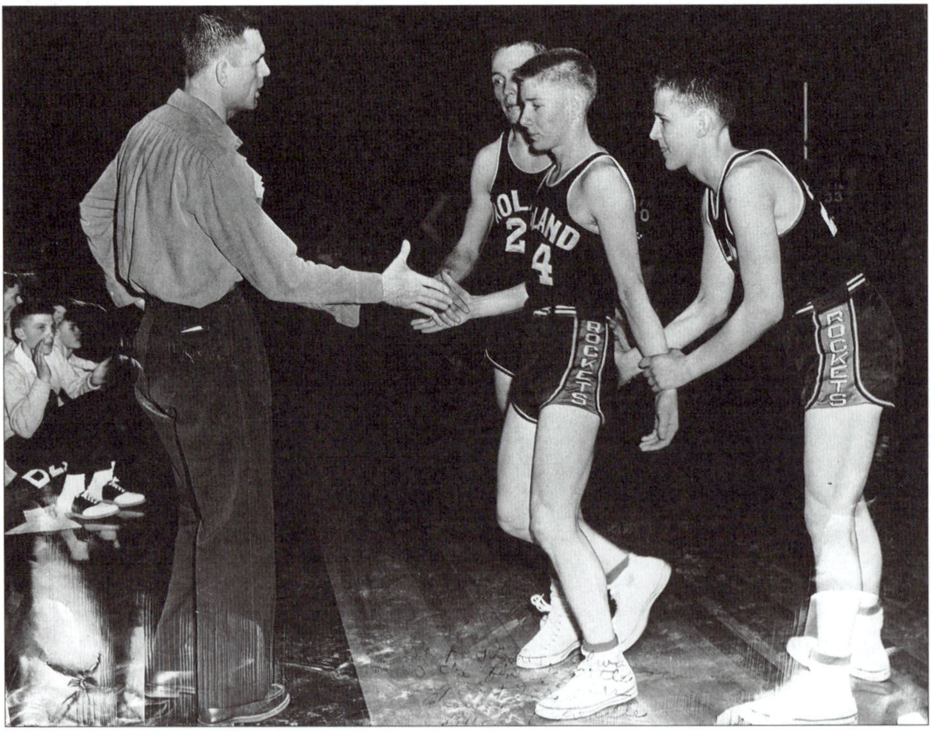

FANS & MENTORS. Three longtime Roland friends and fans of Gary Thompson are (left to right) Harris "Pete" Twedt, Aaron Braathun and Bob Birkeland, all of whom cheered him on in his high school years. They are shown at one of the town signs with the traditional Norwegian welcome. Below, Thompson puts up a hook shot

LIKE A CROWN. When Des Moines Tribune sportswriter Tony Cordaro, known for the unusual hats he always wore, honored his "prep player of the week" one basketball season, he'd snap a photo of the star wearing a coonskin cap and induct him into "Cordaro's Coonskin Cap Club." Gary Thompson is shown when he won the honor for his play with the Roland Rockets. (Photo by Tony Cordaro, copyright 1953, The Des Moines Register and Tribune Company, reprinted with permission.)

SOUVENIR EDITION

The Roland Record, Roland, Iowa

JULY 14, 1957

GARY THOMPSON DAY

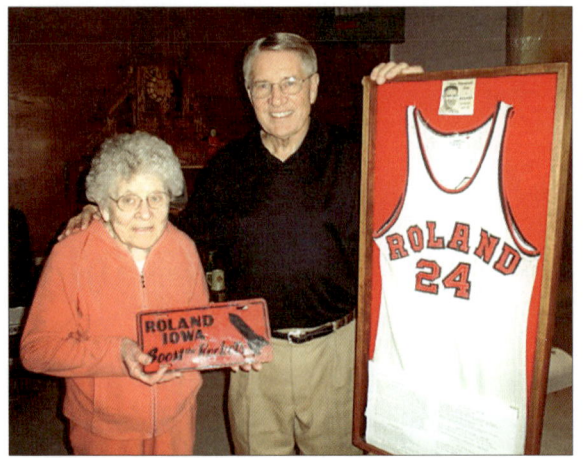

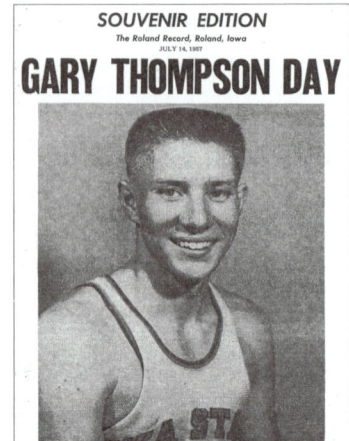

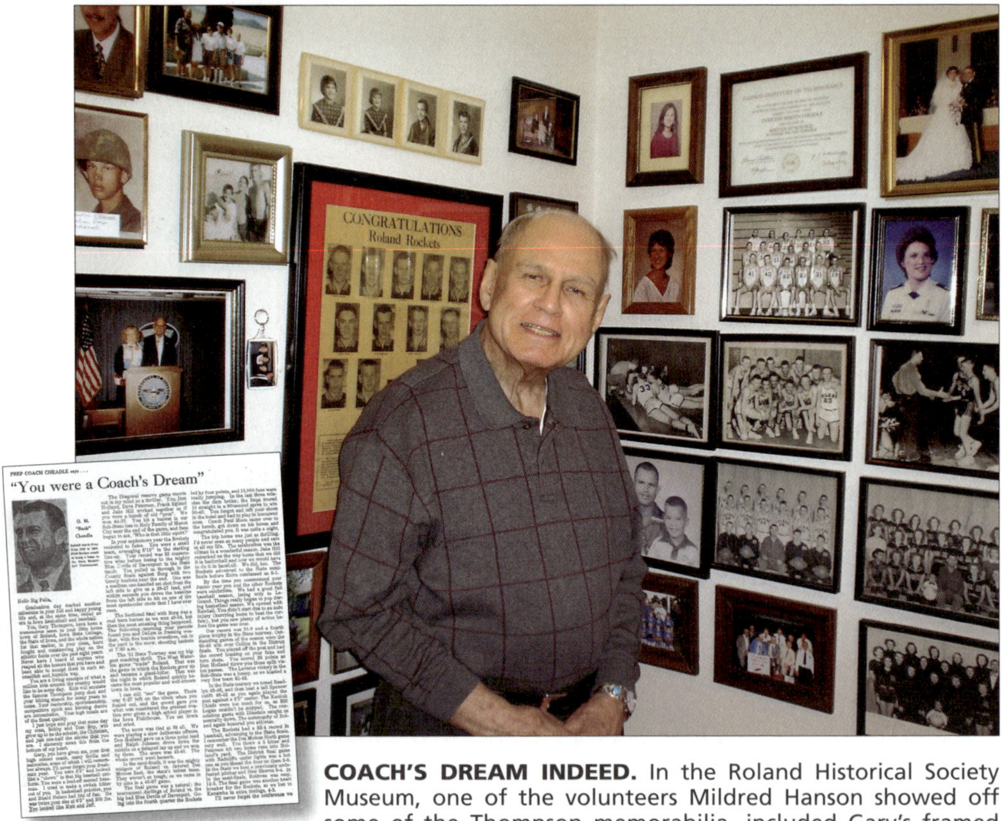

PREP COACH CHEADLE says . . .

"You were a Coach's Dream"

O. M. "Buck" Cheadle

Hello Big Fella,

COACH'S DREAM INDEED. In the Roland Historical Society Museum, one of the volunteers Mildred Hanson showed off some of the Thompson memorabilia, included Gary's framed basketball jersey that Roland High School retired. Below, Coach Buck Cheadle, shown here at 86 years old in early 2005 in his home in Ada, Oklahoma, was Gary Thompson's coach his first three years at Roland High School. He recalls his time in Roland as the highlight of his long coaching career, evidenced by the many team photos on the walls of his home. The newspaper pages are from the Roland Record's special edition in 1957 when the town celebrated Gary's high school and college careers.

would appear in a testimonial advertisement for a concert that would be held Friday night in the Iowa Memorial Union featuring the jazz piano star Duke Ellington.

He said yes. And the ad appeared that week in the student newspaper, the *Daily Iowan*, with a photo of the Roland team and this quote attributed to Thompson: "The Duke's great! I've seen him on TV and heard his records. I'd sure like to stay and hear him Friday night!" The ad also noted that tickets were on sale at the Union for $1.25 each.

A half-century later, Thompson is still wondering "whether I really knew who Duke Ellington was then," but he went along with the fun.

The *Iowa City Press-Citizen* reported another side of the state tournament that was a tradition in the Fieldhouse, but was abandoned when the games were moved to Des Moines:

> Tournament fans see only a brief part of the action on the Fieldhouse court this week. Along about 10 p.m., an all-night session begins, with several hundred youths taking turns at playing on six courts on the center floor and in the gym.
>
> University officials supervise the kids, with one group on duty from 10 p.m. until 2 a.m.. Another group keeps watch from 2 a.m. until 8:30 a.m.
>
> The youths are sleeping in the Fieldhouse this week, and one group plays until it gets tired, then wakes up another group and takes their place in bed, and the play continues until everyone is worn to a frazzle. It's quite a sight, this "night owl" tournament.

Meanwhile, in the real tournament, Roland easily handled Earling St. Joseph in its first-round game, 68-48, with Thompson scoring 26.

The Rockets then faced Clarence, another small-school powerhouse. And that game included one of the most memorable moments in Iowa high school sports history—unfortunately a heartbreaking moment for one young athlete, his team and community.

The Clarence Cardinals, coming from a town of about 1,000 midway between Cedar Rapids and Clinton, were having their best season ever. Coach Bill Holmstrom's team was 27-0 before losing a late game in the regular season, and that just made them hungrier for victories in the tournament.

"We had some really close calls once we started the tournament games," said Merlyn Bixler, a retired farmer near Clarence who was on that team. "We beat Calamus by 1 point in the sectional finals, and we had another tight one with Sabula in the district. When we made the state tournament, everybody was really excited because it was the first time Clarence had ever gotten there."

He was a 6 ft. 2 in. junior who played both guard and forward. Joining him in the starting line-up were seniors Junior Dircks at 6 ft. 4 in., Robert Woode at 6 ft. 3 in., Phil Tuetkin 6 ft. 1 in. and junior Norman "Doc" Paul 6 ft. 4 in.

Paul, who got his nickname because his father was the town's veterinarian, was the team's leading scorer and rebounder, and was an 80 percent free throw shooter. Clarence caught Roland and Gary Thompson having a tough game. "Gary didn't hurt us as much that day," said Bixler. "He was missing quite a few shots."

The Iowa City newspaper's game story noted that "Roland had looked quite inept" and "appeared doomed." When Clarence was ahead by 10 points with three minutes left in the game, it indeed seemed Roland would be bowing out of the tournament. And, in a real switch for the Rockets, the big crowd in the Fieldhouse seemed to be overwhelmingly for the other team.

> *"They could make a bunch of fence posts sing!"*

"The story I always heard—and my memory is that this came from my parents—was that the two schools' cheering sections butted up against each other in the stands, and that my parents were sitting right next to Doc Paul's parents," Thompson said. "In that fourth quarter, when it looked like we were going to lose for sure, Mrs. Paul was even sort of comforting my mother, saying 'Well, Mrs. Thompson, it looks like this is going to be our year, but you have to be proud of all the success your Roland boys have had here.' "

For the account of what happened, let's use a follow up column by sports editor Al Grady in the *Iowa City Press-Citizen*:

Clarence's Doc Paul Unwilling Star of Tournament Tragedy
By AL GRADY, Sports Editor

For a brief moment along about 4 p.m. Thursday, the world seemed to stop revolving for just an instant and came to rest on the shoulders of a 16-year-old kid in the Iowa Fieldhouse.

Most everyone knows the facts by now, of course, but we'll give you a brief recount of them.

Clarence, a Class B club from eastern Iowa, had fought favored Roland, making its third successive tournament appearance, to a standstill and then some for three quarters before falling apart in the final 2 minutes as the Rockets came driving back to regain the lead.

The game that had belonged to Clarence now belonged to Roland. The Clarence cheerleaders were in tears. And the Roland crowd was going wild. And bedlam was breaking loose in the stuffy and over-crowded Fieldhouse. Television cameras were grinding away and the bright spotlights added to the stifling heat.

Many in the crowd of 16,000 had begun to leave when Clarence had a 7-point lead going into the final 2 minutes. But the roar of the fans brought them hurrying back, as Roland surged back with two baskets in 3 seconds time.

They crowded toward the floor, craning their necks to see what was taking place. Those in the seats behind jumped to their feet and shouted for those in the aisles to sit down. Ushers tried vainly to clear the aisles as the crowd surged toward the floor. Fans stood on their chairs, pushed toward the playing floor—did anything to get a look at the hectic action, as the work and effort of an entire season rode on the final seconds.

Now only 2 seconds remained, with Roland in front, 42-41. Roland had two free throws coming and it was obviously the Rockets' game, since Clarence hardly had time to score even if Roland missed both free throws and it got possession of the ball.

But Roland did miss both, and as the ball came off the board, Norman "Doc" Paul leaped high to grab it. The buzzer sounded. The game was over. Roland wins! The Rockets yelled and laughed and stomped and slugged each other on the back.

But wait!

The official had charged a foul on Roland's Alan Erickson just as the game ended. So now it was up to Paul, the 16-year-old junior center of Clarence who had played a magnificent game in pulling Clarence so close to victory.

What went through his mind as he stepped to the free throw line? The game was his. He could win it or lose it. All he had to do was toss the basketball through the hoop. If he could do it just once, it would mean an overtime. The fans from Clarence prayed for the kid to make them. And the fans from Roland closed their eyes and prayed for a miss.

That's when the weight of the world seemed to rest, for just a moment, on Doc Paul's shoulders. The first free throw went up, softly and unhurried. It rolled around the rim—might have gone in—but didn't. Now it was all or nothing at all. Immediate victory was impossible. The second chance could bring only a momentary tie.

The second free throw is up—and short. It hits the front of the rim and bounces off. Roland fans go wild. The Rockets leap for joy. But Doc Paul just hangs his head and tears form in his eyes. The hero of the game, the leading scorer for the season, he had failed when the chips were stacked all the way to the top of the Fieldhouse.

So Roland moves ahead and Clarence goes home. And a 16-year-old kid will probably long remember the chance he had that got away. It's happened before and it will happen again.

It's drama such as that which makes the state tournament what it is. Defeat and tears are as much a part of the game as victory and cheers. At one given moment, nothing in the world may seem as important as putting the ball in the basket.

We know it's only a game. A month from now, next week, tomorrow, it won't seem half as bad. But to Doc Paul, it was tragedy of the highest sort Thursday afternoon.

There is one part of that gripping story that went untold. It's unclear now whether Roland called a time out before Paul attempted the free throws, or whether Thompson called his Rocket teammates together on the floor. But his teammate Dave Twedt remembers what Thompson told them: "Gary told us, 'Forget about the ball, just look at the shooter. Stare at him!' "

And that's what the Roland boys did. Thompson took a spot on the side of the free throw lane closest to Paul. And stared at him. "Some people said later they thought I said something to him, but I don't remember that I did," Thompson said. "I just stared."

Bixler said he and his Clarence teammates "couldn't believe we'd gotten beat. We just couldn't believe it. Of course, Doc Paul has heard about those free throws all his life." But Bixler said he and the other Cardinals quickly realized that at different points of the game, each of them had missed a basket, or allowed one to be scored, that were just as important in determining the final score.

And, no, the missed free throws did not ruin Doc Paul's life. "Like everything else in life, that one incident seemed of paramount impact at that minute," he said in a phone interview from his home in Bonita Springs, Florida. "But, you know, it really didn't stay with me long to shake it off. My big goal had been to get to play basketball at the University of Iowa, and when I got to do that, I was thrilled."

He said he doesn't really remember whether Thompson or the other Roland players were staring at him as he was shooting the free throws. And he had never heard anything about his parents sitting next to Thompson's parents in the stands during that game.

The next year, when Paul and Bixler were seniors, Clarence had another good season but the Cardinals did not make it to the '54 state tournament. After graduation, both Paul and his coach Holmstrom joined the basketball program at the U of I. Holmstrom became a coach of the freshman team while he earned his master's degree. He later coached basketball Iowa City High School and then became athletic director at Clinton High School.

Paul was on the Hawkeyes' varsity squad when the "Fabulous Five" team reached the NCAA championship game in '56. "Iowa had such great teams then that I was on the bench a lot," he said, "but I loved being part of it."

He skipped what would have been his senior season at the university in order to start medical school. He went on to become a general surgeon, practicing for 18 years in Joliet, Illinois, then 18 years in Auburn, Indiana. After retiring, he and his wife Sally have divided their time between homes in

Big Sky, Montana, where both have become avid skiers, and in Florida.

After the unbelievable comeback against Clarence, there was a little more basketball to play for the Roland boys. That meant Gary Thompson was busy on that Friday night when Duke Ellington was performing over in the Iowa Memorial Union. Thompson and the Rockets were playing Clinton St. Mary's in one semi-finals game, with Clinton High and Ottumwa meeting in the other. The whole city of Clinton was going crazy over the possibility of its two high schools playing each other for the state championship, especially since they never met in the regular seasons.

And there was another fascinating sidelight—the team from the small Catholic high school, St. Mary's, was being coached by a 21-year-old! He was Lou Galetich, a native of Madrid in central Iowa who had graduated from St. Ambrose College in Davenport in the spring of 1952. He was in his first year of teaching and coaching in what became a 46-year school career that also took him to Remsen St. Mary's, Carroll Kuemper and back to Madrid.

"Before I got hired at Clinton St. Mary's, one of the priests had always coached the team," said Galetich, now retired in Madrid. "St. Mary's had been respectable the year before I got there, but they hadn't gone very far in the tournament, and nobody said anything to me indicating that we might have some real ball players there. But when I got to know them, I could see that we were loaded. They'd been playing together since they were little kids, and they were really fast. I just ran them to death in practice, got them in great shape and we just out-ran a lot of teams in the games."

But how could a 21-year-old first-year coach lead a small-school team to a state championship in an all-in-one-class tournament?

"Good players," Galetich said, "and a lot of prayers." They knocked off Waterloo East and Sioux Center in their first two games at the '53 state tournament, and that set up the semi-finals game against Roland.

"We knew we were going to have our hands full with Roland, and of course we knew if we were going to have a chance, we'd have to try to slow down Gary Thompson because he was one terrific athlete," Galetich said. "That game went right down to the wire, and we didn't clinch it until Dick Lingle stole a pass and got a quick lay-up right at the end of the game." St. Mary's won it, 57-53. In the other semi-finals game, Ottumwa knocked off Clinton High to break-up an all-Clinton championship game. "We were all kind of disappointed by that, because we had a great relationship between the two schools in Clinton then," Galetich said. "We didn't play each other, but the kids on both teams were all friends."

St. Mary's had a pretty easy time of it in the title game, rolling past Ottumwa 61-44. And in the consolation game, Clinton High handed Roland another loss, 66-37. That Clinton High team had some real talent, too—including Kenny Ploen, who became an All-American quarterback in football for the University of Iowa, and Chuck Vogt, who became a basketball teammate of Gary Thompson at Iowa State.

It was reported after the state tournament that Thompson had been playing in pain all week with badly blistered feet. But, really, he'd had almost as much glory in that Fieldhouse as any one player could ever hope to have. For three seasons, nearly everything had gone his way there—except a state championship, as he always points out.

The next week, Jack North of the *Des Moines Tribune* turned a long, rambling sentence into a very nice farewell to Thompson's high school basketball career:

"A brilliant shooter from far out on the court, and also death on shots from around the free throw lane, Gary Thompson's scoring, floor play, rebounding, defense work and clever passing will long be remembered by the thousands who have seen this great little fellow in action during the last 3 years."

Chapter 5

Growing into That Baseball Uniform

THERE'S a great story about Gary Thompson and his Roland High School baseball career that Coach Buck Cheadle didn't tell Thompson until 50 years after it happened.

"I started at Roland in the fall of 1949 when Gary was going into his freshman year of high school," Cheadle recalled. "I hadn't met him yet, so on the first day of practice for fall baseball, I went out to meet the team.

"I looked at this young boy standing there—he was really little—and I thought to myself, 'Well, I've got a student manager already.' That was the first time I remember seeing Gary Thompson. Little did I know that was an All-American in the making!"

Thompson was only 5 ft. 2 in. then, and Cheadle remembers that Gary's mother Abbie Thompson "had to 'take up' one of our wool flannel baseball uniforms so it fit him a little better."

But in that fall season, and then again in the spring season of 1950, Thompson got considerable playing time on the Roland Rockets varsity that had seven seniors in the line-up. They were 10-2 in the fall, losing in the sectional finals, and were about that successful in the spring, although that season's record is lost.

As Thompson's freshman year was ending, Coach Cheadle gave this assessment of him in "The Rocket" school yearbook: "Gary Thompson—Freshman infielder. A 'little natural.' Plenty of 'baseball sense' and knowledge of the game. Lots of pep and 'chatter.'"

Fall baseball? Spring baseball? Yes, the grand old game was played much differently in Iowa high schools in the 1950s than it is now.

The Iowa High School Athletic Association, which sanctions boys' sports in the state, sponsored baseball state tournaments in the spring from 1928 through 1972. Nearly all schools participated in those spring tourneys, at least until the 1960s.

And since many of the small schools did not have football programs, the IHSAA also sponsored additional state tournaments in the fall from 1939 to 1985. But summer baseball became popular, too, and the IHSAA began sponsoring a summer state tournament in 1946.

A few schools played baseball spring, summer and fall. Gradually, however, more schools started football programs, and that brought an end to fall baseball. As the popularity of track & field and eventually soccer grew, schools did away with their spring seasons. Today, Iowa is the only state in the nation in which the high school baseball season is played in the summer.

Playing in nice summer weather in the Midwest has meant that many schools draw big crowds for their home games, and the tournament games attract even bigger crowds. The week-long state tournament is now divided into four classes and the games are played at the professional baseball stadium in Des Moines, with attendance topping 30,000 for the week.

High school baseball did not get that kind of attendance or attention in the early 1950s. All schools played in the same class, regardless of enrollment differences. Statistics were kept inconsistently, and sometimes not at all. All-State teams were not picked until the 1970s. Most schools did not charge admission to their baseball games, and instead just "passed the hat" at games to help cover the costs of field maintenance and operation of the lights. Attendance for high school baseball games seldom approached the size of crowds for basketball and football games.

> "Most schools 'passed the hat' to cover costs..."

State tournament sites varied from year to year, with such small towns as Manson, Dysart, Williamsburg and Boone, the latter being the IHSAA's headquarters town, all serving as hosts from time to time. Eventually Mason City, which had a nice stadium that was used in the summers for semi-pro baseball, became the site of many of the spring state tournaments, but the fall state tournaments were seldom held in the same town two years in a row.

Baseball was always more popular in Roland than in many communities. As you read earlier in this book, men such as Gary Thompson's father Maurice Thompson played "town team ball" into their late 30s and 40s. Gary remembers good crowds for both adult and high school games, with cars often ringing the outfield fences and horns honking to salute good plays.

"Since the ball park was beside the highway that ran through town, the Iowa Highway Patrolmen would often stop by during games and watch a few innings," he said. "That was a big deal to us back then."

During Gary Thompson's sophomore, junior and senior years, the Roland Rockets—playing in both the spring and fall seasons—gave their fans a whole lot of great baseball.

The team won a total of 51 games, lost only seven and made it to the state tournaments in four of the six seasons. In the spring of 1952, the Rockets played in the state championship game against a Kanawha team led by brothers Donnie and Jack Mewes. Roland lost in two extra innings, 4-3. In their other three state tourney appearances, they were beaten each time by the eventual champions.

The baseball squads generally included the same boys on the basketball squads. Among the Rockets' best ball players during that run were Loren Twedt, a pitcher who was 7-0 in the 1949 fall season; Ralph Johnson, Jake Hill and Dave Peterson, who consistently hit over .400; good defensive infielders Don Holland and Dave Twedt, and of course, Gary Thompson.

As a right-handed pitcher, Thompson was 4-0 and 7-2 in his sophomore fall and spring seasons; lost only two games in the two seasons of his junior year, and was 8-1 and 8-1 in his senior year. He pitched six no-hitters.

By his senior year, he had a good fastball. He also had "a jug-handle curve ball," as sportswriter Brad Wilson described it in the *Des Moines Register*, and he would also throw a nasty knuckleball. He used those three pitches to build some eye-popping statistics.

In the fall season, he pitched 58 innings, had 108 strikeouts and gave up only one earned run—the one that beat the Rockets in the semi-finals of the state tournament. In the spring season, he pitched 64 innings, struck out 134 and allowed only five earned runs.

When he was not pitching, he normally played shortstop, and he was a leading hitter with a career batting average over .450. Statistics like those started attracting a lot of attention.

In a May 26, 1953, letter Gary wrote to his girlfriend Janet Sydnes—and you'll read more about his letters to her in Chapter 7—he talked about his senior baseball season having ended. Then he added: "Guess what? Scouts from the New York Yanks, Brooklyn Dodgers, St. Louis Browns, St. Louis Cardinals and Chicago Cubs have talked to me. I might get a chance to sign a pro contract.

"I want to go to school first, though, and this one scout from the Brooklyn Dodgers said he would wait till I got out of college then. When I was little, I used to think how nice it would be to be able to be signed by a major league ball club, and now I'll get the chance if I want to.

"I was really happy when I heard from all those scouts. I go to the Browns' instructional school at Madrid Thursday and Friday." Then he added—remember he was writing a letter to his girlfriend—this line, quoting a popular song then: "And 'I'm Sitting on Top of the World,' especially when I get to 'go steady' with *you!*"

In that same letter, he told Janet that there was a big difference in how the team was treated for making the state baseball tournament compared to what they'd grown accustomed to when the basketball team made state. For the basketball tournament, the team would stay all week long in Iowa City. For the baseball tournament in Mason City, they had to drive back and forth for the games, and stay at home in Roland.

"We didn't get to stay at Mason City," Gary wrote. "Those jerks wouldn't let us stay. Just think—you get to the 'State Tournament' and they don't let you stay over one night! On the way home, they did let us stop and eat, and just to spend some of their money, six of us guys ordered 18 sandwiches and 12 malts.."

Thompson had been "one heck of a pitcher and shortstop," said Alan Hoskins, a former player in Zearing who is now in Kansas City, Kansas, and has been a lifelong friend.

> *"Scouts for five major league teams contacted him..."*

"Most of the schools around the area were a little more competitive with Roland in baseball than we were in basketball, but we still didn't beat them much. I'm still talking about the time I managed to get a base hit off of him. He was throwing that knuckleball, and I fouled one pitch off to the left, fouled another one off to the right and then hit it right up the middle for a base hit. I've never forgotten it!"

Thompson's teammates knew he had special talent, of course, but they didn't spare him their kidding.

"I'm a year older than Gary, and I was always a reserve in baseball," said Loren Jacobson, a friend since they were little boys. "We were on our way over to Radcliffe for a game, probably in 1951, and Gary and I were kidding back and forth, like we always did. I said, 'The only reason I'm going along on this trip is in case your shoestring breaks, then I can give you one of mine.'

"Well, that happened! He was pitching and broke a shoestring. I took one out of my shoe and he used it. He got back out there on the mound, and I was still kidding him about it. It was pretty easy to make him laugh, and I had him doubled-up laughing on the mound over him needing my shoestring."

Cheadle was the Rockets' coach through the state tournament in the spring of 1952, at the end of Gary's junior year.

"I've never forgotten that after Kanawha beat us for the state championship, we came back to Roland, and the next morning, I was moving my family to Burlington to start my new job there," Cheadle said. "When I was getting ready to load the truck early that morning, here came Gary Thompson and Donnie Holland to help me. That's the kind of kids Roland had back then."

Coach Bob Looft moved to town over that summer and began his Roland High School coaching duties with the fall baseball season.

As good as Gary Thompson was as a high school baseball player, his accomplishments were eclipsed a few years later by his younger brother DeLon, who was a 1960 Roland graduate.

DeLon won his first game as a high school pitcher the season after his eighth grade year. The right hander grew to 5 ft. 10 in. and 185 pounds in his junior and senior seasons, and few high school batters could hit him.

"We didn't have any speed guns back then, but I was probably in the 88-to-91 miles per hour range," DeLon said. "And I threw pretty good sidearm and overhand curve balls, too." He played infield when he wasn't pitching, and he was "a .400 to .500 hitter through high school."

But as you can imagine, it was as a pitcher that he really starred. He pitched "five or six" no-hitters in his senior season. And in a tournament game at Radcliffe, he set a national record by striking out 23 batters in one seven-inning game. How? Twice, his catcher had third-strike pitches get away from him.

In fact, there were three seven-inning games in that tournament. DeLon Thompson pitched complete games in all three, meaning he recorded a total of 63 outs in the three games.

Of those, 53 or 54 of them were strikeouts. Iowa State University baseball coach L.C. "Cap" Timm was in the stands for those tournament games. Little wonder that DeLon Thompson got a baseball scholarship to Iowa State! You'll read more about DeLon later in this book, including about how he gave professional baseball a try.

Of course, big brother Gary did all right in baseball, too, after he grew into that Roland wool flannel uniform.

Chapter 6

Roland Experiences Had Lifetime Effect

LIFE for teenagers in little Roland, Iowa in the early 1950s was a whole lot more than just high school basketball and baseball.

There was serious hanging out to do at Vaughan's Drugstore, where Willard and Helen Vaughan presided. A lot of Roland kids saw television for the first time when the Vaughans set one on the end of their soda fountain.

Solid Rockets backers, the Vaughans gave free malts for players if both the girls' and boys' basketball teams won on home-game nights. That happened so often in Roland that Willard finally had to reconsider that deal.

"I worked all the way through junior high and high school there as a soda jerk," said Marlene Fosse Piel, now of Creston, a member of the Roland High School class of 1953 with Gary Thompson. "It was wild after ball games. Everybody bellied up to the soda fountain, for cherry Cokes, cherry phosphates, 'Green Mountains' and malts."

Piel also worked as a waitress at one of the cafes. There was Fain's Café ("Good Home Cooking and Extra Good Coffee") and the Roland Café ("Chicken Every Sunday"). She got used to serving classmates there, too.

"That Gary Thompson could eat like a horse, and it'd never show on him," Piel said. "I can remember him coming in the café and eating three hamburgers and drinking a malt!"

There were "Bank Night" promotions at the movie theater where, if your name was flashed on screen after a drawing, you could win $25 from the Story County State Bank. There were five full-service gas stations—Phillips 66, Standard, Shell, DX and Sinclair—and the Farmers Co-op had gas pumps, too. Several were hanging-out places. There were also three groceries, and two taverns, the latter definitely not hanging-out places for high school kids.

In fashion, most of the boys were going to the new flat-top haircuts, which they were getting at Con's Barber Shop ("Your Barber Since 1917"). The girls were wearing black & white saddle shoes, not only around town but also as part of the cheerleading, pep club, band and girls' chorus uniforms.

Ah, yes, in many ways, the early 1950s was a great time to be a high school kid in a small Iowa town like Roland. Population was growing with the post-war Baby Boom. Downtown business districts and manufacturing plants were prospering, even in the small towns. All the parents that wanted to could find jobs outside the home. For their kids, that meant money was more readily available for movies, hamburgers, malts and a little gas in Dad's car when he'd let you borrow it.

Teens were star-struck about young movie stars like Tab Hunter and Doris Day. And in that time just before rock 'n' roll erupted, high school kids loved the swing music played by bands led by such directors as Guy Lombardo and Sammy Kaye. There was no dancing in Roland, as you've read earlier, but roller skating became very popular among high schoolers, and you'll read more about that.

Churches and schools were strong in Roland and most other small towns. The high schools were not only important as education centers, but with all their varied activities and programs, they became the social and entertainment centers as well.

"I think we all liked our lives then," said Donna Hagen Henry, now of Colo, Iowa, another member of the Roland High class of '53 and an All-State guard in basketball. "In fact, a lot of us really hated to graduate. We knew it meant separation from each other, having to grow up and get out on our own. We were all very proud to be from Roland. Some kids today in small towns can't wait to leave. It wasn't like that for us back then."

That is reflected in their reunions a half-century later. "In 2003, at the time of our 50-year reunion, there were 21 of us alive, and 20 showed up for the reunion," said Henry. And that's been typical at most of their reunions.

"We hold them every 5 years, and although we're scattered to the four winds, we all try to come back then," said classmate Dave Twedt, who lives in Newton, where he worked 35 years in accounting and payroll for Maytag Corporation. "The town has changed so much, but there still seems to be a hometown atmosphere when we're together."

Three times during their Roland reunions, there have been spirited alumni basketball games.

"Our old guys from my era won each time," Thompson said. "Those games were highly competitive on our part, and we did not want to lose. The last time we played, we only had six guys from our team, and we were a lot older than the other team. We had a few shoving and pushing matches, and the referee said, 'Hey, guys, this is just for fun!' It was fun for us, too, but we did not want any young guys saying they beat us.

"Dave Twedt had had a heart attack prior to playing that game. He was always one of the feistiest players who would not back down from anyone. He was white as a ghost during the game, and I said, 'Dave, you have to sit down or you'll have another heart attack,' but he would not sit down.

"Our classmate Darrel Egemo, who had played on the 'C' team during high school days, had a great line at that game. He said, 'I got to suit up for the first alumni game, the second game I got to play a little, and this time I was the first sub because we only had six players. If we have another alumni game and only five show up, I will get my first start ever for Roland!' "

Since the 25-year reunion, Thompson has led the organizing for the Class of '53 gatherings. Why does he do it?

"Well, I keep telling my classmates, 'Someone else can do this, you know,' " he said. "But the truth is, I enjoy doing it. I love the kids I grew up with. When I look back on it, there wasn't one of them I didn't like. And so many of us married people from around the area that we all knew, that many of our spouses seem like as much a part of our group as the classmates do.

> *"Our music program was stronger than athletics to begin with..."*

"Great story about that—one of our classmates is Cleone Michelson Bowers, and she lives out in California. Her husband Dana has been at the reunions, and at the last one, when I thanked him for coming, he said, 'I wouldn't have missed this for anything. The affection you all still have for each other just makes me feel good. This would not happen in California where I grew up.' "

When you pull out a copy of the 1953 "Rocket" yearbook from old Roland High School and start browsing, you understand why they share such fondness.

All the seniors are listed as having nicknames ("Cuddles," "Bull," "Pud," "Dimples," "Waldo," "Fuzzy"), and all are assigned mottos that probably were thought to reflect their character or personality. When you browse their lists of activities they were involved in over their 4 years in high school, you suddenly realize that in a class of 25 people, they were all in involved in everything. And thus they all became real parts of each others' lives.

Here we see Gary Thompson. Nickname of "Harrigan," for some reason. The yearbook editors suggest a good motto for him would be, "Small but oh so mighty." Besides his athletic accomplishments that you know about, he was also a class officer all 4 years of high school; had parts in both the junior and senior class plays (a bellhop in "Papa Says No" as a senior); was on the staffs of the school paper and yearbook, and also pulled "K.P. Duty" during his junior and seniors years, meaning he had a regular job in the cafeteria.

He and Charlene Hall were selected by their classmates as "Representative Boy & Girl" on "the basis of personality, citizenship, scholarship and participation in extracurricular activities." She was the high-scoring forward on the girls' basketball team, averaging 25 points per game and making second team All-State. Her parents were friends of Maurice and Abbie Thompson, and sometimes when the two sets of parents were socializing, Gary and Charlene would head over to the outdoor basketball & tennis court at the high school, shoot baskets and play one-on-one scrimmages.

"Roland was a great community to be raised in and during a special time," said Charlene Hall Matheny, now of Cedarburg, Wisconsin. "All of our classmates were close. Oh, we had a lot of good times. There just couldn't have been a better place then. I wish my own children would've had an opportunity to grow up in a place like Roland with all we had there."

It's a little startling when you see in the yearbook that Roland High School had only seven faculty members. But when you remember there were only 73 students in high school, it means all were still assured a lot of individual attention from teachers.

The faculty count, by the way, included Superintendent C.P. Thompson and Principal Johanna Finch, although the latter is always referred to in the yearbook as "Mrs. C.R. Finch" or "Mrs. Cecil Finch." They were both administrators who also taught classes. Superintendent Thompson had typing and instrumental music, while Principal Finch taught vocal music and bookkeeping.

"Our music programs were always very strong," said classmate Jerry Twedt, now of Orlando, Florida. "In fact, music was stronger than athletics to begin with. We had 41 boys in high school, and 35 of them were in the boys' glee club. We'd have 60 kids in the mixed chorus, and 50 or 60 in the band.

"And we did a lot of classical music, probably drawing on our Lutheran heritage. If there was a patron saint of the Lutheran Church, it was probably Johann Sebastian Bach.

We all grew up with Bach preludes and Bach compositions. We were introduced to Beethoven in high school band. In chorus, I remember we did 'Going Home' from Antonin Dvorak's 'New World Symphony.' So we learned a lot of very, very good music."

The school's academic reputation was as strong as it had in athletics and music. Buck Cheadle, the basketball coach for Gary Thompson's first 3 years at Roland High, said it was that balance that first got his attention about the community.

"I was in Norwalk before I went to Roland, and it seemed like I saw several stories in the Des Moines papers that indicated that Roland was good in academics, music and sports," Cheadle said. "I thought it must be a special place, and I thought maybe sometime I could get an opportunity there."

Since Thompson was not musical, he didn't take full advantage of the high school's offerings to the extent most of his classmates did. He said he appreciates that faculty members stayed right on him, insisting on academic performance. He wound up being "just above average as a student, probably a low B."

But the Roland High curriculum and extracurriculars gave all in the class of '53 a good launch. At least three eventually got advanced college degrees.

David Fausch graduated from Drake University in Des Moines, then earned a master's at the Medill School of Journalism at Northwestern University in

Evanston, Illinois. After covering business and finance for Business Week magazine and other publications for more than a decade, he wound up as vice-president of corporate public relations for The Gillette Company, and served as Gillette's spokesperson around the world. He now lives in Falmouth, Massachusetts.

Darrel Egemo got his master's at the University of Iowa, worked for a time in Waterloo, became a stockbroker in New York and then spent a long career as a counselor at Cherry Creek High School in the Denver, Colorado, area. He now lives in the mountains near Sedalia, Colorado, where "he built a three-level home board by board, nail by nail at the end of a dirt road with more curves than a snake with hiccups," the *Rocky Mountain News* reported in a profile of him in 2002. "He built the house on an outcropping of pink granite boulders the size of semis."

Jerry Twedt went to Luther College in Iowa, then on for a master's at the University of Illinois. He spent 27 years as a producer-director in television, most of that with an NBC-TV station in Miami, Florida. He directed and served as stage manager for everything from fine arts programming to football, boxing and basketball. Besides writing the book "Growing Up in The 40s" about his boyhood in Roland, Twedt has also published nine plays, several short stories and wrote many television scripts.

Other classmates have had careers across the business spectrum, and one became highly successful in auto racing. Everett Sather, who now lives in Ankeny, Iowa, has been part of the promotion team that has built the Boone Speedway, located in the central Iowa town of Boone, into a major "dirt-track racing" venue, drawing crowds of 10,000 per day for a week of "Super Nationals" racing in early September. He also founded JR Motorsports, a firm that offers high-performance parts, service and cars across the nation.

> *"We still all come back for a reunion every 5 years..."*

Now mostly retired, all the members of the class of '53 have had their share of family, business and health challenges and joys. But the ones I talked to seem to have a genuine happiness that they all discovered together in a small school and small town a long time ago. It came from living close, from knowing each other so well they were almost like family as well as being classmates, and from caring deeply for each other.

That's the legacy of their Roland experience. Maybe the old soda jerk, Marlene Fosse Piel, explained it best.

"You know, I never did like school too much, but I sure enjoyed all the kids," she said. "And the older we got, the more I enjoyed them."

Chapter 7

This High School Romance Worked

THE Gary Thompson story is very much a sports story, of course, but it also is one of the neatest love stories you'll ever come across. It is one of those high school romances that worked, and for life.

Now in their 70s, Gary and Janet Thompson are as devoted to each other as they were when they first started dating in 1951. They have handled the normal challenges that family, careers, finances and health bring to any relationship, learning to lean on one another at all the right times.

They know each other so well now that they complete sentences for one another. There is fun kidding and teasing, and an occasional barb, but always, there is obvious respect for the other. They are much more involved in each other's lives than is common, even among other long-term couples.

And here's how it began.

When Gary Thompson was a sophomore at Roland High School, Hollis Fosse, his teammate and roller skating buddy, "told me there was a girl I needed to meet" at the Skateland roller rink in Ames, Gary recalls.

On their next trip to Skateland, Hollis introduced Gary to Janet Sydnes, of Huxley, a dark-haired beauty just as Norwegian and just as Lutheran as Gary himself.

"Love at first sight," he remembers, as he looks back more than 55 years. "When we met, I just knew she was the one for me. I told Hollis, 'You've got to be crazy! If I were you, I'd have kept her for myself!' "

It was just as quick for Janet. "Right away, I knew—this is the guy for me," she says. "It was like butterflies. I thought he was nice. I liked him. I liked his looks. I just fell in love."

He'd just been the sensation of the 1951 state basketball tournament, and one of the reasons was that he was such a good player while measuring only 5 ft. 6 in. tall.

"He really was pretty small," Janet says, "but I've always been a short person myself, so he was a little taller than I was. I was never taller than anybody."

Skateland became their number one hangout, the place where their relationship really bloomed. "I went skating the next 4 years with her," Gary recalls. "We skated 4 nights a week—Wednesday, Friday, Saturday and Sunday.

"A few Ames kids would come roller skating, but most of us were from the small towns in the county. It was great. There was a live organist playing. They'd have 'Moonlight Skates' and 'Two-Steps.' And, you know, I was a darned good roller skater. Never could dance worth a darn, but I was good at roller skating!"

One of the things they learned about each other was how similarly they had been raised—with strong values, strict discipline and a lot of love. Janet came from a much larger family. She was the fourth of the seven children of Tilmer and Carrie Sydnes, who had an 80-acre farm west of Huxley, which is 9 miles south of Ames.

Carrie, who had attended Iowa State Teachers College after Huxley High School, taught school 2 years before they married. Then came the kids, in birth order, Helen, Carroll, Darlene, Janet, Paul, Sandra and Linda. Darlene was just 2 years older than Janet, and the two were very close. Tilmer died in 1969, Carrie in 1985 and, in 2007, only three of the siblings survive—Janet and the youngest sisters, Sandra Wirtz, who still lives in Huxley, and Linda Lantz, of Seattle, Washington.

When the Sydnes kids were growing up together, "It was a good life," Janet says. "When you come from a family of seven, you weren't the center of attention, and yet we all knew we were important."

Her mother had been one of 12 children in her family, and most stayed in the area. So Carrie and Tilmer raised their own children "with 48 or 50 cousins around here, and we were together all the time—every Sunday, for sure," Janet said. "You just knew that after everybody had been to church and then got home for Sunday dinner, somebody would drop by to visit, so you better have cake and cookies ready. It wasn't unusual at all to have 12 to 15 people stopping by on a Sunday afternoon. We'd take turns being at home, or going visiting. That was our social life, and I loved it."

The Sydneses were members of Lincoln Lutheran Church in Huxley through the kids' early years, then when that church disbanded, they joined Palestine Lutheran east of Huxley.

Life around the farm was simple, by today's standards. In her early girlhood, Janet recalls a fascination with paper dolls, which her mother would help her cut from catalogues. "I'd spend hours playing with those," she says. "I'd get in a room, even on the hottest of days, start playing with the dolls and my imagination would take over. I'd be so involved with the dolls, and so quiet, that my mother would have to come check on me to make sure I was still all right."

She was a big book reader, especially enjoying the "Bobbsey Twins" series. And there were lots of board games, "Monopoly" chief among them. There'd be games of tag around the windmill, including climbing part way up it.

Carrie Sydnes made many of her daughters' dresses, using the patterned fabric sacks that agricultural supply companies had developed during the Great Depression years to ship feed and seed to farmers. In the hardest years, that was the only fabric many farm families could afford.

"I always liked clothes," Janet says. "If some special function came up, I'd always say, 'Mom, hurry—you've got to make me a new dress!' And she'd do it. I never heard her say she couldn't get it done."

The Sydnes kids were not really athletes. "The girls were more interested in music, and our brothers were hunters and fishermen," Janet says. "But we did have a basket at home for basketball. It was an old galvanized steel bucket with the bottom out of it, hanging on a corn crib. We only had one bicycle for the seven kids, and we never fought over it—we just loved it when it was our time to ride."

Tilmer Sydnes assigned all the kids farm chores that had to be done.. One duty Janet had was gathering freshly-laid eggs in the "chicken house," and there'd usually be enough "to take to town and sell on Saturday night." With a lot of chickens around, that usually meant chicken dinners on Sunday, she said.

The family's Saturday night trip into Huxley was a highlight of most weeks. "I look back on Huxley then as being a really good small town," she says. "There were band concerts on Saturday nights, drugstores, grocery stores, implement dealers, at least two gas stations—a lot more businesses than what many small towns now have. We always thought there was a lot to do there. On Saturday nights, we'd normally go to town about 7:30, after chores were done, and I remember we'd all be wishing Dad would hurry up and get done so we could leave. We'd spend a couple of hours in town, and we'd each get a nickel for an ice cream cone."

A big annual event was the Huxley Horse Show, held at Kalsem-Nord Park's outdoor arena, with a festival atmosphere. "I never rode horses myself, except a few times on the work horses we had at the farm, but I loved watching those show horses," Janet said.

At Huxley High School, she was "about an average student" among the 20 in her Class of 1952. In her last couple of years there, she had a teacher, Vera Markt, who taught business and bookkeeping, and "who was instrumental in what I wound up doing after high school."

Among extracurricular activities, "music was my big thing," she says. She was in the mixed chorus, a sextet, girls' trio and did some solo work, qualifying her for a Huxley High "letter." She also was active in the church choir, and she took piano lessons. She enjoyed playing basketball at home, on the outdoor hoop, but never played for the school team. "I loved going to the games," she says, "but I was always a lot happier just being a spectator."

Her church's "Luther League" youth group not only provided additional education and inspiration in religion, but it also became a big part of the social life of high school students in Huxley, just as the Luther League groups did for young people in Roland. There was never any card playing or dancing, as her parents and the Lutheran Church forbade that back then. And Janet "never saw any drinking or smoking by high school students—none."

> *"It was love at first sight..."*

Outings—either with girlfriends or eventually on an occasional date—generally involved going to Ames for movies or skating at Skateland, then going out to eat afterward at favorite restaurants like the new A&W Root Beer stand, Frango's or Tony's Pizza.

It was her sister Darlene who led her to roller skating, which Janet recalls "became real popular" after the new Skateland rink had its grand opening in the fall of 1949. For the small town kids who flocked there, Skateland and the new 20th Century Bowling alley, built next to each other on South Duff Avenue, were entertainment centers almost beyond their dreams.

The investors and owners, the Penkhus brothers, natives of Templeton in western Iowa, had seen roller skating take off elsewhere in the nation's heartland. They were developing seven or eight new roller rinks in Denver, Colorado Springs, San Antonio and elsewhere. They thought the time was right in Ames, which previously only had a rather primitive outdoor roller rink.

"My brother Jerry Penkhus built our original Skateland in Colorado Springs, and it was making pretty good money," said Floyd Penkhus, who spent nearly his whole business career in Ames. "I'd been involved in a Lincoln-Mercury car dealership in Ames for a couple of years, and we weren't doing real well, so I was looking around for something else."

So they built the two new buildings, and brought in another brother, Bob, as a partner. Skateland was a 100-by-150-foot building with a solid maple floor. They installed an organ, and hired Noni Mylenbusch, of Boone, as their full-time organist, having her play whenever the rink was open for public skating.

"That was kind of unusual then, for a skating rink to have its own organist," Floyd Penkhus said. "Noni was just great. She could play almost anything—everything from things like 'Chattanooga Choo-Choo' to World War II two-step stuff to whatever songs were popular at the moment." Her husband Don Mylenbusch was also an organist who played around the area. After his death years later, Noni married again—she's Noni Decker now—and lives in West Branson, Missouri.

Skateland provided a wholesome environment not only for skating but also for young people to meet each other, and one of the reasons was that Floyd and Bob Penkhus had strict rules.

"It seems almost strange to think about this now, the way people dress today, but we had a rule that you could only wear blue jeans for skating on Wednesday nights," Floyd Penkhus said. "I'm telling you, I don't know how we ever got that done, but we did. The girls had to wear dresses or skirts. The boys had to wear slacks, and some would even wear coats and neckties. We wouldn't let a kid in with a T-shirt. They had to have a shirt with a collar, and they also had to be wearing a belt."

There was no rowdy behavior tolerated, either. In a full-page advertisement in the Ames Daily Tribune announcing the grand opening of Skateland in September, 1949, the Penkhuses explained what they called "The Skateland Policy."

The facility, they wrote, "was built with the intent to supply wholesome recreation to the young people of Ames and its adjacent communities. We want our skaters to have fun; to enjoy the fresh relaxation of this graceful recreation; to see and participate in one of America's finest sports. And we realize, too, that we cannot please everyone. We choose, therefore, to please those 9 out of 10 young people who genuinely appreciate a beautiful establishment; who truly regard skating as the pleasure it was meant to be.

"We are glad to say we have enjoyed such type of crowds during the past few weeks of advance operation. We shall not hesitate to suggest to that tenth person, whose conduct on the floor, or whose dress, manner, or conduct are below our standards, that he or she seek recreation elsewhere. We know that only by keeping our establishment on a high caliber of operation will it continue to attract wholesome crowds, to grow, to provide more pleasure for more people. To this policy we shall abide with unrelenting vigor. We know the community we seek to serve wants and hopes that we do so."

Floyd Penkhus said there were two other things he and his brother Bob did with unrelenting vigor—promote their roller rink, and make sure no one got in free!

They worked with the area schools to bring their students for skating during physical education classes, charging a bargain rate then of 15 cents per student. "That was a very popular program, and it got the kids all interested in roller skating," Floyd said. Regular skating prices were 60 cents to skate, 30 cents to rent skates and 30 cents if you just wanted to watch.

On weeknights and Sundays, skating was 7 to 10:30 p.m. On Fridays and Saturdays, there was a second session from 10:30 p.m. to 12:30 a.m. There were also Sunday matinee skates. Skateland was closed on Monday and Thursday nights. The Penkhuses tried to make sure they had a couple of especially skilled adult skaters in attendance, whenever they were open, to give lessons and help chaperone.

There was no smoking or alcohol consumption allowed. "Oh no, none of that," Floyd said. "We didn't even let them chew gum—we didn't want to find it sticking on the floor. We had pop, candy bars and popcorn for sale—that was it—and you had to keep it in the snack room."

Janet Sydnes had been skating at Skateland a couple of years before she met Gary Thompson. She says now that "maybe I'd heard his name from basketball." But she hadn't thought much about him "until his friend Hollis Fosse came up to me and said, 'I need to introduce you to my friend.'"

Gary recalls he came to that moment "with almost no dating experience.

"I was bashful as heck," he said. "My first 'date' was earlier that year. A bunch of us were at the skating rink, and I'd ridden with my classmate Everett Sather. His girlfriend was from Roland, too, and he wanted to take her home that night. So he told me to ask another girl if I could take her home, and the four of us would ride together.

"I said, 'But I've never had a date! I can't ask her!' When Everett said then he was going to ask the girl for me, I went over and asked her myself. It turned out Everett and his girlfriend dropped this other girl and me off at her car in Roland, and she took me right home. That was my big first date."

Janet, however, was "going steady" with another boy when she started dating Gary. She says now she handled the break-up rather abruptly. "I was wearing his ring when I walked up to him," she said of her soon-to-be former boyfriend. "I took the ring off, handed it to him and said, 'Here's your ring, I'm through, I found someone else.'"

The first dates Gary and Janet had were almost always for skating, where he could easily find rides with friends, since he still had no driver's license. Eventually, he would telephone her to see if she were going skating or wanted to go to a movie, but the phone calls were "always to ask for a date, never just to chat," Janet says. "Not many people back then would make a long distance phone call just to chat."

They had a quintessentially-Iowa romantic moment that summer of 1951 when the separate detasseling crews they were on encountered each other in the middle of a cornfield, and Gary and Janet got a few minutes with each other.

Once later on, when he phoned her and asked if she wanted to go to a Halloween Party at Skateland, she said no. He recalls he was startled, and a little upset. But he went ahead and made plans to go skating with his Roland buddies.

What he didn't realize was that Janet had turned him down because she and her cousin Clarice Wee, who was also her classmate at Huxley High School, had arranged special costumes for the skating party, and they wanted to see if their boyfriends Gary and Sam Mathis, of McCallsburg, would recognize them. Their costumes and masks, making them appear to be very young girls, were so good that they indeed won the Skateland costume contest, and also, it took the boys the whole evening before they figured out the ruse.

The more time that Janet and Gary spent skating together, the more they also came to care for each other—and the better skaters they became. Being young Lutherans in that era, dancing was forbidden, as mentioned earlier here, "but we basically just danced on roller skates," Janet recalls. "Frontward, backward, waltz, limbo, two-step. It was really fun, and we both loved it."

They also both bought their own "Chicago" brand roller skates—and they still have them—instead of using rental skates. "You were big time if you owned 'Chicago' or 'Cleveland' brand skates," Gary said.

They continued skating through their high school years and even during Gary's first 2 years at Iowa State College. Janet was working then as a secretary for the Iowa State Extension Service in Morrill Hall on the college campus. They finally gave up skating regularly after they married in the summer of 1955.

"With Gary's sports schedule and keeping up our apartment then, we were just too busy," Janet said.

Floyd Penkhus said Skateland's popularity "was almost amazing" through the 1950s, but by 1960 it "was tapering off." That same year, a tornado ripped off the roof of the building and the accompanying rain ruined the hardwood floor. "We had to take it down after that," he said.

Bob Penkhus moved on to Colorado, and Floyd continued running 20th Century Bowling in Ames until he retired in 1993. And for more than 50 years, he and the Thompsons have taken time when they see each other to recall the stories about when they started their relationship at Skateland.

"I can still remember both of them as teenagers, because they were there so much," Floyd said. "Good skaters, good kids. At first, Gary Thompson to me was just another teenager. Then later we started hearing how good he was in basketball."

Penkhus said he became a major fan of Gary when he was leading the Iowa State Cyclones from 1955-'57. And when the Thompsons eventually settled back in Ames in 1968 and began operation of Gary Thompson Oil Co., Penkhus "became a Phillips 66 customer and have been ever since. When I'd pull up outside his station and be getting gas, if he was there in his office, he'd often come out on the driveway to visit with me. And Janet has always been so kind to me, too. I've always been proud that it was at our skating rink that they met."

"I never could dance worth a darn, but I could really skate..."

Their relationship in their high school years was, for the most part, accepted and even encouraged by their parents. Oh, Gary recalls once his parents joking, as they were reviewing finances, "Can't you find a girl closer to home? These gas bills are killing us!"

But they would have "dates" in each other's homes, having dinner with their parents and sometimes attending each other's Luther League activities.

Janet occasionally attended Gary's home basketball games in Roland, but she never went to his state tournament games in Iowa City. She listened to those on radio, and she also read the newspaper stories about them.

"Basketball then was never the number one thing in my life, and it had nothing to do with my wanting to go with Gary. I was proud of what he was doing in basketball, don't get me wrong. And it was a thrill, of course, getting the paper the next day and reading it to see if anything had been written about him."

He would not phone her from Iowa City, but he'd send a card or two. She says now that Gary would be so focused on the tournament games, she is amazed he sent her anything!

It was not unusual in that era for high school boys from one community to be dating girls from another town, and sometimes that would cause a little friction with their schoolmates. However, Gary's classmate Donna Hagen Henry said she can't recall the Roland girls being upset with Gary that he was going with an out-of-towner. "I never saw anybody give either one of them a hard time about it," she said. "We all liked Janet."

Did it bother Janet Sydnes that, among the fan letters Gary began receiving, some were coming from girls—and in one case a married woman—in far-flung places across the state? One girl sent him a shirt and a bracelet. The woman at first sent a photo of herself alone and suggested she come visit Gary at the skating rink. When he didn't respond, she wrote back that "I'm married anyway," and sent photos of her kids and her husband.

So how'd Janet feel about that? "It wasn't a problem, really," she said. "I suppose I'd have a tinge of jealousy, which would be normal."

The two of them have a precious record of their thoughts and feelings in those early times in a stack of about 50 letters that Gary wrote to Janet over a 3-year period, from his late high school years until they were married in August 1955. Janet saved them, and she kids him now about why he didn't save all the letters she wrote to him, as there are only a couple of hers that are preserved.

In one of those, Janet mentions how one of Iowa's top high school girl athletes of those years was apparently hinting, via letters from one of her girlfriends to Gary, that she would like to date him. "Are you still writing to her?" Janet writes. "She's an athlete, which is more than I can say for myself, I guess. But I'd feel much better if you didn't write to her. I see why you would write back to 'those girls' who write to you, as long as it's only one letter. At least when a guy asks me for a date, I tell him I'm going steady. I bet that's more than you do!"

Gary acknowledged in another letter that he was receiving some odd letters from girls. "(One) invited me down to play horseshoes with her dad this summer," Gary wrote in a March, 1953, letter. "What is she trying to pull?"

And he added: "You should see the way some of these characters write! One says, 'You must have a girlfriend whose name is Mary.' I look down at the signature and it's signed, 'Mary.' Big deal nothing!"

That "Big deal nothing!" was a favorite expression of the teenager Gary Thompson, the letters reveal. He doesn't really remember it, but apparently it was an early 1950s version of today's, "Whatever!"

By his senior year, he was also starting an occasional letter to her like this, "Dear Janet (Beautiful!)..." In another, he writes a line from a popular song then, like it's his own: "I'm in love with a wonderful gal!" And in another, "I love you a bushel and a peck!" In one he mentions, "Gosh, I looked like a painted Indian after I left you Monday night. Good deal, I thought!"

But then there was a letter when he was wondering if Janet had been out with some other young fellow, and writes, "Those Ten Commandments are all right as long as they work *both* ways." And he often said farewell with lines like, "Loads of love..." and "Be good, Darling!"

But as close as Janet and Gary became, they did not attend prom with each other at their schools, and as best they recall, they did not attend each other's high school graduations. "Looking back, I can kind of understand why we didn't go to the proms together, because they were really just banquets—not dances," Janet said. "We'd get all dressed up for the banquet, but it seems to me that a lot of the kids didn't bring dates. It seems odder to me that we didn't go to each other's graduations. I can't remember we even talked about that."

Right after Janet graduated, she accepted the Extension Service job and worked for 18 months on the Iowa State campus. She lived during that time with Clarice Wee from Huxley and two young women from Roland, Eleanor Britson and Marion Egemo, in an Ames apartment. Later, Joan Anderson, of Huxley, joined them, before her marriage to Gary's Roland teammate Ralph Johnson.

"Not many people made long distance calls just to chat..."

Eventually, Janet landed a better paying job with Doane Agricultural Appraisal Service in downtown Ames, working directly for appraisers Neill Thompson and Ralph Olson. One day there in the office, she was suddenly confronted at her desk by students from Roland High School, one of them Gary Thompson, who were supposed to be asking the company for a donation for the "Rocket" yearbook. Gary had to laugh about that in a letter a day or two later. "We forgot to ask Doane's for a donation," he wrote. "Guess I forgot, when we started to talk with you. We really came up to get a donation. Ha! Ha!"

Once he had graduated from Roland High School and enrolled at Iowa State, the public attention on Gary Thompson—and on Janet and everybody else close to him—began to intensify. But in that, she recognized a growth opportunity for herself—and she also recognized a quality in her husband-to-be that she really appreciated.

"I was so timid and bashful growing up, and I'd always blush so quick," she said. "So sometimes, yes, it was hard for me. He was so outgoing in the public, and I wasn't used to that.

"But then I'd say to myself, 'Jan, you have to do something about that yourself.' So I'd make myself get out and meet people, and not hang back. I knew if I didn't do that, I'd wind up being miserable by myself. But he was very careful about making sure I was included, and taken care of. He was always a good person about that, very considerate."

March 24, 1953
Roland, Iowa

Hello Janet (Beautiful),

Gee, what a pleasure!!! I just got done writing 7 letters to people who are dumb enough to write to a guy like me, only 8 left to answer. I got 10 today and 5 yesterday, the one that really counted made it 11 for today. Guess whose? YOURS!

Good night, good looking!

Gary

Chapter 8

Life's Different at Iowa State

THE middle 1950s are generally regarded as having been a time of great calm in the United States, and especially in the Midwest. Under President Dwight D. Eisenhower, the nation was fully re-engaged in a peacetime economy, after the long years of World War II in the 1940s and the Korean War in the early 1950s. It was a good time to be in college, as Gary Thompson was at Iowa State from 1953-'57.

It was Iowa State College then, remember. It did not become a university until 1959. Enrollment was 8,000 in the fall of '53, with a six-to-one ratio of male-to-female students. James Hilton had just taken over as college president, becoming the only Iowa State graduate ever to hold the position.

The Cyclones weren't very good in any sports, although they did have one of the best livestock judging teams in the U.S. In 1954, Cy the Cardinal became the official mascot for the Iowa State teams. In the spring of 1955, the student body surprised the beloved college dean M.D. Helser by secretly pooling 50-cent and $1 contributions, raising a total of more than $7,000 and giving him a brand new Cadillac as a retirement gift.

"When I look back on that time, I think it all seemed very natural to us," said Tom Twetten, a native of Spencer in northwest Iowa who served as president of the Iowa State senior class in 1956-'57 and is now retired in Vermont. "There were a lot of rules. For example, there wasn't any drinking on campus. Oh, a few people knew where to get beer off-campus, but there was no drinking at the parties on campus.

"The girls had a curfew—it seems like it might have been 10 or 10:30 p.m. on weeknights, and maybe midnight on Friday and Saturday nights. The photographs of us back then are funny—the way we dressed, the haircuts. You can get a sense of how different it was then, and how straight we all were.

"The students were not political at all," Twetten continued. "It was not a time of controversies. In a sense, it was a time of extreme optimism and naivete."

Yet, it all played out so differently for Gary Thompson and Janet Sydnes. You could argue that there may have been more pressure on them than almost any people of their young age.

Academics at Iowa State were, of course, much more rigorous and time intensive for Gary then they'd been at Roland High School. As he began leading the Cyclones to heights of success they'd never known before—in two sports—it seemed like everybody in the state wanted some of his time and attention.

When Gary and Janet decided to get married after his sophomore year at Iowa State, they had to figure out how they were going to survive financially—especially with Gary's time commitments in sports and Janet's meager salary as a secretary in Ames.

And they had to deal with a heartbreaking tragedy less than 3 weeks before their wedding. A triple-fatality car accident killed Janet's sister, Darlene Sydnes, who was to be their maid of honor; Darlene's boyfriend Hollis Fosse, the Roland friend who had introduced Gary and Janet at the roller rink and was to be their best man, and also Stan Tjernagel, another of Gary's Roland classmates and teammates.

Their wedding went on as scheduled—Janet's mother Carrie Sydnes insisted on it—but Gary, Janet and most others in their extended families and circles of friends spent a long time in an emotional fog, as you can imagine.

With that ordeal, in that summer of 1955, and with everything else that happened in their lives during Gary's student years at Iowa State, this was one young couple that certainly grew up in a hurry. Truth is, Gary Thompson—for all his sports accomplishments in high school—was just a little green coming out of Roland.

Maybe the best illustration of that is a letter he wrote to Janet on June 7, 1953, from Murray, Kentucky. He had been selected to play in the National High School All-Stars basketball game featuring just-graduated high school seniors from across the nation. He had made the trip to Kentucky via train, traveling with another all-star, Ray Nissen, from Oelwein in northeast Iowa.

"If these trains aren't highway robbery on meals!" Gary wrote, mixing a metaphor. "For $1.70, I got 50 cents worth of food. Then another meal, one egg, three strips of bacon and milk cost me $1.33. Those robbers! We really made a waiter mad when we didn't tip him. We felt we tipped him about a $1 anyway" because of the outrageously high price of those meals!

It's interesting to read, in other letters that Gary wrote to Janet, just how differently a top high school athlete was recruited back then than is the case today. Now, we've seen top basketball players in Iowa committing to play for Iowa State or the University of Iowa as early as eighth grade! They make many campus visits. Top-name college coaches become regulars in the high school gyms, watching the prospects. If one of those prospects has not made up his or her mind by their senior year, the pressure from coaches, media and others can become almost overwhelming. That was certainly not the case back in 1953.

During his senior season, Gary Thompson—who had become the most talked-about Iowa high school basketball player ever—received letters expressing an interest from coaches at Iowa State, Iowa, Kansas, Southern Methodist, Baylor, Rice, Iowa State Teachers College plus a number of small colleges around the state. Iowa State coach Clayton "Chick" Sutherland visited Roland several times, invited Thompson to the campus in Ames, gave him a full tour and had him come to the Sutherland home for a cook-out dinner. Other small-college coaches made personal visits, too.

> "He was recruited by seven major colleges…"

But Thompson had not made up his mind by the end of the basketball season in his senior year. In a letter to Janet on April 6, 1953, he wrote how three of his Roland classmates "are going to Iowa State next year. I wish I could make up my mind as quick as those guys did. I might go to Iowa State if I decide on taking journalism for sure as a major and then physical education as a minor."

By mid-May, he was getting closer to a decision. The University of Iowa had made him a candidate for one of the five Nile Kinnick Scholarships they were offering that year. Those scholarships were named in memory of the Hawkeyes' Heisman Trophy winner from the 1939 football season, and were awarded to promising athletes in various sports. But Thompson was not one of the five picked. His hunch now, all these years later, is "that Bucky O'Connor, the Hawkeye basketball coach, thought I was too small."

He really wasn't all that disappointed in not getting the scholarship at the U of I, as he pointed out in a May 21, 1953, letter to Janet. "I found out today that I wasn't one of the five to get a Nile Kinnick Scholarship, so I don't have to worry about that anymore," he wrote. "I was kind of glad that I didn't get it—don't tell anyone that—because I probably would have gone to school there for sure then. So far I think I like Iowa State the best. They've given me a lot of attention, and showed me around ISC. Dale Williams has offered to help me in journalism by working on the radio with him."

Besides, there were other good reasons to pick Iowa State. His father Maurice had a good job as a carpenter at the university, a job he started before his oldest son became a coveted high school basketball player, by the way. And another reason to pick ISC, as Gary wrote to Janet, "it isn't far from 602 8th Street," which was the address of Janet's apartment then in Ames.

His final commitment to Iowa State was not made until later in June of 1953, when Thompson arrived back from the all-star game in Kentucky and then won a spot on the roster of a semi-pro baseball team in Mason City. That team was being coached in the summers by the Iowa State varsity basketball coach Chick Sutherland.

Actually, Thompson and his former Roland teammate Don Holland had both tried out for the Storm Lake Whitecaps semi-pro baseball team that summer; Thompson was selected by manager Shan Deniston for the Storm Lake team, but Holland was not. Holland went on to Mason City, tried out and made that team's roster. Then Coach Sutherland told Holland he should call Thompson in Storm Lake and invite him to come to Mason City, too. Thompson did just that.

"I always felt bad that I left Storm Lake, after I'd already made that team, to go play for Mason City," Thompson said. "And you can imagine I heard about it when our Mason City team went over and played at Storm Lake."

In the early weeks of that summer, Sutherland got the final commitment that Thompson would come play basketball at Iowa State. (Thompson also played semi-pro baseball the next 4 summers during and just after his college years, 2 years in Marshalltown and 2 in Slater.).

So, in the late summer of 1953, freshman Gary Thompson took his place at Iowa State. He checked into a dorm room in "Spinney House," which was one floor of the Friley Hall dormitory. He soon discovered that the journalism department at that time was emphasizing agricultural journalism and advertising, neither of which interested him. That's when he switched his major to physical education, with a minor in zoology, figuring he might eventually become a teacher and coach.

And it didn't take long before he began having experiences that would have seemed like wild dreams a few months earlier. Five weeks into the school year, he watched a genuine campus riot and panty raid happen right in front of him, and he got caught in tear gas, too. A day later, he was walking along on the edge of a protest march from the campus to City Hall in Ames. Things like that had never happened around Roland!

"My hunch was the Iowa coach thought I was too small..."

The trouble started in a burst of student exuberance when the Iowa State football team, which had a 1-3 record at the time, electrified everybody by upsetting Missouri 13-6 in the Homecoming game in Ames. Missouri had come to town riding high after having beaten the nation's No. 1-rated team, Maryland.

"That Saturday night, we had riots and a panty raid on campus," Thompson recalled. "The students started demanding that we get a half-day off school on the following Monday to celebrate the win over Missouri. But that was not granted, and so as that Saturday night went on, things started getting out of control."

News reports from the time say the students came rampaging off the campus to block the adjacent thoroughfare, Lincoln Way, which in those years also served as U.S. Highway 30. They began dragging old sheds and boxes on to the highway, stacking up old furniture there and setting them on fire.

Thompson missed much of that action. "Janet and I were out on a date that night, and when I was coming back about midnight, there were a lot of cops at the east end of the campus," he said. "They told me that the students had blocked Lincoln Way. I saw one cop there I happened to know, and he said he'd take me back on campus.

"When we got in closer, I couldn't believe what I saw. Students were rocking an old car—standing on its running boards—and the driver just floored it to try to get away from them. It was a wonder somebody didn't get hurt bad or killed in that. When I got up by the Knoll, where the president's home is, more students were congregating there. I stood on the other side of the street and watched.

"It was the first time I'd ever seen anybody defy authority like was happening there. A kid ran up and grabbed a policeman's hat. The policeman ran after him, and students mobbed the police officer! A police officer! I saw him wiping away blood from his face.

"Other policemen ran into the crowd, grabbed the student with the cop's hat, took it away from him and then let him go. There was a lot of pushing and shoving, and then suddenly, there was a 'Boom! Boom!' People were screaming that it was tear gas. I ran over by Lake LaVerne, trying to get away from the gas, but I immediately started to cry. There was gas in the air there, and it was getting me. So I ran back to my dorm. I went into the bathroom, and the windows were open, and the gas was starting to come up there, too."

Finally things calmed down in the wee hours of Sunday morning, after police reinforcements were called in from Des Moines, Boone, Marshalltown, Iowa Falls and Eldora. But they heated back up again on Sunday evening.

"There were announcements posted around campus that there was going to be a march to City Hall downtown," Thompson said. "A group of us in the dorm said, 'Well, we're college kids—let's go see what happens!' So we marched down Lincoln Way to City Hall, and everybody was chanting, 'We want a day off! No school Monday!'"

He said today he has no idea why the students decided to make their demands at City Hall, but they weren't granted, either by city officials or by President Hilton. The Iowa State riot wound up being covered in a three-page photo spread in the national *Life* magazine.

Later on in that school year, Thompson said, "I think the policy was changed so we students would get a half-day off if the football team won the Homecoming game. But, you know, I don't remember us winning another Homecoming my last 3 years as a student!"

Freshmen were ineligible for varsity sports competition in those years, so Gary Thompson did not immediately jump to the attention of his fellow students. He obviously didn't stand out in size—as many basketball players would with their height—or in the way he dressed.

"He had his crew-cut hair, and his white-buck shoes, but we all did," said Bill Duffy, an Iowa State classmate from Ames and a sportswriter then for the

Iowa State Daily student newspaper. "There were a lot of us squares around."

Yet, Thompson was hardly anonymous.

"Every kid in the state back then dreamed of being Gary Thompson," said Al Oppedal, another *Daily* writer who was from the Ruthven area in northwest Iowa. "We were all totally aware of him at Iowa State, but people gave him his space, out of respect for him. Still, he was nice to everybody. He was maybe not unique as an athlete in that regard, but darned unusual."

After his freshman year, Thompson spent the summer of 1954 playing for the Marshalltown Ansons semi-pro baseball team and working for the Bailey Brothers Bottling Company there. Then at the start of his sophomore year at Iowa State, he joined the Alpha Sigma Phi fraternity, the one that is known today for manning and firing the cannon at Iowa State football games. He lived in the frat house that year.

"Two Alpha Sigma Phi alums—Lewis Hawkins and William Stacy—knew my dad from being around the university," Thompson said. "They told him that the chapter was being reactivated, and they convinced him it'd be a good experience for me. They also said they would pay all my initiation fees. So he was talking it up with me, and I can remember telling him, 'Dad, I'm just not a frat guy!' But I went ahead and joined, and I did enjoy it. That's where I learned to play 'Bridge'—we'd play cards over the noon hour there."

Meanwhile, Janet Sydnes became like a sweetheart of the whole fraternity, getting to know all the brothers, riding on the frat's float in the parade for VEISHEA, which is Iowa State's student-run springtime festival.

When basketball started, new varsity coach Bill Strannigan moved Thompson into the starting line-up, and life began to be more hectic for Gary and Janet, with the Cyclones going on long road trips by bus, train and occasionally by plane.

The absences made them appreciate each other all the more, and on Christmas Eve of 1954 in the Sydnes farm home near Huxley, Gary proposed to Janet, "and I said yes right away," she said. "It was kind of a surprise that he asked me then, but I'd gone with him to pick out the ring, so I knew it was coming eventually."

They'd dated for nearly 4 years, had "gone steady" for more than 2 years and were already such "a couple" in so many people's minds that few questioned whether they might be too young, at 20. Both sets of parents approved.

However, Coach Strannigan didn't like the idea of his promising sophomore getting married.

"After Christmas when we got back to school, Coach called me in, said he heard I was engaged and sat me down for a talk," Thompson said. "He said, 'Gary, more good basketball players have been ruined by getting married in college than you realize. The next thing you know, Janet can get pregnant, you'll be having financial troubles and you won't be able to keep your mind on basketball. I've seen it happen over and over.'"

It was pretty blunt talk from a coach that Thompson really admired. "I listened to him," Gary said. "But we still got married the next August."

Years later, when the Thompsons had raised their family and they'd get a chance to visit with retired Coach Strannigan, Janet Thompson enjoyed kidding him about his early objection to their marriage. "Jan would always say to Bill, 'Well, Coach, it didn't hurt Gary too much getting married when he was a player, did it?'" Strannigan, of course, couldn't have been happier or prouder about the way things turned out.

Janet Thompson said that even in high school, "I think Gary and I both just sensed that we were going to get married someday. We knew how each other were brought up, we both knew what we wanted in a marriage, and we both had a strong religious faith and thought that would be important in our marriage."

> *""He proposed, and I said yes right away..."*

The late winter, spring and early summer of 1955 now seem almost a blur to them. Gary finished his first varsity basketball season, was an All-Big Seven Conference selection and moved immediately into the starting line-up of the Cyclone baseball team. In June, he moved back to Marshalltown to play a second season of baseball with the Ansons. Janet was continuing to work in Ames, while planning the wedding they had set for Sunday evening, August 14.

But on Wednesday, July 27, things took a shocking turn in their young lives. Janet's older sister Darlene Sydnes finished her work day at Ames Trust & Savings Bank, and was picked up by her boyfriend Hollis Fosse and their friend Stan Tjernagel, who was driving, after they all got off work in Ames. Their first stop was going to be Roland.

Darlene and Hollis, the young man who had introduced Janet and Gary when they were all in high school, were talking marriage themselves. Hollis had spent 2 years in the military, including a hitch in Germany.

"Hollis and Darlene planned to go apartment hunting that evening," said Marlene Fosse Piel, now of Creston, a sister to Hollis Fosse and a classmate of Gary. "I was working at City Hall in Ames then, and normally I car-pooled to work from Roland with Hollis and Stan, but I'd taken our car that day because I had some other errands to do, and Hollis and Stan were in Stan's car. Otherwise, I might well have been with them."

The three young friends drove north out of Ames on U.S. Highway 69. Just north of Gilbert, they came over a hilltop and were surprised to encounter a road construction project that had traffic backed up. They went skidding right up under a flatbed trailer behind a truck that was stopped in traffic there. Darlene Sydnes and Stan Tjernagel were killed in the crash. Hollis Fosse was rushed to Mary Greeley Memorial Hospital in Ames but died shortly after arrival.

"I'd gone to my parents' home to work on some wedding plans, and my mother and I drove into Huxley that evening to talk to the ladies who were going to be taking care of the food and kitchen at the church after the wedding," Janet said. "When we came home, Gary and his parents were there with my dad, waiting for us. It was Gary and his parents who told us what happened."

It was the most horrific tragedy any of them had ever encountered. "It was like, shock," Janet said. "I thought the world had come to an end, right then."

In addition to the overwhelming grief about the tragedy itself, with the loss of these three young lives, there was also this sorrowful and stunning reality: It was 18 days before the wedding, and the maid of honor and best man had just died.

But within hours, Carrie Sydnes made a decision. "My mother said, 'The wedding goes on,' " Janet said.

The funerals were held separately in the coming days. "The community was wonderful," said Marlene Fosse Piel, the sister of Hollis. "It had been a big tragedy for us all."

Janet Thompson agreed. "A lot of people from Huxley and Roland came to our home," she said. "It was hard for some people even to say anything. They didn't know what to say. Gary was around a lot. He was very supportive, and certainly helped me get through it."

After the funerals, "we all knew that life had to go on," Janet said. Her sister Helen Kochheiser, of Ankeny, agreed to take Darlene's place and serve as matron of honor. Arnie Gaarde, Gary's Iowa State friend and teammate, would take Hollis' place as best man.

> *"Now we had to figure out how to survive financially..."*

Janet said her parents "were so strong through all that. Mother didn't bring it up, about Darlene just having died, and she didn't seem to dwell on it. I think she carried a lot of it inside. Looking back now, I wonder how she dealt with it, other than with her faith. I think their strong religious faith is what got my parents through it."

Sunday evening weddings had become popular in that era in the Huxley and Roland communities, and the Sydnes-Thompson wedding at Janet's family's church, Palestine Lutheran, southeast of Huxley, turned out to be a beautiful and very traditional one. Presiding was Rev. Olaf Holen, the Thompsons' pastor at Salem Lutheran in Roland. He had married Gary's parents Maurice and Abbie as well as baptizing and confirming both Thompson boys.

"There was some sadness at the wedding—there almost had to be after what had happened—but it was a happy time, too," Janet said. It was a call back to good life for all who had been at the funerals and at the wedding.

After the ceremony and reception, the newlyweds Gary and Janet Thompson drove away into the night to start their Chicago honeymoon. Their first overnight stay was at the new L-Ranko Motel, which a family by the name of Rank had opened along U.S. Highway 30 between the towns of Toledo and Tama in east central Iowa.

The Thompsons went on to Chicago for several days, with no firm plans and no reservations made, but they found a motel in the Cicero neighborhood. A murder happened not far from where they were staying, and the killer was still at large, but they went on with exploring the city—including the Brookfield Zoo, an exhibition baseball game between the Chicago White Sox and Chicago Cubs, and the major museums.

Soon they were back in Ames, with their new life starting.

"It was tough to get married-student housing back then," Gary Thompson said. "But the athletics department was able to find us a unit in one of the Quonset huts for married students in Pammel Court, and we figured that's where we'd be. The rent there was going to be something like $20 per month. But my folks had given us a bedroom suite for a wedding gift, and I wanted to measure the bedroom before we bought anything.

"So late that August, we went out there and looked at one of the Quonsets we could get. I'm not kidding—there was a one-inch gap between one window and the wall, and the bedroom floor really sloped down. I told Janet, 'Holy smokes, let's go look for something else!' "

They found a nice apartment on the second floor of a house at 160 North Hyland Avenue, just west of the Iowa State campus—big bedroom, living room, dining room, small kitchen—for $70 per month. Their landlords were Harold and Thelma Rush, who lived on the ground floor.

A year later, the Rushes decided to sell the house, and the young Thompsons were at first worried about who their new landlords would be. But it was purchased by Marion and Gail Fawkes, the operators of a Maid-Rite sandwich shop, who moved in on the first floor, "They were even nicer to us than the Rushes had been," Gary said, "and we've been friends ever since." They had a young son Ed Fawkes, and Gary would occasionally shoot baskets with him.

The apartment, Gary said, "was a really nice place, especially compared to the Quonset huts." The Thompsons needed more furniture than just the new bedroom suite, so they tapped their small savings and went to Ginsberg's, a well-known furniture store in Des Moines, where they wanted furnishings in the very trendy 1955 colors of pink and black.

"We bought a sofa, a swivel chair, two-step end tables, a coffee table, a 9-by-12-foot rug, a floor lamp and two other lamps—all for $249," Gary said. "We were really excited about it—we'd found a neat apartment, we put all this new furniture in it—we had quite a place, for just starting out!"

Janet already had a whole set of Vita Kraft pots and pans, and a set of silverware, all part of her "hope chest." But then "we had to figure out how we were going to survive financially," Gary said.

Janet Thompson was making $80 every 2 weeks at Doane Agricultural Appraisal Service. Gary Thompson joined Iowa State's Army Reserve Officer Training Corps (ROTC) program, for which he was paid $27 per month.

Plus, under terms of his athletic scholarship, he was assigned a job, which was sweeping out the men's gymnasium every day, for which he was paid $15 per month. He also got free lunch by setting up dining tables and working occasionally as a waiter at his fraternity house. Also, per his athletic scholarship, he received free tuition and books. And since he was married and living on his own instead of in a dormitory, he received the financial equivalent of the Cyclones' training table meals, room and board.

Besides that, the young couple "would go to one of our parents' house for Sunday dinner one week, and the other parents' house the next weekend—and they'd always send food home with us, too,' " Janet said. "We lived well. We were happy. Life was a lot less complicated than it got later."

They were even saving a little money. "I was always taught that no matter what you have and whatever amount you are paid, you should put some in savings," Gary said. So when the 1955 World Series was starting that October, he decided they had enough in savings to allow him to go out and buy their first television.

"Janet comes home from work that day and sees this 19-inch TV in a big blond cabinet and says, 'What are you doing?' " Gary said. "I said, 'Well, I'm going to watch the World Series.' She said, 'What do you think you're doing, buying a TV set! We don't have that kind of money!' "

They also bought their first car, a 1948 Chevrolet that had belonged to Roland's Postmaster Richard Christian and his wife Dorothy. A year later, they sold that one and bought a 1951 DeSoto—"a big boat of a car," Gary called it—from his fraternity's housemother, Oma Sermon. "I think we paid $400 for that one, and may have even borrowed a little money to be able to afford it," he said.

Neither Thompson was a drinker or smoker, and that certainly helped them financially, and in a lot of other ways.

"We grew up with training rules," Gary said. "I never was out with any group in high school that was ever drinking beer. Never. And in college? I was married, and I was never out with a group of kids drinking beer. I just didn't drink beer. And I've still never sat down and drank a beer in its entirety. I was never around it. I only remember seeing my dad drinking a beer one time when I was a very young kid, and Mom told him, 'That's the last time or you'll be out of the house!' "

Janet said she, too, grew up in a home where she "never saw any drinking."

Gary's military service began when he enrolled in ROTC at the start of his junior year. "We had classes, had marching drills and I remember having to be in formations at 1 p.m., in uniform," he said. "I was in it 2 years, and had a 2-week summer camp after my junior year, at Fort Sill, Oklahoma."

He was trained as an artillery officer, working with Howitzers. After graduation, he held the rank of Second Lieutenant. He did 6 months of active duty in the summer of 1958, after he had played his first season with the Philllips

66ers, and then spent 6 years in the Army Reserve, with some weekend and summer-camp service commitments.

Al Oppedal, who was one of those *Iowa State Daily* sportswriters who covered Thompson in basketball, was startled when he, too, joined ROTC and learned that "Gary Thompson was my squad leader.

"That was the only thing I ever knew him to do that he couldn't do well," Oppedal recalled. "He could not count cadence when we marched. As a basketball player, he could lead the team so well, stop and go, hang in the air, perfect timing. But when he was trying to call cadence for us when we were marching, he couldn't. We were all out of step most of the time."

Old soldier Thompson was startled to hear that. "What? Oppedal doesn't know what he's talking about!" he said. "I could call cadence, I can guarantee you that!"

As a student, Thompson said he "was average, about a 2.6 or 2.7 on the 4-point system. I look back on that now, and I know myself I could have done better. But it really was hard keeping up in classes with all the time commitments of sports—not just the games but the travel and long practices.

"The athletic department back then didn't have any tutors, like there are today. I can remember coming home some nights, needing to read several chapters of a book and being so tired I'd just doze off. I remembered a lesson from my mother, though, that 'You're always freshest in the morning.' So I'd get up early, and try to get all my studies done."

> *"Life was a lot less complicated than it got later..."*

Thompson said whatever celebrity he had as an athlete did not help him at all in his academic classes at Iowa State, "and in fact, it penalized me at least once. There was a history professor who was openly anti-athletics. And there was a required course in that department, and I kept putting off taking it—until the spring of my senior year—and wouldn't you know that I got the professor who hated athletics.

"We'd be gone on a road-trip all weekend, there'd be no time to read the lesson and he'd make it a point to call on me first thing on Monday mornings. On essay tests that I'd think I did 'C' work on, he was giving me 'Ds' and 'D-minuses'. I was scared I was going to flunk the course."

He said as the time approached for the final exam, he realized the Cyclones were going to be gone on another baseball road trip. He made an appointment with two other professors in the history department, took his papers with him and told them about his concerns. "I told them I was not expecting or asking for any breaks at all, but that I didn't think I was being treated fairly," he said.

One of those professors advised Gary to tell his assigned professor that the baseball trip would make him miss the scheduled exam, and he would need to make it up. The second professor administered the exam, graded it strictly and "I got a 'C' or 'C-minus' for the course," he said. "In recent years, I had a fellow come up to me at some Iowa State event, introduce himself and say he was in that same history class with me, and he said he remembered the professor going after me pretty hard."

The Thompsons' social circle in those last 2 years Gary was a student tended to be family and old friends from home, plus some of Gary's teammates and fraternity brothers and their dates. They spent a lot of evenings at their apartment, playing very competitive card games—"Hearts," "Blackjack," "Canasta" and "Bridge."

Bill Duffy, another of the sportswriters for the *Iowa State Daily*, got a good look at the Thompsons' lifestyle in the apartment when he came to interview them for a feature story that he sold to *The Iowan* magazine in Gary's senior year. "They seemed settled," Duffy recalls. "Like a traditional couple. Like older people would be."

So, they were pretty "straight," as Gary's classmate Tom Twetten said early in this chapter. But nearly everybody was, back in that era of the mid to late 1950s.

Fifty years later, it sure seems like they received good foundations at Iowa State. Twetten, for example, had a 34-year career with the U.S. Central Intelligence Agency, winding up as chief of its "clandestine services," working most of his career in Africa, South Asia and the Middle East. He retired to Craftsbury Common, Vermont, where he repairs and trades in antiquarian books—"something about as far from clandestine operations as you can get," he said with a smile.

The Class of '57 also included Roy Reiman, a native of little Auburn in west central Iowa who founded and turned Reiman Publications in Wisconsin into one of the most successful magazine publishing companies in the nation. He was the lead donor funding the creation of the gorgeous Reiman Gardens at the south end of Jack Trice Stadium at Iowa State, as well as a new alumni center. He and Thompson have become good friends in recent years.

> "Looking back,
> I wonder how Mom
> dealt with it…"

And there are a lot more loyal and successful Iowa Staters in that class. When they had their 50th reunion in the spring of 2007, they set a record for a "class reunion gift," with 375 individual classmates donating $125,000 to endow scholarships for ISU sophomores, and also making a major contribution for a new veterinary medicine teaching hospital. Co-chairs of the fund drive were Thompson and Gerry Leader, a classmate who now is an emeritus professor of management at Boston University after earlier career stops at Tulane, Stanford and Harvard.

"Gary Thompson was a class hero and a model citizen, someone we all looked up to," said Twetten. And they still do. But that's a feeling shared by more than just his classmates.

Funny story about that: In 1970, Leo Milleman, a native of Spencer in northwest Iowa, was a scared first-year student in Iowa State's College of Veterinary Medicine.

"Vet school back then was a no-nonsense experience, neckties and lab coats every day, big black notebooks, very serious," said Milleman, who eventually went on to medical school, became a urologist and practices in Ames, where one of his patients is Gary Thompson. "I was a real serious student, and I had no money, so I was cooking and washing dishes at a frat house, working all the time, not really paying much attention to anything but my studies.

"Well, the professors at the vet school decided that we students needed to be in command at all times of all the knowledge they were giving us, not just cramming for the big tests. So they told us they were going to start giving us unannounced quizzes that could cover anything, and we were all scared to death of those.

"I was taking a class in histology, taught by Bernard Skold, who was very strict, came from a military background. One morning, when I walked into his class, I was expecting we were just going to be continuing to dissect this horse we'd been working on. But Professor Skold said it was 'exam day,' and he told me to report to his office. I went in, and the quiz question he gave me was, 'Who was the Roland Rocket?'

"It just stopped me cold," Milleman continued. "I thought, 'Oh, my God, who or what was the Roland Rocket? The guy who invented penicillin? The vet who did the first heart surgery on a dog?' I finally just told Professor Skold I didn't know.

"He said, 'Milleman, you may be bright enough to get the grades you need, but you've got to be more well-rounded than that. The Roland Rocket is Gary Thompson, Iowa State's greatest basketball player, an All-American. One thing you have to know is who Gary Thompson is!'"

Chapter 9

New Era for Iowa State Basketball

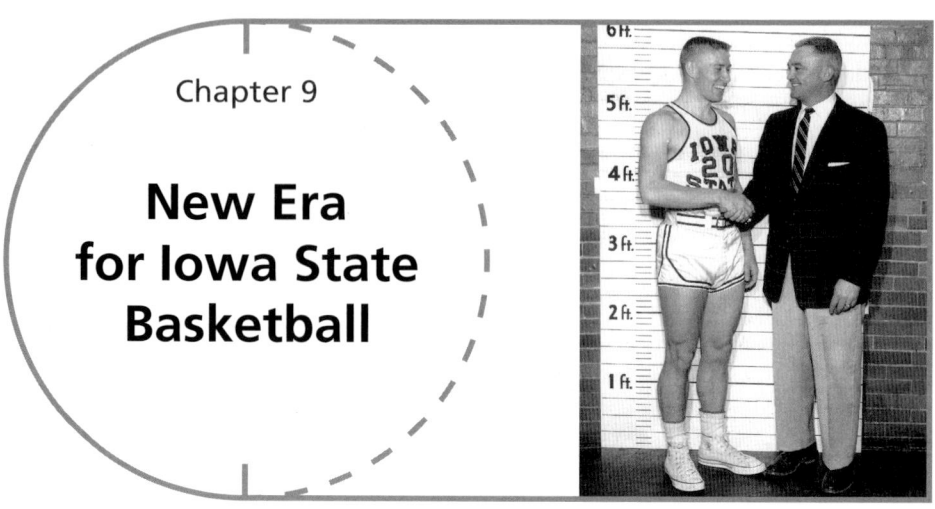

BEFORE Gary Thompson started playing varsity basketball at Iowa State in the 1954-'55 season, it had been nearly a decade since the Cyclone teams had stirred much excitement.

Earlier, there had been a pretty good run through the 1930s and first half of the '40s. From 1933 to '35, the Cyclones of Coach Louis Menze came to power using the strength and height of Waldo Wegner. He was a 6 ft. 4 in. "giant" from Everly in northwest Iowa, who decided to try out for the team after seeing the coach's advertisement for players in the *Iowa State Daily* student newspaper.

In the 1934-'35 season, Wegner led the team to a 13-3 record and the school's first Big Six Conference championship, and he was named to the All-American team, the first Cyclone basketball player to achieve that honor. Jack Flemming, a sophomore on the '35 champions, played 2 more years and was named an All-American in 1937. Menze's teams also won conference championships in 1941, '44 and '45.

And in that '44 season, when teams across the nation were short of talent because of all the men gone to military service during World War II, the Cyclones reached the NCAA semi-finals before losing to Utah, which went on to win the championship. Menze, who took on additional duties as athletic director in 1945, had one last hurrah as Cyclone coach in the '47-'48 season when the team went 15-8.

In the fall of 1948, the Big Six Conference became the Big Seven with the addition of Colorado University. And that year, Menze turned the basketball coaching reins over to Clayton "Chick" Sutherland, who stepped up from being freshman coach.

Six consecutive losing seasons followed, including the 6-15 finish in 1953-'54 when Gary Thompson was a freshman. NCAA and conference rules then prohibited all freshmen from playing varsity sports.

"We played some games as a freshman team, but I can't remember who we played," Thompson now says. "We also had a Varsity vs. Freshman game that year, and the varsity nipped us right at the end of the game."

Though Sutherland's varsity squads weren't very successful, there's no denying that he helped Iowa State get the corner turned in basketball—by landing Thompson as a recruit. And when Sutherland was dismissed as coach in the spring of '54 by Athletic Director Menze, he was allowed to stay on at Iowa State as an instructor in physical education and eventually retired there.

In seeking a new coach, Menze made a move so bold that he surely must have done so with approval, if not encouragement, from Iowa State President James Hilton: He went after one of the nation's brightest young coaching prospects, Bill Strannigan, of Colorado A&M. It was a clear signal that Iowa State wanted to start a new era in basketball.

Born in Scotland but raised in Rock Springs, Wyoming, Strannigan had been a superstar athlete in basketball, football and baseball at the University of Wyoming from 1940-'42, including being named to the All-American basketball team of 1941, as a 5 ft. 10 in. guard. He went on to star in AAU basketball for the Denver American Legion team that won the 1942 national championship, and he was named an All-American at that level. He then joined the U.S. Navy for war-time duty.

After military service, Strannigan taught and coached high school sports in Loveland, Colorado, for at least 2 years. Then he landed the head basketball coaching position at Colorado A&M, the college in Fort Collins that later would be re-named Colorado State University. In 4 years as the Rams' coach, he directed his teams to a 60-56 record. In the 1953-'54 season, he attracted national attention while leading A&M to the championship of the Skyline Conference and a ranking of 13th in the U.S.

Strannigan was 36 years old when he became head coach at Iowa State. News stories then described him as "personable," "effervescent" and "a public relations genius." Basketball instantly became fun for the Cyclone faithful.

"There was an overnight change in the program," said Arnie Gaarde, who was between his sophomore and junior years as a guard. "It was especially exciting for a guard because we pressed, we'd fast break—the pace of our game really picked up. The other part of it, he designed our offense around our starting guards, Gary Thompson and Larry Wetter. Chick Sutherland's style of play had been so much more methodical—pass, pass, pass, try to get it inside. Bill Strannigan's game was so much faster and more fun to play. It was like a light going on for us."

Strannigan's starting line-up in his first year, the 1954-'55 season, had Thompson, who was just a sophomore, joining four seniors—all of them from Iowa. They were Wetter, from tiny Rinard; Stan Frahm, from Manning; Chuck Duncan, from Atlantic, and Don DeKoster, from Spencer. The key reserves that year included juniors Gaarde, from little Armstrong, Gerald Sandbulte, from Sioux Center, and sophomore Chuck Vogt, from Clinton.

Thompson loved everything about being a varsity athlete. There was the acceptance by the older fellows on the team, the camaraderie. He recalls how when they made the trip about Christmastime to the Big Seven Conference pre-season tournament in Kansas City, "Chuck Duncan and Stan Frahm took me to the Pioneer Grill across the street from the Muehlbach Hotel, and they showed me how they'd eat two scoops of ice cream in a bowl of Wheaties. By gum, it was pretty good! I love ice cream, and I still *alamode* everything," although never his Wheaties in later life.

Gaarde, who often kids Thompson that he always got preferential treatment from the coaches, tells a story that Strannigan didn't think his players should be eating ice cream on their Wheaties, that it was an unnecessary extra expense. "Strannigan caught me with ice cream on my Wheaties and started to chew me out, saying it'd probably cost 10 to 15 cents extra," Gaarde says. "But then he looked down the table and saw that Gary Thompson had ice cream on his Wheaties, too, and so he said, 'Well, I guess that will be O.K.' "

Thompson also remembers how, after he'd won his spot on the varsity team at Iowa State, getting in touch with his old Roland High School coach Buck Cheadle, who was by then coaching in Burlington. "When I was in high school, Buck never let us drink pop or eat candy bars," Thompson said. "I told him at Iowa State, they had pop for us right in the dressing room!"

> *"They showed me how to eat ice cream on Wheaties…"*

He experienced other new kinds of training. "The first time I ever lifted a weight was at Iowa State," he said. "No one was doing that back then. But the University of Iowa physical education people were doing a study on how weight training could increase a player's jumping ability. So our coaches decided we'd participate. We'd lift barbells and then do duck-walking with them—the worst thing you could do, we learned later. That lasted about a month, and that was the first and last time I ever lifted weights."

Players' uniforms back then had a very different look from what fans are accustomed to now. The Cyclones' uniforms in the mid-1950s featured the very short trunks that were popular in that era. "I look at photos of how we looked back then, and see how players look today in the real baggy shorts, and I think that the ideal is surely something kind of in-between," Thompson now says, with a smile.

The sneakers nearly everybody wore were the Converse Chuck Taylor All-Stars, the same brand Thompson wore in high school. Teams had warm-up outfits that were a jacket, some with a back flap that could be zipped into a hood, and trousers—made of either satin-like material or a softer fleece-like fabric.

The team generally used either trains or buses on road trips. Once or twice, they traveled by airplane—Gary specifically recalls a DC-6 flight home from a game at Colorado. Team practices were in classic old State Gym, which today looks just about the same as it did in 1954.

"This baby is just like it was then," Thompson told me when we were walking through it. The dressing rooms—for both the Cyclones and for the visiting teams—were on the lower level. However, the games were being played four blocks north in the Armory, which was the ROTC facility on campus. It had a wood basketball floor that could be set down on the dirt surface inside the building. The somewhat-rickety wood bleachers could accommodate 5,000 fans.

The best illustration of how different college sports was in the 1950s, from what we know in this new century, may be what would happen on basketball game evenings.

"We'd get to State Gym about 5 p.m., get taped up, get into uniform and maybe go up in the gym to work on some last-minute thing," Thompson said. "The visitors would be over in their dressing room, also in State Gym. But then when it came time to go over to the Armory for the game, both teams and all the coaches would go out and get on the same city bus, and ride together to the Armory.

"We'd each have a ROTC classroom over there that served as a meeting room for pre-game and halftime. After the game, same thing—we'd all go out and get on the same bus, and ride back together to State Gym, where we'd shower and get back into our street clothes."

I was astounded when I heard that story. The opposing teams would ride on the same bus? Would the Cyclone players talk to the players on the other team?

"Oh, no, we'd keep our game faces on, both before and after the game," said Thompson. "At least that's how I remember it."

After he had played a couple of years against some of the opposing players—Missouri star and later coach Norm Stewart would be an example—they'd often talk to each other when they were away from the court.

But not on the bus going to and coming from the basketball games? "Well, in Norm's case, I might have smiled at him a little," Thompson said.

Of course, it would be cold walking to and from that bus. "We'd have our warm-ups on over our uniforms, and when it was really cold, we'd also wear those hooded parkas that the football team had, too," Thompson said.

There were also some attempts at psyching out the opponents, via that bus ride. "In my sophomore or junior year, we were playing Kansas in Ames, and after we got dressed at State Gym, we went upstairs to work on a little zone defense we were going to use," Thompson said. "Then we went back down to the dressing room, and we think we're ready to go to the Armory, but Coach Strannigan says, 'No, sit down for a while.' He might have gone outdoors for a smoke. Then Dick Harp, who was the Kansas assistant coach, comes to our dressing room and says that their head coach Phog Allen is ready to go. But Strannigan had come back, and after Harp left, he told us to stay sitting down.

"Then Harp came back in about 5 minutes and said, 'Hey, Phog's ready to go—the boys are on the bus and it's cold out there!' So then Strannigan told us to go on out to the bus. Phog was sitting out there on the bus, fuming. Strannigan was just trying to do a psych job on Kansas!"

Another unusual thing about the Armory is that late in the afternoons, even on game days in the wintertime, the ROTC cadets and their instructors would often have outdoor training exercises with big Howitzer cannons. When the ROTC classes were done for the day, they'd pull open the huge garage-like doors on one side of the Armory, and wheel the Howitzers back to their storage area inside the building.

"That cold air would come rolling in there on us when the big doors were opened," Thompson said. "And there'd be so much dust get stirred up from the Armory's dirt floor that it would settle on the wood basketball floor. We'd have to wash our hands after warm-ups to get the dirt off."

That '54-'55 Iowa State team raised eyebrows when it beat perennial power Kansas twice and had a winning season, with a record of 11-10. Twice they scored over 100 points.

Late in the season, in a game against Nebraska in Ames, they thought they were in trouble when the 6 ft. 5 in. Chuck Duncan, who was the starting center, came down with the flu. Strannigan shocked everybody by telling the 5 ft. 10 in. Thompson to move inside and play the post.

"How the coaches could see that I might do all right playing inside against taller players, I don't know," Thompson said. "Buck Cheadle had me do that a few times in high school, but that was high school. At Iowa State, I'd played some one-on-one in practices against Strannigan himself. I guess he must've thought that the big guys weren't as active on the floor, and that with my quickness and hook shot, I might do all right inside there."

Against Nebraska that day, "I missed my first five or six shots, but then I settled down and I got 29 points," Thompson recalled.

It was not unusual during his next 2 years at Iowa State for Thompson to slide inside, get the ball and see if he could out-maneuver opponents' big men for baskets. Or perhaps they'd foul Thompson, and send him to the free throw line.

People across the nation were buzzing about that.

"I first became aware of Gary Thompson when he was playing at Iowa State, and I was a young assistant coach at Air Force," said Dean Smith, who as a player had been a reserve on the 1952 national championship team at Kansas and later as a coach won national championships at North Carolina. "You know, there wasn't much basketball on TV then, but I do remember we watched him once or twice in televised games.

"We'd never seen a player before quite like him. What was he, 5 ft. 10 in. or 5 ft. 11 in.? And he was playing a key role in the inside game. He'd go in there and post-up on much bigger men, and he'd be shooting those hook shots!

He had so much basketball savvy, he could make it work. I'd never seen a little guy do that before, or since then, either. And of course, he could really shoot it from outside, too. He could take people all over the floor."

Normally, however, Thompson was playing guard, initially teaming up on the perimeter with the Cyclones' veteran guard Larry Wetter.

"As a sophomore, Gary had great improvement in his game, and became a solid all-around player," said Wetter, who had played against Thompson in high school. "He was deceptively quick, he had very strong hands and good peripheral vision.

"Since Gary and I were the guards, Strannigan had us go one-on-one against each other, and sometimes those match-ups would get a little brutal. But that gave me a lot of respect for Gary, and frankly helped my game a lot, too. I've always regretted that we got to play together just that 1 year, because then all of us seniors were gone."

Wetter said he'd "have given an eyetooth to have been able to play one more year." He is now retired in Oregon, after a distinguished business career with JELD-WEN, Inc., makers of doors, windows and other construction components.

Duncan, who was 6 ft. 5 in. and one of the centers on the team, said he's always been proud of how "that senior year of ours, with Strannigan coaching and Gary in the line-up, was the beginning of the turn-around in Iowa State basketball. I remember speaking at a high school athletic banquet after that season and telling the kids that if Iowa State could pull a team together around Gary the next couple of years, he would become an All-American—and he did."

> *"I loved everything about being a varsity athlete..."*

Duncan is now retired in San Antonio after a long career as a project engineer with Black & Veatch Corporation, a global engineering, consulting and construction company. Stan Frahm is in Rancho Santa Fe, California, and DeKoster is in Louisville, Kentucky.

Strannigan indeed set out to "pull a team together around Gary the next couple of years," as Chuck Duncan predicted. He went on a recruiting binge the likes of which Iowa State basketball had never known.

Lyle Frahm, younger brother of Cyclone starter Stan Frahm, was finishing a stellar high school career at Manning in western Iowa, and remembers the impact of Strannigan's recruiting.

"I believe when Bill Strannigan came to Iowa State, it was just a new era," said Lyle Frahm, now retired in Montana after a career that included coaching basketball and then working as a sales manager with Converse athletic shoes. "I rather doubt that all of a sudden the recruiting budget grew by leaps and bounds, but it wouldn't surprise me if Bill just spent whatever to get the job done. I think for many years, the program was just stuck with Iowa players, and

I doubt that Chick Sutherland felt much like getting into the recruiting wars.

"So, my freshman year, the fall of 1954, was really an interesting and almost overwhelming year. We had All-State players from all over—New York, Wisconsin, Illinois, Wyoming, Colorado, Iowa and possibly some other states I'm not remembering. There were 30 of us freshmen who showed up for the first practice. A few were on full scholarships, some on half scholarships, some on tuition only—like me—and some were walk-ons."

Frahm rattled off names of as many of those players as his memory provides: Don Medsker, Englewood, Colorado; Walt Bradley, also from Colorado; Al Lowery, Homewood, Illinois; Larry Swanson, Oshkosh, Wisconsin; Leroy Whiteside, Joliet, Illinois; Ron Hain, Westmont, Illinois; Terry Ecker, from Wyoming; John Crawford, New York City, and other players from Iowa, like Bud Bergman, of Grundy Center; Bill Meyer, of Davenport; Dick Farwell, of Clinton, and Dave Young, of Ottumwa.

Of all those, the one who got the Cyclone fans' immediate attention was Crawford, the school's first African-American basketball player and eventually one of its most popular students.

Crawford had been named the "most outstanding player" in New York City's tough high school basketball leagues during his senior year at the New York School of Printing in Manhattan, a high school with about 1,000 students. He had averaged 32 points per game that year. He stood 6 ft. 5 in., weighed 185 pounds—"same as now," he told me proudly 50 years later. He had excellent speed and was as good a defensive player and rebounder as he was a scoring threat on offense.

How the heck did Strannigan find him, and then convince him to come to Iowa State? "I believe Bill Strannigan heard about me from a former player or friend of his at Colorado A&M who was working in New York City," said Crawford. "That guy made arrangements for me to talk to Strannigan, and we hit it off. He talked to my mother, and she liked him, too. He was very personable."

Crawford had letters offering scholarships "from 30 or 40 schools," he recalls. "St. John's in New York and Temple in Philadelphia were both really after me, but you know, I just wanted to leave the city. I wanted to try somewhere else. I got an offer from UCLA, which had a good pharmacy program and I was thinking about that back then. The University of Hawaii recruited me a little. And I heard from most of the historically black colleges and universities, too.

"Strannigan told me he had a great shooting guard—he meant Gary Thompson—and that he was building a team around him. He said this guy was just a great player, but I had no idea then just how good he was."

The thought of living in Iowa, a rural state with a very small black population, did not bother him, and it didn't worry his mother Cleonis Crawford. "Strannigan promised he'd look out for me, and he always did," John Crawford said.

And the coach also recruited another African-American player to come to Iowa State at the same time.

"He was Stacey Arceneaux, who was a friend of mine who had played at a different New York City school—Taft High in the Bronx," Crawford said. "He came to Ames with me, but I don't think he ever actually enrolled at Iowa State. When they were checking his records, they discovered that somehow he had not completed enough high school credits to enroll. So they were arranging it so he could go to Ames High School and take whatever course or courses he needed. But Stacey was also in love with a girl back in New York, and that was his excuse to go back home."

Arceneaux, incidentally, went on to become a star player for several years in the professional Eastern Basketball League, a minor league that operated in New York and other eastern states, and he was picked up briefly by the old St. Louis Hawks of the National Basketball League.

Coming out of New York City, did the two young men feel like they were on the other side of the moon when they got to Ames?

"Not at all," said Crawford. "We rode out on the train, and I was already used to wide open spaces. I was born in South Carolina, and my parents moved us to New York City when I was 5 years old. As I grew up, I spent a lot of summers with my grandparents, aunts, uncles and other family around a little town of Ellenton, South Carolina. So I already had a little experience in small towns."

> *"Iowa State was the first place I lifted weights..."*

Crawford said he "had a very good freshman year. We felt as a freshman team that we could have beaten the varsity, but our coach Herb Cormack had so many of us he had to play, that we couldn't just play our best against their best."

In that school year of 1954-'55 when Crawford and Lyle Frahm were freshmen, "the NCAA allowed universities to hold 4 weeks of spring practice after the regular season was over," Frahm recalled, "and thus the coach could see what he had coming back already for the next year. Those spring drills were only allowed for 1 or 2 years, and then that was it.

"But of those 30 of us who started that school year together as freshmen basketball players, all of them pretty much hung around until spring," he continued. "It was after that spring practice, that I received my full scholarship for the balance of my career, and a few others did, too. Then the roster narrowed down considerably by fall, as players either saw the writing on the wall or were cut by the time fall practice began."

Of the 30, incidentally, only six were still playing when they were seniors—Frahm, Crawford, Medsker, Swanson, Lowery and Farwell. Of that group, Medsker had another of the more unusual routes to Iowa State.

"I had a pretty good high school career in Englewood, Colorado," Medsker said. "I played center and some forward, and I was a starter from my sophomore year. By my senior year, I made All-State in Colorado, and I probably averaged

22 to 23 points per game. So Bill Strannigan, who was then at Colorado A&M, had recruited me to go there and play for him.

"He was a charmer. He had a real way about him, especially with your parents, and most especially with your mother. He could convince any mother that he was going to take great care of her son. So I was all signed up to go to Colorado A&M with him, and then after my senior high school season, he suddenly called and said, 'You know, Don, I think I've got a better opportunity for you. I want you to come to Iowa State with me.' So I did!"

> "Both teams rode on the same bus to the Armory before and after games then..."

Crawford, Medsker and Lyle Frahm all moved into the starting line-up as sophomores, joining juniors Thompson and Vogt, for the 1955-'56 sesason. As the season went on, senior Arnie Gaarde also started several games at guard. "I never figured out how I got to start," Gaarde said. "But when I did, I was wise enough to know that it wasn't really about me, it was about me getting the ball to Thompson."

The Cyclones got off to a fabulous start, with relatively easy non-conference victories over North Dakota State, Texas Tech, Tulsa and Colorado A&M, before being upset by the University of Denver, 65-62.

Then came one of the biggest victories in Iowa State basketball history, an 87-76 upset of No. 6-rated Vanderbilt. Thompson scored his career high of 40 points to thrill the hometown fans in Ames. "Coach Strannigan had me go into the post position, and I think three different Vanderbilt players who were guarding me fouled out," Thompson said. "I hit 18 free throws in that game."

Frahm said he's "always thought that win over Vandy was the real start for us."

The Cyclones began believing they could beat anybody. After a 5-1 start to the season, they went to the Big Seven Conference holiday tournament in Kansas City. They rang up successive victories over Kansas State, Colorado and Kansas, and won the tournament championship. Thompson scored 20, 18 and 22 points. Those three victories allowed Iowa State to soar as high as No. 5 in the national rankings.

The team had captured the imagination of basketball fans across their home state. Iowa Governor Herschel Loveless, who attended the championship game in Kansas City, asked Thompson if he wanted to fly back to Des Moines with him on the state's airplane.

However, Thompson was married by then, and his wife Janet was in Kansas City with his parents Maurice and Abbie Thompson. So Gary declined the governor's invitation, saying he'd stay with the team and his family to enjoy the victory celebration. But he also gave Gaarde, his normal roommate on road trips, the boot that night so that he and Janet could have their own hotel room.

Iowa State then went into the regular season Big Seven games, and lost two of their next three. When they played at Missouri, Arnie Gaarde was playing with a little too much spirit in the first half, and was called for a technical foul. As the team left the floor for the halftime break, Gaarde was still upset, approached the official who'd called the technical, and said, "Boy, you've made a lot of bad calls today!" The official didn't miss a beat, smiling and responding, "Oh, you're just upset because our team is ahead!"

The Cyclones got back on their feet against Colorado in Ames, with another memorable Thompson performance. He hit a half-court shot at the end of the first half. Then at the end of the game, Iowa State held for a last shot, and Gary drilled it for a 70-68 victory.

The Cyclones went on to win seven of their next nine to finish an 18-5 season, the most wins in a season ever by an Iowa State team. They did not qualify for post-season play in the NCAA tournament, because back then, only the conference champion advanced, and the Cyclones had finished second.

But Gary Thompson was the talk of the Big Seven. There was the personal letter from Kansas coach Phog Allen, quoted in full in Chapter 1, saying how the coach had "always been most favorably impressed with your great skill on the basketball court." He also said Thompson's play had "bordered on the phenomenal."

Even opposing players knew they were seeing something special.

"Gary was a heck of a player, one who knew so many ways to beat you," said Norm Stewart, the former Missouri star player and coach, and a friend of Thompson for more than 50 years. "When you're a player as small as he was, you have to be in better condition than everybody else, you have to know the game, and you have to develop other skills. Gary did all that."

But there was something else about Thompson that made opponents respect him, even enjoy being around him, and it was something Stewart shared, too.

"Gary had come out of little Roland, and I'd come out of Shelbyville, a town of about 750 in northeastern Missouri," Stewart said. "The small town is one of the commonalities he and I share, and probably is one reason we've always been friends. When you grew up in a small town back then, you had to figure out a way to survive. And you learned to care for other people—that it wasn't just all about you." That helped their games, Stewart said, and it helped make them better people.

Phil "Red" Murrell, who came out of tiny Linneus, Missouri, and became a 3-year superstar at Drake in Des Moines from 1955-'58, played 2 years against Thompson. By the time he graduated, he'd become Drake's all-time leading scorer and also broke Thompson's career-scoring record for a college player in Iowa. Then Thompson and Murrell became teammates for the Phillips 66ers in AAU ball, and both were in the 66ers starting line-up.

"From playing against Gary in college, I knew he was really quick with the ball and was very strong for his size," said Murrell, who was 6 ft. 4 in. and, like Thompson, played all over the floor. "But the things that really made him special were that he was such a smart player, he was always hustling and he was so competitive. Later, when we were teammates, I learned he was a hustler and competitive in everything he did—even playing gin rummy!"

Iowa State fans were relishing the start of the 1956-'57 basketball season, Thompson's senior year. He'd been named to the All-Big Seven Conference first team the previous two seasons. When the NCAA Record Book came out previewing the season, Thompson was the player featured on the cover. Iowa State's sports information director Harry Burrell was calling the upcoming campaign the "Go with Gary!" season.

The Armory was given a complete renovation. The direction of the playing floor in the building was shifted from north-south to east-west. That, plus a new "crow's nest" balcony, allowed room for 2,500 more seats, expanding the capacity to 7,500 for games. Dressing rooms were added, ending the one-bus commutes from old State Gym for the Cyclones and their opponents.

"The crowds were bigger, but the bleachers were still so close to the floor that it was like the fans could almost reach out and touch you," Thompson said. "And the bleachers were steel, too, so when the fans would start stomping their feet, it was really noisy. The Iowa State pep band would play 'Happy Trails to You' when an opponent fouled out. And when somebody from the other team was shooting free throws, our crowd would chant, 'Bounce! Bounce! Bounce! Shoot!' The Armory became one of the toughest places to play in the conference."

That is confirmed by Max Falkenstein, the radio voice of the Kansas Jayhawks for nearly 60 years, who recalled the Iowa State Armory in that era as being "a crappy place to play," a gym he remembers mostly for requiring "a laborious climb up into the rafters to reach the broadcast booth."

Of course, Iowa State broadcaster Dale Williams recalls the Armory "as an exciting place to play, one where there was always a lot of enthusiasm," and he says he loved the view "from the broadcasting loft they built above the floor." He was starting his 15th season as the radio play-by-play voice of the Cyclones, a position he held for 26 years without ever being paid for it. It was just an add-on to his radio and TV job with the Iowa State College Extension Service, which had him doing daily farm reports and features, as well as serving as a livestock judge "at nearly every county fair in Iowa."

He became famous for his shout of "Holy Cow!" when something went the Cyclones' way. "I guess I get the blame for coming up with that expression first," said Williams, who is retired in Ames, "although Harry Caray—the broadcaster for the University of Missouri and in major league baseball—made a lot more money using it than I ever did!" He said he recalls people across the state being excited for Gary Thompson's senior year. "When I'd be out around the state on farm stories, everybody would be asking me about Gary and the team," he said.

The turn-out for Iowa State home games from Thompson's hometown of Roland was, of course, huge. In fact there was practically a "Roland Section" in the stands. His wife Janet Thompson would usually sit halfway up in the stands on the south side of the floor with Gary's parents Maurice and Abbie Thompson and often their younger son DeLon, who was a freshman at Roland High School and starting to make a name for himself in sports.

"I was usually fairly relaxed at Gary's games," Janet recalls. "I always just knew he was going to do fine, that he wasn't going to make some big mistake out there. I'd get excited and yell, just like all the other fans, but never anything too wild." They would not make eye contact during games, she said, adding, "Gary was so concentrated on basketball."

The Cyclones' starting line-up was generally the same as in the preceding season, with Thompson, Vogt, Lyle Frahm, Crawford and Medsker. As the season went on, John Krocheski, a 6 ft. 7 in. sophomore from Ames, became more of a factor and an occasional starter.

They opened the season with consecutive victories over Michigan State, Houston (Thompson scored 35), Brigham Young University, Texas Tech and Tulsa.

"One thing I've never forgotten about that trip in December '56 to play Texas Tech and Tulsa was that it was one of those times when we ran into some real racial discrimination against John Crawford," said Thompson. "On that trip, we first went into Dallas, where we were going to work out and then check in at a hotel around 6 p.m. We had reservations at the hotel, but when we got there, the clerk looked at our group, saw Crawford and said to Bill Strannigan, 'Is he with you?' When Strannigan said that, yes, John was one of our players, the clerk said, 'Well, he can't stay here.'

"Strannigan shocked everyone by starting Thompson at center..."

"Strannigan came right back at him and said, 'Well, if he doesn't stay here, none of us do!' The clerk kind of backed off, and probably saw a whole lot of business about ready to go out the door. Then he said, 'Well, if he will stay in a ground-floor room and doesn't use the elevator, he can stay.' That was ridiculous, but John said it was O.K., so that's what we did. But that wasn't all he had to put up with.

"When we went to Texas Tech to play, he was whistled for three fouls in the first 6 minutes of the game, and had to sit out. When we went to Tulsa and played, same thing—they called a bunch of quick cheap fouls on John."

Finding a place where Crawford would be allowed to eat on that trip was also difficult.

"We were only getting about $2 apiece to eat a meal on then, and we generally couldn't afford to eat at the hotels," Thompson said. "So a small group of us, including John, walked down the street to find a restaurant. I'd go to the manager and say, 'We're the Iowa State basketball team, and we've got a player who is a Negro—that's what we called blacks then—and we'd like to eat here.'

"We went to five or six restaurants, and it was awful what most of the managers were saying back to me. But two of them said they did have a back seating area in their restaurants, and we could eat there if we wanted to. So I picked one of those, and I just told the guys that's where we'd go. I didn't say much to them about what really happened because I didn't want it to hurt John, but I'll tell you, I was really mad about it myself."

The first loss for that '56-'57 team was to top-ranked Kansas in the first round of the Big Seven holiday tournament, 58-57. That was the first time Iowa State had played against Kansas' 7-ft.-tall Kansas phenom, Wilt "The Stilt" Chamberlain, a sophomore.

That loss was disappointing to Cyclone fans. Then a few days later, they got a real scare when Thompson badly sprained an ankle in practice.

"I didn't know if I was going to be able to play," Thompson recalls. "But our trainer, Beryl Taylor, taped me up so tight I wanted to cry. It about cut off circulation to my foot, but Beryl knew what he was doing. The tape loosened up when I was on the floor. I could go straight ahead fine, but I had a trouble cutting on it. But still, he kept me in the line-up."

Taylor could be pretty rough, Thompson says. "He was a professor, actually, who taught athletic training in the physical education department. He was smaller than I was, but he had huge arms on him, and he had the strongest hands. I remember getting a charley horse one time in my leg, and he'd come out and knead the cramp out. I'd be screaming from the pain, and it seemed like he was just delighted. 'The pain's all in your head!' he'd say. I'd say, 'No, Beryl, the pain's in my leg!' He'd laugh and then keep kneading until the cramp was gone."

Victories followed over Kansas State and Nebraska before a loss to Missouri.

Then on January 11, 1957, in the first college game played in the new Veterans Memorial Auditorium in downtown Des Moines, Iowa State beat Drake, 97-71. Thompson scored 27 points, including the 1,000th point of his career. But Drake's Red Murrell took the game's scoring honors with 28.

Three days later in Ames, the Cyclones upset top-ranked Kansas 39-37 in the historic game mentioned in Chapter 1, a game which is profiled in full in Chapter 10.

It was a wild season the whole rest of the way. In order, there was a victory over Oklahoma, a loss to Missouri, another win over Oklahoma and then a rematch with Kansas in Allen Fieldhouse in Lawrence.

Sports Illustrated basketball writer Jeremiah Tax did a feature story previewing the game called, "The Battle on the River Kaw," after a river that flows through Lawrence. More than 17,000 fans were there, with another 2.5

million watching a telecast of the game carried on four stations throughout the Midwest. Kansas won it 75-64, with Chamberlain getting 19 points, but being outplayed by Thompson, who scored 21 and pulled down seven rebounds.

A one-point victory over Colorado was next, then a rematch with Drake, this time at the Armory in Ames.

"We were getting ready to play a 'Box & 1' defense on Drake, with Lyle Frahm chasing Red Murrell," Thompson recalls. Frahm, incidentally, remembers Murrell as being "mean as a hornet," but he followed Coach Strannigan's orders and stayed right on the Drake star, while Iowa State raced to a 92-71 victory.

Drake threw a defensive surprise at Iowa State, too, but the Cyclones handled it well. "It turned out they put a 'Box & 1' on me, so I just started hitting the open guy with passes all the time," Thompson said. "Chuck Vogt hit five or six in a row from the corner for us. He ran down the court after he hit several in a row, shrugging his shoulders, like he was saying, 'I don't believe this!' I think I only had 6 points at halftime, but I ended with 31. When people focus their defense on you, you don't fight it—you go to someone else. They'll lose interest later, and then you can go back to your normal game."

In subsequent games, the Cyclones were upset by Colorado, then beat Nebraska and lost to Kansas State at Manhattan 86-77, with Thompson hitting 29.

Those two teams then made their way back to Ames for a rematch a week later, in Thompson's last home game as a Cyclone on March 2, 1957. It turned into a huge event, a special send-off night for Thompson and his senior running mate Vogt. *The Iowa State Daily* newspaper put out a 16-page edition with a special section recounting their careers and the season.

Strannigan was quoted at length about what made Thompson so special as a player.

"He's the greatest little man I've ever seen," the coach said. "He's a fierce competitor and a fine team leader. You get to feeling that he has reached his peak, and then he comes up with something entirely new in the next game. He has great basketball sense, a very fine touch and every shot in the game. Gary is not fast, but he's very quick, and above all his desire is tremendous."

And here was the student newspaper's lead editorial, characterizing the play and impact of the team:

> Well, what can we say? Iowa State has produced a basketball team that is rated as one of the best in the country, and things look pretty good for next year—even though we'll sorely miss Vogt and Thompson.
>
> The team that we are honoring with this congratulatory issue has done more, however, than just win ball games and praise. This bunch, along with their coach, has brought back a real interest in college sports at Iowa State.
>
> The telegram that was sent to Kansas, the student financing of television presentation of the game, the frenzied support given at

every Cyclone home game, the renewed alumni interest, and the long Commons discussions of Saturday night's game that are so frequent—all of these things, and many more less obvious or tangible were prompted by this team simply because they were a team.

Here's a gang that deserved every thrilling win they obtained, and—the way some of us look at it—deserved to win some of the close ones they lost.

And this man Thompson! Time after time, he's come through with that extra scoring spurt just when things looked bad. His floor play and scoring ability have made him the favorite subject of many sport writers around the state.

And even elsewhere in the country, the name Thompson is synonymous with good basketball. His coolheaded stall in the closing seconds of the 1955 Colorado game will never be forgotten by those who saw his last-second basket rip the net and win the game.

His split-second decisions when the crowd could hardly think were always a factor in winning the close ones, and when the team lost, no one in the stands could do anything but shake their heads and wonder how any team could try so hard and still lose a game.

Then there's Chuck Vogt, the man who drove Drake fans wild as he fired in point after point to send the Bulldogs skittering to a stinging defeat. No one could try harder nor be more valuable to the team.

Well, let's just put in this way. For what it's worth, the *Daily*, on behalf of the entire student body, wishes all of the team members and Bill Strannigan and the coaching staff all the success they deserve—and thanks for a great basketball year.

The paper also announced that the team would be saluted post-game with a free dance for all students in the Great Hall of the Iowa State Memorial Union.

Thompson scored 16, helping Iowa State to a 69-67 victory in overtime over a strong K-State team that featured two players who became All-Americans—6 ft. 7 in. Bob Boozer, 6 ft. 9 in. Jack Parr—and another standout 6 ft. 3 in. Roy DeWitz.

After the game, Strannigan surprised Thompson, who was summoned back out on the floor before the sell-out crowd. "You'll never see No. 20 on this floor again," Strannigan said over a hand microphone. "We are retiring that number."

Thompson was so startled he began battling tears. After regaining his composure, he took the microphone and did his best to thank his school, coaches and fans. "Iowa State did better by me than I did for it," he said. "The 12 players, no, I mean the 13 players…" and then he hesitated and said, "You know, I only got a 'C' in speech."

Janet Thompson, who was sitting up in the stands, recalls that it was all a surprise to her, too. "I remember that night well," she says now, "and I was very proud."

Gary's last game as a Cyclone was at Nebraska, and the Cyclones lost 67-58. They closed the season with a 16-7 record, tied for second in the Big Seven and thus ineligible for the post-season tournament.

Meanwhile, the honors rolled in—All-Conference for the third year in a row in the Big Seven and the conference's MVP for '56-'57, Iowa State "Athlete of the Year," and best of all, Associated Press first team All-American. The other AP All-Americans, as mentioned in Chapter 1, were Wilt Chamberlain of Kansas, Lennie Rosenbluth of North Carolina, Chet Forte of Columbia and Rod "Hot Rod" Hundley of West Virginia.

> *"The pep band played 'Happy Trails to You' when opposing player fouled out..."*

That honor resulted in all five being featured on the famous "Ed Sullivan Show" on network television.

"It was a live television show, and when Ed Sullivan introduced each of us, we were supposed to dribble out from behind the curtain and shoot at this make-shift basket they had on stage," Thompson said. "They had these old basketballs, some so old they even had laces on them. I was supposed to dribble out and shoot a lay-up, and I felt like it was the most pressure to make a gol-darned lay-up I'd ever had, but I did make it. Wilt picked up the ball, jumped up and jammed it. Then Lennie Rosenbluth, a real cocky guy who played on North Carolina's national champions that year, was going to dunk it, too. But he dribbled the ball—one of those with the laces—and it bounced crooked off the laces, took off and rolled behind the curtains. Lennie ran back there to try to get the ball, but it was totally dark back there. The other four of us got a real kick out of that—sort of a 'couldn't happen to a nicer guy' thing, we all thought."

Thompson got a second appearance on the "Ed Sullivan Show" that spring with the All-American team that *Look* magazine picked. That was a 10-member first team that included Thompson, Chamberlain, Forte, Hundley, Rosenbluth, Elgin Baylor of Seattle, Frank Howard of Ohio State, Jim Krebs of Southern Methodist, Guy Rodgers of Temple and Charlie Tyra of Louisville.

All those young college guys appearing on that week's Sullivan show got an extra thrill when a very popular young singer, Julie London, was there to perform. "We all knew her from her song 'Cry Me a River,' and it was fun to meet her," Thompson said. "She was probably 8 or 9 years older than most of us were, and one thing I remember about her was how nervous she was before she went out to perform. They were actually going to have her lip-sync a song, and she was worrying how that was going to go. She told us, 'I'm so nervous,

I've got to keep going to the bathroom!'"

Some of those five 1957 All-Americans, Thompson among them, were reunited by the NCAA at the 1982 Final Four in New Orleans, as the "Silver Anniversary All-American team." They were honored then not only for having been outstanding players in 1956-'57, but for their career accomplishments.

> *"He'd be shooting those hook shots over the big guys..."*

Two of the 1957 Associated Press All-Americans are deceased. Forte, who had a great broadcasting success as director of "NFL Monday Night Football" on ABC-TV, died of a heart attack in 1996. Chamberlain died of heart failure in 1999.

The other three of those AP All-Americans still survive—Thompson; Rosenbluth, who is retired in Florida, and Hundley, who continues a long broadcasting career as the play-by-play voice of the Utah Jazz in the National Basketball Association.

Thompson got a surprise phone call in July, 2008, from Barbara Chamberlain Lewis, of Las Vegas, a sister of Wilt Chamberlain. She was just a year younger than her famous brother, and the two of them were the closest of the nine Chamberlain siblings.

She'd been slowly going through Wilt's collections. "People are surprised when I tell them that Wilt saved everything—every note, every letter, every program—going clear back to his high school years," Lewis said. "It has taken me forever, but I've been going through it all, and just recently I came across a stack of letters he'd received from those guys on the 1957 All-American team. I saw the name 'Gary Thompson,' and I was thrilled. I was a great fan of Gary, except for him beating Kansas, of course.

"But the reason I called him is that all the letters from those guys reflected something you don't hear about much in sports now. They all really cared for each other, and they honored each other on their accomplishments, not only in basketball but in their careers. I loved that about those guys—so what if one guy whipped you in basketball, you could still be friends. So that's why I called Gary, just to remind him about those letters and to thank him for caring about Wilt."

As the All-American and other honors were being bestowed back in that spring of 1957, Thompson got to play in two more college games—the East vs. West College All-Star Games in Kansas City and New York City. At Kansas City, he led all scorers with 16 points, made the winning basket and was named MVP.

"Thompson was the star of the show, as far as the crowd was concerned," wrote Bert McGrane in the *Des Moines Register*. "An estimated 8,500 fairly lifted the roof when he was introduced and gave him an even greater ovation at the finish."

A long-lasting and fun measure of what a state hero Thompson had become back then is that at least three baby boys in Iowa were named after him, so enthralled were their parents with his story.

One is a namesake, Gary Lee Thompson, who was born in 1958 to Stuart and Mary Thompson in Newton.

"I'm a great basketball fan," said Stuart Thompson, who now lives in St. Charles, Iowa "I admired Gary Thompson a lot when he played at Roland and Iowa State, and that's why I named my son after him. Later on I enjoyed him as a basketball announcer, too. I never did get to meet Gary in Ames, but I know he's quite a guy."

Stuart's son Gary Thompson, a tool & dye maker in Newton, said he did get to meet his more famous namesake once, and they had a good laugh how Gary Lee Thompson in Newton had received a tax bill on payments for basketball broadcasting that should have gone to Gary Lee Thompson in Ames.

"I told him I wouldn't mind paying his taxes," said Gary of Newton, "but I'd want to have his income, too."

Another man named after Thompson is a Lutheran pastor, Rev. Gary Grindeland, who was born in 1954 in Ames and grew up in the same Bethesda Lutheran Church where the Thompsons have been long-time members.

"My dad and mom, Roger and Naomi Grindeland, who still live in Ames, were real fans of Gary Thompson when he was playing at Roland," said Rev. Grindeland, who now is a vice-president with Lutheran Social Services in Wisconsin and Upper Michigan. "In fact, Dad would go watch him play in Roland, and that's how I wound up being named after Gary."

Gary Grindeland grew up to become a starting guard on outstanding Ames High basketball teams before he graduated 1972, then went on to Luther College in Decorah and Luther Seminary in St. Paul. In 1980, he served a year back home as assistant pastor of Bethesda Lutheran while he was working on a Ph.D. at Iowa State. His pastoral career has taken him as far east as New York City. In 2006, Rev. Grindeland returned to Ames and Bethesda as a guest minister for a weekend.

"When I saw Gary Thompson attending a service that weekend, I was able to thank him from the pulpit for my name, and it was very cool being able to do that," said Rev. Grindeland.

But Thompson may have been more touched than the minister was. "It was a real honor for me, just knowing he was named after me," Thompson said later, "and then there I was, receiving communion from him."

The other boy named after him, Gary John Yungclas, got his middle name in honor of another Cyclone player, John Crawford. He was born in February, 1956, to former Iowa State students Bruce and Patty Yungclas. Tragically, Gary John died when he was only 14 years old, in a tractor accident in August, 1970.

"We've always been a real Iowa State family," said Patty Yungclas, who now lives in Webster City. "My dad was Ralph Olsen, from Ellsworth, and he was a big supporter of Cyclone sports, and particularly a fan of Gary Thompson and John Crawford. Then I married Bruce Yungclas, who'd come back after serving in World War II to go to Iowa State. The Yungclases were as much of an Iowa State family as the Olsens were. After our student years, we went back and were farming at Ellsworth where we raised the kids, and we were big fans of the Cyclones.

"When Gary John was born, it was during the basketball season, and I had to miss one game while I was in the hospital having him. So we decided it was appropriate to name him after Gary Thompson and John Crawford. We regarded them almost like members of our family. Maybe the best part of the story is that we've stayed friends with Gary and John and their families through all the years since then."

Bruce Yungclas died in 1970. Another son he and Patty had, Alan Yungclas, now lives outside Webster City with his family. Bruce and Patty Yungclas' daughter Leah Maass and her family are on the Olsen home farm. After the Thompson playing era ended at Iowa State, Coach Strannigan stayed 2 more years with the Cyclones. His last teams had records of 15-8 in 1957-'58 and 9-16 in '58-'59 before he was recruited to return to his alma mater, the University of Wyoming, where he coached until his retirement in 1973. He and Thompson stayed close through the years.

"Coach was just trying to put the psych on Kansas..."

Strannigan died in the fall of 1997 while on his way back to Wyoming, after attending ceremonies at Iowa State in which Thompson was inducted into the university's Sports Hall of Fame. Thompson flew to Wyoming to speak at his old coach's funeral.

Thompson has stayed amazingly close to his old teammates, too, even organizing many of their reunions through the years. Their appreciation of him has grown through the decades.

"Gary was the ultimate teammate," said Chuck Vogt, now retired in Bonita Springs, Florida, after a long career in the awards and advertising specialties business. "How do you describe that extra something that he had? You know, I got to play with another great athlete in high school in Clinton—Kenny Ploen, who went on to become an All-American quarterback at the University of Iowa.

"Gary and Kenny were alike in that they were leaders by doing, not by shouting at you, or by acting like they were the star. At Iowa State, Gary was clearly the leader, but he wasn't in your face about it. He was a class act then, and he's demonstrated that same characteristic in his success later on in life."

Don Medsker, retired in Centennial, Colorado, after a 35-year career as a lawyer, said Thompson "was in a different category than most players back then. I always told people if they thought he was good in the Iowa State games, they should have seen him in practice, where he was always doing sensational stuff. He wasn't a showboat, or anything, but he was doing stuff with the ball that none of the rest of us could. You didn't see his kind of ball handling back then. Today, all the great players handle the ball like he did, but nobody else did back when he was playing."

John Crawford is retired in Westport, Connecticut, after nearly 42 years as a teacher and administrator in the New York City public schools. He said that as he has reflected over time about what his friend Thompson accomplished as an Iowa State athlete, he thinks he has been able to put it in perspective: "Gary really was what every man wishes he'd been, what every boy wanted to be."

Chapter 10

Sweetest Time to Be a Cyclone!

IOWA STATE'S upset, 39-37 victory over No. 1-ranked Kansas on January 14, 1957, stands as one of the two most-talked-about basketball games ever played in the state of Iowa.

Of course, because this is Iowa, you can probably guess that the other legendary game that nearly all older fans still talk about was a six-on-six girls' basketball game. In fact, it was the 1968 girls' state tournament championship game, with the Union-Whitten Cobras and Denise Long winning 113-107 in overtime over the Everly Cattlefeederettes with Jeanette Olson. About 14,000 packed Veterans Memorial Auditorium in Des Moines, and fans in nine states watched the telecast of that game.

But 11 years earlier, the KU vs. Iowa State game was mighty big.

The Jayhawks were 12-0 and ranked No. 1 in the nation. The Cyclones were 9-2 and had been ranked as high as No. 7.

Kansas' sophomore sensation Wilt "The Stilt" Chamberlain was making his first trip to the other schools around the Big Seven Conference, and the 7-footer was averaging 31.8 points and eight blocked shots per game.

The *Des Moines Register's* Maury White, in his game preview story in that Monday's newspaper, said there'd never been such public focus on a game at Iowa State. "The basketball menu here tonight is pure caviar," White wrote. "Wilt Chamberlain & Co. against Iowa State, the only team to come within a point of undefeated Kansas in 12 games.

"On a statewide basis, it is safe to say that no basketball game ever played at Ames has had as many Iowans excited. The 7,800 Armory seats have been oversold for weeks, and tickets are considered pure gold."

Among those who managed to come up with a ticket was young Johnny Orr, then boys' basketball coach at Dubuque Senior High School in northeast Iowa—a person who eventually wound up in a lot of other big Iowa State games, as coach of the Cyclones in the 1980s and '90s.

Fans took outrageous chances to get to the game, despite a blizzard and extreme temperatures. Barry Benson, now a writer in Des Moines, was 14 years old and a huge fan of Gary Thompson in the town of Nevada, east of Ames.

In 1997, Benson wrote an op-ed column for the *Des Moines Sunday Register*, recalling his trip to the Kansas game 40 years earlier. "Snowstorms had been raging, and outside the old Armory gym in Ames that mid-January night, it was 15 below zero," Benson wrote. "We barely made it. Blizzard conditions were forecast, but ISU administrators decided not to call the game.

"Six friends, my younger brother and I all crammed into Mom's 1950 yellow Ford sedan. She was night operator at the Nevada telephone office, having been transferred to Nevada in the spring when Story City's office was closed. Our new Nevada friends told their parents Mom was driving us the 9 miles to Ames. They lied. I was the 14-year-old driver of that old Ford without a heater, without windshield wipers, without a horn. Of course, I was also without a license. I could barely see pavement markers on old Highway 30. I kept rubbing the frozen windshield to glimpse curb or ditch images along old Lincoln Way.

"New friends, Mike and Steve Collis, brought stogies. Steve Schmidt, Cal Halliburton and Keith Cherryholmes puffed away, making it harder on the eyes. Only Chuck Sutherland, future All-State forward and Drake Bulldog, abstained. Somehow we made it."

Meanwhile, WOI-TV and seven radio stations were broadcasting the game live to fans across the state. The atmosphere in the Armory during the game was as intense as anybody could ever remember it.

"The Armory's seats were on steel risers, and when a game got particularly exciting, people would be stomping their feet and making a tremendous noise," recalled Marv Stromer, a retired professor of animal science at Iowa State. He was a third year student at Iowa State at the time of the Kansas game in '57, and he attended with his girlfriend Shirley Roepke, eventually his wife.

"Our seats were on the north side of the floor on the lower set of risers, but we had a balcony riser above us, and that balcony had lights hanging down from it, with big glass globes on them," Stromer said. "As the game went on, all of us in the crowd were standing and cheering most of the time. Once when we were getting up to cheer again, I saw an odd flicker of light out of the corner of my eye. I glanced up and just as I did, the glass globe over the light let go and dropped—right on us! I reached up and caught it! It was a good 10 or 12 inches in diameter, so it would've made a real mess, right on our heads, if I hadn't caught it."

Did Shirley and the other fans around him give him an ovation—or at least pats on the back? "Frankly, no one said very much at all," Stromer said. "They were so into the excitement of the game, they glanced at the light and the globe, and then immediately refocused on what the team was doing out on the floor."

The fans were thrilled with the upset victory, particularly because it was over the No. 1-rated team in the country. And everybody was just fascinated by Chamberlain. He was the tallest man most Iowans had ever seen, and everybody wanted to get a close look at him.

"I remember after that game, sticking around to see Wilt come out of the locker room," said Alan Hoskins, a friend of Gary Thompson from their high school years in the neighboring towns of Zearing and Roland, and by then a student at the University of Iowa. "When he did come out, I remember thinking, 'I knew you were big, but I had no idea you were that big!'"

Tom Emmerson, then an Iowa State journalism student and a writer for the *Iowa State Daily*, decided before the game that he wanted to try to have a personal interview with Chamberlain—sort of a sophomore-to-sophomore encounter—to see what the most talked-about college basketball player in America was really like. It's yet another illustration of how different times were then from today, just how accessible and open Chamberlain proved to be for Emmerson.

> "Snowstorms were raging, but the game was a complete sellout..."

"The KU team arrived in Ames on that Sunday, and I went to their workout and asked if I could interview Chamberlain," said Emmerson, who still lives in Ames. "They said I could, but that I should come by the hotel later on Sunday or else on Monday morning." It turned into an adventure that Emmerson loves re-telling, as he did often during his 40-year career as an Iowa State journalism professor.

So, later on that long-ago Sunday, young Emmerson grabbed a copy of the pre-game coverage the *Iowa State Daily* had published in its Saturday edition, and he headed for the Sheldon-Munn Hotel in downtown Ames, where the Kansas team was staying.

"I can't imagine now that I just knocked on his door," Emmerson said, but that's his recollection. "I was really pleased to get the interview. Heck, Wilt was probably 18 or 19, and I was probably 19 or 20. I thoroughly enjoyed the session. Wilt was soft-spoken and cooperative—not full of himself and verbose. As I remember, we might have talked 40 minutes or more. I even had the impression that all of this 'press stuff' was relatively new to him. I know that seems odd, but I wonder how often before that he had been interviewed one-on-one for any real length of time."

Chamberlain was willing to let Emmerson take a couple of photographs of him sprawling on his hotel room bed, with his feet extended off the mattress.

In fact, they got along so well that Emmerson asked Chamberlain if he would autograph the *Daily's* pre-game sports section for his girlfriend Linda Murray, a sophomore in architecture, now Emmerson's wife of more than 40 years. Chamberlain obliged. "To Linda, girl architech," Chamberlain wrote, with a slight misspelling of "architect." And then the young star player added this: "He really wants you—you know who." He signed it, "Yours in sports, Wilt Chamberlain."

Emmerson's story was published in the next edition of the *Iowa State Daily*, on Tuesday, which also reported the outcome of the game. Here it is, just as it ran then:

"Ivy League" and Conga Drums; That's Wilt
by Tom Emmerson

WHEN he opened the door of his hotel room, he was in his stocking feet. His size 14 shoes were placed neatly by the bed. He bent over and looked through the door. We shook hands and I introduced myself.

We started talking. His initial answers were short and to the point, but as we got further along, he began to loosen up and relax, telling about things people often overlook with a celebrated sports figure.

That's how I met Wilton Chamberlain. Conversation started with food, then it drifted to the woe of most college students—eight o'clock classes.

"I've got five a week and I hate 'em."

"Do you have any trouble getting up?"

"Nope, I room with a human alarm clock."

An economics major, Wilt hopes to enter the law field. He hasn't decided whether he prefers business or corporation law. Chamberlain is carrying 16 credit hours this semester, including five of economics, three of accounting, three of western civilization, three of religion and two of English.

At present Wilt is "dating no one in particular" and has "no special girl at home" (Philadelphia).

Disagreeing with the idea that tall men are at a disadvantage, Wilt explained it this way: "It's not as inconvenient as some people think. You get used to ducking. I really don't have any trouble buying clothes; living in a large city helps, and cars, seats and desks aren't any problem."

For a man as big as Wilt (he says he's 7 feet tall in his stocking feet) he's not out of proportion physically. Wilt gets most of his added height in his legs. Wilt says he grew between 13 and 15. "I put on 3 inches in 2 months once. At 15, I was 6 ft.11 in."

For recreation, Wilt enjoys ping pong, swimming and bowling. Chamberlain bowls in an all-college league and has a 172 average.

"I like music, too." (Chamberlain really lit up on music.) He thinks Elvis Presley is "all right" but prefers Harry Belafonte and Fats Domino. "I really like any music; rhythm and blues, jazz and all the rest."

As favorite songs, Wilt presently lists Belafonte's "Banana Boat" and "Calypso," Domino's "Blue Monday" and "Green Door" by Jimmy Lowe.

On the other side of music, Wilt sings (a throat operation this fall has stopped him recently) and "fools around with the drums." "I've got a Conga drum. You play it with your hands, like this," he said, going through the motions of playing a make-believe drum.

A sharp dresser, Wilt strongly believes in the "Ivy League" look. When I noted he was "quite Ivy League!" Wilt quickly replied, "It's the way to be." Chamberlain's "Ivy League" caps have taken the KU team by storm. When they arrived Sunday, every member of the team, including coaches, trainer and manager had an "Ivy League" cap.

Personally, Wilt could outfit the whole team with caps. He owns "11 or 12 of them." He only brought one to Ames.

Statistically, Wilt is 19 years old, a graduate of Overbrook High School and one of nine children. His older brother is 6 ft. 5 in. and his younger brother (12) is about 5 ft. 4 in. His six sisters, four older and two younger, are all fairly tall. "Tallness runs in the family."

At the age of 6, Wilt was severely bitten on the shins by poisonous mosquitoes. The left shin took eight years to heal and nine years for the right one to heal. The scars and bumps of his unpleasant episode with mosquitoes still mark his legs.

The infected shins have never really cleared up completely. It is feared if Wilt were to cut his shins again the infection would reoccur. For this reason Wilt wears knee socks when he plays.

The most surprising thing I learned about Wilt was the rubber band he wears on each wrist.

"It all started when I was in junior high, playing basketball. We wore knee socks and they kept slipping down. So we kids began putting rubber bands around the socks. Well, this worked fine, but sometimes a rubber band would break in a game and the socks would end up around our ankles.

"Someone got the idea of wearing one around his wrist, just in case one should break. It just got to be a habit with me. I've had a rubber band on my right wrist for over 6 years now. This one," he said, pointing to the band presently on his right wrist," is about a year old."

"Don't you ever take them off, even in a game?"

"Nope. Never have."

"Any superstition involved?"

"None at all. It's just a habit."

Wilt wears his wrist watch over the rubber band on his left wrist when he isn't playing ball. When I finally decided that the rubber band on his left hand was there as a spare in case the one on the right hand should break, Wilt threw back a quick, "Yeah, now you're working."

With that, we shook hands, and while I put my coat on, Wilt put some drops in his eyes. Then he walked four flights of stairs to the lobby and onto the bus with the team.

Emmerson was plenty excited about his interview and his story, he says now. "I heard later from a student friend that one of my professors, Bill Ames,

(Continued on page 153)

Iowa State & Phillips 66ers Years

HE EVEN INSPIRED ARTISTS. Gary Thompson's sports career at Iowa State is chronicled in old clippings, photographs, films of games—even artwork. Left is a salute from nationally syndicated sports cartoonist Murray Olderman of the Newspaper Enterprise Association. Above and right are drawings of Gary by Kevin Richards, an artist in Jefferson, Iowa, from a collage he did in 1997 of the inaugural inductees into the ISU Athletic Hall of Fame.

JANET & GARY THOMPSON (right) married in the summer of 1955, when Gary was between his sophomore and junior years at Iowa State and Janet was working as a secretary in Ames. They became the most recognizable young couple in the state. (Photo copyright 1957, The Des Moines Register and Tribune Company. Reprinted with permission.)

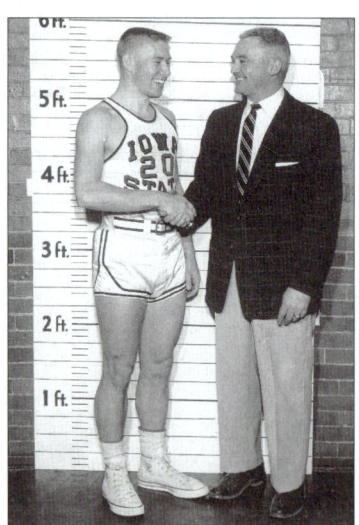

ALL-AMERICAN SEASON. Right, Iowa State's team in Gary Thompson's senior season, 1956-'57, when he was first team All-American. Left, with Coach Bill Strannigan, an All-American player at Wyoming in 1942. The coach was "checking if Thompson 'measures up' to being an All-American," he said. (Photo copyright 1957, The Des Moines Register and Tribune Company. Reprinted with permission.) Above left, Strannigan and Thompson in 1997 at ISU Hall of Fame induction.

BRIGHT LIGHTS. One fun part of being on college basketball's All-American first team, back in the 1950s was going to New York with the other honorees and being introduced on the "Ed Sullivan Show," the nation's favorite TV show. Left, Thompson is shown while being questioned by Sullivan. Below the All-Americans were (left to right) Wilt Chamberlain of Kansas, Lenny Rosenbluth of North Carolina, "Hot Rod" Hundley of West Virginia, Thompson of Iowa State and "Chet the Jet" Forte of Columbia.

FULL COURT. Gary Thompson was the rare player who was used both "outside" as a guard and "inside" among the post players. He was only 5 ft. 10 in. tall in his Iowa State years, but he was so athletic and savvy about basketball that his coaches built plays around him all over the court.

EMOTIONAL FAREWELL. Left, Gary Thompson sheds tears after his last home game in 1957 when it was announced his No. 20 was being retired. (Copyright 1957, The Des Moines Register and Tribune Company. Reprinted with permission.) At right, old State Gym still stands at Iowa State. In Gary Thompson's era, the Cyclones practiced at State Gym but played their actual games a few blocks north at the Armory. On game days, the Cyclones and their opponents used the dressing rooms at State Gym, then players and coaches from both teams rode together on the same city bus to and from the Armory.

BIG MOMENT & BASEBALL GLORY. Upper left, the defense is shown that the Iowa State Cyclones used in their January, 1957, upset of Wilt Chamberlain (13) and Kansas. Right photo, Iowa State baseball coach L.C. "Cap" Timm (left) is shown with Gary Thompson (center) and Arnie Gaarde, of Armstrong, infielders for the Cyclones. Left, just above, Coach Timm and Thompson (center) with another top Cyclone player Dick Bertell, of Des Moines, who had a 10-year career in pro ball with the Chicago Cubs and San Francisco Giants. (Last photo from Iowa State University Library Archives.)

PROTÉGÉ AND A PRODIGY. Left, Ron Baukol, of Downers Grove, Illinois, who was just starting his Iowa State sports career as Gary Thompson was finishing his, "sometimes passes as a double for the Cyclone star," the Des Moines Register reported in May, 1957. Baukol was an all-conference basketball player and top scholar athlete in his senior year of 1959. (Copyright, 1957, The Des Moines Register and Tribune Company. Reprinted with permission.) Right, Gary Thompson in his varsity baseball uniform.

PHILLIPS 66ERS STAR & COACH. Above left, Gary Thompson was an AAU All-American player for the Phillips 66ers 1957-'62. He was MVP of the '62 national tournament, won by the 66ers. From '64 to '68, he coached the team. Above right, at a reunion in 2004, Gary (second from left) was dwarfed by his former players (left to right) Kendall Rhine, Bill Kusleika and Bobby Rascoe. Above, Gary vents frustrations over refs' calls with North Dakota U. coaches Jimmy Rodgers (second from left) and Bill Fitch (fourth from left). Right, 1965-'66 Phillips 66ers, with Coach Thompson at left.

L–R Coach Gary Thompson, Jim Kerwin, Lou Skurcenski, Bill Kusleika, Ray Carey, Bobby Rascoe, Tom Black, Darel Carrier, Kendall Rhine, Warren Rustand, Tom Patty, Harold Sergent, Tony Cerkvenik, Manager Wayne Rountree.

Won: 47 Lost to Detroit Ford Mustangs in finals of National AAU Tournament
Lost: 6   in Denver, Colo., 71–67.
Phillips AAU All-Americans: Carey, Rascoe, Sergent, Rhine.

SHAPING PHILLIPS CAREER. Gary Thompson began his career with Phillips Petroleum right after graduation at Iowa State, "working the drive" at Hibbs' Brothers Phillips 66 in Ames. Left, Jim Hibbs checks on the All-American gas jockey. Right, Thompson's mentors at company headquarters in Oklahoma included Pete Morrison (top) and George Durham (bottom). Middle, at a 66ers reunion, Gary with teammate Bobby Plump, whose high school basketball story inspired the movie "Hoosiers."

PHILLIPS ICON. The old "Phillips Tower" is still an iconic part of the company's headquarters in downtown Bartlesville. Just left, when Gary Thompson was coaching the Phillips 66ers from 1964-'68, one of the "ballboys" for the team was young Ricky Thompson, Gary's son. Now Rick Thompson is vice-president of Gary Thompson Oil Co., which is the Phillips distributor in the Ames area.

STARTING TOGETHER. Gary Thompson and Janet Sydnes were married in August, 1955, in Palestine Lutheran Church near her hometown of Huxley. Upper left photo, they are shown after Gary was named Iowa State's 1956 "Athlete of the Year," the first junior so honored. Just above, Gary and Janet are shown after Gary's graduation in 1957 receiving the keys to a new Pontiac from Ames auto dealer Art Skeie. In the other photo, Gary and Janet are shown in 1961 with the first two of their three children, 3-year-old Kim and 16-month old Ricky. (Family photo by Tony Cordaro, copyright 1961, The Des Moines Register and Tribune Company. Reprinted with permission.)

had commented along these lines, 'You'd think he'd just interviewed God.' Maybe Bill was right. And, actually, at that time, Wilt was pretty close to the super force of collegiate basketball."

Another member of the *Daily* staff, sportswriter Al Oppedal, also gave readers an inside look at Chamberlain and his Kansas teammates, in his "Sports Slants" column. Oppedal wrote the first half of the column before the game, predicting that the Jayhawks were "prime for an upset." He then took a break, went to the game and then afterward wrote the rest of the column for readers of the Tuesday edition.

Here is Oppedal's column, just as it appeared in print:

"Sports Slants"
by Alan Oppedal

ALONG with a few of my contemporaries, I strolled up to the Armory Sunday afternoon to watch the highly touted Kansas cagers work out. The main reason for taking this walk in such cold weather was Wilt Chamberlain, of course.

As you watch the Kansans go through their warm-up drills, you cannot help but be impressed by the long frame of Chamberlain. He so thoroughly overshadows everyone else that it seems as the other four members of the team must be on the floor only because a basketball team has been traditionally composed of five men.

As Phog Allen once remarked, "I could win 75 percent of my games with four co-eds and Wilton Chamberlain." You gape at the reed-thin Chamberlain's high altitude, you could not help but feel that "The Foghorn" had some basis for his remark.

All was not impressive about the Kansas workout, however. They did not all look like a team that was on the eve of a game with an opponent which had lost to them by only one point in a previous encounter. Even Wilton looked lackadaisical, nothing at all like the superstar that I had expected. He missed a few shots just like any other human.

He also spent a good share of the practice period brushing up on 40-foot set shots, instead of practicing shots from a more logical distance. The attitude of the Kansans was in direct contrast with the Cyclones, who held their practice earlier in the afternoon.

The Cyclone cagers went through their drills in a methodical, business-like fashion. They wound up their practice with a talk by Coach Bill Strannigan.

The Kansans come out for their drill by twos and threes—I do not believe the entire squad was on the floor at one time during the whole drill. They also left singly and in pairs.

Their practice consisted of a little three-on-three drill by the lower echelon of the squad with the higher-ups occupying their time with shooting practice. There were no free throw drills, although weaknesses at the free throw line almost cost Kansas the game when they met Iowa State in the Big Seven tournament.

Because of this contrast in squad attitude, I believe the Jayhawks are prime for an upset. (This is written about 3 hours before game time.) I'll check in with you after the game and give my comments on why I was right or wrong—whatever the case may be.

I was right!!! But what can you say about a team such as Iowa State that plays the coolest brand of basketball ever exhibited in the tall corn state. All the superlatives between the covers of an unabridged dictionary wouldn't begin to describe the brilliant display of basketball perfection put on by the Cyclones last night against the top-ranked team in the nation. It wasn't the ineptness or the lackadaisical manner in which Kansas played which spelled the difference in last night's game.

Rather it was a terrifically coached, tenacious defending Iowa State team which kept the pressure on the Jayhawks from the start. The Cyclones refused to concede anything to Kansas. Even in the rebounding department where Wilton Chamberlain has held forth in such spectacular fashion for Kansas in previous games, the Cyclones were not to be denied.

And Gary Thompson—if ever there was an All-American, Gary was last night. In fact, every man that played for Iowa State looked like an All-American. John Crawford was terrific—that's the only way you can describe his play off the boards. Chuck Vogt, Lyle Frahm and—well, I saved Mr. Drama himself for the last spot because he waited until the last second last night to uncork the most dramatic shot ever launched in the Armory. Of course, that would be none other than Don Medsker.

A great deal of the credit for the victory last night must be awarded to Bill Strannigan. His defensive setup for the Jayhawks was absolutely the last word in coaching genius. If any other coach has ever been awarded a Cadillac for his coaching feats, then Bill Strannigan deserves a gold-plated one.

All in all it was about as terrific a game as a person could expect to see in one lifetime. Wow—man—hot dog—woof! What more can you say? Hats off to the Cyclones and I sure wish there was no school today. Woof? Ah, student journalists!

Actually, Oppedal's column is a good reminder of a significant change that had occurred in Kansas Jayhawks basketball coming into the 1956-'57 season. The legendary coach Forrest C. "Phog" Allen, who had coached 49 years at Kansas, was forced into retirement after he turned 70 years old. Allen had recruited Chamberlain to Kansas, but never got to coach him at the varsity level. Dick Harp, who had served as an assistant to Allen for 8 years, was named head coach, and Allen—bitter about the forced retirement—resumed his earlier practice of osteopathic medicine.

Max Falkenstein, the legendary Kansas broadcaster, said there was often "a strain" between Harp and Chamberlain, and that was part of the reason Chamberlain eventually decided to by-pass his senior year at Kansas and play for the Harlem Globetrotters, before he went on to a long career in the National Basketball Association.

In both the late Allen years and the early Harp years, the rivalry between Kansas and Iowa State was

"I had no idea Wilt was <u>that</u> big!"

a terrific one. Their first game in the 1956-'57 season resulted in a one-point Kansas victory over Iowa State in the Big Seven holiday tournament in Kansas City, and that set-up the classic game in Ames in January.

Probably the best analysis of how Iowa State was able to control Chamberlain and get the victory in Ames was a story written a week after the game by Des Moines Tribune sportswriter Bill Bryson, for the national weekly sports newspaper, The Sporting News. Bryson's account:

Cyclones Fence in Wilt on New Defense
By Bill Bryson

AMES, Ia.—Ordinarily a coach would be justified to grow smugly satisfied with a defense that had held wondrous Wilt Chamberlain to 12 points. Yet no sooner had Iowa State achieved this stunning achievement against Kansas' 7-footer on December 26 than Coach Bill Strannigan was beginning to figure out how he could change that defense for their next meeting.

"Next time" was January 14 in the Iowa State Armory jammed with more than 8,000 onlookers. Strannigan did, indeed, change his defense and while Wilt stuffed in 5 more points this time, Iowa State dealt Kansas its first defeat in 13 starts, 39 to 37. The 29 points in two games represented just about half of Chamberlain's average.

Strannigan was dissatisfied with his original 1-3-1 zone defense because, although it wilted Wilt, it allowed other Jayhawkers too many easy set shots in their first-round game of the Big Seven pre-season tournament at Kansas City.

So Bill set out to correct that deficiency, even though Kansas hadn't won until Gene Elstun hit from 15 feet out with 6 seconds to play. That put the Jayhawks on top, 58 to 57.

The finish on January 14 was practically a duplicate, but with a reverse twist. Don Medsker, hitherto "just the other center," popped in a soft 15-footer; the ball was in the air at the final buzzer.

In the tournament, Strannigan posted the 6-8 Medsker, his tallest man, behind Wilt to keep him from the basket. One of the forwards, 6-6 Chuck Vogt or 6-5 John Crawford, stayed in front of Chamberlain and one of the quick and handy guards, 5-10 Gary Thompson or 6-2 Lyle Frahm, "sagged back" to make it a three-man fence around Wilt.

The big change for the second meeting was in stationing Medsker in front of the mobile tower from Philadelphia, with the forwards alternating in protecting from the rear.

"Actually," said Strannigan, "it was a 2-3 zone, with the forwards 'dropping off' in a more normal way. The weak side forward in the zone would go behind Wilt to block his path.

"The guards didn't drop back this time. They stayed out front to contain the other shooters. And Thompson and Frahm turned in the greatest job of outside coverage I've ever seen."

Strannigan said a widely circulated story that the defense had come to Assistant Coach Bob Lamson in a dream 2 nights before the game "was pretty far-fetched. Bob helped on it, of course," said Bill, "but it was something we'd been working on a long time.

"Anyway," Strannigan added, "it wasn't any blackboard strategy that beat Kansas. It was five kids going out there with the most determination and competitive fire that I've ever seen."

Bill said that movies of the game "showed that we really made lots of mistakes. But those kids simply covered them up with their tremendous scrapping."

The Cyclones had been looking ahead to the return match ever since December 26. In fact, they were so intent upon Kansas that they failed to concentrate on Missouri and were upset in their conference opener, 77 to 59.

"We had to keep trying to talk ourselves into being 'up' for Missouri," said Thompson, the supercharged little guard who now has twice outscored Chamberlain. "But we just couldn't help looking ahead to 'the big one.'"

It was Thompson, the smallish guard from the nearby little town of Roland, who quarterbacked Iowa State's ball-control against Kansas. The Cyclones had to maneuver for good shots. They knew that, if they missed, they wouldn't get a rebound chance against the board-sweeping Chamberlain.

As a result, Iowa State triggered only 38 shots—just 13 in the last half, when the Cyclones erased a 19 to 17 Jayhawk lead. But they missed a mere five times in the tense second period after failing on 20 or 25 during the first half.

At the same time, they limited Kansas to 46 shots and, like Iowa

State, the Jayhawks cashed 13. Wilt's five field goals all came in the second half—two "dunks," two rebounds and one lay-up. That was two more than the fabulous sophomore earned in their first meeting.

Chamberlain, a notoriously poor free thrower, showed he was a clutch player when, with 9 seconds left, he dropped in two gift shots for a 37 to 37 tie. Wilt had missed seven of 13 free tosses in the first game with Iowa State and had failed on half of his 10 previous tries on January 14.

Wilt visited the Iowa State dressing room after the game and congratulated each Cyclone personally. "You played a fine game and deserved to win," he said. Asked about Thompson, who had pumped in 18 points, Chamberlain said, "He's great, that's all."

Of course, everybody in the Armory had expected that the Cyclones would try to get the ball to Thompson for the final shot in the game—and they did try. Chuck Vogt threw the ball in-bounds to Lyle Frahm, who looked first to pass to Thompson. But when Chamberlain and another Jayhawk were covering Thompson, that left Don Medsker open and Frahm snapped a pass to him.

Fifty years later, during the celebration of 100 years of Iowa State men's basketball, the *Des Moines Register's* Rick Brown talked to Thompson about the play, and about how the victory over Kansas victory still stands as one of the "key Iowa State basketball moments," as Brown called it in his February 12, 2008, Register story.

"This was back when No. 1 was really No. 1," Thompson told Brown. "Now, we've got 20 teams that can be No. 1 on a given week. Kansas was undefeated and had the player of the half-century in Wilt."

After Chamberlain had hit the two free throws with 9 seconds left to tie the score at 37-37, Iowa State called timeout to draw up its final play. When action resumed, the Cyclones set two screens to try to break Thompson loose on the in-bounds play.

Did it weigh heavily on him, or jangle his nerves, that he was the player who normally took the game-breaking shots? No, he told me, because his coaches had prepared him for it.

"As a player starting back in high school, I was never afraid to take the 'tough shot' and in fact wanted the ball in those situations," Thompson said. "When you are playing 'the game,' if you have any other thoughts than executing what the coach has outlined, you certainly are not focusing in the right direction."

So, he "pretty much knew when Coach Strannigan called a timeout and we were heading to the bench with the score tied, that something would be set up for me to take the last shot against Kansas. But as players, you react to what the other team does, and Lyle Frahm did just that. Not trying to 'force' the ball to me was the smart play because I was double-covered and Don Medsker had an uncontested shot."

Thompson said it didn't bother him a bit that a teammate had taken the fateful final shot, instead of shooting it himself.

"My only reaction to Medsker taking the shot was exactly the same, I am sure, as our entire team and all the fans—'I hope it goes in, because then we win the game and beat the No. 1 team in the country!' " Thompson said. "I never played a game thinking about myself. The only thing that counts when your team is out there is winning!"

Medsker, now retired in Centennial, Colorado, a Denver suburb, after practicing law for 35 years, said it's somewhat ironic he wound up taking the shot, because he had not done much offensively during the game.

"I think I played the whole game, but I'd scored no more than 4 points up to when we took the timeout with 5 seconds left. It was obvious that we were going to try to set-up Gary for the last-second shot—he was our best player and he'd really done well in that game. But when we put the ball in play, Lyle Frahm saw Gary wasn't going to be open, and I was there at the top of the key. He threw me the ball, and I put it up—just that quick."

When I pressed him for details on the shot, Medsker finally said it was "a jump shot." And how did it go through the hoop? Did it brush the rim? Or possibly come off the backboard? He laughed. "Well," he said, "of course it swished!"

Bedlam broke out in the Armory. Medsker was mobbed. Then he and John Crawford, who'd played such a great defensive game, were carried off the floor on the shoulders of the Iowa State students. "It truly was crazy," said Medsker, "and really fun!"

The students continued their revelry and devilry for hours. First a huge crowd gathered in Campus Town, then about 300 of them marched on "The Knoll," the home of President James Hilton, chanting "No school tomorrow!" Later they blocked Lincoln Way, which was also U.S. Highway 30 back then, starting bonfires and interrupting traffic—until the fierce weather eventually drove them back to their dormitories, fraternities and sororities.

"After beating the nation's No. 1 team, the Cyclones climbed to No. 3 in polls..."

With the stunning victory that week, Iowa State climbed briefly to No. 3 in the polls, still the highest ranking they've ever held.

Medsker clearly enjoys reminiscing about his most famous shot, and the win it brought over Kansas, but it's not like he's been obsessed by it through the decades.

"Oh, it's always been there, something that a few people around me know about," he said. "But I've got to tell you, since I wasn't living in Iowa during my career, it's not been that big a deal. When I was practicing law, every once in a great while someone might ask if I didn't hit that shot. But it happened so infrequently that it wasn't something I was really thinking a lot about myself.

"But a few years ago, we were having a reunion of the 1956-'57 team that Gary had put together," Medsker continued. "I couldn't believe how many people came up to me that weekend in Ames and said, 'Hey, aren't you the guy who hit the shot to beat Wilt?' I was amazed!"

It still makes a lot of old Cyclone fans smile, that's for sure. In 2004, the senior citizens' organization in Ames was having a program on "Radio at Iowa State," and asked Iowa State's retired play-by-play broadcaster Dale Williams to make a special appearance.

"They wanted me to re-create the last 2 minutes of the victory over Kansas in 1957, just like I'd called it back then," said Williams, who was in his late 80s. "So I went to the microphone, and talked through all the players in the line-up. Since I had 2 minutes to fill, I had them passing the ball back and forth, one player to the other, and then calling the timeout. Then when they came back from the timeout, I had Lyle Frahm looking for Gary Thompson, but then having to pass to Don Medsker. As exciting as I could make it, I had Medsker taking the shot, the ball going through the net and the crowd going wild. And then I ended it the same way I had back in '57, with my trademark 'Holy Cow!' "

The crowd indeed went wild—again now as senior citizens—just like they had nearly 50 years earlier when they'd been witnesses to the sweetest moment in Cyclone basketball history.

Chapter 11

Helping Cyclones to Baseball Glory

IN the 1950s, college baseball was played almost in anonymity, especially if you compared it to the spotlight sports of football and basketball.

"For home games on the campus in Ames, we might get 100 to 150 fans," the late Harry Burrell, who for decades was Iowa State's sports information director, said in an interview before his death in early 2005. "We didn't even charge admission. You could just walk over, sit down wherever you wanted and watch the game."

And, of course, it's always been tough just to play college baseball in the upper Midwest, where springtime weather is so iffy.

In Gary Thompson's first 2 years as the starting shortstop on the varsity team, 1955 and 1956, the Cyclones had records of 9-11 and 9-9.

He was actually playing more games and a faster brand of baseball in the summers, with semi-pro teams in the Hawkeye State League. The summer after his freshman and sophomore years, he was among the college all-stars and experienced older players in the line-up for the Marshalltown Ansons. After his junior and senior years, he played with the Slater Nite Hawks.

Playing with those teams brought a "salary" of $250 per month, plus a job with some local company. The summer teams Thompson played with always seemed to be contending for the state semi-pro championship in the tournament held at the end of the season in late August, and he helped Marshalltown win a title.

Travel budgets were never big, either in semi-pro baseball or at Iowa State, and meal allowances were meager. For example, Thompson said the college baseball teams rarely ate steak when they were on the road. But he remembered one fun story about a time when they had it.

"We were on a road trip in 1956, went to a cafeteria in Omaha on a Friday night and we all ordered steaks," he said. "Charlie Rasmussen, a former player from Exira who was by then an assistant coach, had eaten two or three bites of his steak, when one of our players, Dick Bertell, said, 'Charlie, you're Catholic—what day is this?' We all knew Catholics weren't supposed to eat meat on Fridays back then. Charlie looked right down at that steak on his plate and said, 'Swim, you SOB, swim!'"

Thompson, always a huge baseball fan, never missed an opportunity to talk about the game and its great players.

"One year, we were on a baseball trip, traveling by train, and we had a 2-hour layover in the depot in El Reno, Oklahoma, which is just west of Oklahoma City," he said. "We were sitting in the lobby, and we saw Allie 'The Chief' Reynolds, who'd been a great pitcher for the Cleveland Indians and New York Yankees. His playing career was just over, and he was a working as a scout for the Yankees.

"We asked him all kinds of questions about being in the major leagues, and he was full of stories. Somebody asked him if pitchers would intentionally throw at batters to move them back from the plate. He said, 'Oh, sure.' Then somebody asked, 'Well, would you throw at Roy Campanella?' He was a great catcher for the Brooklyn Dodgers. Reynolds said, 'Oh, yeah.'

"Then I asked him about one of my own heroes, Jackie Robinson, who had to overcome so much when he was the first black player in the majors. I asked Reynolds if they'd throw at Robinson, too. 'Oh, no, you wouldn't throw at Jackie. With him, it's better to let a sleeping dog lie. If you knock him down, I can almost guarantee you that he'll get right back up and get a base hit off you. That's the kind of competitor he is.' We kept asking him questions like that until we had to catch our train."

There was always that kind of camaraderie and fun in being on a college baseball team. But who would have thought that Thompson's senior baseball season at Iowa State, in the spring of 1957, would actually provide a storybook ending to his illustrious two-sport playing career for the Cyclones?

In fact, after he'd just been named first-team All-American in basketball, it's somewhat a wonder he decided to play another season of college baseball. But he liked baseball nearly as much as basketball, and he still had some hope that he might get signed to a professional baseball contract. So he was eager as ever when Cyclone baseball coach LeRoy C. "Cap" Timm put his lads on the ball diamond and started Big Seven Conference play.

What ho! Iowa State battled its way to the conference championship—its first in 21 years—and became the first Cyclone baseball team to qualify for the College World Series in Omaha. They played their way to third place in that double-elimination tournament, with their only losses being the two to the University of California, which won the national championship.

Thompson was named third-team All-American, and four other Cyclones from that team were named all-conference—Bertell, the catcher from Des Moines Roosevelt; second baseman Jack Taylor from Auburn, Iowa; leftfielder Dan Peters from Manning, Iowa and first baseman Jerry McNertney, from Gilbert.

Both McNertney and Bertell went on to careers of 9 and 7 years as catchers in Major League Baseball, and McNertney later served as a bullpen coach for two major league teams. Bertell, who later in life was a salesman, died in 1999. In addition, Bob Locker, a freshman pitcher from George, Iowa, couldn't play varsity ball that spring of 1957 because of NCAA restrictions against freshmen participating, but he was on the full Cyclone squad, and he also wound up in the majors, as a pitcher.

So that '57 team had a lot of talent on it. The team's success "was a matter of a bunch of good baseball players working their way up through school, and all kind of peaking together that year," said Peters, who has retired back to his hometown of Manning.

"We were thrilled to make it to the College World Series, because we had to fight pretty hard to win the conference championship. As I recall, we lost several close games during that year, and we almost lost the conference title in the last series of games that year, I think they were with Colorado. But we hung on to win it. What I'm saying is that our 17-10 record for the year maybe doesn't indicate how strong we really were."

> *"Four major league teams wanted to sign him..."*

Peters was a 26-year-old junior on that team. He had played on Manning High School's great state championship basketball team in 1948, the year they knocked off mighty Davenport for the title, and he finished high school a year later. He worked briefly for the railroad, then went into the military during the Korean War. When he came out of the service, he used the G.I. Bill to start his college education at Iowa State.

"Let me use an old baseball adage, 'strong up the middle,' to tell you why that 1957 Iowa State team was good," Peters continued. "At catcher, we had a future major leaguer, Dick Bertell. We had an All-American Gary Thompson playing shortstop and an all-conference second baseman in Jack Taylor. And we had a darned good pitcher, Phil Groth, who now lives down at Pella. So we were pretty 'strong up the middle.' "

Peters did not continue his baseball career after Iowa State. "I was 27 years old, married and had three little kids when I graduated," he said. "I couldn't very well be spending time bumming around on a bus trying to make it in minor league baseball. I had to get to work! I was a forestry management major, so I went to work for the National Forestry Service in Colorado, hoping they were going to let me hunt and fish all the time. But they had a few other ideas on what I was going to do for them. It still was a good career, though." He returned to Manning in 1991.

Taylor, the second baseman, also had an interesting career. After service in the U.S. Navy, he joined Boeing Aerospace in New Orleans and worked on the Apollo Moon Landing Project. Later he joined Peat Marwick Mitchell and supervised construction and staffing of the first oil refinery in the Middle Eastern nation of Kuwait. In 1969, he moved to Steamboat Springs, Colorado, where he started a real estate company and eventually became a partner in a coal mining operation. He became active in politics and government, and was elected as a Republican to four 2-year terms in the Colorado House of Representatives, and in 2008 completed his second 4-year term in the Colorado Senate, after which the state's term limits law required him to step down.

Gary Thompson, in that senior year, hit .311 with four home runs and had 18 RBI in the 27 games. How good was he?

"With the skills he had, and with his competitive nature, I think he'd have been a major league shortstop if he'd decided to go in that direction," Peters said. "When he was through at Iowa State, he had a choice of becoming a professional baseball player, or a professional basketball player, but instead he chose amateur basketball with the Phillips 66ers. For Gary, that turned out to be a real good choice, but I'll always believe he'd have been a major leaguer if he had gone after it."

Four major league teams wanted to sign Thompson in '57—the Chicago Cubs, New York Yankees, Chicago White Sox and Cleveland Indians. But a "bonus money rule" then in effect in professional baseball would have limited his signing bonus to $4,000 if he was to be assigned to a minor league team. He had more financial security waiting for him in the corporate world and amateur basketball, as you will read in the next chapter.

Of course, the other factor that made the Iowa State team good was that Cap Timm had one of the best baseball minds in the country.

He was a Minnesota native who had played at the University of Minnesota, then came to Iowa State soon after he graduated. He taught physical education and coached in both baseball and basketball over the years, eventually attaining the rank of professor in the physical education department. His career at Iowa State was interrupted after the 1942 season, for service in the military in World War II, and then he returned to the college in 1947. He coached until retiring after the 1974 season. He died in 1987.

"Cap was barely in his 30s when he started coaching baseball here," Harry Burrell told me. "I had never known anybody who studied the game as much as he did. He knew all the rules by heart, and he would look for ways to use them to his team's advantage. I think there wound up being a couple of rules changes made, just because Cap had figured out how to turn them more to Iowa State's advantage than was fair."

Timm taught his base runners how to slide past a base, roll over and then grab the base with their hand—all to elude the baseman trying to tag them out. He was notorious with opponents for his double steals: With Cyclone runners on first and third, he'd have the runner on first walk off the bag toward second base; when the pitcher turned to make a play on that runner, the other runner on third base would bolt for home, and often scored. He had one signal for his pitcher to intentionally walk a batter, and another signal that meant "look like you're intentionally walking him, then throw a hard strike and have the catcher jump back in behind the plate to catch it."

Ultimately, the NCAA put him on its Baseball Rules Committee, and he was a leader in not only refining the rules but also improving player safety. He served in 1958 as president of the American College Baseball Coaches Association, coached the 1959 U.S. team in the Pan-American Games and was twice named national coach of the year—in both the years that he took Iowa State teams to the College World Series, 1957 and 1970.

By the 1970s Timm had come up with a first-base pick-off play that became the talk of the nation. It involved the Iowa State pitcher, eyeing a runner who was leading off, stepping off the rubber and then faking a hard throw to first base. The first baseman would yell like he'd missed the throw, turn and scamper back toward the sideline fence as if to retrieve the ball. Meanwhile, the relief pitchers in the Cyclone bullpen along that sideline were standing up, rattling the fence in front of them and excitedly yelling, as if to the first baseman, "Over here! The ball's over here!" Often the baserunner was indeed faked out and ran for second base. The Cyclone pitcher, who was hiding the ball in his glove, would make a snap throw to second and the runner would be out by a mile.

Ah, yes, that was Cap Timm baseball! He even involved sports information director Burrell in some trickery—a story which Burrell delighted in telling the rest of his long life.

"One year, Cap had me sit right next to him in the dugout, while I was keeping the scorebook," Burrell said. "He would say softly whether he wanted a player to steal a base, and I would give the actual signal by the position I was holding the scorebook. The other teams' would be watching Cap real close, or they'd watch the base coaches, trying to pick up our sign. But who'd ever think the humble publicity man was giving the signals!"

Since Burrell was keeping the "home" scorebook, that made him the "official" scorekeeper for games in Ames, per the baseball tradition at the time.

In the 1955 or '56 season, Missouri's ace pitcher Norm Stewart—later to become the Tigers' long-time basketball coach—had a no-hitter going against Iowa State late in the game. The Cyclones' Arnie Gaarde came to bat and slapped a ground ball toward the shortstop. The Missouri fielder struggled with fielding the ball just long enough that Gaarde was able to beat his throw to first base—and Burrell ruled it was a clean base hit.

"It was the only hit Norm gave up the whole day," Gaarde said. "He and his shortstop both started arguing with Harry's decision right away. After the game, both of them were still arguing with him, saying it should have been an error and Norm should have had a no-hitter. Harry refused to change it."

In fact, Stewart would occasionally still bring up that play decades later if he saw Burrell or Gaarde when his Missouri basketball team was playing in Ames!

A memorable—and at first frightening—play that Gary Thompson was involved in occurred during the spring of 1956, when the Oklahoma Sooners played in Ames. They were closing in on winning the Big Seven championship, and they had their No. 1 pitcher, right hander Tony Risinger, on the mound when Thompson came to bat.

Bob Burr, Oklahoma's first baseman then, later became an employee of Phillips Petroleum in Bartlesville, Oklahoma, at the same time Thompson was coaching the Phillips 66ers basketball team, and they became good friends. It's been during a conversation they had in recent years when Burr, who now lives in Houston, told Thompson the "Oklahoma side" of what happened during that long ago baseball game.

In a follow-up interview, Burr recalled that his teammate Risinger "went into his wind-up and threw a fastball. Gary hit a line drive right back at the mound, and it hit Tony somewhere in the lower abdomen or below. It hit him so hard, he dropped straight down like he'd been hit with a 30.06 rifle shot.

"He was just lying there, and I went running right over, figuring he might be hurt bad. I leaned over him and he said, 'God, Burr, it hit me right in the cup!' I said, 'Well, Tony, thank God you're wearing a cup or otherwise this would really be serious!' I suppose it took him a good 5 minutes before he got his wits back about him. But he was tough enough that he stayed in the game, and he might have even finished it."

Back then, the protective cups that baseball players wore were made of a hard aluminum, and they would slide into a special athletic supporter that had a pouch covering the player's genitalia.

"After the game, Tony pulled that cup out of his supporter, and that thing was absolutely concave where Gary's line drive hit it," Burr said. "Tony picked up a baseball and it fit right into the caved-in part. All the rest of us looked at it and were amazed."

> *"He hit a 375-foot home run against Notre Dame..."*

Risinger went on to a long career as a school superintendent in Oklahoma public schools, and the two have not been in touch "for nearly 40 years," Burr said. "But I'll bet there are times when he still thinks about that line drive coming at him, and I'll bet he's still glad he was wearing a cup that day, too!"

Perhaps the most remarkable story that Thompson figured in, happened in the Cyclones' first-round game in the '57 College World Series against Notre Dame. Early in that game, he hit a 375-foot home run, one of the longest he'd ever hit anywhere, and through much of the game, it looked like the Cyclones were in control.

"We were three runs ahead, 8-5, going into the bottom of the ninth inning, but our pitcher got wild and had the bases loaded with two outs," Thompson recalled. "All that season, our relief pitchers had been wild as March hares So Cap Timm called time out, started walking out to the mound and called us infielders together. I was thinking he was going to ask us which of our wild relievers we thought he should put in to pitch. But he took the ball from Gene Lafferty, who had been pitching, looked at me and said, 'Gary, here's the ball—I know you'll get it over the plate for me.'

"I had not pitched since I was a sophomore, and that was only one game, more than 2 years earlier! I thought, 'Well, O.K!' and started warming up. So, I faced the first batter, and one pitch I thought I could throw was a knuckle-drop ball. So I threw it, but this one didn't knuckle and it didn't drop, and the guy blasted it. Three runs scored to tie the game, and the guy's on third base representing the winning run for Notre Dame. But I somehow got the third out, and we went into the 10th inning."

Iowa State then exploded for a five-run rally and a 13-8 lead. "In the bottom of the 10th, Cap put me back to shortstop," Thompson said. "One of our normal relief pitchers came in, did a good job, shut them down and we won."

After the game, the sportswriters surrounded Cap Timm, asking what he was thinking, bringing Thompson in to pitch in such a critical situation when he had not pitched for so long. Thompson's old high school coach Buck Cheadle, who was in Omaha watching the game, was just as curious.

"I'll never forget what Cap told the sportswriters and told me, too," Cheadle said. "He said, 'I wasn't going with Gary's arm in that situation, I was going with his heart.'"

"Named All-American in baseball, too..."

Thompson said "that situation that Cap put me in has meant as much to me as any athletic moment. Why? He was saying I was the ultimate competitor and that is what I've always strived to be."

Ironically, Thompson now says with a smile, since he was still the pitcher of record when Iowa State took its commanding 10th inning lead, he was credited as the winning pitcher. "So I'm 1-0 as a pitcher in the College World Series!" he said.

In subsequent games there, Iowa State lost to California 8-2, then beat Connecticut 5-2, then lost to California 9-1 and bowed out. It was a nice ending to Thompson's collegiate playing career.

And it was one of the high points in Iowa State's baseball history. Followed by a low point:

Thompson and many other Cyclone players were shocked in 2001 when the university ended the baseball program as a way to save on athletics department expenses. A nice club baseball program has grown since then, but many of the alumni of the intercollegiate baseball program still talk of helping Iowa State re-instate the sport on the varsity level.

But back to 1957. One more special event was held in Gary Thompson's honor when his collegiate career came to an end.

On Sunday, July 14, that year, his ol' hometown of Roland celebrated

"Gary Thompson Day." The *Roland Record* weekly newspaper published its first-ever "Sunday edition," a special tabloid celebrating all of Thompson's accomplishments in his high school and college years.

More than 2,000 people turned out in Erickson Park in a town with a population of 687, including Iowa State President James Hilton, Gary's coaches at Roland High and Iowa State, his pastor Rev. Olaf Holen from Roland's Salem Lutheran Church, and others. The master of ceremonies was Tommy Thompson, Roland's native son who was making a name for himself at WHO-TV in Des Moines. And Roland Mayor Willard Vaughan declared Gary Thompson to be "Honorary Mayor of Roland," and presented him with the key to the city.

Gary's family, coaches, teammates and fans then starred in a "This Is Your Life" program. Their voices would be heard over a public address system, coming from behind a curtain, and Gary had to guess who the mystery person was.

The show-stopper was when one of them said in a lilting voice, "When I found out he could roller skate, I knew he was the one for me!" It was, of course, his wife Janet Thompson.

And it was a moment Gary Thompson will never forget.

Chapter 12

Stay Amateur? Or Go Pro?

THINK of a first-team All-American in college basketball today. If you could find such a player still in college in his senior year, one who was actually going to graduate, do you suppose he would choose a career option which would have him starting out that summer pumping gasoline for customers at a full-service station in the town where he'd played his college ball? Not likely.

That's the option Gary Thompson chose in late March or early April, of 1957, when his selection as an All-American and other honors were stacking up for him at the end of his Iowa State Cyclone basketball career. And that's another reminder of just how different things were 50 years ago.

Pro basketball was barely an option for Thompson. The National Basketball Association (NBA) did exist, and he did get drafted in the fifth round by the Minneapolis Lakers, who years later would move to Los Angeles and become one of the league's marquee franchises.

But in 1957, NBA salaries for players of his caliber were running about $10,000 to $12,000 per season, which wasn't bad unless you got hurt—then your paycheck and financial security were immediately gone. That was a big consideration in the mind of Thompson, who with Janet, had plans to start a family.

Far more attractive to him and most other top college basketball players across the U.S. in the era from the mid-1940s to the mid-1960s was signing with one of the teams in the National Industrial Basketball League (NIBL). Those teams were sponsored by large companies which used their basketball squads as promotional tools. The teams would play all over the nation, or in whatever the company's trade territory was, against top colleges and universities as well as other amateur teams.

The players would attend receptions for the companies' dealers and customers. Those NIBL teams were paying good salaries, and when a player got a position on an NIBL team, he also got an actual job with the sponsoring company. Best of all, that job would continue after the player's basketball years were over, provided he was a good employee.

Another meaningful enticement to high-profile players like Thompson was that since the NIBL players' salaries were for their 8-to-5 jobs with the companies, they were still regarded as "amateur" basketball players by the Amateur Athletic Union. Thus, they would still be eligible to be on the Olympic teams. In that time, professional athletes were not eligible for Olympic competition, at least not in the U.S. Thompson wanted badly to play for the U.S. in the 1960 Olympics.

His desire to maintain his amateur status also guided his decisions to forego two other opportunities.

"The Harlem Globetrotters would put together a team of college all-stars, all seniors, after our college season was completed—like in April—and barnstorm around the country playing them," Thompson said. "The Globetrotters offered me $5,000 to play a 10-game tour that spring. That was really attractive, but I couldn't do it because the rules were so strict on amateur status."

Those rules also kept him from giving professional baseball a try. Scouts from a half-dozen major league baseball teams had been following him since his senior year at Roland High School. Eventually, rules were changed so athletes could be professionals in one sport and amateurs in another. And then in the 1990s the Olympics began allowing professionals to compete, too. But in the 1950s, if you signed a professional contract, no matter what sport, that eliminated you from amateur competition in all sports.

"I was always a little disappointed that I couldn't play professional baseball, but I knew where my bread and butter was." Thompson said, "It was a decision I have never regretted."

He knew the better future for him was the Phillips 66ers and the Phillips Petroleum Co., both based in Bartlesville, Oklahoma.

"I was getting recruited by several of the Industrial League teams—the Akron Goodyears, Peoria Catepillars, Wichita Vickers, Denver 'D-C' Truckers and the Phillips 66ers," Thompson said. "My Iowa State coach Bill Strannigan was telling me all along that Phillips was 'the Cadillac of amateur basketball.'

> *"He was drafted by NBA in fifth round..."*

"The heck of it was that all the other teams offered me $50 a month more in salary than Phillips was offering, and the others were offering to pay for my move. But my big financial goal in life, up till then, had always been that someday I'd make $5,000 a year, which I knew is what my old high school coach Buck Cheadle had worked up to.

"That seemed like an awful lot of money back then, and Phillips' offer put me a little over $5,000. Plus, one of their recruiting pitches to me was that 80 percent of all the players who had played with the 66ers were still with Phillips, and several of them had executive positions. That meant a lot to me. And they also said they would start my job off with a training program that summer in Ames."

Being in Iowa that summer was good for Gary and Janet Thompson for several reasons. It let them take a little more time to plan their move to Bartlesville in the fall of '57. He could play another summer with the Slater Nite Hawks in semi-pro baseball. And the company was also honoring Gary's military commitment, which eventually was going to require 6 months of active duty.

Phillips Petroleum was a company that believed in having its employees learn its operations from the ground up. Thus, Thompson was assigned to go to work for the company's "jobber" in the Ames area, Charlie Sorenson of Sorenson Oil Company, owner of the local stations. Thompson was told to report to work in mid summer at the Phillips 66 station operated in Ames by brothers Jim and Herb Hibbs, and do whatever they told him.

So on July 23, 1957, he began his Phillips career by "working the drive," which meant pumping gas, washing windows, fixing tires and handling other tasks as assigned by the Hibbses. "They were two great guys," Thompson said. "They really taught me a lot."

Of course, when word got out that the favorite and most famous athlete in the whole state would fill your car's tank at Hibbs 66, it didn't hurt business a bit! Thompson was indeed quite a draw that summer. His star status wound up letting him get a hot deal on a brand new car.

Art Skeie, owner of Skeie Pontiac in Ames, had always been "kind of awestruck by Gary," recalled his son L.J. Skeie, now of Litchfield, Connecticut. "We all were. I was a kid on the basketball team at Welch Junior High in Ames when he was at Iowa State, and all of us on the team emulated Gary. Our whole family had watched in awe when he was on the 'Ed Sullivan Show' on TV with Wilt Chamberlain, Hot Rod Hundley and the other players on the All-American team. My dad was from Radcliffe, Iowa, just north of the Roland area, and many times he would talk about when Gary and the Roland Rockets were in the state tournament."

Art Skeie and Thompson had a mutual friend in Paul Rod, a Roland native who was a Post Office employee in Ames. In that summer of '57, Skeie asked Rod to tell Gary and Janet Thompson that his dealership would give them a very favorable price on a brand new Pontiac as a special promotion. Skeie had never participated in offering coaches or other officials at Iowa State new autos for their use, but he was excited about the possibility of having Thompson driving one of his cars.

Rod arranged a golf game for Art and L.J. Skeie with Thompson, who was just taking up that sport. They all met at the Grand View Golf Course in Des Moines. "Gary had only been playing a few weeks, and I actually beat him—and I was in junior high school!" L.J. Skeie still remembers. "I still think about that, and how years later, when Gary was in his 60s, he won the Iowa Golf Association's State Seniors Championship. I couldn't believe it! That tells you what an all-around athlete he's always been."

During that '57 round of golf, Art Skeie told Gary he would sell him a new Pontiac at dealer's cost, plus taxes and license fees. In exchange, they'd have a photo taken of Skeie handing over the keys to the Iowa State sports hero. Gary and Janet Thompson agreed, borrowed some money, came to the dealership and picked out a burgundy and cream colored Star Chief, a real eye-catcher. The photo was displayed prominently in the news pages of the Ames Daily Tribune and subsequently in Skeie Pontiac ads.

Art Skeie told Thompson he'd never given a customer that good a deal. "It was a very favorable price, all right," the old dealer's son L.J. Skeie said recently, recalling the deal in a phone interview from his home in Connecticut. "Mom might have killed Dad if she'd known how favorable the price was!"

The younger Skeie has corresponded with Thompson occasionally over the years, always signing his letters, "L.J. Skeie, Superfan." In a 2005 letter, he recalled how he viewed Thompson that summer of '57. "I can remember sitting in Jim Shipley's barber shop talking with Jim about the Kansas victory,

"I saw along the way gas was 27¢ a gallon..."

with Ross the other barber spitting tobacco into his tin can spittoon," Skeie wrote. "Suddenly I saw you and Janet coming from your apartment on Hyland to go somewhere in your beautiful '57 Star Chief. I thought, 'Wow! Gary has everything a guy could want—a beautiful wife, a fantastic All-American basketball career and, of course, a great car!' And after all these years, I haven't changed my mind."

Come September, of 1957, the Thompsons drove that Pontiac Star Chief south to Oklahoma to allow Gary to begin his new job with Phillips Petroleum and continue his basketball career with the Phillips 66ers.

He says there is one thing about that trip that sticks in his memory.

"I've never forgotten looking at the gas gauge when we were driving through Coffeyville, Kansas," Gary said. "I saw gas prices there at 27 cents per gallon, and I knew it was just 35 miles on to Bartlesville. I thought gas was bound to be cheaper where Phillips was headquartered. It turned out to be 37 cents a gallon in Bartlesville. I found out Coffeyville was known for always having a gas war."

Gasoline at 27 cents per gallon? Or even 37 cents?

It was indeed a very different time from today.

Chapter 13

Golden Era For Phillips And 66ers

WHEN Gary and Janet Thompson arrived in Bartlesville, Oklahoma, in the fall of 1957, it was a "happening" place, maybe one of the most vibrant small cities in America. They found themselves in a community that had grown to become one of the most important centers of the petroleum industry, with a population of about 35,000, nearly half of them younger than 35 years old.

After oil was discovered in 1897 in that area of northeast Oklahoma, it was hard to imagine development happening more quickly than it did in Bartlesville. By the 1950s, the petroleum companies with major presences around the city included Phillips, Sinclair, Skelly, Cities Service (Citgo), Barnsdall and Getty. And there were many industry support companies, such as REDA Pump and H.C. Price International Pipeline Company, the latter of which had hired famed architect Frank Lloyd Wright to design and build its Price Tower headquarters building.

Phillips Petroleum Company had been founded in 1916 by brothers Frank and L.E. Phillips who had come to Bartlesville from the Iowa towns of Conway and Creston, and in the late 1950s, their company was the corporate kingpin of the city.

"Back then in the late 1950s, we had about 9,000 employees here in town, with three major buildings in downtown Bartlesville and at least 30 different office facilities around town," said G.J. "Pete" Morrison, who eventually became vice-president of marketing for Phillips and was one of Thompson's most important mentors in business. "There were just a whole lot of young people around then. It was a fun company. In fact, I tell people I worked for Phillips when it was fun to be there.

"I don't think it's quite that fun today. I don't mean that we didn't work hard, because we sure did. It was 7 days a week, 24 hours a day, if necessary, but I remember there being a common goal—do whatever it takes to get the job done. There was so much more personal contact in business then, where now it's so much e-mail and computers."

George Durham, who died in early 2008, talked in earlier interviews about coming to Bartlesville when he was 25 to become sports editor of the *Bartlesville Examiner-Enterprise*. In 1948, he joined Phillips as publicity director for its Phillips 66ers basketball team and later became the company's sports director.

"In the late 1950s, when Gary Thompson got here, it was really a young town," said Durham. "And at that time, Phillips had an *esprit de corps* you wouldn't believe. A lot of that had to do with our basketball team. There was a whole lot of pride in that team."

The 66ers had made Iowa State All-American Gary Thompson their top recruit in 1957. He joined a basketball program that had started in 1920.

"Back then, K.S. 'Boots' Adams had played basketball at Kansas University when he was a student there, and then he hooked up with Phillips Petroleum," said Durham. "He was working in the company's treasury department, and he wanted to start involving athletes in the company, so he organized a team. At first, they'd just play pick-up games.

"But then Frank Phillips, who was president then and later became chairman, saw a possible public relations gimmick in having a good basketball team. He thought they could travel the company's territory, playing games and building good relations with dealers and customers."

Boots Adams succeeded Frank Phillips as the company president, and he made the basketball program even stronger. They would try to recruit the top graduating senior players at colleges and universities across the country, knowing their names would help draw crowds and bring public attention.

The biggest incentive they offered was that with a spot on the basketball team, came a full-time job with Phillips Petroleum, and if you were a decent employee, you'd still have the job when your playing career ended. Many of the company's top executives through the years had earlier been players on the 66ers.

The team barnstormed the country, playing such other corporate teams as the Denver Safeway Stores, Wichita Cessna Aircraft, Oakland (California) Bittners, Peoria Catepillars, Denver American Legion, Seattle Buchan Bakers, Milwaukee Allen-Bradleys and later the Denver-Chicago Truckers, Wichita Vickers, Akron Goodyears, Cleveland Pipers, Detroit Ford Mustangs and others.

Eventually those corporate teams formed the National Industrial Basketball League, which had a caliber of play that for years was regarded as being as good as, or better than, that of the fledgling professional league, the National Basketball Association.

The NIBL teams, especially the Phillips 66ers, would also play many college and university teams, some of the best of them and some not so strong, and the 66ers tried to play games at or near the colleges that produced the players on their rosters. They also played teams from the U.S. military services.

Beginning in the middle 1930s, the post-college teams were all joining the Amateur Athletic Union, which began staging a national tournament at the end of the season, with the site for more than 30 years being in Denver, Colorado.

At one point, there were more than 60 such teams in the AAU, and its national tournament became a highly-selective invitational, so the level of basketball being played there was outstanding. The Phillips 66ers won their first National AAU championship in 1940, and won 10 more before the company ended its basketball program at the conclusion of the 1968 season.

In years when the Olympic Games were to be played, there would be an additional tournament to determine which amateur team would represent the United States. The Olympics playoffs would include the National AAU tournament winner; the NIBL winner; the champion collegiate teams from the National College Athletic Association tournament, the National Invitational Tournament and the National Association of Intercollegiate Athletics tournament, as well as the top teams from the various branches of the U.S. military.

"The Phillips founders came from Iowa..."

Whoever coached the winning team in those playoffs became the U.S. Olympics coach, and he would assemble a squad of all-stars, generally built around the nucleus of his own team. Twice, in 1948 and 1956, the Phillips 66ers won those playoffs and represented the U.S. in the Olympic Games.

The more successful the 66ers became, the better players they attracted, and the more resources the company devoted to the program. Their uniforms and warm-up suits were always the latest basketball styles. The team generally stayed in the best hotels in cities and the players' meals allowances were generous. When Phillips built a new headquarters building in 1950 and named it after Adams, they included in it a classy new gymnasium with 2,600 seats—or 3,000 when bleachers were added for big games.

In the years just before Gary Thompson joined the team, among the stars in the Phillips line-up were 7-footer Bob Kurland, who'd been college player-of-the-year as he led Oklahoma A&M to back-to-back national championships in 1945 and '46; Chuck Darling, a 6 ft. 9 in. Colorado native who had played center for the University of Iowa and who was a great Phillips player from 1952-'57; Clyde Lovellette, a 6 ft. 9 in. three-time All-American at Kansas who played the 1952-'53 season with Phillips before going pro, and the great Burdette "Burdie" Haldorson, a 6 ft. 9 in. center who was an All-American at Colorado from 1952-'55, and then a five-year superstar with the 66ers.

George Durham, the former publicity director for the team, recalled that in 1957, when Thompson was joining the team, "AAU basketball was about at its high point, and the Phillips program was real strong, too." The coach of the team was Gerald Tucker, who had been an All-American player at Oklahoma, a star for the 66ers, a player on the 1948 U.S. Olympic team and coach of the 1956 Olympic team.

"We were well aware of Gary Thompson at Iowa State, especially that he'd beaten Wilt Chamberlain," said Durham. "We went to see his coach, Bill Strannigan, whom we knew from when he'd been a player at Wyoming, and he helped us with Gary. And it seems like we had Phillips staffers from Bartlesville and from the Des Moines office follow-up."

He described Thompson then as "a good lookin' little guy, with that burr haircut, but he didn't have a whole lot to say. He came close to being bashful."

As much as the 66ers wanted Thompson, they did not move him right into the starting line-up when the 1957-'58 season started. He had joined a squad of veteran players who had gone 23-8 the previous season, winning the NIBL and losing in the semi-finals of the National AAU tournament.

Among the established stars ahead of Thompson on the team were Joe Dean, a guard from Louisiana State who'd been a three-time All-Southeastern Conference selection; Gib Ford, a former Texas Longhorn who had captained the 1956 Olympic team; Ray Steiner, a steady guard in his fourth year from St. Louis University; and another taller guard, 6 ft. 4 in. Bill Hougland, who had been on Kansas' 1952 national championship team and was on the Olympic teams of 1952 and '56. And, of course, in the middle was Haldorson.

"I got the season off to a great start," said Thompson. "I came off the bench in the first five games, and I played really well, and scored 16 to 24 points a game. I kept thinking after each game, 'Well, I'll probably get to start the next one.' But after the fifth game and I still didn't get to start, I was really disappointed. I came out for the sixth game's warm-ups with a poor attitude, just going through the motions, no enthusiasm at all.

"That's when Ray Steiner, who was playing his fourth year, a real veteran, did me a favor. He sidled up to me and said, 'Gary, you need to change your attitude. You know, and I know, that you should be starting, but you're not going anywhere with that attitude. So, pick it up until your time comes.' It took a real man to step up and say that, because he was trying to help me, and it was his playing time that I was taking away.

"You know, as I think back over the years, I think that was probably the only time in my sports career I had a bad attitude, but it only lasted 30 minutes."

Thompson followed Steiner's advice well, made an attitude adjustment, played hard and was soon in the starting five.

He missed a couple of games later in that first season when he separated his shoulder in a game in Peoria—and it was the night before the 66ers were scheduled to play the Sanitary Dairy AAU team in Cedar Rapids. That AAU team included many former Iowa Hawkeye players, including most of the "Fabulous Five" Iowa team that had finished runner-up in the 1956 NCAA tournament. It would have been a big return for the former Iowa State star to his home state.

At a subsequent game, he was still feeling low about the injury, and was dressed in street clothes and sitting at the end of the bench. "Boots Adams came down and sat next to me during the game," Thompson said. "As we talked, he told me he was sure glad they had me on the team and with the company, and that if I worked at the job, I could have a great career with Phillips. That gave me a real lift right then."

That '57-'58 team wound up 43-12, sharing the NIBL title with the rival Wichita Vickers and reaching the semi-finals of the National AAU tournament before losing to the eventual champion Peoria Cats. Both Haldorson and Thompson were named AAU All-Americans.

Thompson got quite a surprise during that national tournament. He called home to talk to Janet, who was then caring for their infant first-born, daughter Kim.

"Janet said the U.S. Army had written with orders telling me to report for duty for the next 2 years," Gary said. "I was shocked. I knew I was supposed to spend the next 6 months in training at Fort Sill, Oklahoma, as part of my Army Reserves duty that came after my ROTC program at Iowa State. But 2 years! I knew if I had to do that, it'd probably ruin my career at Phillips."

He called Colonel Harold Dye, who commanded the ROTC program at Iowa State, to ask what he should do. Dye was a well-connected military officer, having served in the Korean War and being among the witnesses to the signing of the peace treaty at Panmunjom that ended the fighting in 1953

"Colonel Dye called the Fifth U.S. Army Headquarters in Chicago and somehow got it resolved, but I had to make a trip in there for the paperwork," Thompson said. "What was going on, it turned out, was that the military services had been watching their teams in the National AAU tournament, and they wanted to improve their chances of winning, so they were trying to stockpile athletes in the active services. Luckily, I was able to prove that my agreement was for 6 months active service, and then several years in the Reserves."

The Thompsons did move in May to Fort Sill that summer, renting an apartment there, and living the military life. During 6 weeks of that hitch, Gary was assigned to Fort Leonard Wood, Missouri, to serve as a lieutenant in a basic training brigade.

"We got all these young kids from Iowa and Missouri coming in there for their basic training, and it was supposed to give us young lieutenants a little experience commanding troops," Gary said. "I knew enough to know how the Army operates—it's not the generals who get things done but the sergeants. So, one of my drill instructors was a Sergeant Nipper. I told him, 'Look, you know a lot more about what's supposed to happen here than I do. I'm trained in artillery, and I'm only going to be here 6 weeks. So you run it, take care of me and I'll back you up."

Janet and Kim joined Gary there to live in "a pink mobile home" located between the town of Waynesville, Missouri and Fort Leonard Wood. "The bedroom was so small, we had to climb over each other to get in and out of bed," Gary said. "There was barely room for Kim's crib in the living room."

But they all made it through the 6 months of active duty—and then his weekend duty with the Reserves the next 6 years, initially in Oklahoma, later in Iowa. The Thompsons moved back to Bartlesville in the late fall of 1958, just in time for Gary to return to work and start working out for his second season with the 66ers.

During the next 4 years of his playing career, the team went 33-20, 41-13, 28-21 and then 45-8 in 1961-'62. He bowed out in a nice way, with the team winning the '62 National AAU tournament, in which he was named the MVP, and he was also again named AAU All-American. He also became the 66ers' all-time scoring leader, among guards, with 2,348 points in five seasons.

In Thompson's second season, 1958-'59, Omar "Bud" Browning had taken over as head coach of the 66ers.

Browning was already one of the best-known figures in American basketball. A native of Enid, Oklahoma, he became a two-time All-American player for the University of Oklahoma in the mid 1930s, then was also an AAU All-American in four years playing with the 66ers. He wound up coaching the team 12 years, in three different stretches, around his increasing business responsibilities in the company's general services department.

"Bobby Kennedy tossed ceremonial jump ball…"

He became the coach for the first time with the 1943-'44 season and directed the 66ers to five consecutive National AAU tournament championships. He then stepped down for 4 years, came back as an interim coach for the 1953-'54 season, and then in his last stint coached from 1958 through 1963-'64. His career coaching record was 489-100.

With his accomplishments as both a player and coach, Bud Browning was thought by many to be "Mr. Phillips 66ers basketball," in the description of Durham, the former publicity director. Browning not only knew the game of basketball, he also understood how the 66ers program fit in the corporate operation, and he was great at bringing along young men as both basketball players and company employees.

"Before or after our games, there'd often be receptions, where the local jobbers or other Phillips employees would come meet us, and sometimes bring their best customers along," said Thompson. "They'd be pretty excited, because a lot of our players were really well-known as basketball players. But I remember Bud Browning giving us some great advice about meeting the fans or Phillips dealers at those receptions. He said, 'Don't be talking about yourself or the basketball team. Instead, you learn about their business, and if they want to talk basketball, they'll bring it up.'"

That was a great lesson for young star athletes in how to be effective in making business connections.

Browning was also an excellent recruiter. In the 5 years of Thompson's playing career with the 66ers, his teammates included such former college stars as Bill Evans of Kentucky, Tom Fuller of Oklahoma State, Phil "Red" Murrell of Drake, Bobby Plump of Butler, Dallas Dobbs of Kansas, Don Matuszak and Wally Frank of Kansas State, Tom Robitaille of Rice, H.E. Kirchner of Texas Christian University, Al Bunge and Charlie McNeil of Maryland, Denny Price of Oklahoma, Jim Spivey and Jerry Shipp of Southeastern Oklahoma State College, Ron Altenberg of Cornell College in Iowa, Charlie Bowerman of Wabash and Don Kojis of Marquette. A few of them went on to play in the NBA, most notably Kojis who had a 12-year career in the pro league.

When Red Murrell came from Drake to join Phillips for the 1958-'59 season, it meant the 66ers' following among Iowa fans greatly increased—with both Thompson and Murrell normally in the starting line-up.

Another player of special note in that list is Bobby Plump, who also joined the 66ers in the '58-'59 season. You may not immediately recognize his name, but you probably know the story of Plump and his high school team from little Milan, Indiana. That story was made famous in the 1986 movie "Hoosiers," which fictionalized their 1954 state championship victory over one of the state's larger high schools, Muncie Central. The state title was clinched when Plump hit a long shot to beat the gun. The true story of that season is told in the 1997 book "Bobby Plump: The Last of the Small Town Heroes."

He went on to be a college star at Butler, in Indianapolis, playing for the legendary coach Paul D. "Tony" Hinkle, called "Mr. Hinkle" by nearly everyone. Plump set Butler's one-game scoring record (41 points) as well as the career scoring record.

Plump said Phillips' Bud Browning "had never seen me play, and had never even seen any film of me." During a "tryout" in Bartlesville, Plump "shot around about 10 minutes. Bud came in, looked at me and said to his assistant, 'If Mr. Hinkle says he can play, hire him.'" And so Plump joined the 66ers, becoming the other starting guard with Thompson.

"Gary Thompson and I had barely heard of each other—maybe we'd known a little about what we'd done in college but that was it—before we met at Phillips," said Plump, now semi-retired in Indianapolis where he has an insurance and financial planning agency with his daughter and son-in-law, and also has a well-known restaurant, "Plump's Last Shot."

As they got to know each other, Plump continued, "Gary and I realized our personal stories kind of mirrored each other. We had a lot in common—coming from small towns, being recognized throughout our home states because of doing something big with small-school teams. That's probably why we got along so well, and we became great friends."

Their styles were so similar that publicity director Durham and Browning started calling their guards the "Katzenjammer Twins," after the brothers "Hans" and "Fritz" who were stars of a popular, long-running comic strip "Katzenjammer Kids" in the newspapers at the time.

Thompson and Plump were both sharp-shooting, ball-hawking guards. Both sported flat-top haircuts. Plump, standing about 6 ft. tall, and Thompson, at 5 ft. 10 in., would "argue all the time about who was taller," Plump said. "So when you talk to him now, just tell him I said that I was so much taller than I could eat soup off his head."

Thompson would kid him right back, often saying, "If the Roland Rockets had beaten Davenport for the Iowa state championship in 1951, we'd have been the 'Hoosiers' story and no one would have ever heard of you."

Actually, they really admired each other's play. Thompson "was a good shooter and defensive player, but he was like me, a real competitor," Plump said. "In fact, our competitiveness is what we were really known for. Nobody wants to lose, of course. But competitors like we are, we'd go the extra step and figure out ways not to lose. Gary was very good for me. I think we both got better by playing with each other."

Life for the 66ers ranged from fun to hectic to almost crazy.

Some of the games were wild, like the night in March, 1960, when Phillips scored 152 points and beat the Cleveland Pipers NIBL team by nearly an 80-point margin. "Cleveland was a good ball club," Thompson said, "but we caught 'em in Bartlesville on one of those nights when everything went right for us and we couldn't miss, and they couldn't even hit lay-ups."

But then there was the night in 1959 when the arch-rival Wichita Vickers team beat the 66ers 142-78. "They wound up beating us by 64 points," Thompson noted, "but their fans were clamoring, 'We want 66! Beat 'em by 66!' "

Most seasons stretched to more than 50 games—all over the U.S. and sometimes beyond.

"It seemed like we traveled every way except by swinging grapevines," Durham said. "First we were traveling by train or bus. Then we went to the regular airlines, then to charter flights and then the company bought a DC-3 that we used for nearly all games. That airplane had been specially fitted with comfortable sofas and a card table, and a steward traveled with us serving food and drinks.

"The schedules could be crazy, depending on where the company wanted us to be representing them," Durham continued. "I remember one night we played at Madison Square Garden in New York City, and the next night in little Bolivar, Missouri. Our jobbers and sales people were always wanting the team to come into their territories."

The top AAU teams, like the 66ers, normally drew big crowds. And you never quite knew who was watching.

Gary Thompson said he was surprised, years later, when legendary basketball coach Bobby Knight, who was at Indiana University and later Texas Tech, told Thompson he'd seen him play with the 66ers in Akron, Ohio, against the Akron Goodyears.

"I was in high school back then in Orrville, Ohio, and that's halfway close to where those games were in Akron, so I'd go in on Sunday afternoons and watch them play," Knight told me. "I knew who Gary Thompson was because I could remember when he was at Iowa State and they beat Wilt Chamberlain. So I was interested in seeing him play with the 66ers. I remember him being quick, tough, a good shooter—an all-around good player."

Anytime the 66ers played in or around Iowa, Thompson would get lots of special attention. In November of 1958, the team played a mid-week exhibition game at the brand new high school gymnasium in Fort Dodge in northwest Iowa against the McDonald Scots AAU team from Lakes Charles, Louisiana. Both Thompson and Murrell were in the starting line-up, and the *Fort Dodge Messenger* reported that a crowd of 3,284 packed new Dodger Fieldhouse to watch Phillips win 88-77, with Thompson scoring 17 points and Murrell 10.

"Fort Dodge mayor challenged Gary to horseshoes match..."

But of special note was that just before the game, Fort Dodge Mayor Marvin Vedvig challenged Thompson to a horseshoes pitching match at halftime!

"The mayor was apparently pretty good at horseshoes, and he knew Gary had been a junior horseshoes champion at the Iowa State Fair when he was at Roland High School," said George Durham. "He'd arranged to have an indoor horseshoes pit, with rubber horseshoes, set up on the gym floor at halftime. Gary loved the idea, and accepted the challenge."

The outcome? "The Mayor took an early lead, but 'choked' under the pressure," the Messenger reported in its post-game coverage.

Another memorable game was an exhibition in a state prison in Indiana. "For that game, we divided up our squad and we played a game against ourselves with the prisoners being the crowd," said Thompson. "During the National Anthem, we became aware of a ruckus happening at one end of the stands, and over our shoulders, we see five guards wrestling one inmate down from the bleachers and out of the gym.

"Later we were touring the prison, and that same inmate was handcuffed down on a concrete slab in 'The Hole.' Seeing those young people in so much trouble, and hearing those doors lock behind us, I always thought if junior high kids could all be taken on a prison tour, it'd be quite a deterrent for them about getting into trouble."

Typical road trips for the 66ers were a week long, but some extended to 3 weeks and there were the occasional international trips—one to the Middle East lasted 7 weeks.

A lot of the players were married, and several had young children. Janet Thompson recalled that in the middle of one long road trip, the 66ers' plane landed back in Bartlesville "just long enough for all us wives to come to the airport and bring the guys clean underwear and shirts."

Gary Thompson said, "We kissed them and said 'hi' and 'goodbye.' " Maybe it was on that trip when Bobby Plump's young daughter, who hadn't seen her father for some time, tugged at the trousers of Murrell, smiled and yelled, "Daddy!"

The wives quickly became close friends, always ready to help one another.

"We were all young, a lot of us had babies and we all got pretty close," said Ruthann Steiner, whose husband Ray was the veteran guard that helped break-in Gary Thompson. She and Janet Thompson shared a hospital room as they awaited delivery of their children Mark and Kim in 1958.

Then in late February, 1960, when Janet was about to give birth to her second child, son Rick, the 66ers had a game in Cleveland and were flying back to Bartlesville right afterward, with Gary hoping he'd be there by the time Janet was delivering.

"But we ran into a big snowstorm around Indianapolis, and our flight got turned back to Cleveland," Gary recalled. "So we were in a hotel and I was rooming with George Durham. In the middle of the night, the phone rang, George rolled over and answered it. He said, 'Huh? Oh!' handed me the phone and said, 'It's a boy!' "

Gary got all the details from Janet, who was being watched over then by Kay Haldorson, the wife of player Burdie Haldorson. "When I went into the delivery room," Janet recalled, "they had Kay go out in the 'waiting room' with all the fathers whose wives were having babies. Kay told me later they were all looking at her like, 'What are you doing here?' "

Back in Cleveland, a proud Gary Thompson managed to fall back asleep in the hotel room. Suddenly the phone rang again. George Durham answered, grunted and said to Thompson, "This one's a girl!" Before Thompson could get too shook up, Durham confessed, "Nah, it's just the wake-up call!"

Ruthann Steiner looks back on that era as "an exciting time in Bartlesville because the company was growing and the entire town was excited about the basketball team."

Janet Thompson said "it was like we were all a big family." There were lots of programs for employees' families, like free swimming in the company's pool in the new Adams Building, and big dances in the gym. There were lots of company parties as well as team parties.

Most of the events did not involve alcohol, since Oklahoma was a "dry" state then. But occasionally some of the players and their wives would go out for dinner at a restaurant named "Marie's" that was operating like a key club. "It was one of those places where you had to knock on the door, someone would open a little window to see who you were, and then let you in," said Ruthann Steiner. "They'd serve alcohol with your dinner." Fancier events were at the Hillcrest Country Club.

But team members and their wives never got out of line in public, Janet Thompson said. "We conducted ourselves with the idea that we were 'Phillips people,' and that the men especially were always representing the company."

They were good representatives, too.

The U.S. State Department occasionally sent the 66ers on goodwill missions to other countries, like for a five-game series in Mexico in 1959, and a 7-week tour of the Middle East from mid-October to early December of 1961, with games in Israel, Egypt, Lebanon, Jordan, Greece, Cyprus and Italy. In addition, Thompson joined other college and AAU all-stars on USA teams that played in the Pan-American Games in Chicago in 1959, in a series of exhibition games in the former Soviet Union in 1961, and in the World Games held in the Philippines and Taiwan in 1962.

"I've never forgotten that I got to travel the world—free—to play basketball," said Thompson. "I've always been grateful for that."

He also got to meet some very interesting people along the way.

In an All-Stars game against a Soviet team at Cole Fieldhouse at the University of Maryland, there was a ceremonial jump ball to start the game—and throwing the ball up was U.S. Attorney General Bobby Kennedy. Thompson said he was surprised, when he met the 5 ft. 9 in. Kennedy, to find somebody on a basketball floor shorter than he was. "I remember thinking at the time that if I could play on a team of Bobby Kennedys, I'd be the center!" Thompson said with a laugh.

In the Pan-Am Games of 1959, he was on a team with young Jerry West who, as a junior at the University of West Virginia, had already become one of the nation's best college players. "What I remember most about those games," said West, "is that we were playing in the DePaul Fieldhouse in Chicago, and staying in the DePaul dorms, and nothing was air-conditioned. It was incredibly hot—oh, man, it was hot!

"The games were extremely physical, and with all the heat and humidity, it was almost impossible to keep the floor dry. After that experience, I always noticed, over the years, when Gary Thompson would pop up as one of the commentators on a college basketball game on TV. It would make me think back to playing together that summer in Chicago."

West went on to a great career as a player, coach and executive in the NBA, retiring in 2007 after serving as president of basketball operations for the Memphis Grizzlies.

"Jerry West is one of the great guys in the game," Thompson said. "When he was playing with the Lakers in the NBA, sometimes we'd have doubleheaders in Madison Square Garden in New York—they'd play one of the NBA teams and we'd be playing another AAU team as a preliminary game. We'd be staying at the same hotels, and Jerry was always good to sit down and visit for a half-hour or hour."

Another basketball legend Thompson became pals with during international competition was Jerry Lucas, superstar for Ohio State and later the New York Knicks. Lucas had helped Ohio State win consecutive NCAA championships in 1960 and '61, and in May, 1961, he and Thompson became teammates and roommates on the 3-week-long tour by the USA All-Stars teams—men and women—playing against teams in the Soviet Union.

The men's team was coached by the legendary John McClendon, who'd had National Association of Intercollegiate Athletics championship teams at African American colleges and later became the first black coach of a professional basketball team in the U.S., the Cleveland Pipers and later the Denver Rockets.

Before the start of that trip, the team was practicing in New York City, and Thompson took a phone call for Lucas, who was out of their hotel room right then, from a radio show host who wanted to interview Lucas. "It was Howard Cosell," said Thompson, "and I didn't know him from a bale of hay at that point." It turned out that Cosell, who became famous a few years later for his coverage of boxing and Monday Night Football on ABC-TV, asked Lucas to meet him at Yankee Stadium, and Lucas asked Thompson to go with him.

"Cosell treated us great," Thompson recalled. "He took us down on the field during batting practice, and we're standing there talking to Mickey Mantle, Roger Maris, Whitey Ford, and a lot of the other great Yankee players. I wanted to talk to them about baseball, but all they wanted to talk about was basketball!

"One thing I haven't forgotten about being on the field there was that Yogi Berra came by. Cosell introduced Jerry and me to him and said we were getting ready to go play basketball for the U.S. in the Soviet Union. Yogi just kind of grumped at us, shook hands and walked on. I thought to myself at the time, 'Well, Yogi doesn't have much personality,' but he probably just had his 'game face' on.

"Years later, I met him again after a baseball game in Kansas City, I think in 1984. I was down there with the Kansas City Royals broadcaster Fred White, whom I did some Big Eight basketball games with, and our producer John Crowe. We went to dinner at Stroud's Restaurant after the baseball game with Dick Howser, the Kansas City manager; Rocky Colavito, a former Kansas City player; Hank Bauer, the Yankee great who was later a manager and was retired in the Kansas City area; Mike Ferraro, who was a Royals coach, and Yogi, who was manager of the Yankees then.

"Over dinner, Yogi started telling stories and was the life of the party. My whole opinion of him changed. He was famous for twisting his words and thoughts around, you know, and that night, they were telling how he'd walked down a hotel hallway, and checked in with some Yankee players who were watching a movie. Yogi asked the players, 'Who's in the movie?' The players answered the star was Steve McQueen. He'd died recently, and Yogi said, 'Steve McQueen, huh? He must've made that movie before he died.' "

But back to 1961 and the memorable night at Yankee Stadium. Broadcaster Cosell took Lucas and Thompson to dinner in the Press Club at the stadium, and they also had a chance to visit with Yankee broadcasters Mel Allen and Red Barber in their radio booth.

When the team got to Moscow to begin its series of games, they noticed during warm-ups for one game that a big section of seats was roped off right at center court. There was no explanation why until the game was just about ready to start. Suddenly the public address announcer told the crowd that there would be a special guest, and introduced Yuri Gagarin, the young Soviet cosmonaut who, just weeks earlier in April, had become the first human to go into space. The crowd went wild as Gagarin came into the arena flanked by high-ranking Soviet government and military officials.

"We were all impressed," Thompson said, "but one thing I'll never forget is that after the game, a guy came up to us with a newspaper. I asked our interpreter what he wanted. And it turned out the newspaper had a story that the U.S. had just put our first astronaut in space, Alan Shepherd. But the Soviet man wanted to point out that Shepherd's flight was 'sub-orbital' and not an 'orbital' flight like Gagarin had made."

It was clearly a time of great competition, and frequently tension, between the world's two superpowers, the Soviet Union and the United States. Thompson and his teammates were among the first Americans to be admitted to the Soviet Union, and they were invited to come under a sports and cultural exchange program.

"That was in the middle of the Cold War, kind of an unusual situation to be in for a bunch of young people like we were," said Jerry Lucas, who now heads his own memory enhancement seminars and courses, with operations in southern California and Ohio.

Thompson has often wondered what happened to the team's first interpreter in the Soviet Union. "He was a 19-year-old man named 'Volvo' who could speak six languages," Thompson said. "He told us that he hoped his language skills would some day be his ticket out of that country. We really got along with him well. He'd carry a briefcase for his maps and paperwork, but when we'd be away from the hotel, the guys on the team gave him some blue jeans—which the Soviet people loved—and T-shirts, and he'd stuff them in there.

"I remember one night in the hotel, a bunch of us were talking with him about our countries," Thompson continued. "He asked us about the racial segregation in the United States, and somebody asked him about what he thought of the Communist Party. He said immediately, 'The Communist Party is the greatest institution there is, and will eventually rule the world!'

"Then he pointed up around the ceiling, telling us there were people listening to our conversation. We all thought, 'Wow! They've bugged the rooms of a little old basketball team!' Other Soviet officials were always observing us, though, and soon, Volvo was replaced as our interpreter. We were told he'd been doing too much fraternizing with us."

The team played two games in Moscow, one in Kiev, one in Tbilisi and one in Leningrad (now St. Petersburg).

In Tbilisi, Thompson recalls, they were getting ready for an outdoor game in a soccer stadium—where a portable basketball floor had been put together—with a crowd of 20,000 in the grandstand. Typical of everywhere they played in the Soviet Union, there were also bouquets of flowers and baskets of fruit in their dressing rooms, symbols of the friendship the Soviet people were extending, and incentives that made the American players want to put on a good show.

> *"I got to travel the world—free—to play basketball…"*

But there in Tbilisi, "It started to sprinkle, and we were slipping and sliding, so we said we couldn't play right then and would have to wait for the rain to stop," he said. "We were sitting in the dressing rooms, and all of a sudden, men started carrying buckets of sawdust out and dumping it all over the basketball floor to soak up the moisture. Then a bunch of women came out with brooms and started sweeping off the sawdust. The rain had stopped, so we started playing again, but only got in another 6 or 7 minutes before it rained so hard we had to cancel the game. We hated not being able to play, when all those people had come out to watch us."

Lucas said that "in Moscow, like in a lot of big cities, the people were always hurrying everywhere and were not very friendly, but the farther we got away from Moscow, the friendlier the people got. I just loved the experience.

"I think I was the only player who was still in college," Lucas continued. "All the others were AAU players, like Gary Thompson, so it was a good experience for me to play with them. I remember him as being fun, good to be with and a really good basketball player."

Thompson said the team, which won all its games in the Soviet Union playing several "national teams" and basketball clubs, "was able to do a lot of relationship building while we were there, and that was really our purpose in going."

Most remarkable of all his international basketball experiences, undoubtedly, was the long trip through the Middle East in the late fall of 1961. That trip was chronicled in a series of stories that George Durham wired to the *Bartlesville Examiner-Enterprise*.

"As far as the Phillips 66ers are concerned, the Glory that was Greece is still glorious," Durham wrote in his first story for the fans back home. "After arriving here Saturday night, the 66ers had a chance Sunday to tour some of the ancient ruins of Athens. The Acropylis, the Parthenon, the Temple of Athens, the Greek Amphitheatre—all were getting a fine perusal from the wide-eyed Phillips crew."

He told of the players floating in the Dead Sea, bobbing around like unsinkable toys in a swimming pool. In Jordan, Palestinian refugees built an asphalt basketball court just so the 66ers could play in their Aquba Jaber camp.

In Cairo, Egypt, as the team's bus approached a sports club, where they were to play the Cairo All-Stars, they found a mob of 7,000 boisterous, unruly fans crowding the fences around the club, insisting on being admitted immediately. Mounted policemen, waving swords, tried to part the crowd in front of the main gate to allow the 66ers to enter, but the crowd became even contentious. So the officers asked the 66ers if they would mind climbing over a 6-foot-high back wall—and they did! A little later, the crowd was allowed into the stands.

In that game, according to Durham's story, the Cairo players began running and dribbling right at the 66ers, colliding, and then fouls were being called against the visitors, even after they'd been knocked down.

"One of the biggest mistakes the Cairo players made was to get Captain Gary Thompson mad," Durham wrote. "After an Egyptian had run smack into Tom Robitaille, and a foul was called on Robitaille, the little veteran guard boiled up to the nearest referee, demanding to know what constituted a charging foul. When the referee tried to turn away, while saying only the captain could speak to him, Gary got angrier. 'I'm the captain, and I want to know what's going on!'

"Well, as you can imagine, Thompson didn't get enough satisfaction—right then, that is. However, the next time an Egyptian tried to drive, he got run under, decked, clobbered, and smasherooed by the usually mild-tempered 66er. But, the veteran of much international play thought quickly. The only histrionics the Egyptian could get into was a loud 'Ooof!' when he hit.

"Then Thompson had him back up on his feet in a split second, brushed the sand—yes, the court was sand—from him, patted him on the back and smiled. The crowd went wild over the sportsmanlike gesture. The playing of the game straightened out immensely after that."

The team won all 14 of its games on the tour, and all but two of them were played on outdoor courts. From Jerusalem, Durham wrote, "Playing an intrasquad game outdoors at night with the Mount of Olives in the background will have to go down as something new for the Phillips 66ers."

The fans in the Middle East were wowed by the precision of the 66ers' game.

"The people applauded any good play by either team," Durham reported from Port Said, Egypt, "and just about went into hysterics when the 66ers pulled off five or six quick passes right under the basket before putting the ball in the hoop."

They also conducted clinics for local players, and made visits to U.S. embassies.

They arrived back in Bartlesville at mid-day on a Thursday in early December, 1961, and started their regular season at home against the Denver-Chicago Truckers from Colorado on that Saturday night. Fifty-two games later, they beat the same team for the championship of the '62 National AAU tournament, and Thompson's playing career ended—with his teammates carrying him off the floor on their shoulders as the tourney MVP.

Was it difficult for him to give it up? "He never indicated it was hard," Janet Thompson said. "He has always been one to go on to the next thing."

Gary said that with Janet managing two children—then 4 and 2 years old—he was definitely ready to end the extended road trips. "I'd had a good run," he said. "It was time for other guys to get their chance."

He left with only one real disappointment, that he was unable to tryout for the 1960 U.S. Olympics team. A pinched nerve in his back had forced him into a hospital for a week right before we went to the National AAU tournament in Denver, and then the Olympic trials were right after that.

Even considering that, it's hard to imagine anybody getting much more out of playing basketball than Gary Thompson had.

Chapter 14

Playing Days Over, Back to Iowa

WHEN Gary Thompson's playing career with the Phillips 66ers ended in the spring of 1962, the Phillips Petroleum Co. had prepared him well to take over a sales territory in eastern Iowa with a base in Cedar Rapids.

Recall that in his first weeks with the company in the summer of 1957, just after he graduated from Iowa State University, he had stayed in Ames and "worked the drive" at a Phillips 66 station there. That station's operators had him pumping gas, checking oil, airing up tires and washing windows.

It was all part of the company's insistence that employees who were thought to have bright futures would be schooled in all phases of the business. That kind of hands-on training continued in the fall of '57 in Bartlesville, Oklahoma.

"Phillips had a service station downtown there in the same neighborhood as the company headquarters," Thompson said. "They started a lot of us off working at that service station. You'd get to know a lot of the Phillips executives while you were doing that, because they'd drop by the station and buy their gas there. After a while working at the station, then they'd move you into the office, and you'd go through training programs in the departments there. As players, we got accelerated training programs that other employees might take 6 to 10 years to qualify for."

During most of Thompson's 5 years as a player, he had a full-time day job in the sales and marketing department in Bartlesville.

The company would also occasionally send young sales employees back into their home territories for additional experience, and Thompson spent the summer of 1959 in the Des Moines sales office, while living in Ankeny. There he came under the direction of a strong Phillips manager, Andy Riggs, who was a graduate of Des Moines North High and knew the Gary Thompson story well. Riggs took a special interest in helping develop Thompson's marketing and other business skills.

In Oklahoma, Thompson got to know another North High grad who was with Phillips 66, Ed Beisser, who had played college basketball at Creighton University and then with the Phillips 66ers from 1945-'48. Fast forward to 1965, when Thompson was back in Bartlesville as coach of the 66ers, Beisser helped him try to recruit one of the most promising players in the country, Rick Barry, who had just finished his All-American career at the University of Miami in Florida.

"Ed hosted Rick Barry at his ranch during his recruiting visit," Thompson said. "Rick wanted to ride one of the quarter horses, something he had never done before. He rode it only a short ways before he fell off." Barry subsequently turned down the 66ers, signed with the Golden State Warriors of the NBA and went on to an outstanding career as a pro player. Thompson, recalling Barry's long-ago fall from the horse, notes "his NBA career could have ended in Bartlesville that day!"

In terms of an exciting business environment, the 1960s proved to be "absolutely the best time to be with Phillips," Thompson said. "The interstate highways were just coming into existence, so there were going to be a lot of new service stations built. My job in sales was to take proposals for new properties that were coming in from the field offices, and then do a quick development of a plan to buy properties and start stations. We were also looking at the Department of Transportation plans for all the states, and then buying options on places we thought would be good properties. I got a great background then in real estate and legal work."

In one of his biggest projects, he did the presentation to corporate management of a proposal that led to Phillips 66 purchasing a 250-foot frontage on the Las Vegas "strip," with land stretching back a half-mile or more from the frontage, adjacent to the popular Stardust Hotel and Casino.

"The proposal came in from our western division office, for our jobber out there, Jack Cason Oil Company," Thompson said. "Cason Oil was starting to operate stations that not only didn't have locks on the doors, they didn't even have doors—they were open 24 hours a day, 7 days a week. That was the first time I'd heard of anything like that, but in Las Vegas, you can imagine there'd be customers all night long."

Thompson said the Vegas deal was "by far" the biggest financial project he'd worked on to that point. "My memory is that the total cost for the land and for building the station was going to be about $250,000, which was about three times the cost of what a normal first-class unit was back then," he said.

He checked and double-checked on the real estate titles and building specs, presented the proposal to the executives at Phillips 66, won their approval, the deal went through, and the station was built and opened. Eventually, the extra land the company had purchased behind the new station was sold, "because it was so valuable, they couldn't afford to hold on to it anymore," Thompson said. "When they sold it, they got a lot more for that piece of property than the original cost had been for all the land and building the station."

As enthusiastic as he was for some areas of corporate life, he "saw some things on the corporate level I didn't like as much," he said. "I'd see what I perceived to be some individual getting promoted because of a personal relationship with someone within division management. That just happens."

That probably shaped some of his thinking that, eventually, he wanted to operate more independently. His former boss, G.J. "Pete" Morrison, remembers thinking Thompson would be successful in whatever position he wound up in, whether it was with Phillips Petroleum, some other corporation or even his own company.

> *"He started out pumping gas, checking oil..."*

"Gary had a natural ability of being able to get along with people in the business world," Morrison said. "And he also had a natural ability to look at a business opportunity and say, 'This is a good one,' or 'This one has some problems.' He studied and worked at it to perfection, and his enthusiasm was always a plus. He's a guy who in business never gave up—just like he was as a basketball player."

Thompson said he learned a great piece of management philosophy from Morrison. "Pete always used to say, 'If I can teach and train people to the point that they surpass me in the company, then I've done the ultimate job for Phillips,' " Thompson said. "I always thought that showed how loyal to the company he was."

Another strength Thompson had in the corporate world, he could follow orders.

"One time when I was still in Bartlesville, the company was getting upset because they thought our Phillips employees were buying gas at cut-rate unbranded stations instead of at our own stations," Thompson recalled. "The bosses came into marketing and sent us out to check. They told us to go to competitors' stations, be careful not to get on their property, but write down license plate numbers of people buying their gas there.

"So I was assigned a station out on one corner, and there was a grocery store parking lot abutting the station's location. I sat in that grocery lot in my car, with a pair of binoculars, and I'm writing down license plate numbers. After a little while, the service station guy comes out and says, 'Hey! I know what you're doing! You better get out of here, or I'll call the sheriff!' I said, 'Sir, I'm just doing my job for Phillips.' I didn't want to lie about it.

"About then, another customer drove into the station. The guy working there yelled to the customer, 'Hold it! Don't put any gas in yet!' Then he ran over there and slapped a chamois over the license plate! So I was pulling up the binoculars to see if I could see the rear license plate of the car, and then the driver comes over and says, 'I know what you're doing, but this is my neighbor's car! I buy Phillips Flite Fuel all the time.'

"He turned out to be an employee. After he visited with me, I told him I was going to do him a favor and not turn him in this time, "but you better stay out of these unbranded stations because Phillips is checking them. Oh, by the way, you can take that chamois off your license plate now."

Thompson said the result of his survey, and those taken by his colleagues at other locations around the city, was that "80 percent of the Phillips employees who were buying the competitors' gas were our technical people and research people."

But he said there was one other result worth noting, too. "A sheriff's deputy came out and got three of us who were doing these surveys," Thompson said. "We were taken to the courthouse, and Phillips had to send down its attorneys to get us out of there."

Besides all the training Gary Thompson had, there were two other things that gave him a real advantage going into his new sales position in the Cedar Rapids area in that summer of 1962. One, he came in with real celebrity status that made everybody in the area feel like they knew him. And, two, Cedar Rapids-based Nordstrom Oil Co. was one of the fastest-growing Phillips 66 distributorships in the nation, and the father and son partners, Floyd and Bill Nordstrom, were anxious to do business with him.

Even though Cedar Rapids and Iowa City are in the heart of Iowa Hawkeye territory, and at that point Thompson was arguably the most identifiable Iowa State Cyclone of all time, eastern Iowans had still become fans of his during his All-American college career. And they had packed gymnasiums in eastern Iowa when he occasionally played there with the Phillips 66ers from 1957-'62. Many also remembered him as the great high school basketball hero with the Roland Rockets, the most popular team in Iowa from 1951 to '53 when Thompson led them to three consecutive state basketball tournaments that were played then at the University of Iowa Fieldhouse in Iowa City.

"The Cedar Rapids media people all knew Gary so well, and they all did stories and columns that welcomed him to the community," recalled Don King, a longtime basketball coach in Cedar Rapids, first at Coe College and later Cedar Rapids Washington High School, who became a close friend to Thompson in those years. "Tait Cummins, Ron Gonder and Bob Brooks from the TV and radio stations, and Gus Schrader at the Cedar Rapids Gazette—they all were doing features on him. That helped make the people genuinely excited to have Gary and Janet living in the city."

Iowa State graduates who were active in the community—like Dr. Russell Anthony, Al Sorenson and Tom LeBuhn—made the rounds of the service clubs and organizations with Thompson, introducing him to the leading citizens of Cedar Rapids.

King felt like he already knew Gary Thompson, too.

"I had been the basketball coach at Nevada High School from 1957 to 1962, and that's Story County, the same county that Roland is in, so it was the heart of 'Gary Thompson Territory,'" King said. "By that time, Gary was in Bartlesville, but his younger brother DeLon was playing for Roland then, and we'd play the Rockets several times a year. When we'd play at Roland, we'd see Gary's retired jersey, the big photo of him and all the state tournament trophies there. So I definitely knew who Gary Thompson was and what he'd accomplished.

"That summer of '62, I was succeeding Bill Fitch as the basketball coach at Coe College," King continued, "and about the middle of that summer, my wife June and I moved to Cedar Rapids. June went to one of those 'Welcome Wagon' gatherings they used to have in towns to welcome newcomers, and she met Janet Thompson. They hit it off immediately, both being newcomers to Cedar Rapids and both having a lot of basketball interests. Within a couple of days, the four of us got together, and that was the first of a whole lot of get-togethers over the next 2 years—at their house, our house, playing bridge or a little golf now and then. And we've been friends ever since."

Later that fall, when Gary felt like he'd gotten his bearings on the job, he started visiting Don King at the Coe College fieldhouse and occasionally working out in the gym.

"We talked a whole lot of basketball on those visits," said King. "We watched a lot of film of games together, too, talking strategies. He brought along films of several of the Phillips 66ers games, and we got out the old one of the 1951 state tournament game between Davenport and Roland. He'd also work with some of our Coe players, and even jump into a few scrimmages with us. It was great for our young people to have Gary around, with all the experiences he had. He became a good Coe fan, too, and attended a lot of our games."

"Some areas of corporate life were questionable..."

Meanwhile, Thompson was grooming his business relationship with the Phillips 66 distributors and station managers in the area, as well as working on new station development.

The Nordstroms had come from the Minneapolis area to Cedar Rapids in 1953 to start Nordstrom Oil Co. Floyd Nordstrom had experience with Phillips 66 earlier, and he began his own company as a distributorship, selling Phillips products, tires, batteries and car accessories to service stations in the area. His son Bill Nordstrom joined the company in 1955 and they eventually expanded the business to serve 35 service stations and two truck stops in Iowa and Nebraska, as well as bulk gas and fuel oil plants.

As Phillips distributors, they had hosted 66ers basketball games in the Cedar Rapids area when Gary Thompson was in the line-up.

"There was the AAU team in Cedar Rapids called Sanitary Dairy, and the 66ers played them a couple of times in Gary's era," Bill Nordstrom said. "One of those games was the first time I'd ever gotten to see him play, since I'd been raised in the Minneapolis area and then had been away in the Navy. He got his jump shot going, and he was fabulous that night. I couldn't believe how good he was. I think we might have had the game at Washington High School there in Cedar Rapids, and the crowd was huge, and it was clear to me—Gary Thompson was a legend around Iowa.

"Then lo and behold, he retires from basketball and becomes our district representative from Phillips. I remember so clearly him coming up and introducing himself to us as our new sales rep."

Thompson took a very active interest in Nordstrom Oil's growing accounts, making sure they had all the Phillips products they needed. It's a business relationship, incidentally, that has continued in different forms for 40 years, as you will read later.

There were also a lot of athletic and social get-togethers between the Nordstroms and Thompsons.

"Gary's always been very competitive, and I'd often needle him about it," Bill Nordstrom said. "One time we were playing golf in a little tournament somewhere in Iowa, and he was so serious about it, I started in on him. I said, 'Jeez, we can't even have a beer or a sandwich!' He looked over and said, 'O.K., let's get a sandwich.'

"Another time, I heard someone mention that Gary had been a state champion in horseshoe pitching in high school, and I kidded him about that. Then it came out that I was playing a lot of handball at the YMCA in Cedar Rapids, and he'd never played it. He said, 'Tell me about this handball,' so I took him over and showed him how to play. I'd been playing for years, but by the time he'd played for about 6 weeks, he was beating me. So I switched to tennis, and said, 'Thompson, please leave me alone in this sport.'"

They still kid each other about the night, early in the relationship, when Gary and Janet Thompson invited Floyd and Bill Nordstrom and their wives out to dinner, suggesting they all gather first at the Thompson home.

"We knew the Thompsons didn't drink, but they wanted to be sure we were comfortable," Bill Nordstrom said. "So when we came in, Gary said, 'O.K., what's everybody drinking? We've got about everything,' Dad and I looked at each other, and Dad said he'd drink a bourbon and soda, and I said I'd like a scotch and soda.

"So Gary ran out to the kitchen, fixes the drinks and brings them back to us. I took a drink, and it was so sweet I couldn't believe it. I said, 'Gary, I think you got some sweet soda in here instead of regular soda.' He said he was sure it was regular soda, so I said, 'Let me see your soda bottle,' and it was a sweet soda, not a club soda."

The Thompsons were mortified. "I didn't know the difference between sweet soda and club soda, and I was embarrassed," Gary recalled with a laugh. Bill Nordstrom told him the drink would be just fine, but Gary Thompson wasn't going to let his mistake go uncorrected. He ran out of the house, drove to a nearby store and bought the right kind of soda to go with Nordstrom's Scotch.

"Ever since then," said Bill Nordstrom, "I've told people, 'I'm the guy who taught Thompson how to drink!' " Nordstrom knows that what makes that especially funny is that Thompson never did start drinking.

Gary worked hard at expanding sales in his territory, and he helped get new stations developed near Interstate Highway 80 in West Branch, Coralville and a few other locations.

He said so many of his business contacts were wanting to discuss deals while playing golf, that he checked back with his bosses to make sure he wasn't spending too much time at golf outings and not enough in the office. They noted the growing sales figures and told him to play on, and use his best judgment.

Of course, Thompson didn't completely give up playing basketball, either.

Late in the 1962-'63 season, his first one away from the Phillips 66ers, he in fact played against them. Knowing what great promotions the team's games were for Phillips dealers and products, Thompson decided to organize a game for them in Cedar Rapids again.

He turned to his friend Don King, the Coe College coach, and ask if he'd put together a team of former Iowa college all-stars to play against the 66ers, and Thompson volunteered to be one of the guards.

"That turned into such a neat event," said King. "My memory is that we had 17 players from around Iowa on that team, and that was probably too many for an all-star game like that, but it sure added to the crowd."

The fans overflowed the stands in the gym at old Cedar Rapids Regis High School. Besides Thompson, King's all-stars included former Iowa Hawkeye players Joel Novak, Nolden Gentry, Bill Seaberg and Dennis Runge; former Iowa Staters Gary Wheeler and Terry Roberts, and from the smaller colleges Bob Tidgren of Simpson, John Carle from Central and Dick Keel from Coe.

> "After 6 weeks, he was beating me at handball!"

The 27-year-old Thompson led all scorers with 26 points, but his former Phillips teammates prevailed, 90-80. That 66ers team, by the way, went on to win a second consecutive National AAU tournament championship.

King said that after the game in Cedar Rapids, "there was a big gathering—maybe it was at Elmcrest Country Club if I remember correctly—for all the players on both teams, and for any of the fans that wanted to attend, too. Gary put all that together, and it was a really fine event and a great promotion for Phillips."

Maybe it was Thompson's involvement in that event—maybe it was hanging out with Coach King—but before long Thompson said he "was getting itchy, thinking I just have to coach. As a guard in basketball, I'd always been close to my coaches, and so I was always interested. I liked my job just fine, but I just had this feeling."

In the spring of 1964, the University of Iowa hired a new basketball coach, the highly respected Ralph Miller, who came from Wichita State.

"One day when I was in Iowa City, I went over and talked to Ralph about coaching," Thompson said. "As we talked, I remember telling him, 'I'm just going to have to coach somewhere,' although at that point, I didn't have anything in mind."

Before long, that same idea was stirring in the minds of some of Gary Thompson's biggest fans—in Bartlesville, Oklahoma.

Chapter 15

Coach Thompson And the Phillips 66ers

GARY THOMPSON'S interest in coaching, as he has said, probably grew out of the close relationships he always had with his basketball and baseball coaches.

As a student at Iowa State, he initially thought he'd go into sports writing, but then discovered the college's journalism program emphasized agricultural reporting and advertising. So he went on to major in physical education, with a minor in zoology, thinking he would teach and coach.

The first time he acted on that interest came "during my second or third year as a player at Phillips," he said. "A basketball assistant coaching job opened up at Iowa State."

Glen Anderson was the head coach by then, and Bob Lamson was the top assistant, and both had been there as assistants when Thompson was playing for the Cyclones. Anderson had been promoted to head coach when Bill Strannigan moved to his alma mater, the University of Wyoming, in 1959.

Thompson said he called Anderson about the assistant coach position. "Glen discouraged me and said, 'Oh, Gary, you don't want to get into coaching basketball—it's a rat race,'" Thompson said. "But I told him I'd like to look at it, so I came back to Ames to talk about it."

He met with Anderson, and got a rather cool reaction, which surprised him. That's when Lamson, the assistant, took Thompson aside and asked, "What are they offering you?" When Thompson told Lamson the salary figure he'd been quoted, Lamson said, "Well, they could afford to pay you a lot more than that. But they don't really want you. They think having you here would put too much pressure on them if they lose."

Apparently Anderson's thinking was that, if his team wobbled, there might be a public outcry to make the popular Thompson the head coach.

So Thompson went back for a couple more good years as a Phillips 66ers player and continued his career in business with the company. And he says he harbored no grudge at all toward Anderson or Iowa State for not hiring him as an assistant coach.

"Actually, I've always appreciated that Bob Lamson would come forth and tell me the truth about that situation," Thompson said. "He kept me from what could have been a bad situation in the end. Immediately after Bob told me that, I said I was no longer interested in the job and headed back to Bartlesville."

Anderson and Lamson are now both deceased, Anderson dying in 2008 and Lamson in 1967.

A much better coaching position came at Thompson "out of the blue" in late September, 1964, when he and his family were happy in Cedar Rapids.

In Bartlesville, the 66ers veteran coach Bud Browning, citing increased responsibilities on his regular Phillips job, decided it was time to turn the coaching over to someone else. He called Thompson and said, "Gary, I hear you want to coach. I want you to come back and coach the Philllips 66ers."

Thompson said he has wondered ever since if Ralph Miller, the coach of the Iowa Hawkeyes with whom he had discussed getting into coaching sometime, "had made a phone call to Browning. I never found that out."

Regardless, "getting to coach the Phillips 66ers allowed me to have my cake and eat it, too," he said. "I wanted to coach, but I really did not want to leave the Phillips company."

When the 66ers coaching change was announced, Browning told the *Bartlesville Examiner-Enterprise* that, "to be truthful, I realize I will miss coaching. However, it will be a nice change to be able to spend more time at home with my family. And, knowing that the team will be in such capable hands makes it easier to bow out. Gary Thompson was one of the finest players and gentlemen we have ever had on a Phillips team. He is a great student of the game, and I know he will make a great coach."

Thompson, then 29, had accepted the position after meeting in Bartlesville with Browning, Phillips sports director George Durham and officials in the sales department, which administered the program.

"I am very happy to have this opportunity to coach the 66ers," Thompson told the newspaper. "In my mind, it is one of the finest athletic programs in the country. And it looks like Bud Browning is turning over the ingredients of a fine team. While we'll have only three veterans, we have a flock of good-looking rookies."

Janet Thompson initially was not enthusiastic about the move.

"We had already moved around so much," she said. "Later on, I counted up that in the first 15 years we were married, we moved 11 times. And there in Cedar Rapids, we had bought our own house for the first time, and we were pretty settled. Then the chance for Gary to coach came up.

"I didn't have any problem with the thought of living in Bartlesville again, or with Gary being back at the Phillips headquarters. We always liked living in Bartlesville, and the company was great to us. It was just the thought of going through the disruption of moving again, and knowing that when he was coaching, he'd be gone a lot."

In addition, Janet was pregnant with their third child, Scott, who was born the following April. Daughter Kim was 6, and Rick was 4, on his way to becoming a 66ers ballboy later.

"All three of our kids were born in Bartlesville," Janet said. "I'd always say I'd get pregnant in Iowa and have babies in Oklahoma!"

Actually, it wound up being a happy move for Janet. She discovered that she became something of a coach herself—with the young wives of the 66ers players and their families.

"A lot of them would gather at our house, or some other place, nearly every night, and we'd play Bridge, " she said. "It wasn't a lonely time at all. In fact, after a while, I'd think back to how worried I'd been about making the move and I'd think, 'What were you even whining about?' "

Kim and Rick kept her very busy with school, Brownie Scouts, church activities, swimming and diving lessons, and more.

Another person Thompson consulted about the move, and about going into coaching, was Bill Nordstrom, his good friend and customer in Cedar Rapids.

"He called me the day he got the offer to be the Phillips coach," Nordstrom said. "He asked me what I thought, and I said, 'What's your ultimate goal?' He said it was to be a Phillips distributor in Ames, just like I was in Cedar Rapids.

"I told him if he went down to Bartlesville and did a good job running that basketball program, it would help him with the Phillips executives when it eventually came time to decide whether he'd get the distributorship in Ames. I told him, 'The fella who is the basketball coach for Phillips Petroleum sort of sitteth at the right hand of God, as far as management is concerned!' "

With the coaching job came an off-season position in the Phillips advertising department in Bartlesville, and that gave him additional experience in that area of the business.

Thompson was certainly a good custodian of the Phillips 66ers heritage as the best AAU basketball program in the U.S. His teams over the next four years had a combined record of 159-36, always reached at least the quarter-finals of the National AAU tournament and twice played for the championship.

He coached a United States all-star team in the World Games in Santiago, Chile, in 1966, and earlier that same year, coached the 66ers during a three-week tour of Puerto Rico with games against several teams there.

He learned a lot.

"You know, you're really not ready to coach just because you've played," he said. "It's so much more than Xs and Os. The psychology of it is one of the biggest things. I made some mistakes with players, of course, but I also got some to play at a whole new level.

"One valuable lesson came after I told the players I'd have an 'open door policy,' and that they could come in and talk about whatever was on their mind. One of our good players, Bill Kusleika, came in after that and said, 'I think I can help you.' He went on to tell me that when I'd get upset and jump on Darel Carrier, 'he just melts.' But he said I could continue to ride another player, Ray Carey. He said, 'When you jab Carey, he plays better.' Then he said, 'You just can't treat all of us the same.' Kusleika was right. I followed his advice and both Carrier and Carey became better players."

And there were some big changes in basketball and in society that Thompson had to try to deal with, too.

In the early 1960s, network television discovered professional basketball. There were at least weekly telecasts of such storied teams as the Boston Celtics, New York Knicks, Philadelphia 76ers and others. The TV audiences grew, so did attendance at games, and the NBA franchises gained strength as businesses. The salaries and contracts the teams would award to players became more lucrative and offered more long-term security, too.

Then the NBA began adding teams, growing from the eight that had played through most of the 1950s, and that meant they had to recruit more players. And in 1967, the rival American Basketball Association was started by master promoter Abe Saperstein, and pro basketball just mushroomed.

All of that was eroding the popularity of AAU basketball with the fans, and it was killing the interest among players to stay in the "amateur" ranks after college.

For the Phillips 66ers new coach Gary Thompson, it meant finding good players was increasingly a challenge. No longer were first-team All-Americans looking to play in the National Industrial Basketball League.

In addition, he said, "the NAACP (National Association for the Advancement of Colored People) put pressure on Phillips to recruit blacks, both for the company and for the team. Phillips had always been pretty much all-white. The executives knew it was time to change, and they were committed to it.

"They told me to be on the look out to recruit a black player who was a good player that could be a starter on our team, but could also be a quality employee. That became real difficult to find the right guy, because if the player was good enough to be a starter with us, he was commanding more money from the pros and wanted to play there, and wasn't interested in the job security we could offer him. And if we found someone who would be a good employee, he usually wasn't quite the caliber of player we needed. We didn't want a token sitting on the bench."

One black player Thompson wanted to recruit was Gene Littles, an NAIA All-American at High Point College in North Carolina. "I talked to a lot of people about Gene, and I knew he was a quality guy and a really good player," Thompson said. "But he just wasn't interested in playing AAU ball and working for a company."

Littles instead decided to go pro, turning down the New York Knicks of the NBA to play for the Carolina Cougars in the ABA. He later served as an assistant coach in the NBA, and had three brief stints as a head coach—with the Cleveland Cavaliers, Charlotte Hornets and the Denver Nuggets.

There was also a concern among some black players, as well as players from other minority groups, about being trailblazers, especially in the South.

Thompson really wanted to recruit Larry Brown, the former University of North Carolina star who later would become a highly successful coach at UCLA, Kansas and in both the ABA and NBA. For two seasons, 1963-'65, Brown starred for the Akron Goodyear Wingfoots in Ohio, leading them to the AAU national championship in '64.

"I got word that Larry wasn't wild about the tire business and was thinking about leaving Goodyear, so I tried to recruit him to come join us at Phillips and play with the 66ers," Thompson said. "I was excited to try to get him on the team because I thought if we had Larry as point guard, we could win a couple of championships with him.

"He came to Bartlesville for a visit, and I had a great conversation with him about the team. But I learned 40 years later from a mutual friend that on that visit, when Larry also talked to one of our executives about the job, he'd felt some concern whether he would be accepted in the Phillips organization as a Jew. I never thought it would be a problem—I knew the company was opening up."

> *"Gary, I want you to coach the Phillips 66ers…"*

Actually, said Brown, the puzzling treatment he got from Phillips 66 came in 1963, immediately after his college playing career.

"Coming out of North Carolina, I got drafted by the Baltimore Bullets of the NBA then, but in that era if you tried out for the pros then, you were automatically a pro and precluded from playing AAU ball," he said. "So Baltimore came to see me, but they said, 'You know, Larry, you're smaller than we thought.' They doubted a 5 ft. 9 in. guard could make it in the NBA.

"So my coach at UNC, Dean Smith, had a lot of friends at Phillips He was a Kansas grad, and Kansas had always sent a lot of its players on to play for the 66ers. He said he'd send me to Phillips to play there, and I thought that was where I was headed. But then at the last minute, Coach Smith called me in and said, 'Larry, I don't know what happened, but there's some problem at Phillips, and so I'm sending you to Goodyear instead.' Lo and behold, I got to Goodyear, and we won the AAU national championship and I was named the MVP of the tournament."

The next year was Gary Thompson's first season as coach of the Phillips 66ers. "Gary was wonderful with me, but by my second year, when we were talking, I just felt enough loyalty to Goodyear, that felt I shouldn't jump to another AAU team," said Brown.

But he did make a move, becoming an assistant coach briefly at his alma mater. Then he resumed his playing career in the ABA, becoming one of the new league's top players from 1967 through '72 with New Orleans, Oakland, Washington, D.C., Virginia and Denver. Following that, he started his long coaching career in the college and pro ranks, and he's had national championship teams in both. In the 2008-'09 season, he is in his ninth NBA head coaching job, with the Charlotte Bobcats.

Does he feel being a Jew kept him from being a Phillips 66er back in 1963?

"I would hope that's not true," Brown said. "I was all set to play for them, but at the last minute, something came up on their end of it. My career turned out fine anyway. And I will say that when Gary Thompson was talking to me about playing there, he couldn't have treated me any nicer."

Thompson was not getting completely shut out in the recruiting battles, though. He knew where to turn first for help in finding good new players. In November of 1964, as his first 66ers team was starting into its schedule, he wrote a letter to alumni of the Phillips basketball program. Here is that letter:

Dear 66er,

Well, whether you know it or not, yours truly is now coach of the 66ers. Bud decided he had had enough of the traveling, etc., and with his other duties, the coaching was just too much. I felt honored to be considered for the job, and I hope I can meet the challenge.

I wanted to let you know how much we will appreciate any support you can give us. If you know of any outstanding player, either at your own school or at a school in your present area, please let us know about him. That is, if you think he'll fit into our program. Obviously, we can't know about every good player, and we usually get to see only those whom we play against.

A 1965-'65 schedule is attached, and we hope that you'll find time to drop around to see us if we are anywhere close to you.

As to our team, there are a lot of questions to be answered, since nine of our 12 men are new. Bobby Rascoe from Western Kentucky will be playing his third season and Ken Saylors (Arkansas Tech) and Tony Cerkvenik (Arizona State U.) will be playing their second. All three are 6 ft. 4 in. The only thing old on the team is George Durham. So now, there's Old Crow, Old Charter and Old Durham.

Our new players are Tom Black (6 ft. 10 in., South Dakota State U.), Scottie Pierce (6 ft. 7 in., West Texas State U.), Ray Carey (6 ft. 7 in., U. of Missouri), Lou Skurcenski (6 ft. 6 in., Westminster College, Pa.), Tom Patty (6 ft. 6 in., Texas Tech), Ken Ryan (6 ft. 5 in., Loyola of the South), Darel Carrier (6 ft. 4 in., Western Kentucky), Jim Kerwin (6 ft. 3 in., Tulane U.) and Houston Frazier (6 ft. 1 in., East Tennessee State U.).

Well, that's about it. We are going to try our best to get a letter out to you about the first of each month and one after the National AAU tournament. We hope to see you.

Sincerely,
Gary Thompson

That year's schedule, incidentally, was typical for the 66ers—playing 44 games in places stretching from Oklahoma to North Dakota, Montana, Washington, New Mexico, Texas, Louisiana, Georgia, South Carolina, Virginia, New York, Massachusetts, Ohio and points in between.

What was Thompson like as the coach?

"He was very intense, always has been at whatever he does, and now today it's golf," said Jim Kerwin, who came to the 66ers from Tulane where he had been the leading scorer and player-of-the-year in the Southeastern Conference. "He was very disciplined, a no-nonsense guy. He demanded we play hard. But I think he was very fair in treatment of us players, too."

Kerwin has good perspective on what it takes to be a good coach. After his four-year Phillips playing career, he went on to coach basketball at high schools in Kansas and Oklahoma, then at two junior colleges in Oklahoma, then as an assistant to Oklahoma University coach Billy Tubbs from 1984-'90.

Kerwin moved to become an assistant to Kansas State coach Dana Altman for 2 years, and wound up his career as head coach at Western Illinois University for 11 years. He brought his Western Illinois Leathernecks to play in the Iowa State Cyclones' early-season tournaments a couple of times. He retired in 2003 and moved to Norman, Oklahoma.

"Actually, I turned out to be the same kind of coach as Gary Thompson," Kerwin said, "pretty much a disciplined, no-nonsense approach to the game. But, you know, as I look back on what Gary did when he was coaching at Phillips, there was probably a lot of pressure on him. He was succeeding Bud Browning, who had been a national champion and Olympic coach, and here he wasn't much older than his players."

He recalls that Thompson "used to jump right in and play with us a lot in practice, and he was better than we all were. Being a guard, I'd try to play defense on him, and he'd get 20 points on me every time."

Thompson's team offense was fairly deliberate, with set plays, and the defense was man-to-man, Kerwin said. But with all the talent the 66ers had, they also loved to fast break.

"We always had 12 good players at Phillips," said Kerwin. "We all had been college stars—all-conference, a few All-Americans. With that much talent on the same team, we'd play maybe 20 minutes apiece in the games, so everybody would stay fresh. We could hold our own with about anybody."

Was it fun?

"Oh yeah," he said. "We were a bunch of young guys in our 20s, a lot of us were single and we loved Bartlesville. There were a lot of single women around, and we had a couple of guys who liked to get parties started. There'd be a party every other Friday night—with maybe as high as 150 people there—and let me tell you, Gary Thompson definitely didn't go for that!"

Kerwin recalled that he "missed three or four weeks of one season with a bad thigh. So one night, a bunch of us were at a club in Bartlesville, and I'm out on the dance floor, dancing away. All of a sudden, one of the other players came up and said, 'Gary Thompson is here!' I said, 'Nah! No way!' The other guy said Gary was right over by the door, and I looked—and sure enough! The following Monday, he called me into his office and said, 'So, you're too hurt to play, but you're well enough to dance? Explain that.' I was pretty embarrassed."

Kerwin said Thompson took firmer control after police had to break up one of those big Friday night parties at a Bartlesville hotspot. "Gary laid down the law after that one," Kerwin said. "It was 'No more parties, and no more going into establishments in Bartlesville.' If we wanted a few beers, we had to go to a neighboring town, Dewey."

Work rules at Phillips Petroleum were strict, and when the team was in town during the season, the players would have to be in the office by 8 a.m., put in a full day and then have practice at 5:30 p.m. for up to two hours.

"We had to be there by 8, even if we hadn't gotten back to town from a road trip until 3 or 4 in the morning," Kerwin said.

That reminded him of a rugged morning following a road trip to Georgia. "Six of us had missed curfew there," Kerwin said. "Curfew was like 11 at night, and we were out at one of the local establishments until about 1 in the morning. Gary caught us because he was looking for one of us to do a television interview that night, and we were gone. He didn't say anything to us right then.

"The next night was our game, and we played great and won big. Then we flew back to Bartlesville, and didn't get there until 3:30 or 4 a.m. When we got to the Adams Building, we were all ready to head home for some sleep, but he said, 'I want those six guys who missed curfew to be in the gym in 15 minutes for practice.'

"We started practice at 4 a.m., and he ran us 'til 5:30 a.m. Then he told us we still had to be at work by 8 a.m. After that, we nicknamed ourselves 'The Dirty Half-Dozen.'"

Thompson said as he looks back on his coaching years, "it seems almost unbelievable that I was doing bed checks on guys who were college graduates," he said with a laugh. "But at the time, I was a big believer that when we were on the road, we were representing Phillips Petroleum, and we couldn't embarrass the company."

The players would get pretty creative when they occasionally tried to break the rules. Thompson said one night, he was walking to his hotel room, and saw the door ajar of a room where two of his players were staying. So he knocked on the door, looked in and asked if they knew their door was open.

"Tom Patty jumped up quick out of bed, and I said, 'Did you know your door is open?' " Thompson said. "He said no. So I said, 'Well, turn off the TV and get to sleep—you know, we got beat last night.' I glanced in and saw the other bed, with two pair of feet sticking up under the covers, so at first I thought his roommate Ray Carey was there, too. But then as I was walking down the hall I realized I'd only talked to Tom. I thought to myself, 'Well, that didn't look real. These guys aren't going to fool the old coach.'

"So I went back there, the door was still ajar, I knocked and said to Tom, 'Is your roommate in?' Tom kind of put his head down and sheepishly said, 'No, Coach, he isn't.' I went in to look, and Ray had propped up his basketball shoes under the covers, so it looked like he was in bed—but he was gone!"

Thompson said afterward, he figured he better check all the players' rooms, so the two wouldn't think he was just picking on them. "I pretty well knew which players might likely be gone," he said. "I knocked on one door, no answer. I knocked again, no answer. So I went down to the desk clerk, got a key and went back up to the room. I went in and one guy was gone. But the other guy, one of our big centers, Scotty Pierce, was there asleep, snoring, hadn't heard a thing."

Carey, Houston Frazier and Tony Cerkvenik were all suspended for the next game, Thompson recalls. "I had a rule that if they were suspended, I wouldn't let them suit up, that they had to wear street clothes and sit on the bench," Thompson said. "That would hurt their pride a little bit, but players will always come up with something. Ray Carey later told me that he told the other two, 'O.K., when we leave the floor, limp like we're hurt!' "

Another player who was a challenge, but also became one of Thompson's favorites, is Bill Kusleika. He was mentioned earlier here for using the rookie coach's "open door policy" to give him some ideas about how to best handle some teammates. Kusleika was a 6 ft. 3 in. shooter who came to the 66ers after finishing his college career at Tulsa University. He was originally from Duquesne, Pennsylvania, and spent a year at Mansfield State Teacher's College in Pennsylvania, then a year at Bacone Junior College in Oklahoma, and then Tulsa.

He joined the 66ers in the 1965-'66 season and played the team's last 3 years. "Bill Kusleika couldn't run, couldn't jump but had the quickest hands I'd ever seen and he could find a way to beat you," said Thompson. "I didn't have a lot of confidence in him right at first. But later, Bill became our go-to guy many, many times."

Kusleika, retired now in Tulsa after a career teaching and coaching in high schools in that area, recalled that "every day after practice, Gary would have us run laps around the gym in the Adams Building. He would get out in front of us and say, 'Follow me!' Then he'd start running and the rest of us would follow along. I finally figured out that after a lap, I could duck into a broom closet when we went by it, and then when the guys would come by the door, I'd open it up, wave from the closet at a few of them and then close the door again.

"Eventually Gary would yell, 'O.K., one more lap and then you all have to pass me.' I'd jump out of the closet right after he came by, run the extra lap and then sprint right past all those guys who were 6 ft. 8 in. and 6 ft. 10 in. and were worn out—and then I'd pass Gary. At first he'd say, 'Kusleika, man, you're not fast, but you can go all day long!' I don't know how long that lasted before he caught me, and I'm sure I paid for it."

He said the players really admired Thompson, even though he was tough on them. "We all knew he was a real Phillips man, and he was going to do everything by the book," Kusleika said. "But when it came to coaching, he could really show you the ins and outs of how to play the game. He was always a professional about it, but he was also your friend at all the right times. And he knew when to straighten you up, too. I can still hear him saying, 'Son-of-a-biscuit!' You knew he was really mad when you heard that!"

> *"We moved 11 times in first 15 years of marriage..."*

The team had a great year in 1965-'66, finishing with a 47-6 record. Early in that season, the 66ers had a victory which did not seem like such a big one at the time, but by the end of the season, stood out as a huge one—and it's one they've talked about a whole lot in the decades since. On December 6, 1965, they faced little-known Texas Western College, of El Paso, Texas, in an exhibition game played in Hobbs, New Mexico. Phillips won 68-59 over Coach Don Haskins' TWC Miners.

That is the historic Texas Western team that, generally playing with an all-black line-up, did not lose again until their final game of the regular season, a 74-72 loss to the University of Seattle. Then the Miners got hot in the '66 NCAA tournament, winning the national championship over an all-white University of Kentucky team. Texas Western's record for that remarkable season is recorded as 29-1, with the loss to the Phillips 66ers not counted because the 66ers were an AAU team and the game was regarded as an exhibition.

Bobby Rascoe, one of the 66ers put that game in perspective years later in an interview with a sports publication at his alma mater, Western Kentucky University. "Of course, we on the 66ers had all been college players and had already graduated, and we were playing against Texas Western guys that weren't quite as experienced as us," Rascoe was quoted in the "Hilltopper Haven" of June, 1998. "...but they went on to win the NCAA that year, and I think that may have been the only one, or one of the very few, maybe two or three games, that they lost all year long."

Why was the game played in Hobbs, New Mexico? "Hobbs was a great basketball town," said Moe Iba, who was an assistant coach on that Texas Western team and later went on to become a head coach at Memphis State,

Nebraska and Texas Christian. "That's where Ralph Tasker was the basketball coach at Hobbs High School and won about a million games and had a slew of state championships. There was a real active booster club there, and they'd promote games like the one we played with Phillips as fundraisers for their high school sports programs."

(For the record, Tasker's teams didn't really win "about a million games," as Iba said. But his record must be one of the greatest ever among high school coaches. In his 52-year coaching career, 49 of those years with the Hobbs Eagles, Tasker's boys had 1,116 victories against only 289 defeats, and they won 12 state titles. He died in 1999 at age 80, a year after he retired.)

Phillips' coach Gary Thompson, sensing that Texas Western coach Don Haskins had a great team developing, was proud of that victory, and he and Haskins struck up a friendship.

"The next year, they brought us in to play them on their campus in El Paso, and we beat them again," Thompson said, of the 67-61 overtime victory on February 22, 1967. "That Texas Western team was so quick, there was no way we could cover them playing our normal man-to-man defense, so we played zone most of the game, and we almost never played zone."

Thompson said he still enjoys the idea that he "was 2-0 against Haskins." Their friendship would be important years later when Thompson was trying to help find his alma mater, Iowa State, a new men's basketball coach, as you will read later in this book. And they remained friends until the time of Haskins' death in late summer, 2008.

Those 66ers of 1965-'66 also made a memorable road trip to Grand Forks, North Dakota. There they played the University of North Dakota Fighting Sioux—in the middle of a blizzard. It was a very good North Dakota team that was an NCAA Division II national champion. They were coached by Bill Fitch, a Cedar Rapids native who eventually wound up with a long career as a coach in the NBA.

His assistant at North Dakota then was Jimmy Rodgers, a former star player at the University of Iowa who also eventually coached in the NBA. One of their Fighting Sioux players was Phil Jackson, who later coached the Chicago Bulls and Los Angeles Lakers.

"They had 6 or 7 feet of snow on the ground up there, from all the storms and wind," said Thompson. "It was so bad that the North Dakota team had stayed all night in the gym. We flew into Grand Forks and somehow made it to the gym, but the regular referees couldn't get there. So they found one high school referee and one sporting goods salesman to call the game, and I want to tell you, we really got jobbed. It was ridiculous!"

At one point, Thompson stormed off the bench, yelling at the officials and pointing at Fitch while berating him, too. "I told Bill Fitch, 'If you want this game that bad, we'll forfeit and just quit!'" Thompson said. "He just looked at me with a blank face, like he thought I was nuts, and didn't say a word."

A local news photographer snapped a picture of that angry scene. Later, Fitch sent a copy of the photo to Thompson in Bartlesville with this caption scribbled across the bottom of it: "Phillips' Goodwill Ambassador to Grand Forks, N.D.!" And he also attached a sticker of corporate rival Texaco's "Star" logo.

The '65-'66 season ended with the 3-week-long road trip to Puerto Rico.

"Phillips Petroleum entered into a $400 million business deal on a new chemical production complex to be built in Puerto Rico," Thompson recalled. "Back then, the people of Puerto Rico were just nuts about basketball, and their leadership made it part of the business deal that Phillips Petroleum had to send the 66ers to play some basketball games there, spread out over 3 weeks, so we played all over the island. All our wives got to go on the trip, too."

How'd the families manage that, with all their small children back in Bartlesville?

"Our youngest, Scott, was just a year old then, Kim was 7 and Rick was about 5," said Janet Thompson. "As much as I was looking forward to the trip to Puerto Rico, I was so worried about being gone from the kids that long. But my mother (Carrie Sydnes) came down from Iowa to stay with them while we were gone, and that helped me feel better about it. As much fun as we had, I was really glad to get home to them."

Some of the fun on the trip was due to the efforts of one of Gary Thompson's former college opponents.

"In my Iowa State years, I had played against an excellent guard at Kansas State, Juan 'Pachin' Vicens, who was from Puerto Rico," Gary said. "He was the quickest player I'd ever gone up against. Pachin had played some professional ball after K-State, but by 1967, he was back working in the banking industry in Puerto Rico. We got in touch, and he said he wanted to arrange something special for us.

"When we got there, we discovered that Pachin was really the whole island's hero, and everybody wanted to welcome us. He'd lined up two big yachts to carry all of us on the 66ers and our wives out to a separate island, where the island caretaker prepared this fresh lobster feed for us. We were all just in awe!"

Years later, incidentally, when Tim Floyd was coaching at Iowa State and was considering a couple of good high school basketball players in Puerto Rico, Thompson worked the "Pachin connection" again, and his old friend helped the Cyclone coach scout the players.

Jim Kerwin, who played all 4 years that Thompson coached, said he thinks the following year's 66ers "was probably our best team in Gary's era, even though we didn't have the best record."

That 1966-'67 group finished 42-9. They were runners-up in the National AAU tournament to the rival Akron Goodyears. Two of the 66ers, Johnny Beasley from Texas A&M and Harold Sergent from Moorhead State in Kentucky, were named AAU All-Americans.

"We had six players from that team that went to the ABA," said Kerwin. And that meant Thompson faced a huge rebuilding project for the team's final season of 1967-'68. It became a season with a "secret," too.

"By the mid 1960s, with the NBA improving their contracts and the ABA getting ready to start up, we couldn't get the caliber of players we wanted," said George Durham, the sports director.

Sometime during the 1966-'67 season, he had been summoned by G.J. "Pete" Morrison, the vice-president of marketing. "Pete told me that the company's executive committee had decided it wanted to stop the basketball program," said Durham. "We talked about the difficulty in getting the players we thought we needed and knew it wasn't going to get any easier.

> *"After 4 years, I'd satisfied my desire to coach..."*

"I asked him to please give us one more year because I had already scheduled the whole season of games for 1967-'68. He agreed to that. So we played the whole last season knowing it would be the end of it. We felt like we had to keep it from the players, to hold on to the ones we had. And we didn't do any new recruiting.

"We left it up to Gary Thompson to tell the players when the season ended. But he could give them at least a little good news with the bad. He could tell them, 'Well, it's all over, but you've still got your jobs with Phillips.'"

Through that whole season, said Kusleika, the former player, "We weren't really aware of it being the last. Normally, Phillips did most of the real recruiting in April, so we didn't really notice that they were backing off on making contacts with new players earlier. It seems like maybe after Christmas that year, maybe there was some speculation, because I can remember guys were talking about going to try out for NBA or ABA teams."

Kerwin said he "didn't have the slightest idea about it. It seems odd thinking about it now. There was no special ceremony, and no farewell game, in Bartlesville. I kept all the newspaper clippings, and I don't remember that there was any big write-up about Phillips disbanding the program."

Everybody was a little sad about it, of course. "Yeah, it was sad," said Morrison, the vice-president of marketing.. We were giving up something that we'd grown accustomed to having, something we enjoyed and was good for the company. And then it was gone. But times had changed."

He said as he thinks about the corporation running a major league basketball program for so long, "It's kind of unbelievable how much the program cost, but also unbelievable how much good it did. Everywhere the team went, there'd be sell-out crowds of Phillips customers."

The program had also developed many good basketball players into real successes in the business world and beyond. Three Phillips Petroleum CEOs were former players—Boots Adams from Kansas, Bill Martin from Oklahoma University and Pete Silas from Georgetown.

Ray Steiner became Phillips vice-president of sales. Gib Ford became chairman of Converse Inc., the makers of basketball shoes and other sporting goods equipment. Joe Dean was an assistant to Ford at Converse, then became the lead broadcaster on radio and TV coverage of Southeastern Conference basketball, then in a third career became athletic director at his alma mater Louisiana State University.

Mickey Wittman, a University of Miami star who played on the last Phillips team, wound up with Goodyear Tire & Rubber Co., managing assignments for the Goodyear Blimps at major sporting events and festivals around the U.S. Charlie Bowerman, who played three years in the early 1960s, had a 38-year career with Phillips Petroleum, becoming executive vice-president and a member of the board.

The Bowermans, the Skurcenskis, the Steiners and others that remained in Bartlesville for careers became social leaders in the community. In fact, nearly all the former 66ers players did well in life. And they've generally been thankful for all the experiences that playing for Phillips gave them, a point that has been made over and over when they've gathered for the eight or nine Phillips 66ers reunions held since 1968.

Gary Thompson said being the coach when the program ended did not bother him so much. Like at other major turning points in his life, "it just seemed like it was time to move on to something else."

He knew he did not want to continue coaching.

"No, I had satisfied my desire to coach," he said. "I liked it those 4 years, but I wasn't excited about chasing kids all over the country, recruiting. And if I had tried to stay in it, I might have had trouble with all the discipline problems that came along later in basketball. I was a pretty no-nonsense guy, stressing the fundamentals, and demanding that you be a good role model to young kids. I was kind of old school that way."

He and his family were ready to head home to Iowa.

Chapter 16

An All-American Turned Entrepreneur

"I'M competitive." I've heard Gary Thompson say that a dozen times in our interviews for this book.

He's told me how competitive he has been in far more than just basketball and baseball. He has always been one to get right after it, in everything from academic courses, to roller skating, horseshoes, bowling, the card game "Bridge," golf, ping pong, even the planning of his high school reunions ("I always try to get every single classmate there!") and, as you might already expect, in business.

Those who have observed Thompson's work patterns as the president of Gary Thompson Oil Company over the last 10 to 15 years, really have no idea what a dynamo he was in earlier years.

In recent years, his son Rick Thompson and son-in-law Tom Wierson have taken over the day-to-day leadership of the company, which operates convenience stores, has about 50 employees and does commercial property development around the Ames area. Gary Thompson typically arrives at the offices on South Duff Avenue about 9:30 a.m., after an hour of coffee and conversation with a group of old friends at the Dutch Oven Bakery on the east edge of downtown. He generally leaves the office for lunch, returns in the early afternoon and sticks around for another couple of hours. Then he leaves for golf, or for meetings about some causes or project at Iowa State University, or he joins his wife Janet to follow the school and sports activities of their grandchildren.

There was also a time, when he was at the height of his side career as a color commentator on telecasts of college basketball, that he'd be gone as much as 4 to 5 days per week, traveling to and from games around the Midwest and beyond.

"I was fortunate here," he said. "When I bought the business, it was a going business, and I was the leaseholder and supplier for gas stations that were already operating. That's why when I eventually started broadcasting, it was easy for me to be gone like I was. Plus, I've always had good, dependable people around me."

However, in the earliest years of Gary Thompson Oil Company, there were very few days away from the office and the hours were long.

He bought the business in 1968 when he was a 33-year-old entrepreneur, in a time before anybody was using that word. Up till then, he had worked 11½ years with Phillips Petroleum, with most of that time being at corporate headquarters in Bartlesville, Oklahoma.

Now, he was going out on his own, buying a Phillips "distributorship," or "jobbership" as some referred to it. He would take over the lease of stations in the Ames area that were owned by Phillips, and he would have the exclusive right to sell Phillips 66 gasoline and other company products in that area.

Gary Thompson came back to Ames with a great reputation, an unusual list of experiences from his basketball travels around the world, keen insights into the corporate environment at Phillips headquarters, and a real fire-in-the-belly to succeed in his own operation.

At home, he had Janet and three children—age 10 and younger—cheering him on, and depending on him, too. He did not want to fail in the city where he was a sports hero. He fully understood that while his sports experience might help him in business, it did not guarantee his success. He was going to have to work hard, and work smart, to be as successful as he wanted to be.

Actually, his resolve was tested before he got back to Ames. He had to make a strong stand for himself at Phillips headquarters, just to get the opportunity to buy the Ames distributorship. Thompson felt he had been promised in early 1968, after the longtime Ames distributor Charlie Sorenson died unexpectedly, that he would be given an opportunity to present his credentials and financial plan to buy and operate the Ames jobbership.

He said he expected that he would at least be interviewed for the opportunity. But by whom? The interview wasn't happening.

"I'd been really impressed with Gary Thompson in the sales department," said G.J. "Pete" Morrison, now retired in Bartlesville, who had become assistant general sales manager at corporate headquarters in 1959, and general sales manager a few years later. "It didn't matter what assignment we gave him, he did it to perfection. We had him driving projects for new gas stations, making proposals for new locations. It was a period of real growth and expansion for us. Plus, Gary never met a man who didn't like him. I knew he had a great future in the business."

As they became better acquainted, Morrison said, "We talked about Gary's home in Iowa, and he said if the opportunity ever presented itself, he'd like to go back to Ames as a Phillips jobber. I told him I'd help him get that opportunity eventually."

During the 1967-'68 basketball season, when Thompson was coaching the last 66ers team, he was surprised to learn that Sorenson, who for 30 years or more had been the Phillips "jobber" in the Ames area, had died of a heart attack while watching the Bob Hope Golf Tournament in Palm Springs, California, where Sorenson was spending the winter. In fact, Sorenson and Thompson had talked between 1962 and '64, when Thompson was a Phillips district representative in the Cedar Rapids area, about Thompson joining the Sorenson Oil Company in Ames. But Thompson had turned that down when Sorenson's offer did not include an option to buy the business eventually.

"I really wanted to do that," Thompson said, "but when Charlie said he couldn't grant me the buy-in option, I thought I had too good a future with Phillips to leave for something that would not provide us with as much family security. It was a business decision, and Charlie and I remained good friends. I would visit with him when we came back to Ames on vacation."

Now in the late winter and spring of '68, Thompson found himself "negotiating with Phillips to come back to Ames as the Phillips jobber. When I had talked to Pete Morrison during the season, he assured me again I'd get the opportunity to go back and talk to the division manager in Iowa about buying the business in Ames."

> *"He didn't want to fail in the city where he'd been a sports hero…"*

After basketball was over, Thompson was working in the Phillips advertising department in Bartlesville, but he was also "talking back and forth with people in Des Moines about when I was going to come up and see about buying the jobbership," he said.

"I think it was in late May or early June, I called and talked to the division manager. He said they wouldn't know anything for 2 weeks, because Sorenson's attorney was working on some details and he would be on a fishing trip for the next 2 weeks. The next day, I was at work and my boss Floyd Burk, the regional manager who oversaw that divisional office in Iowa, said, 'Gary, they're making a decision up in Des Moines, and you probably are not going to be really happy about it. I received a letter in the mail this morning, and you're not going to be awarded the Phillips jobbership.' They were going to give that jobbership to somebody else!"

Thompson said he has "always been one to go up a tree when people lie to me or lie about me. The guy in Des Moines had just told me '2 weeks,' and he knew that day when he was talking with me that he'd already sent in his recommendation!" Thompson went immediately to his mentor Morrison, the company vice-president of marketing in addition to being the sales manager.

"I was really hot when I went in to see Pete," Thompson said. "I told him that I felt I'd been promised the opportunity for that jobbership, and then told him what was going on in the Des Moines office. I said, 'Pete, I know what I'm going to say could get me fired, but I'm not worried about that because I've got a job with another company waiting for me if I want it. And if that guy in Des Moines is an example of the kind of people Phillips has in management, I don't want any part of Phillips!' I just unloaded on him."

Morrison said, "Now, Gary, wait a minute. Simmer down here." He calmly repeated his earlier assurance to Thompson and asked him one question, "Did they visit with you about the jobbership in Ames like I promised you?" Thompson said no. Morrison said, "Gary, go back to work, and I'll get back to you soon."

Morrison recalled in a later interview, "What had happened is that we had an assistant sales manager in Iowa who wanted to put another person in as the new jobber in Ames—not Gary. I overruled him. It was one of the best business decisions I ever made, because Gary through the years has done an outstanding job there."

Thompson says he has spent nearly 40 years thanking Morrison. "Pete was always known as a man of real integrity and real fairness, and he proved it to me back in 1968," Thompson said. "Every year when I send him a Christmas card, or any other time I write him, I always add a P.S. saying, 'And thanks again for giving us the opportunity to live in Ames, Iowa!' "

So when the deal was agreed upon for Gary and Janet Thompson to buy the jobbership, they obtained financing from Dean Knudson at the old University Bank and Trust in Ames. Knudson had been another person who'd gone out of his way to help Gary Thompson through the years, beginning with conversations they had during Gary's student years at Iowa State.

On August 1, 1968, Gary Thompson Oil Company took over from Sorenson Oil Company in Ames.

Thompson Oil then began supervising three local Phillips 66 gas stations, which were still owned by Phillips Petroleum but leased to Thompson. The actual station operators were called "Phillips dealers," and they hired their own employees. Thompson Oil was their supplier of Phillips gasoline products. In addition, Thompson Oil was contracted to be Phillips supplier for three other stations that were owned independently by Carroll Rex, Clarence "Scoop" Small and Jim Inglis.

Two employees came with the deal—Virginia Beese, a part-time secretary and office manager who continued to work for Thompson Oil for more than 35 years, and Jim Inglis, one of the independent station owners who also supplied the car batteries and tires that Thompson Oil offered at its stations.

The company's first office was behind one of its stations at 508 Lincoln Way in Ames, in a complex shared with a Mayfair Cleaners that is still there. New boss Gary Thompson didn't bring any radical new business philosophy to the operation. "I never had anything written down, like a mission statement, but I just tried to grow the business," he said.

And he began using a personal touch whenever possible.

"In those years, when customers used credit cards, we'd have each billing card to confirm the numbers, and then we'd send it to Phillips for mailing to the customers with their total bill," Thompson said. "So I'd take time to write a note on the card, thanking the people by name for their business and then signing it. They'd be mailed out to customers that way from Phillips, and we got a lot of comments back about those notes."

He recalled that his competitiveness "caused me some real headaches in my second or third year of business.

"I was pushing one of my station dealers too hard," Thompson said. "One day he said, 'Here are the keys, I quit,' and he walked out. Well, I was standing there realizing I was going to have to find a new dealer for the station, and that would take some time to find the right person. The guy who quit was probably thinking I'd have to close down the station in the meantime, and I just wasn't going to let that happen.

"So I operated it by myself for a month, and it about killed me. I had to work 20 hours a day doing that! I'd get up at 5 in the morning, open up the station at 6, work the drive and the cash register until 11 o'clock at night when I'd finally close. Then I'd have to do the books for the day's business.

"I was crawling into bed about 1 in the morning, then getting up again at 5 and starting all over. I couldn't even leave for meals. Either Janet would bring me something, or I'd find somebody who would run over to a Henry's Hamburgers stand that was nearby and they'd buy me a sack of the 15-cent hamburgers. But I was able to keep the station operating until I finally got another dealer hired."

Despite how busy he was at work, Thompson took time in his first years back in Ames to join with 10 men and start the community's first Little League Baseball program.

Among them were Judge John McKinney, Ames Tribune publisher Verle Burgason, former high school coach Ev Cochrane, then-Ames High School football coach Phil Johnson, William Carroll, Bob Case, Richard Matt, Howard Mullica and Arnie Zediker. Not only were they the program's founders, most of them also served as coaches of the teams in those early years. The players who went through that program included their own sons and a lot of other Ames boys—and many of them are still talking about the experience nearly 40 years later.

"Gary Thompson and John Nervig were my coaches on the 'Gary Thompson Oil Tigers' in the Ames T-shirt league when I was 7 years old in 1972, and I can still tell you we wore red T-shirts and red wool ball caps—how's that?" recalled Bob Gostomski, a food broker in Des Moines who also does play-by-play on KRNT radio of high school sports in the capital city.

"Of course, I didn't have any idea back then that Gary was anybody but my friend Scottie Thompson's dad, and one of our neighbors," Gostomski continued. "But he and Mr. Nervig were great coaches. What they gave us, at that young age, was all the baseball fundamentals, and they made it fun. I do remember that they also gave us pretty good 'incentives,' too. After the games we'd sit around the 'team cooler' and all of us have a Shasta pop, and sometimes they'd treat us at the Baskin-Robbins Ice Cream store, too.

"But beyond the baseball, the bigger things they taught us were that we should play hard, and that we also needed to learn how to win right—and how to lose right, too. I remember all that stuff vividly to this day, and it's helped shape my life."

A core group of players from those earliest Thompson Oil teams were in the line-up for Ames High's baseball teams a decade later, Gostomski said. And he personally became so enchanted with baseball that while he was going to Iowa State University, he coached 5 years of Little League baseball himself.

By the early 1970s, leaders around Ames were realizing what a dynamo Gary Thompson was becoming as a businessman, how involved he was getting in the community, and how everyone in the territory seemed to know him. In 1973, they elected him president of the Ames Chamber of Commerce.

He enjoyed that experience, and stayed active in Chamber affairs, but when people began pushing him to run for elective office, he drew a line. "I had people asking me to run for mayor," Thompson said, "but you know, I've never been a political guy, except to vote and occasionally give a candidate a little money."

As the years went on, one of the reasons he became more successful, he said, is that he became "a good copier" with his business. He had maintained a friendship he initiated with the Nordstrom family in Cedar Rapids from 1962 to '64, and they had developed a chain of about 40 service stations that eventually was turned into today's HandiMarts. In August of 2007, Casey's General Stores bought 33 of the HandiMarts in Iowa.

> *"I'd take time to write a personal note with each bill..."*

"The Nordstroms are in their fourth generation in the business and have always been excellent operators, real innovators," Thompson said. "So I'd call Bill Nordstrom, who was running their company back then, and ask him about things they were doing in their business.

"When they started putting in 'mini-service' islands in addition to full-service, I asked him if he minded me copying that. He said, 'No, go right ahead—that's flattering.' They put in car washes, and we did, too. And on business and promotion ideas, Nordstroms were great to work with."

Thompson, who knew the value of good promotional work from his years in sports, loved doing promotions for his new business.

"Phillips was pretty good at coming up with ideas and merchandise to use," he said. "One year, they had one with new glassware to use at meals. So we bought all this glassware in advance. Then one Saturday, a bunch of our dealers, friends and I went door to door all over Ames, giving every home a free glass wrapped up in paper, telling them they could get another free one each time they came to one of our gas stations and got at least an 8-gallon fill-up. You could complete your 'set of eight' free glasses by coming in seven times.

"In that group we had Herb Hibbs, "Scoop" Small, Carroll Rex, Si Jacobson and Roger Smiley, and my memory is that it took us most of the day to cover the town. That glassware was pretty good, and the promotion worked, too. Janet and I later went to a dinner party at a banker's house, and they used our glasses!" (The Thompsons didn't mention anything to the banker about recognizing the glassware.)

They did cross-promotions with Jim Miller and his Kentucky Fried Chicken restaurants. "We'd hand out tickets that you could get two KFC dinners for the price of one if you bought at least 8 gallons of gas from us," Thompson said. "Later, he went into roast beef sandwiches, and we did the same kind of promotion again. We learned that it's always good to do promotions with food, because nearly everybody understands the value of the food item you're using."

One promotion went awry.

"We had a group within the Ames Chamber of Commerce called 'Cyclone Ambassadors' that was trying to help the athletic department at Iowa State," Thompson said. "One of the ambassadors, Sam Jennison, came up with an idea for a new tradition to make football games a little more fun at old Clyde Williams Field, and Sam got Ted Tedesco and me involved.

"We borrowed this beautiful black horse from somebody and nicknamed it 'Cyclone.' Then we had one of the members of the Rodeo Club at the university come to the games with the horse. When the football team would score, the rider would get on the horse and gallop it up and down the sideline, waving an ISU banner. We thought it'd also be a good promotion for the Chamber and for us as business owners, too.

"That went O.K. until the third or fourth game," Thompson continued. "Then some guy on the sidelines took a couple of steps backward without looking, and the horse ran right over him. And that was the end of that tradition."

There was another promotion that had Thompson wondering for a few frightening moments if he might be risking his whole business in some foolishness—but then it turned out fine.

"In our early years of business, Iowa State was playing Nebraska at Clyde Williams Field, and I had what I thought would be a great idea," he said. "We hired a helicopter, and we met 'Cy,' the Iowa State mascot, somewhere away from the stadium. The plan was to put Cy in the helicopter, and we had arranged with ISU to let us fly him right into the stadium and deliver him to the football field, just before the game. We'd have our Phillips 66 signs out there on the field around where the helicopter was going to land.

"So I'm sitting in the stands, really pretty nervous about whether this would work, and here comes the helicopter coming in real low over the top of the stadium. But instead of Cy being safety-belted into his seat, Cy has his leg hanging out of the helicopter door, holding on with one hand, waving to the crowd with the other! The crowd goes absolutely bananas, and I'm starting to think, 'What if he falls out of there and gets hurt bad, or dies on the field? What if we killed Cy?' Well, the helicopter landed on the 20-yard line and Cy jumped out on the field without any problem. The place went absolutely nuts, and I took a big deep breath that we got through it."

Everyone was talking about Gary Thompson Oil Co. and Phillips 66 for weeks to come. Thompson said that, years later, "a young man came walking up to me at an ISU sports event, shook hands and said, 'Gary, remember the promotion when you flew Cy into Clyde Williams Field? I was the Cy!"

Gary didn't know whether to hug and thank him, or give him a long overdue scolding.

The Broadcasting Years

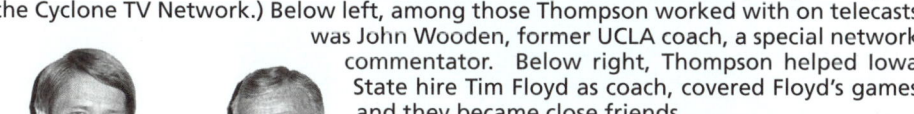

GAME TIME IN PRIME TIME. Gary Thompson ended 34 years of commentary on telecasts of college basketball on March 2, 2005, covering an Iowa State victory over Missouri in Ames. For that broadcast, the Cyclone Television Network reunited Thompson with Jay Randolph, play-by-play man from St. Louis, for 19 years Thompson's partner on "Big Eight Conference Games of the Week." They are shown opening coverage of the game in front of a camera operated by Michael Ericson. (Photo by Roger Riley, of the Cyclone TV Network.) Below left, among those Thompson worked with on telecasts was John Wooden, former UCLA coach, a special network commentator. Below right, Thompson helped Iowa State hire Tim Floyd as coach, covered Floyd's games and they became close friends.

HELPING TELL THE STORY. Gary Thompson's television work allowed him to work with some very well-known coaches and athletes. Clockwise from upper left, he's shown with Don Haskins of Texas-El Paso, Johnny Orr of Iowa State, Larry Eustachy of Iowa State cutting down the net after a big victory, Bobby Knight of Indiana and Texas Tech, and former Iowa State player Julius Michalik. The latter photo was used on the cover of an Iowa State basketball media information booklet. Said Knight: "Gary always wanted to know things that might happen in the game, so he could explain them better to the viewers. He understands coaches so well, he'd know just what questions to ask to get the information he wanted."

THE 1970s STYLE. During Gary Thompson's long broadcasting career, the game of basketball changed a lot—and so did fashions! In the top photo at the right, check Thompson's suit as he chatted pre-game with his fellow commentator John Wooden, the former UCLA coach. In the middle photo, there was a lot of the mid-1970s style when Gary interviewed Notre Dame coach Digger Phelps before a non-conference game at Kansas, with the KU coach Ted Owens waiting his turn.

WORKING WITH THE BEST. Gary Thompson not only did game analysis on the "Big Eight Conference Game of the Week" telecasts, but he also was frequently assigned by the networks to do top national and regional games, especially during the tournaments. On those broadcasts, he often worked with some of the nation's best known play-by-play commentators, like Dick Enberg (shown here), Bob Costas, Don Criqui, Charlie Jones, Fred White, Jack Buck, Gary Bender, Tom Hammond, Ray Scott and others.

FRIENDSHIPS & AWARDS. Gary Thompson made a lot of friends during his broadcasting career. He made a special point of always trying to get to know the production crews he was working with, and he is shown in the top photo visiting before a game with camera operator Michael Ericson of the Cyclone TV Network. (Photo by Roger Riley, of the Cyclone TV Network.) He became friends with Lute Olson (center photo) while covering Olson's games when he was coaching at Iowa, and their friendship remained after Olson moved on to Arizona. Below, Thompson (second from right) is shown being inducted into the Iowa Broadcasters Association Hall of Fame near the end of his television career. With him are, left to right, Ray Cole, general manager of WOI-TV in Des Moines, who nominated Thompson; Bill Wells, general manager of the Des Moines Radio Group, who was president of the IBA at the time, and Jim Field, general manager and sports director of KJAN Radio in Atlantic, who was IBA vice-president.

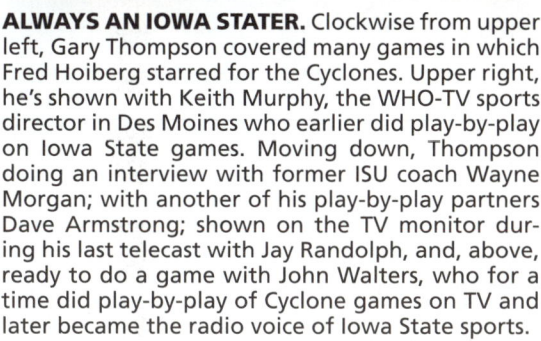

ALWAYS AN IOWA STATER. Clockwise from upper left, Gary Thompson covered many games in which Fred Hoiberg starred for the Cyclones. Upper right, he's shown with Keith Murphy, the WHO-TV sports director in Des Moines who earlier did play-by-play on Iowa State games. Moving down, Thompson doing an interview with former ISU coach Wayne Morgan; with another of his play-by-play partners Dave Armstrong; shown on the TV monitor during his last telecast with Jay Randolph, and, above, ready to do a game with John Walters, who for a time did play-by-play of Cyclone games on TV and later became the radio voice of Iowa State sports.

STORIES WERE THICK. The morning of Gary Thompson's last college basketball telecast in March, 2005, there was a fun coffee gathering in Ames that brought together (left to right) Thompson, Jay Randolph, former Missouri coach and Tigers' TV analyst Norm Stewart, Missouri play-by-play broadcaster Chris Gervino, and former Iowa State football coach and broadcaster Jim Walden. The last telecast also enabled the reunion, shown in the second photograph, of four people who had teamed on broadcasts of dozens of games in earlier years—Thompson, former Ames mayor Ted Tedesco who worked as a statistican for the TV games, broadcaster Jay Randolph and producer Bob Helmers.

TAKING A BOW. Above, referee Scott Thornley, of Pocatello, Idaho, a top basketball official, was working Thompson's last college broadcast and wished him well. Left, Gary makes notes in a media briefing, with Janet Thompson listening, too.

SAYS IT ALL. Iowa State officials surprised Gary Thompson at halftime of his last college basketball broadcast by calling him to the floor for special recognition. When that happened, the Iowa State students in the "Cyclone Alley" cheering section hoisted letters to spell out their appreciation. (Photo by Roger Riley, Cyclone TV Network.) Right, during the ceremony Thompson got a big hug from "Cy," the Iowa State mascot. (Photo from ISU Sports Information.) Above, broadcast partners Jay Randolph and Thompson. (Photo by Roger Riley.) "I'm not going anywhere," Thompson said that night. "I'm just moving to a seat about 15 rows up. I always said, I wanted to leave while they were still wanting me to continue, rather than waiting for them to ask me if I was going to retire. You want to get out ahead of the broom!"

GENUINELY GRATEFUL. Gary Thompson waves in thanks to Iowa State fans after he was recognized at halftime of his last college broadcast in 2005. His wife Janet was on the floor with him. Near the end of the game that night, play-by-play broadcaster Jay Randolph congratulated Thompson, who responded: "Jay, I'll repeat what I said here 48 years ago when they retired my number. What I said then, I say again now—Iowa State has always given me more than I've been able to give back. But I'm going to keep trying, and see if I can catch up!" (Photos from ISU Sports Information.)

Chapter 17

Thompson Oil Grows and Diversifies

IF you're a person who doesn't cope well with change, you probably have not been working in the petroleum marketing business the last 40 years, or at least not working in it for very long.

When Gary Thompson Oil Co. was launched in Ames in the summer of 1968, gas stations still had attendants running out to pump gas into your car, check the oil levels and wash your windows. In fact, when Gary's son Rick Thompson started working in the stations as a 14-year-old high school kid in the mid 1970s, he did all that. He remembers that "the rest of the business was always called 'TBA'—tires, batteries and accessories."

About that time, change started happening, fast, and has continued happening. Phillips Petroleum sold all its stations in 1977, with many "jobbers" like Thompson stepping up to buy them.

Within a couple of years, "mini-service" islands began appearing, where you could buy gas for a penny or two cheaper per gallon, but you had to wash your own car windows and had to ask if you wanted your oil checked.

By 1982, when Rick Thompson (shown above in his earlier days as a ball boy) joined his father's company full-time, they were studying the idea of transforming their gas stations into the convenience stores we all know today. Doing so required more property. The family formed TOMCO, a limited liability corporation to begin investing in commercial real estate around Ames.

By 1985, Rick was named vice-president of the company and began functioning like a chief operating officer might in a larger corporation, as well as doing most of the gasoline purchasing and marketing. In 1986, they had torn down one of their original stations at 414 South Duff Avenue in Ames and built their first convenience store there. Later they moved their company headquarters to a suite of offices on the south end of that building.

In 1989, Gary Thompson Oil Co. changed the name of its stores to "Swift

Stops," while retaining the oil company name for its overall operation.

In 1994, Gary's son-in-law Tom Wierson joined the company as operations and personnel manager after a dozen years in the insurance business in Des Moines. And Scott Thompson, youngest of Gary and Janet Thompson's three children, left an accounting firm in Des Moines to start his own CPA firm in the Ames area, with his office among those at Gary Thompson Oil Co. He began doing some of the family businesses' accounting, too. His company is named Tax Pros/Scott Thompson CPA.

In 1996, Thompson Oil moved from being exclusively a Phillips 66 marketer to begin also offering AMOCO products from the company formerly known in the Midwest as Standard Oil Co.

Meanwhile, competition has steadily increased, with the large convenience store chains—QuikTrip, Kwik Shop, Casey's General Stores and Kum & Go—all leading the market. When they open larger stations, with more store inventory, brighter lights and colors, and bigger parking lots, the smaller operations like Thompson Oil have to do the same.

> *"It gradually became a family business..."*

It has been a time, as Kum & Go co-founder Bill Krause of West Des Moines once told me, when "you don't want to fall in love with your assets." New street and highway developments could quickly make today's hottest convenience store location into a forgotten corner, and just as quickly turn some weed patch into your best store property.

So Gary Thompson Oil Co. and TOMCO have proved themselves to be nimble, acquiring properties that they might eventually develop into their own store properties, or possibly as commercial developments where they lease space to several retail firms. They owned 15 such properties around Ames in 2008, Rick Thompson said.

A very attractive example of how they develop commercial properties, and not include a convenience store, is on South Duff Avenue in the south part of Ames, which they completed in 2007. Several national or regional chains lease space there—Cold Stone Creamery ice cream, Sport Clips haircuts, Pancheros Mexican Grill, Check 'n' Go financial store and Jimmy John's gourmet sandwiches.

My goodness, they've now moved their company headquarters four times over the years and decided in 2007 to close the flagship convenience store adjacent to the company headquarters at 414 South Duff "because the store had gotten out-of-date and the lot didn't have as much room as we think a convenience store now needs," Rick Thompson said.

"So we remodeled the store space, and leased it to U.S. Cellular," a national marketer of cell phone services and other communications products. He said the option of moving Thompson Oil's offices to a new location is always under consideration. But they spent a lot of time and money making improvements in the summer of 2008, after the offices were flooded in late May and early June, the result of several days of heavy rain in Ames and to the northwest.

The number of employees has grown from three in 1968, including Gary Thompson, to more than 50 today.

They have six convenience stores, five of them in Ames and one on the northwest corner of the Des Moines metro area—the latter one is located along busy Iowa Highway 141, just north of the interchange with Interstate Highways 80 and 35 as they loop around Des Moines. That location, Gary Thompson said, "needs to be rebuilt but it's so busy it's been hard to plan a project there."

They also supply three other convenience stores owned by others—a Phillips dealer in Boone and two BP stores in Ames.

Rick Thompson said the company decided long ago to hire common carrier trucking companies to deliver gasoline to their stations. "Owning trucks seemed like another area of the businesses we didn't want to get into," he said.

Among the employees, stores supervisor Mike Fitzgerald has been with the Thompsons since they hired him in 1989 to run their first convenience store. They'd had a business relationship with the Fitzgerald family that started even earlier, when Thompson Oil began supplying the station Fitzgerald's parents owned in Boone.

Denise Van Marel has been a part-time bookkeeper since the early 1990s, and receptionist Liz Parker is the newest office employee, having joined the company in 2006.

"When you get out at the store level, there is a lot of turnover at the entry level clerk positions," said Rick Thompson. "From managers on up, the jobs are pretty stable."

Larry Parr, manager of the north Swift Stop near North Grand Mall in Ames, has been with the company for more than a decade. Gail Warren and Brad Hurd are also long-time store managers for the company.

For as much as Thompson Oil has grown through the years, it is still a small company with very much a "family" feel, especially within the headquarters. And they all got a real jolt on June 23, 2006, when Jayne Nelson, their secretary and receptionist for 10 years, was killed in a car accident on her way home from work to Roland.

"Jayne's death was a real shock," Rick Thompson said. "It really hit us hard. It was not only a matter of dealing with the emotions of losing someone who everybody liked, but there was the challenge that the business could not just stop. She had done a whole lot of jobs, and done them really well, probably more than we realized before her death. And in a small company like this, you don't really have back-ups for people, you know? Oh, we can fill in for each other for a short time when one of us goes on vacation, but when you lose somebody as involved as Jayne was, you've got to find a good replacement right away."

Gary Thompson recalls fondly how Nelson, after her first year on the job, once told him, "Your family all works together in the office, eat lunch together, go to all the basketball games together, do all the holidays together, and you still get along. That doesn't happen in most families."

The Thompsons have always been good promoters, especially in connection with activities at Iowa State University or around the Ames area, and on in-store promotions. Rick Thompson acknowledges they've been slow to figure out how to use the Internet for promotional purposes, but they use it extensively in pricing and research.

Thompson Oil got a fun burst of publicity nationally in 2004 when one of their customers, Gary Denner, then 35, of Nevada, Iowa, won a national drawing to shoot four free throws for $40,000 in a Phillips Petroleum-sponsored contest at the halftime of a semi-finals game in the Big 12 men's basketball tournament in Dallas, Texas. Not only was the TV coverage nice on the sports channel ESPN, but the Iowa media had fun with the story when it turned out that Denner had never been a basketball player.

So, former Iowa State All-American Gary Thompson and Iowa State assistant coach Bob Sundvold scheduled a couple of practice sessions for Denner at Hilton Coliseum, home of the Cyclones, and coached him on how to shoot free throws. In Dallas, with Thompson on the floor with him, Denner made one of his four free throws and won $10,000. "But I hit the rim on all of them," Denner later bragged to his hometown newspaper, the *Nevada Journal*.

When you study Thompson Oil, and get acquainted with the key players, you can begin to identify three key things that have made it successful: 1) The staff members seem to enjoy their jobs; 2) they genuinely enjoy dealing with the public, and 3) they have pretty well stayed with Gary Thompson's generally conservative approach to operations and investments and that has helped keep the company from over-extending.

"When I was growing up in the 1940s and '50s, it seemed like I would hear so many adults saying they just hated their jobs," said Gary Thompson. "I always thought that must just be awful to feel that way. I made up my mind it wasn't going to be like that for me."

And it hasn't been, his wife Janet Thompson said. "Gary has always loved going to work," she said. "He's loved every job he's had."

He was somewhat concerned about their son Rick wanting to join the company in 1982, after Rick had completed his associate degree at Des Moines Area Community College.

"Both Janet and I wanted him to join the business, but we wanted to be sure that that is what he really wanted, and we didn't want to push him," Gary said. "I'd seen from Phillips that father-and-son combinations can be very good or very bad.

"But it didn't take long to see that he really wanted to be here. In fact, his mother has had to tell him a few times over the years to slow down and spend more time with his family. I hate to say this, but he's far-better versed in business than I am."

Rick Thompson says it was easy to immerse himself in the business "because I liked it so much. What I do is different every day, and it seems like there's a new challenge every day. In my role, I'm overseeing the marketing and distribution of the gasoline—and that changes constantly—and I oversee the commercial properties, looking for tenants, working on the leases and contractors.

"It may seem like tedious, detailed work to somebody else, but I've always thought it's really interesting. Especially in those earlier years, I felt like there was so much I wanted to do and learn, I couldn't get here early enough or stay late enough."

Tom Wierson said he was wearying of the daily commute to Des Moines from Ames the dozen years he worked with Allied Insurance, and he had mentioned to Gary in the early 1990s that "if they were ever considering growing the staff at the oil company, I'd be interested. Being in a family business, after being in a larger corporation, sounded good, and being in Ames sounded great."

He said he's liked doing the "employee hiring, firing, discipline and wage administration" in a close environment that has him working directly with people. "I seem to do a lot of trouble shooting," he said. "I'm kind of the fix-it guy with the company."

Wierson said it has been neither intimidating nor awkward working with his father-in-law as his ultimate boss because of Gary's manner and his business experience.

"I realized early on that Gary has a real keen business sense," Wierson said. "He has a real ability to read people, and an ability to get right to it. He listens to Rick and me when we're briefing him on something we're considering doing, and after he asks just a few questions, he seems to understand it completely. He'll listen with an open mind to how we think things are, and then he can add his experience to what we're thinking, and that is really valuable."

Gary Thompson said Wierson "has been a real asset to our company, particularly in the area of construction. When we're building new properties, he makes sure they're built the right way, and has saved the company a lot of money with his expertise in construction."

The Thompson Oil headquarters staff also seems genuinely to enjoy dealing with the public.

"We don't really have a motto, but I've always talked a lot about 'Cleanliness & Friendliness,'" Gary Thompson said. "If your place is clean and everybody is friendly, the public likes coming in and trading with you."

From the boss on down, they'll all stop and visit, something that is increasingly rare in business.

For the 20 years that their flagship convenience store was in the same building as the company headquarters—with gas pumps out front on the driveway—"we'd get to see a lot of people when they were coming in for gas or stopping in the store," Rick Thompson said. "Since we closed the store and leased the space out, it's seemed a little lonely here in the offices, actually."

Gary Thompson has always had the office up front in the headquarters and, when customers could see that he was there, more than a few would stop in for a quick "hello" and chat. His generally conservative approach to business and finance has been key.

"When Rick was coming into the business, I told him that if you work hard, and treat the money like it's your own, you won't have a problem," Gary said. "We've also talked a lot over the years about how, when we're considering something new, that it's a good idea to imagine the worst-case scenario and then ask yourself, 'If that happens, can we cover it?' If we can, then it's probably a deal we should do."

Rick Thompson said "a phrase that all of us Thompson kids have heard all our lives from Dad is 'Save your shickles! Save your shickles!' I swear, we're going to put it on his tombstone. We'd all get to an age where we'd finally say, 'Dad, just what is a shickle?' But after being in on the decision making in the business, I've come to believe that 'Save your shickles!' is a pretty good idea."

How has he viewed his parents as business owners and mentors?

"Well, I don't know if 'frugal' is the right word," Rick said. "Maybe 'conservative' is more accurate. They certainly do their homework. They look at every angle before they move. Everything is well thought-out. Dad doesn't ever do things on a whim.

"He has to slow me down on things, now and then, and it's usually turned out to be a good idea to slow down a little. He's got such a good business sense, and while his basic business philosophy is to grow the company, he never goes overboard. He has never tried to grow too quick."

> *"You all work together, and you all still get along…"*

Gary Thompson was starting into the gas station and convenience store business about the same time that a few other Iowa families did, too—the Krauses and Gentles with Kum & Go, the Lambertis with Casey's General Stores, the Pesters with Pester Derby Oil, the Nordstroms with HandiMarts. Those families operated their companies with more aggressive growth plans. Did Thompson ever want to make his business substantially bigger?

"No, not really," he said. "You know, when I first got into the business in Ames, I was wholesaling gasoline. Then I started getting involved in broadcasting, and because I was a wholesaler, I could be gone when I needed to be for games. I liked what I was doing with TV, and we had enough units to live like we wanted to.

"Plus, we didn't know then if the kids would want to come into the business with us. Once they did, they've really taken our business to another level. But instead of trying to add a lot of stations, we've decided to diversify, and get into the commercial property investment and development. Earlier, I was investing in the stock market, and it seemed like I'd go for a while making pretty good money, and then I'd lose money. I decided I wanted to be involved in something I could control a little more.

"It's my conservative nature, which I think I got from my mother, who was always saying, 'I'd rather have something than nothing.' So that's when we started into commercial property. Now, what we try to do is have a more balanced portfolio."

Interestingly, they've never really exploited the Gary Thompson name like they could have, especially in the first 30 years of the company, when his name and face were so well known from basketball and broadcasting.

The gas stations were never called "Gary Thompson's Phillips 66," and never had signs showing him dribbling a basketball, as you might have expected. As noted earlier, in the new era, the convenience stores are called Swift Stops. For years you had to look hard at the company headquarters before you would finally see "Gary Thompson Oil Co." on the outer door and its small awning. In the last year, the company's proper name did go up in a little larger letters on the front of the office building.

Why was his name been underplayed on the business for so long?

Early on, Gary himself thought the "Phillips 66" brand, shield and colors were more of an attraction for customers. Besides, this is a fellow who all his life has remembered his mother's admonition against getting "the big head." And he's also remembered his father's line that, "if you have to tell people what you've done, then it's not worth as much."

In later years, Rick Thompson said, "everyone in the industry was looking for catchy names that emphasized a fast in-and-out experience for customers, and a name that people would remember. That's why we came up with 'Swift Stop.' "

There's no question Gary's name, persona and accomplishments have helped bring customers into the stations and stores. They still do.

"We've all grown up thinking he's just normal ol' Dad," Rick Thompson said. "I can remember at some age thinking, well, it must be normal that your dad has played basketball with Wilt Chamberlain and Oscar Robertson and Jerry West. Then you get a little older, and you're thinking, 'What? My dad played with them?'

"Then the older we get, the more we realize just how many people he knows—and who know him—not just in Ames but all over everywhere. That's helped our business in so many ways to be successful."

Chapter 18

Getting His Start in Broadcasting

HIS side-career as a commentator on television and radio coverage of college basketball games had Gary Thompson working coast to coast in the biggest arenas, in some of the biggest games and alongside some of the most popular play-by-play broadcasters of his era. He was so good at color commentary in the sport that, when he retired from the microphone in 2005, he was named to the Iowa Broadcasters Association Hall of Fame.

When you consider all that, it's especially fun looking back at how he got started in the field. You might say it was the same place his early development as a basketball player happened—in the gymnasium at old Roland High School.

"When I was in high school, we'd get overflow crowds for our games in Roland," Thompson said. "Our boys team was good, but so were our girls. So one night, we had a particularly big game, and the gym was already packed by the time the girls' game started, and they had people sitting back in the lunch room."

School officials scrambled. They rigged up a microphone in the concession stand, which was just outside the north end of the gymnasium and had a view of the action through a screened window. They tied the microphone into the school's intercom system.

"They had me do play-by-play of the girls' game for the people in the lunch room," he said. "I guess that was kind of a broadcast—my first one!"

In his junior and senior seasons, from 1951-'53, he often got to see and hear real broadcasting pros at work—as they interviewed him. As an established star player who was already known across the state, he was often sought out for interviews by such well-known sportscasters of that era as Dale Williams, who did play-by-play of Iowa State Cyclone games and also did the high school state tournaments for WOI-AM radio in Ames; Harry Burrell, who was the sports information director at Iowa State but also did color commentary on Williams' broadcasts of the high school tournament games, and by the young Jim Zabel, who in 1944 had started what has become a career of more than 60 years with WHO radio and TV in Des Moines.

"I hold the distinct honor of having broadcasted games in that Roland gymnasium when Gary Thompson was a player there," Zabel said. "We were doing a high school 'game-of-the-week' on our FM station at WHO back then, and I not only did games from Roland, I also remember doing them in gyms all over the state—as far away as Algona, Villisca and even Davenport."

Does Zabel have specific memories of broadcasting the games in Roland? "Oh, yeah," he said. "First of all, Gary Thompson was just a ball of fire as a player, a great natural shooter—he would have been fabulous in the later era of the 3-pointer."

Williams, who had started his radio and TV career at WOI in 1943, also did some of the Roland Rockets' home basketball games, besides covering them in the state tournaments of 1951, '52 and '53. "I did some of those Roland regular season games when Gary was playing because KFJB in Marshalltown asked me to fill-in for them, and they were carrying some of them," said Williams, who remained in Ames after his retirement in 1968.

His recollection of Thompson as a high school player?

"What I remember most was his determination," Williams said. "He wasn't the fastest, or the biggest, but he was a good shooter and he could find some way to beat you." And as the subject of an interview? "Well, at first he was a very bashful kid, but later he got over some of that," Williams said. "He was always very humble, though, even when he was in college."

Williams and Burrell both figured they had a bit of a role in Thompson deciding to attend Iowa State and play his college ball for the Cyclones.

"Everybody in central Iowa was anticipating that Gary would come to Iowa State, and Chick Sutherland, who was the basketball coach, had talked to him several times," Williams said. "So sometime during Gary's senior season at Roland, or maybe that spring, when I was talking to him, I mentioned that if he came to Iowa State, he could work for me when I did my broadcasts of Cyclone football games. I told him he could be a 'spotter' for me—picking out the players who made the tackles, that sort of thing—and you know, I think that helped Gary decide to come to Iowa State."

"Started in radio, transitioned to TV..."

They worked side-by-side in the radio booth at those Cyclone football games, Williams said, "but it took Gary a long time before he quit calling me Mr. Williams and started calling me Dale."

In his college years, of course, Thompson became increasingly comfortable around the media, since he was asked to deal with them so much.

Another prominent young broadcaster he came to know then was Dick Greene, who had been a Cyclone baseball player, then became a sportscaster after following around Williams and Zabel and helping them when they'd let him.

"I'd grown up in Glidden in western Iowa, and I'd sent Jim Zabel some game results from time to time, and I got to be friends with him," said Greene, who now lives in Bushnell, Florida, after a long career in broadcasting, then agri-business and later construction. "When I got to Iowa State, I backed up Zabel on some of his broadcasts of high school basketball games, including some of those in Roland when Gary was playing."

Greene had finished his studies at Iowa State by the time Thompson was becoming a factor there, and he became sports director at WOI-TV, holding that position from 1955-'61. He did back-up of Williams on the play-by-play of Cyclone basketball, and he also did some play-by-play of Cyclone baseball games, including the 1957 College World Series, which Thompson helped the team reach.

But the most fun connection between Greene and Thompson was on a wildly popular, non-sports show that WOI-TV featured, "Seventeen," a live dance show for central Iowa teenagers, kind of a local version of the nationally-famous "American Bandstand" show that Dick Clark had started in Philadelphia. It gave Thompson a whole new kind of broadcasting experience.

Greene, besides his sports duties, had become one of three hosts of the "Seventeen" show, which would gather teen dancers at different locations around the Ames area on Saturday late afternoons. His partners were Betty Lou McVay, whose main job at WOI-TV was hosting the station's legendary "Magic Window" show for children, and Ron Scott, whose real job at WOI was in advertising sales.

"I was 26 or 27 years old at the time, Ron Scott was a couple of years younger than me, and Betty Lou might have even been younger," Greene said. "We were having a ball doing the show. Besides spinning 45-rpm records for the dance music, we'd do interviews with the kids who were there and we'd do reports on teen fashion.

"So in 1957, our program director at WOI, Dan Norton, came to me and asked what we could do to help spruce up the show a little bit. I said, 'Well, I know Gary Thompson, from doing games, and I think maybe we could get him to come on the show and make appearances with us.'

"Of course, everybody knew Gary then—he was an All-American basketball player—so Norton liked the idea. I got a hold of Gary and told him what we had in mind. We said he could take over the interviews with the kids, and also do some of the fashion bits." Thompson agreed to give it a try.

How was he, in his first experience as an interviewer instead of an interviewee?

"Nervous," said Greene. "We started him out with little vignettes at first, and they were a little rough. But, you know, he had a knack for it, and after one or two shows, he really became good at it. As he became more comfortable, we had him doing more things to get involved with the kids. I can remember him being in a bubble gum blowing contest with some of the teenagers."

Thompson also saw first-hand that even "seasoned old pros" like Greene could make mistakes, which sometimes made the live telecasts all the more fun for the audience. Greene recalled how one of the show's sponsors was "Curlee Clothes," a national brand sold at many local clothing stores back then; in fact, the "Seventeen" hosts all wore red blazers during the show, and those coats carried a patch for "Curlee Clothes" on the breast pocket. Teenagers who wanted to attend the show had to pick up a free pass from a store that sold the Curlee apparel.

"We were doing the show on VEISHEA weekend, right out in front of the Memorial Union at Iowa State, and we must've had 3,000 kids out there dancing," said Greene. "It came time for me to do a commercial for Curlee Clothes, so I was telling the audience that, 'If you'd like to appear on the WOI-TV 'Seventeen' show, all you have to do is pick up a pass at a Curlee Clothes dealer…'

"But I got things twisted up, and I suddenly heard myself saying, '…all you have to do is piss up a pack at a Curlee Clothes dealer…' And then I just cracked up. Luckily, I'd been in broadcasting long enough that it didn't totally stop me. I just kept going."

That probably just helped the show's ratings with central Iowa's young people.

Betty Lou McVay later married James "Red" Varnum, who also worked at WOI-TV. She had a 40-year career at the station, hosting a variety of educational and public affairs programs.

"Unlike Dick Greene and Ron Scott, I'd come to Iowa from Wisconsin, so I didn't know as much about Gary Thompson as they did," she said. "But I was really impressed at how easily he got into his role on the show. He was kind of a natural, and he didn't have any of the bad habits that some young broadcasters had. We'd show him what to do, and he'd do it. Of course, everybody knew who he was, and it helped that he was very much admired and respected, both on the campus and around Ames."

But surely Thompson—who was never a dancer, you'll recall—must have seemed just a little stiff in that setting, at least at first.

"Oh, I don't remember that he was, at all," Betty Lou said. "I think he was as groovy as any of us, to use an old phrase."

She and Thompson have been friends ever since—often seeing each other in the Dutch Oven Bakery in Ames, where both have been part of coffee klatches.

And Thompson and Greene have enjoyed visits over the years, too.

"I can remember a few years ago, Kansas was playing basketball at Iowa State, and I went to a press conference for the game," Greene said. "Gary came in there, saw me and made everybody aware that I was the guy who got him into broadcasting. Of course, I enjoyed hearing him say that."

But a full 10 years lapsed between the "Seventeen" show experience and Thompson's next experience in the field.

That came in the late 1960s, after Gary had completed his playing and coaching careers with the Phillips 66ers, and returned to Ames to start Gary Thompson Oil Co. He began a friendship then with Ted Tedesco, an Ames insurance agent and later the mayor of the city—a friendship that grew through broadcasting and is still strong today.

"I was from Council Bluffs and played basketball at Abraham Lincoln High School, a year behind Gary," said Tedesco. "We made the state tournament one of those same years that Roland did. So, even though I was a sliver-getter on the bench, I did get to observe him play. Then I went to Iowa State, and I got to know him just a little bit in our student years.

"Then when he came back and settled in Ames in 1968, we got a lot closer," Tedesco continue. "Even though I was working in insurance, I always liked being around sports, and I was doing radio with Skip Nelson of KASI on the Ames High basketball games. Skip did the play-by-play, and I was keeping stats and doing a little bit of color.

> *"He soon got a call to work with Jim Zabel..."*

"I told Skip we ought to get Gary to come on with the two of us—that Gary could do most of the color—it'd be a natural. So we did Ames' games in the Central Iowa Conference, and we followed them to the state tournament, too. I guess we probably worked high school games, off and on, for 3 or 4 years."

When word got out that Thompson was interested in broadcasting, others started calling.

Jim Zabel, whose career had mushroomed at WHO in Des Moines, was doing not only the play-by-play of Iowa Hawkeye games, he was also doing nearly all the games of Iowa State and Drake men's basketball. And he was calling some high school tournament action. He recalls that during the 1969 season, he did play-by-play for an amazing total of 129 basketball games!

"I had Sharm Scheuerman (a former University of Iowa player and coach) with me doing color on the Iowa games back then, and I wanted to find an Iowa State guy to help me on the Cyclone games," Zabel said. "Harry Burrell suggested Gary Thompson." They worked together on the radio coverage of Iowa State games for about 3 seasons.

"One funny thing during those years that I'll never forget happened when Gary and I were doing a Missouri game at Iowa State," Zabel said. "Missouri had been rated No. 2 in the nation, but they'd gone to Kansas State a couple of days earlier and got beat. Then Iowa State beat them by a couple of points. Norm Stewart, the Missouri coach whom we all really liked, got so mad at the end of the Iowa State game that he kicked over the water cooler, stormed off to the locker room and said he would only talk to certain reporters.

"But I knew he liked Gary—going back to when they were playing against each other in college—so I sent Gary off with a tape recorder to get an interview. Gary goes into the Missouri dressing room, and he got the interview with Norm, all right. But when he came back to the booth, he said, 'Boy, you better preview this tape!'

"It turned out Gary had asked Norm what had happened that Missouri could get beat at Iowa State, just like it had at Kansas State. Norm's answer was, 'Same thing happened here as at Kansas State—we got (expletive)!' Well, we didn't air that, of course, but we were able to use the rest of the interview."

Thompson said as startled as he was when Stewart said that, he held his composure pretty well for a relatively inexperienced broadcaster. "I just said, 'Oh, well Norm, are there any other comments you'd like to make?' I just went on like nothing unusual had happened. Then Norm laughed and said, 'O.K., now let's do it right,' and we started again."

Zabel said he carried the Stewart interview tape with him for a time, sharing it with other coaches and sports media.

"Illinois was playing at Iowa a few nights later, and during my pre-game interview with Lou Henson, the Illinois coach, I told him about the Stewart tape, played it and we got a big laugh out of it," Zabel said. "So, Iowa goes out and beats Illinois by two points. After the game, I sent Sharm Scheuerman into the Illinois locker room with a recorder, and he asked Lou Henson what happened. Lou said, 'Sharm, you go back and tell Zabel that the same thing happened to us tonight that happened to Missouri at Iowa State the other night!' "

By the early 1970s, WHO had decided to drop its play-by-play of the Iowa State games, and in 1971, Thompson was asked to become color commentator on the Big Eight Conference's television network coverage of its member schools' games.

"Mickey Holmes, who was an assistant commissioner in the conference, had been listening from the Big Eight office when I was doing those games with Jim Zabel," said Thompson. "He called Harry Burrell and asked if he thought I could make the transition from radio to TV." Burrell gave the idea a ringing endorsement.

As you'll learn in the pages ahead, Gary Thompson reached the big time in college sports television.

Chapter 19

Hit Bigtime in Network TV

NETWORK television coverage of college basketball games was still a relatively new idea when Gary Thompson got involved in the early 1970s. During his collegiate playing career in the mid-1950s, only a few single games were televised by ambitious local stations.

The first coverage on a network of stations occurred in 1957, pioneered by television executive C.D. Chesley in North Carolina. Knowing the popularity of basketball at the University of North Carolina, Chesley decided to arrange a telecast of the Tar Heels' games in the NCAA Final Four tournament in Kansas City.

He put together a network of five TV stations in the states of the Atlantic Coast Conference to carry the games. Then in the 1957-'58 season, he produced an "ACC Game of the Week" on 11 Saturday afternoons, with the games being carried by 12 stations in the southeastern U.S.

In the early 1960s, Jim Corbett, Louisiana State University athletic director, helped organize a network of stations to carry basketball games in the Southeastern and Mid-American Conferences.

In 1965, Eddie Einhorn, a Chicago lawyer with both business and television interests, founded the TVS television sports network, to offer more college basketball coverage on regional networks, like Chesley and Corbett had put together for ACC and SEC games. Einhorn quickly negotiated deals to take over "Game of the Week" telecasts for the SEC, MAC and also the old Southwestern Conference (SWC).

His network and his reputation spread far, wide and quickly, especially after TVS did a nationwide telecast of the 1968 "Game of the Century." In that storied game, the University of Houston upset perennial champion UCLA 71-69 in the Astrodome in Houston, in front of 52,693 fans. Einhorn had arranged a network of more than 100 TV stations around the country, making that game the first to be televised to a truly national audience.

The Big Eight Conference's first network TV package for basketball coverage was negotiated by Commissioner Wayne Duke in 1968. Max Falkenstein, who also did radio play-by-play coverage for the Kansas Jayhawks, anchored most of the weekly basketball telecasts from '68 to '71.

Then Duke moved on to become commissioner of the Big Ten Conference, and Chuck Neinas succeeded him at the helm of the Big Eight. One of Neinas' first tasks was renegotiating the conference's network TV contract for basketball, and he awarded the package to Einhorn and his TVS network.

For the 1971-'72 season, Einhorn hired Merle Harmon, a young broadcaster who seemed to have real potential, to become the Big Eight network's play-by-play man, and Gary Thompson, to be the color commentator. Their producer was John Crowe, a Texan who had worked for Einhorn on SWC and MAC telecasts.

Harmon had grown up in Illinois, served in the U.S. Navy during World War II and then began his college years at Graceland College, which was then a 2-year school in Lamoni, Iowa. He finished a degree in radio at the University of Denver. He came to TVS and its Big Eight Network after doing some of the broadcasts for University of Kansas sports, as well as doing play-by-play of baseball in Kansas City—first for the minor league Kansas City Blues and then for the major league Kansas City Athletics when they were moved in from Philadelphia—and in Milwaukee.

Thompson said he will never forget their debut on the Big Eight telecasts.

"It was a Missouri-at-Nebraska game," he said. "Merle and I got all ready to go, the game started and the crowd continued to stand—none of them sat down—and they were blocking our view. When we asked some of them closest to us if they'd please sit down, they looked at us like, 'Are you crazy?' We were trying to look around them and over them, and come up with some kind of description of what was happening on the floor. After 5 or 6 minutes, when Nebraska finally scored, everybody sat down around us. We didn't know until after that game that the tradition there was for the fans to stand up until the Cornhuskers scored."

Thompson received no special training for the job. Instead, he relied on what little TV and radio experience he'd had, plus some good quick coaching from Harmon, and of course his deep knowledge of basketball.

"They just started me out, with no training and with very little direction from the crew," Thompson said. "I'd get really nervous when we were about to go on the air. And I'd get sweaty armpits when I had to do a 1-minute interview. I'd ask a question and then I'd look down at the floor director for hand signals on how much time was left during the answer.

"Finally, Janet told me, 'You're jerking your head all the time—stop doing that! What are you doing?' At first, I had no idea how long it would take to ask questions and get answers. Eventually I learned that two or three questions and answers would be about as much as you could cover in any on-air interview.

"After the first few games I did, I'd come home, look at the tapes and be so embarrassed. I was just awful. Part of it was that that I enjoyed being able to do the games so much that I didn't want to screw up, and I'd wind up maybe trying too hard."

Crowe, the producer, remembers that Thompson "was a little frightened, but he had a great reputation in the Big Eight Conference. All the coaches knew him. And he was the one coaches wanted doing the color commentary, because he knew the game so well and he knew everybody involved in the conference."

Thompson's first TV season included doing the color commentary on the NCAA tournament first-round games played at Hilton Coliseum in Ames—the only time Iowa State has hosted an NCAA men's game. The four teams were Louisville, Southwest Louisiana, Texas and Kansas State.

Harmon and Thompson were the Big Eight broadcast team for two seasons. And Thompson was part of a prank that the TV crew pulled on Harmon when the Big Eight network was in Ames to do an Iowa State game in early 1973.

"Iowa State had a great wrestler back then, Chris Taylor," said Thompson. Taylor was a two-time NCAA champion at heavyweight, with his weight fluctuating between 410 and 450 pounds during his career. He had a career record of 87-0-1 for the Cyclones.

> *"I'd look at the tapes and think I was just awful!"*

"Everybody knew who Chris Taylor was at that time," Thompson continued. Taylor, who died of a heart ailment in 1979, "was also just the greatest kid, always fun to talk to and a great interview. So our plan was that Merle Harmon was going to interview him on videotape before the basketball game, and we'd use the interview as a special feature during halftime. So John Crowe, our producer, and I decided we'd have a little fun with Merle.

"We got to Chris early and told him that during the interview, he should keep a straight face, only answer questions with a 'yes' or 'no,' and be as stiff as he could. So, when the lights went on, Merle started asking Chris questions, and that's exactly what happened. You could tell that Merle was starting to scramble, back-tracking, re-asking questions, trying everything he could to get Chris to open up, but Chris wouldn't crack. "Finally, John Crowe and I started breaking up about it and laughing. Merle saw us, stopped the whole interview and said, 'O.K., now I see what's going on here!' We all had a good laugh, then Merle and Chris went back on videotape and did a great interview for the halftime show."

Going into the 1973-'74 basketball season, Einhorn moved Harmon over to do the play-by-play on his network doing the Big Ten Conference games. Harmon later went on to other major jobs in broadcasting, including the National Football League, NCAA football, the Winter Olympics and more.

Brought on board to do the Big Eight play-by-play with Thompson was

Jay Randolph, who had moved from broadcasting the pro football games of the Dallas Cowboys, to joining the staff at St. Louis' radio sports super station, KMOX. There he was working with such well-known sportscasters as Harry Caray, his son Skip Caray and Jack Buck—doing everything from St. Louis Cardinals baseball, to University of Missouri sports, to St. Louis University basketball.

After 3 years at KMOX, Randolph was wooed away by the NBC-TV affiliate in St. Louis, KSD Channel 5, which made him its sports director and anchor. He also continued doing play-by-play on telecasts—sometimes for his station, sometimes for the NBC network—in football, basketball, baseball, professional golf and even the Olympics. He held that position for 21 years, while he was also doing the Big Eight basketball telecasts with Thompson.

"Gary and I hit it off magically, right from the beginning," Randolph recalled. "Our styles seemed to complement each other. From January through the end of the Big Eight post-season tournament, we spent nearly every Saturday together for 19 years."

Besides being broadcast partners, they also became great friends—and still are.

Jay Randolph is certainly one of the most interesting people in Thompson's life. He is a West Virginian by birth, one who got "a great love of sports, especially college basketball" from his father Jennings Randolph, who had been a star player at old Salem College in Salem, W.V. The father began his professional career as a sports writer, then became athletic director at Davis & Elkins College in Elkins, W.V.

In 1930, Jennings Randolph ran as a Democrat for the U.S. House of Representatives and lost. In 1932, he ran again and was elected. He served 14 years in the House, then was defeated and became a college speech and business instructor for 11 years. In 1958, he was elected a U.S. Senator from West Virginia and served 27 years, until his retirement in 1985. His major legislative contributions include the 18-year-old vote, the interstate highway system and the development of the aerospace museum in Washington.

Because of his father's long service in Congress, Jay Randolph grew up in Washington, D.C., "and that was back when Washington really was sort of a small town," he said. "A lot of my friends' fathers were members of Congress, worked in government agencies or were in the service. There were just a lot of opportunities there for a kid growing up."

But he also knew his native West Virginia well. "I'd go back with my dad when he'd be campaigning," he said, "all over the state, every nook and cranny."

Senator Jennings Randolph and his contemporary Senator Everett Dirksen, the legendary Republican from Illinois, were two of the most respected orators in their years on Capitol Hill. Jay Randolph says hearing his father speak so often, and so well, inspired him to learn to use his voice, too.

Jay Randolph also became a good young golfer. He finished as a quarter-finalist in the U.S. Amateur tournament one year, and nearly turned professional in 1954. That was during his student years at Salem College, where he became the fourth generation of his family to graduate.

In 1958, he was in West Virginia helping in one of his father's campaigns "when I stumbled into the radio business." He took an announcer's job at a 250-watt station in Clarksburg, W.V., working for $1.25 per hour and $10 per game for broadcasting high school sports. By "being in the right place at the right time," he found the broadcasting opportunity in Dallas, and eventually St. Louis, where he's lived ever since.

When he and Thompson were working together through the 1970s and '80s, "it was like the golden age of sports on TV," Randolph said. "Today, you can get several college basketball games on television every day, but it was not like that at all back then. In the 1970s, there were no cable companies. Throughout most of the Midwest, there was only one college basketball game on a week—and it was our 'Big Eight Game of the Week.' People would be calling their local TV stations during the week to find out what game we were going to be covering on Saturday."

Their producer through most of those years was Crowe, "a big burly Texan, a lovable guy," said Randolph. "And he really knew how to work with the technology we had available."

When they started their telecasts together in the 1973-'74 season, they'd never have more than three cameras to use for different angles during the game. The technical equipment to relay the telecast was typically set up under the bleachers in the noisy fieldhouses, "and it would be so loud we couldn't hear anything down below there," Crowe said.

"We had no instant replay equipment back then, of course. We'd use a tape machine, recording the whole game, and then if we wanted to show a replay, we'd get to a commercial, back the tape up, save it and then show the highlight when we came back on the air. But there was no slow-motion to it. We had to run it back in real time."

Crowe had found a production truck and willing crew at WIBW-TV, Channel 13, in Topeka, Kansas, and for years they traveled all over Big Eight Conference territory, doing the "Games of the Week."

The main sponsor, in the early years, was Shell Oil, later replaced by Phillips 66.

Of course, that switch in sponsorship was especially nice for Gary Thompson, who, besides being the color commentator on the Phillips 66 "Game of the Week," was also Phillips' distributor back home in the Ames area.

The audience for the games on TV—and the hunger of fans for more Big Eight basketball—grew rapidly in the 1970s. The technology was improving just as fast. And the budget, style and fun of the telecasts kept growing, too.

"We'd typically fly in on Friday, limousines would pick us up at the airport and we had generous expense accounts," Randolph said. "We had great camaraderie with the coaches, the sports information directors (SIDs), the athletic directors (ADs), even the university presidents. They'd make it seem like a big deal when we were coming in to do the 'Game of the Week' from their campus. When we'd get to town, the newspaper and radio reporters would often want to talk to us."

Crowe remembers "we'd watch the teams practice Friday afternoon, do some pre-game interviews and then we'd usually go to dinner with the coaches and SIDs. I can remember when we were at Missouri to do a game against Kansas State. On the Friday evening Norm Stewart, the Missouri coach, had us come over to his house for a cocktail before we went to dinner, and he had Jack Hartman, the Kansas State coach, come, too. I don't think that kind of thing happens anymore."

Randolph recalled that he, Thompson and Crowe went to Stewart's house before a Kansas game one time, too, "and Ted Owens and all his Kansas assistants were there. When we'd go to Nebraska, we'd go to the Elks club there in downtown Lincoln, and we'd drink with Joe Cipriano," then the Nebraska coach.

When Randolph was telling those stories to Thompson's morning coffee gathering in Ames during a visit in 2005, Thompson interrupted him. "I want all of you here to know that I was the designated driver!" he said, reminding his pals that he's never been a drinker.

Randolph's point, though, was that "when Gary and I started working together, the Big Eight was very much a coach's league—and we had great coaches—and they pretty well all got along with each other. With the pressure on coaches today, with the games under such a microscope, there's just not as much camaraderie. But Gary Thompson and I still think of a basketball game as a pleasant experience."

Crowe said it was fascinating watching old pros like Harmon and then Randolph "work with Gary, and develop him into a first-rate color commentator. Gary was very lucky in that he got to work early on with two real pros, and he got better and better, every year. He had so much confidence in Jay that it helped him have confidence in himself. And as the years went by, Jay kept giving Gary more and more responsibility in the broadcasts."

"Coaches often got together for dinner before games back then..."

Randolph and Thompson often would debate each other's roles, however, each saying the other was more important to the telecast.

"I always felt that a color guy was brought in to help fill time and share some insights," said Thompson, "but the play-by-play announcer was the guy."

Randolph, however, said he always looked at himself, doing the play-by-play, "kind of like the conductor—I'd get us on the air and get us to the commercials at the right times. I'd inform the audience of the score, talk about the lead changes and do the promos.

"All of that is kind of a lost art today. A lot of that now is done with all the graphics and other bells and whistles that are available with technology. I'd always tell Gary that I was just going to try to let the game breathe, that I'd give the audience just enough information to give them perspective, because they could already see for themselves what was happening. Some player would take a shot and score, and I might not even say he made the basket, but instead say something like, 'He's already got six points above his average today.' Then Gary would take it as the player ran down the floor, maybe telling the audience how this player was doing it.

"I'd tell Gary that if he's telling a story, not to worry about having to stop for me to describe a basket; instead, be succinct but finish the story, and then I could catch-up everybody after he was done. We developed a nice rhythm that way. Actually, when he and I started working together, he already pretty well knew what he was doing. All we had to do was, like dancing, get into step together."

Randolph said that both he and Thompson "were over-preparers in the way that before the games, we'd do our homework on the teams. We'd both dig up all kinds of statistics and stories to use, and a lot of times he'd get frustrated because a game would be over and he hadn't used half of the material he had put together. But I'd tell him that you always want to have it, just in case something happened and we'd be asked to fill 15 or 20 minutes of air time. 'Be ready to tap dance,' we'd say."

As a color commentator, Thompson "was always trying to analyze, to teach. He was a straight-shooter, a no-nonsense guy, and I think he made it easy for the fans to absorb the intricacies of the game. He was concise and bright."

He would also admit his rare mistakes in analysis. In later years, the frequent use of instant replay technology in broadcasting often shed new light on officials' calls.

In an early 1980s NCAA tournament game between Coach Joe Hall's Kentucky Wildcats and the University of Alabama at Birmingham Blazers coached by Gene Bartow, Thompson remembers saying that one official's call "was a bad one." Bartow thought the same thing and threw such a fit with the officials that he got a technical foul.

Meanwhile, Thompson and NBC play-by-play broadcaster Bob Costas kept looking at different camera angles of the play, on replay, and ultimately, Thompson told the audience, "Well, I'm wrong there—and you can see why basketball is so difficult to officiate!" He said that a minute or two later, there was another stop in the action, and the referee who'd made the controversial call "sidled up to me, there at our broadcast booth on the edge of the floor, leaned over and said, 'Gary, how was that call?' I said, 'You're O.K.'"

In terms of broadcasting style, Randolph noted that Thompson "was not flamboyant. He never had that wild, catch-phrase call that in later years, color commentators like Dick Vitale or Bill Rafferty started using."

Thompson said Vitale and other similarly boisterous commentators "have been good for the game, but they like to draw attention to themselves, and that just wasn't me. I never wanted to be anything but plain vanilla—just plain mashed potatoes and gravy, I often said."

Joe Castiglione, who was athletic director at Missouri back then and later moved to the same position at Oklahoma, also used the food analogy in describing Thompson's style. "Gary gave you the meat and potatoes, when a lot of guys would just give you the whipped cream," said Castiglione. "Gary was all about substance. I thought for viewers, he helped them understand what was really going on."

Thompson told Phil Anderson, in a 1985 story in the Topeka Capital-Journal, that he just could not force himself to do the kind of non-stop, rabid commentary during games that some color commentators were doing. "I'm not big on that," Thompson said in the story, "and I wouldn't be myself if I tried to do that. You have to be yourself."

Mel Bracht, who did occasional columns on the sports media for the Tulsa Tribune in that same era, wrote that "Thompson's low-key style plays well in Big Eight Country." And Bracht quoted Jay Randolph saying that, "Gary is different from some people in that he is not a critical person. He feels strongly that isn't his role. Most of these kids aren't going to play professionally. They are just trying to get a college degree."

That's not to say Thompson didn't have fun on the air.

Norm Stewart, the Missouri coach, whom Thompson had known since they played against each other, once erupted in anger at a call by an official, jumped off the bench and just as he did so, the basketball bounced right to him. Stewart, a former pitcher in baseball, grabbed the ball and threw a one-armed fast-ball back to the referee. Thompson's quick description: "Well, Norm hasn't lost his high hard one!"

Stewart "figures in a lot of stories through my career," Thompson said. "When he would be coaching, he always had this kind of a smile that was really more of a sneer. So we were doing a Missouri game, and when we had a shot of Norm on the bench, I said something about his 'sneer-smile.' Later in the game, another camera picked up a photo of Norm standing beside the court with that look on his face. The producer says in my ear piece, 'Say something about Norm,' so I said the first thing that came to my mind, which was, 'There's Norm with that sneer-smile again!' Since I had already used that line once, I realized as soon as I said it again that I had committed a no-no."

The next time they ran into each other, Stewart didn't sneer, he snarled! He walked up to a group of reporters watching his Missouri Tigers practice, and said directly to Thompson, "You, you little shit, I'll talk to you afterward. And I'll tell you later what everyone else won't say to your face!"

Sitting with the group was Buddy Epps, the trainer for Missouri. Thompson said that when Stewart walked away, "I told Epps that if Norm thinks he's going to intimidate me about something I said during our coverage of the basketball game Wednesday night in Ames, he might as well forget it. But if he wants to get on me about my using that 'sneer-smile' twice, I'll take everything he wants to give me because I have it coming."

Epps got up and walked over to the bench where the players and Stewart were sitting during their practice. "I saw Epps talking to Stewart," Thompson said, "and Stewart never said anything more to me about it." The old pals patched things up quickly.

It was double the fun for Thompson and Randolph any time they were doing a game between Missouri and Nebraska, since the Cornhuskers' Cipriano was just as much of a character as the Tigers' Stewart.

Stewart is still telling the story about how in the mid 1970s, which was a rough time of protests and violence on many college campuses, he was just starting to put his team through an afternoon workout in the old Nebraska Coliseum, before a game that night.

"All of a sudden, we hear this 'Boom!' that sounded just like a gunshot," said Stewart. "A couple of my players dropped down like they were trying to get away from any shooting, and I was about as scared as they were. Then we heard this laugh coming from over under the bleachers. It was Cipriano, and he'd thrown a cherry bomb out there just to shake us up!"

In a timeout during one of the games, Cipriano walked from his own huddle of players alongside the floor to where the Missouri players were gathered around Stewart. Cipriano reached into his suitcoat pocket, grabbed a set of bad-looking costume teeth he'd brought along, slipped them in his mouth, stuck his head in the Tigers' huddle and said, "How we doing, guys?".

> *"The official asked me, 'Gary, how was that call?'"*

Thompson recalls that their normal broadcast pattern, especially for their Saturday "Big Eight Game of the Week," was to interview the winning coach after the game—if there was enough time left from the network.

"Coaches always wanted to get to do that post-game interview when they won," he said. "Cipriano and Stewart even started fiddling around with that. I remember doing one of their games which was being played at Nebraska, and Nebraska was winning it in the last couple of minutes of the game. It got down into the last minute, and Missouri didn't have any chance to win, but Stewart still called a time-out.

"Then he glanced at his watch, looked over at Cipriano and just smile, like he was saying, 'You ain't getting on TV this time, Joe!' Of course, Cipriano would do the same thing if they were playing at Missouri and, late in the game, Missouri was winning it. He'd call a time out, too, just to send a little message over to Stewart."

There were occasionally outrageous incidents that Thompson would do his best to try to describe, in a fair way if he couldn't put a positive light on them. Many happened during games between the great rivals, Kansas and Kansas State.

"Kansas State had a good player named Curtis Redding, who was from New York and pretty cocky," Thompson said. "So when we were doing their game at Kansas, and Redding was introduced, the Kansas fans were throwing hotdogs out on the floor.

"Then there was a game at K-State, there was a prank that unfortunately had a touch of racism in it. Kansas had several black players, and when they were introduced, the K-State fans threw bananas on the floor. They squished when they hit, and the officials had to hold up the game for 20 minutes to get them cleaned up, and the TV production people were going crazy with the delay.

"I can also remember games against Kansas when the K-State fans threw or dropped chickens from the rafters, all painted up like they were Jayhawks, and the home fans would chant, 'Here come the Chickenhawks! Here come the Chickenhawks!' When those things would happen, we'd have to talk about them, because the fans at home could see them. But we'd generally talk about how that stuff really has no place in college basketball and is dangerous, too."

Producer Crowe, in telling about how well-known Randolph and Thompson became to Big Eight fans, said "Jay had a love-hate relationship with the student bodies. They loved him, but they'd make so much fun of his hair," which he was wearing slicked-back on the sides. "They idolized Gary," Crowe continued, "absolutely idolized him. If we'd go into the student union buildings, it seemed like Gary would speak to every person we saw, particularly to black athletes. I think he wanted to try to make them feel welcome in the Big Eight."

Eventually, the "Big Eight Game of the Week" package became two games per week, generally on Wednesday nights and Saturday afternoons. The telecasts would also include the post-season conference tournament. Thompson said in his busiest years of broadcasting, he was doing "as many as 40 to 42 games a season."

He would typically work at his Gary Thompson Oil Co. in Ames on Monday and Tuesday morning, then leave Ames to fly or drive to the site of a Wednesday game. He'd watch practice, prepare during the day Wednesday, do the game that night, then head home either right after the game or early Thursday. He'd spend Thursday in his business office, then leave again early Friday morning for the Saturday game, returning home late Saturday night or early Sunday morning. Gary's son Rick Thompson was getting quick on-the-job training in how to run the business, and doing a good job of it.

One thing that made Gary Thompson's travel schedule a little easier was his friendship with Mike Millett, a professor in engineering at Iowa State, and his wife Esther Millett, an elementary school teacher in Ames, who had a single-engine Mooney airplane. They would often fly Thompson to his Saturday TV games. The Milletts were not basketball fans. They just enjoyed visiting the college campuses while Thompson was doing the game broadcasts, and then they'd fly him back to Ames right afterward, allowing him to get home much quicker than if he had to rely on commercial airlines.

That busiest period in his broadcasting career began in the late 1970s, when in addition to the Big Eight regular season games, Randolph and Thompson would also do the conference's post-season tournament. They also began being summoned by NBC-TV to do telecasts of NCAA regional games in far-flung places around the nation. Occasionally they'd work those games together, but often they would split up and work with other broadcasters. The two of them did the third place game in the NCAA Final Four in 1978 in St. Louis, and then Thompson was the analyst on three more third place games before the NCAA discontinued them in 1982.

On those special assignments, Thompson got to work with and around some of the biggest names in college basketball broadcasting—Costas, Dick Enberg, Don Criqui, Charlie Jones, Fred White, Jack Buck, Gary Bender, Tom Hammond, Ray Scott and others.

The great UCLA coach John Wooden joined Thompson twice as a special guest commentator on games that were picked up for national broadcast by NBC-TV. And he also worked with some of the up-and-coming play-by-play broadcasters on the NCAA games—Wayne Larrivee, Kevin Harlan, Ron Franklin,

Early-on, Thompson would be a little in awe when he'd work with one of the nation's most prominent broadcasters. But he quickly learned that they went about their jobs just like he did, and sometimes they wound up leaning on him for help.

In 1980, Buck was going to travel from St. Louis to join Thompson on the broadcast of the championship game in the Big Eight Tournament in Kansas City, matching Kansas State and Kansas.

"I'd never met Jack Buck before," Thompson said. "So I was waiting for him at the hotel, where we were supposed to meet, but then I got a call that he'd missed his flight from St. Louis, and they told me to head on over to the arena. The crew and I went ahead and started getting things ready for the pre-game opening segment we'd always do.

"Then we heard that Buck was in Kansas City but he was tied up in traffic. The producer said, 'Gary, you're going to have to do the opening yourself.' Just as we were about ready to start, Jack came running into the arena. He came over, jumped in and we were about to start, but then the band played the National Anthem, so we delayed a little more.

"When we finally went on the air, Jack wasn't very focused at all. He got all mixed up and had Rolando Blackman, who was the great K-State player, in the Kansas line-up—that kind of thing. But we made it to the first commercial, and during that break, we managed to get Jack straightened out. Then he was great the rest of the way. Sometime later on, he sent me a photo of himself that he'd signed: 'Gary, this is me leaving for a basketball game—the one you totally carried me on. Thanks! Jack Buck.' "

Ray Scott, who had built his broadcasting reputation doing the pro football games of the Green Bay Packers, was assigned to do a mid-week Big Eight Conference game with Thompson.

"I was really looking forward to working with him, but when he came in, he said, 'Gary, do you have a game program? I need to get brushed up on these players,' " Thompson said. "I didn't have one, because I'd done all my preparations by working up the information you get talking to the sports information directors and the coaches.

"Ray found a program, started looking it over and asking me about players listed there—some of them weren't even playing any more. Here was a guy who'd been a great professional, but he was getting near the end of his career, and he came into a game not really prepared. It was disappointing, and probably a good lesson for me. But Ray was still a great guy, and I had a good time working with him."

In 1983, Criqui and Thompson were doing an NCAA game involving the Iowa Hawkeyes in Iowa City. Brad Lohaus, a 6 ft. 11 in. Iowa freshman who was still developing as a player, broke loose on the baseline, went up to dunk the basketball but lost control when the ball hit the bottom of the rim. Criqui's immediate reaction on the air: "Gary, now there's a classic case of white man's disease!"

Thompson said that "as soon as Don said it, I knew he was in trouble. Something like that just wasn't said back in that time. So I tried to cover for Don a little bit, saying something about Lohaus being a young player and that he hadn't learned yet about getting his legs underneath him before he tries to make a play like that." Nevertheless, in the days after the game, Criqui wound up making a public apology for the remark.

Enberg, who is still active and living in San Diego, remembers Thompson from that era as "a serious, sincere and solid person who was very well-prepared when it came to doing games. I knew what a great player he'd been, because I graduated from Central Michigan about the same time he played at Iowa State. Anybody who had anything to do with college basketball back then knew who you were talking about if you mentioned Gary Thompson. He was one of the top guards in the country.

"But what made him so enjoyable to work with was that he was such a nice guy, a real people person," Enberg continued. "I think of a line the great Marquette coach Al McGuire once used about somebody else and apply it to Gary—'If you don't like Gary Thompson, there's something wrong with you.' "

In 1981, Enberg and Thompson were just finishing an NCAA game in which Oregon State, coached by Ralph Miller, had beaten UCLA, coached by Larry Brown. "I really had to scramble on that one," Thompson said. "I raced down to the end of the floor right after the game, to do a quick interview with

Miller. I was wearing my ear piece in my right ear, and the way we were lining things up, we were putting the ear piece in Miller's left ear, so it'd be hidden from the camera. But just as we were getting ready to go on the air, Miller said, 'Gary, I'm deaf in that ear—I can't hear anything!' I had to grab my ear piece, shift it over to my left ear, put Miller's in his right ear, and then change our standing positions—but we got everything re-arranged just in time!"

The schedule would always seem hectic at NCAA tournament time.

"One time Fred White and I did the championship game of the Big Eight Tournament in Kansas City, then we left the arena right away with a police escort to catch a red-eye flight out to Las Vegas," Thompson said. "We were doing a game between Marquette and UNLV that was starting at 10 a.m. local time that next morning. We got to the hotel at 5 a.m.

"They had a room reserved for Fred, but they didn't have one for my wife Janet and me—she was traveling with me on that trip. They found us a parlor room with one pull-out sofa bed, and it didn't have a bathtub or a shower. I got about an hour of sleep, took a sponge bath and then had to be at the arena for a 7 a.m. meeting with the producer and director.

"They didn't know yet who I was going to interview at halftime— they said they'd find somebody for us. Halftime came, I went out on the floor and they still didn't have anybody lined up. I told Fred, 'I'll go down there and see what happens.' Right then, they saw Sammy Davis Jr. walking along the court, and asked me over my earpiece to grab him for the interview. I went right over to him and said, 'Sammy, we need an interview here during halftime—would you come on with us?' He said, 'Sure.' I had no chance to do any background work on him, so I just had to wing it.

"He was a pretty small man, so when we got on camera, I just dwarfed him, and it was kind of awkward," Thompson continued. "But he was such a nice guy. I asked him if he'd just finished his shows from the night before, since it was so early, and he said, 'Yeah, I did, but I really like basketball, and I like Jerry Tarkanian (the UNLV coach), so I decided to come to the game, and I can sleep later.'

"I asked him if he'd ever played basketball and he laughed and said, 'Oh, no, I couldn't play, as small as I am, but I've always loved the game.' It turned out to be a really fun interview. Later, we saw his show 'Bo Jangles,' and what a talent he was!"

Doing those NCAA games meant Thompson was dealing with some of the best coaches around the country—like McGuire, who won a national championship at Marquette in 1977.

"I was assigned by NBC as the analyst for all of Marquette's tournament games that year until the Final Four, which included their first round game in Omaha, then two at the regional tournament at Oklahoma City," Thompson said.

"I went into the first one a little worried, because I'd always heard that Al McGuire was kind of a cocky guy, and I was guessing he could be difficult to cover.

But he turned out to be just great. He was a fun, genuine guy and he'd take all kinds of time before the game and fill me in on what they had planned and things I should watch for. That really helps you as an analyst, of course, and it meant a lot to me that McGuire trusted me with the information before the game."

Sometime later, Thompson had a layover at the Dallas-Fort Worth airport on a trip home, and he was browsing in a newsstand. "All of a sudden I heard somebody say, 'Gary, what are you doing here?' and I turned around and there was Al McGuire," he said. "It impressed me even more about him that he remembered me and went out of his way to say hello. It turned out he was on his way to Iowa to do a speech at Fort Dodge St. Edmond High School, and was on the same plane I was, going to Des Moines. We sat together and visited all the way."

Among other nationally-known coaches Thompson covered were Bob Knight at Indiana and later Texas Tech, Dean Smith at North Carolina, John Thompson at Georgetown, Tarkanian at UNLV, Roy Williams at Kansas and later North Carolina, and Lute Olson at Iowa and later Arizona.

"I think Gary did four or five of our games over the years, and he was always good, always very professional," said Knight, who finished his career at Texas Tech. "He always wanted to know things that might happen in the game, so he could explain them better to the viewers. I would never volunteer any information before the games, but with Gary, I would answer his questions. He understands coaches so well, he'd know just what questions to ask to get the information he wanted."

> *"Gary sat on plane next to Al McGuire and visited all the way..."*

Thompson and UNC's Smith had known of each other for a long time, going back to when Smith was finishing his stellar playing career at Kansas in 1952, just before Thompson began his college years at Iowa State. They formally met during Thompson's Phillips 66ers years when several former Kansas players were on that AAU team with Thompson. They got to know each other better years later, when Thompson was on the broadcast team doing some of the games Smith's UNC teams were playing in the NCAA tournaments.

"I remember once when we were doing one of UNC's regional games in Salt Lake City, I was walking down the run-way to the arena floor, and Dean came walking toward me," Thompson said. "He said, 'Are you working these games out here?' When I said yes, he said, "This is your last chance with us.' I said, 'Huh?' He said, 'We've never won with you doing our games.' That reminded me again how long good coaches remember little details. But then Dean smiled and said, 'I don't think you're the reason we lost.'"

Smith, who retired from coaching in 1997 and is now an ambassador for the UNC athletic department, says that while he does remember Thompson broadcasting several UNC games, he doubts they actually lost many, if any, of them. "We had quite a run, you know," Smith said. "I'm pretty sure that game in Salt Lake City was in '81. We beat Utah there and went on to the Final Four."

What made Thompson so successful as a broadcaster, Smith said, is that "he had the savvy for basketball from playing the game like he did, both in college and with the Phillips 66ers. Not many commentators have that kind of experience."

Thompson recalled that in 1994, when he was going to attend the NCAA Final Four being held in Charlotte, N.C., he wanted to try to play golf on the famous Pinehurst Golf Resort courses, where major national tournaments have been held. He called and tried to make reservations and was told none were available.

He then put in a call to Smith, who was still the head coach at UNC, and asked if he had any connections at Pinehurst. Smith said he would see what he could do, and soon, one of his assistant coaches called Thompson. Smith had arranged for Thompson to play as his guest on the Pinehurst National Golf Club, playing the famous Pinehurst No. 2 course, as well as two other courses at the resort. When he tried to pay, the club pro told said, "There won't be any charge, Mr. Thompson." Astonished, he later sent Smith and his assistant coach nice gifts from Iowa.

Roy Williams and Thompson knew each other very well during the 15 years Williams was coaching the Kansas Jayhawks in the Big Eight and later Big Twelve Conference, 1988-2003.

"One of my favorite stories about Roy tells you just what decent people a lot of these coaches really are," Thompson said. "I always admired his coaching so much that I told him that sometime I'd like to get my picture taken with him. He brought his team to Ames back in about 1993, and I wasn't working that game on TV, so I went over to the Kansas practice during the afternoon and reminded him about getting a picture. He said, 'Let's do it right after the game tonight,' and I said, 'Oh, we'll get it another time, you'll probably be too busy then.' But he said, 'No, you be here right after the game, and win or lose, we'll get the picture taken then.'

"Iowa State did beat Kansas that night, and so afterward, I was thinking that Roy would really not want to mess around with photos. But I did go down to the Kansas dressing room, and with me were my son-in-law Tom Wierson and grandson Matthew Wierson, who was about 8 then. We waited around for Roy, and when he got finished up with his players and the media, he came right out and said, 'O.K., Gary, let's get that picture taken now.'

"He was so congenial you'd have never known whether he won or lost the game. Tom took the picture of Roy and me together, and, you know, I really wanted to have him pose with Matthew, too, but I just couldn't bring myself to bother him more. Then, as we were standing there saying goodbye, all of a sudden Roy kneeled down beside my grandson and said, 'Matthew, could I have my picture taken with you now?' What a class act!"

Lute Olson said he first got to know Thompson "early in my time at Iowa," which began with the 1974-'75 season and continued for nine years. "I was well aware of his accomplishments as an Iowa State player, but I first met him when he did a couple of our games," Olson continued. "The thing that everybody knew about Gary, even back then, was that he's a very fair-minded person. He'd be bending over backwards to be fair to the Hawks, even if our Hawk fans might not have always thought so.

"I always enjoyed it when he was doing our games because, when it came to Xs and Os, he could talk right along with me or any other coach. A lot of guys who have gone into those color commentator jobs in more recent years have been expected to be so critical, and to try to be entertaining. Gary never did that. He always analyzed games in the right way. If something wasn't going right, he'd spot it and explain it to fans.

"He knew his basketball, and he presented it in a way that fans could really understand. He was really good at explaining what would be happening in the next few minutes in a game—what players to watch. He could really open up the game to the average fan, to things we coaches and players are thinking about and doing. I'll tell you, in the history of college basketball, Gary would be right up there with the all-time best game analysts."

Olson noted that he and Thompson also "became good friends over the years. As you know, Gary got to be pretty involved with coaching changes at Iowa State, and we talked often about potential coaches. It impressed me that his first question to me about somebody always seemed to be, 'What kind of person is he? Will he represent Iowa State well?' "

Thompson said an important Iowa Hawkeye tournament game in 1980 was one in which he "really made a great call" as a game analyst.

"Iowa was playing Georgetown in Philadelphia on a Sunday, with the winner going on to the Final Four," Thompson said. "It really was a hectic weekend because that Saturday night, Don Criqui and I did an NCAA Regional in Tucson. As soon as we got done in Arizona, they had an NBC Lear jet waiting to take Criqui, myself and a couple of tech people to Philadelphia to do the Sunday game, which was starting at noon there.

"On those tournament weekends, it's a challenge, because you've got to be preparing for several teams that might be advancing. I remember I went into that weekend studying the media books of eight different teams. But I already knew Iowa pretty well from watching and reading about them all season."

The great Georgetown player Eric "Sleepy" Floyd had the Hoyas on a roll.

"With 10 minutes to go in the game, Iowa was down by about 12 points, and the game was about to get away from the Hawkeyes," Thompson said. "Lute Olson called timeout, and Don Criqui asked me on the air what I thought Iowa had to do to get back into it. I said, 'They have to keep the ball out of Sleepy Floyd's hands, and try to force turnovers by the other four Georgetown players.' It turned out that's exactly what Lute had Iowa do. They made a great comeback and won it," 81-80.

Other broadcasters have been complimenting Thompson ever since on that bit of game analysis. Incidentally, at the conclusion of that game, NBC was picking the game's MVP. Sleepy Floyd and Iowa's Vince Brookins had led their teams in scoring—Floyd had 31 for Georgetown, and Brookins had 22.

"But my pick as MVP was Steve Waite, one of the Iowa centers," said Thompson. "He and the other center, Steve Krafcisn, hadn't done anything the whole first half, but then Waite scored 14 in the second half—including the winning basket. So that's who I picked, but I found out later NBC overruled me and gave it to Sleepy Floyd, on the losing team. That's the Eastern press for you."

He said he took some good natured kidding from Iowa Hawkeye fans before that game, who were saying an old Iowa Stater like himself would have to work awfully hard to be fair to the Hawks in the broadcast. But that was never a problem for Thompson when he picked up the microphone.

"We couldn't see the game—the crowd stood up and blocked our view..."

The best testimony that he was able to maintain his neutrality in broadcasting situations is that Missouri hired him to do the color commentary on the Tiger basketball network from the mid 1980s into the early '90s.

Castiglione, then the athletic director, said "part of my role at Missouri was to oversee our radio and TV coverage, and I wanted to try to put together a TV package to do the games that were not being covered in the Big Eight Conference package.

"To get this going, I basically had to do it on my own—lease the production equipment, arrange the satellite feeds, hire the crew, hire the talent. I was so impressed with the job that Jay Randoph and Gary Thompson were doing on the Big Eight games that I decided to ask them to do as many of our other games as they could.

"We were trying to give Missouri basketball some credibility, and we knew it'd really help if we had the conference's best broadcasters coming in to do some more of our games. Some people wondered about Gary's Iowa State ties, but Norm Stewart and Gary always got along so well, and Norm was all for Gary doing our games."

Castiglione said Randolph's schedule with NBC "was getting so heavy that we couldn't get him as much as we wanted, and we could usually only get Gary six to eight games a season. But we used them as much as we could right on into the early '90s. To fill for Jay, we'd get other play-by-play people like John Rooney, who did baseball for the Chicago White Sox; Tom Dore, who did the Chicago Bulls basketball games, and sometimes others from around the Big Eight like Joe Buck, from St. Louis, and Dave Armstrong, from Kansas City.

"We wanted Gary on as many games as we could get him, and I remember there were times when we'd try to move a game from Wednesday night to Tuesday night, just so I could get Gary. He brought so much to it—professionalism, charisma, his vast knowledge. He helped give our Missouri TV package a little bigger feel."

It was quite a sight when Thompson worked games with play-by-play man Dore, a former Missouri player who at 7 ft. 2 in. tall towered over everybody, including the 5 ft. 10 in. Thompson.

"When we were getting ready to do the pre-game show, with the two of us standing right next to each other, the crew brought out a box for me to stand on," Thompson said. "Tom Dore said, 'Gary, do you mind doing that?' I said, "No, Tom, I don't mind at all—I've been small all my life!' We got along great."

Of course, Missouri Coach Stewart enjoyed needling Thompson now and then at those Tiger games.

"Every once in a while," said Stewart, "I'd walk over to him and say, 'Hey, be careful—ol' Cy is sneaking out on you!' We had a lot of fun together in those years."

Chapter 20

In the Eye Of Some Iowa State Storms

GARY THOMPSON'S 23 years as the color commentator, or analyst, on the old Big Eight Conference's telecasts of the men's basketball games must have set some sort of record for TV longevity. Of course, you don't go that long in any career pursuit, and especially in media, without being involved in a controversy or two.

But remember, Thompson is a man who has led a very charmed life, nearly controversy-free. That may help explain why two squabbles during his time on the Big Eight broadcast team—the most recent of them more than a dozen years ago—were still so frustrating to him in 2008.

It's not just that there were a couple of conflicts, or even that the second one led to him giving up his conference TV position. It's that both situations involved athletics directors at his alma mater, Iowa State, trying to oust him.

The late Lou McCullough, the Cyclones athletics director from 1971-'82, tried and failed to have Thompson removed as the basketball analyst in the 1978-'79 time period. Then McCullough's successor and disciple, Max Urick, who was ISU athletics director from 1983-'93, took his shot.

That occurred soon after Urick had moved on to finish his career as athletics director at Kansas State. From that position in the 1993-'94 time period, he was able to get the number of games Thompson would broadcast on the conference TV network drastically reduced, so much so that Thompson just bowed out.

"What was the most frustrating thing to me was to have people from my own university not telling the truth about me," Thompson said. The disputes that led to those two flash points were direct hits at the epicenter of Iowa State University and its athletics department.

The university's presidents were involved, as were other key administrators, major donors and the head coaches from several Cyclone sports. There was an attempt to drag down an Ames business leader who later became mayor for 8 years, along with Thompson.

There were at least two marriage break-ups, rumors of romantic affairs, allegations of sexual harassment, charges of financial mismanagement, petitions from faculty members, heated meetings of the ISU Athletics Council, as well as the old Faculty Council and later the Faculty Senate. The athletics directors from the other universities in the conference were contacted. The conference commissioners got involved. There were calls to the NCAA. There were lengthy stories in the *Des Moines Register* and other Iowa media.

It was ugly.

The bottom line on it all, probably, is that McCullough and Urick both got fired at Iowa State, although they announced their own "resignations." And Gary Thompson today remains one of the most respected and involved Iowa State alums there is.

"Yeah, that should tell you something," said Buck Turnbull, a retired sportswriter who covered some of the fusses for the *Des Moines Register*, when we talked in 2005.

And, yet, both episodes still grate on Thompson.

In August, 2006, he and Arnie Gaarde, of Ames, his friend since they were teammates at Iowa State in the mid 1950s, were driving to a benefit golf tournament in Wisconsin. "On the way up there, Gary started talking about his conflict with Lou McCullough and Max Urick, and he must've talked about it for 50 miles," Gaarde said. "You could tell it still bothers him. It's amazing to me to think it ever happened."

How, and why, did it?

That was the subject of more than 25 interviews over a 2-year period with those who were involved both directly and peripherally. Thompson, while "not wild about the idea of opening old wounds," said he'd discuss the feuds after being told that Urick had agreed to be interviewed.

"All I want is for the truth to be told," Thompson said. "I've always said that I don't care what people say about me, as long as it's true."

McCullough's side of the story is largely unknown. He went on from Iowa State to become commissioner of the Trans America Athletic Conference, founded in 1978 by smaller universities in the southeastern U.S. He moved the league's headquarters from Shreveport, Louisiana, to Athens, Georgia, the latter city one that he had always told Iowa friends was one of his favorite spots in the nation. He retired in 1991, and died of a heart attack in September, 2000, when he was 75 years old. (The Trans America Conference, incidentally, changed its name in 2001 to become the Atlantic Sun Conference.)

Urick, who retired as athletics director at Kansas State in 2001, still lives in Manahattan, where that university is located. He talked openly in a long interview.

In about March of 1979, when Urick was McCullough's young assistant in the Iowa State athletics department, he was summoned by his boss to be "a witness" during a confrontational meeting between McCullough and Thompson.

Urick described that "as almost like an out-of-body experience for me," as he watched an argument that "was like two billy goats butting heads." He said "when I walked out of that meeting, I thought to myself, 'What have I just been through?' " He said he "was never comfortable around Gary Thompson after that meeting. There was never any animosity, just not a good feeling."

Urick said when he was leaving Iowa State and interviewing for the job at K-State, he knew administrators there were asking Thompson for his opinion about Urick. They knew Thompson well through his TV work, and they knew he usually has inside information about most matters at Iowa State.

"One of the administrators who was interviewing me at K-State asked me, 'What is the issue between you and Gary Thompson? He certainly doesn't have anything good to say about you,' " said Urick. "I had three or four different people here ask me things like that. I felt like Gary must've been trying to torpedo me. But I got the job, and for me it was like, 'Take that, Gary Thompson!' "

> *"Maury John said, 'Goodbye, Gary'..."*

He went on to tell how, as the new K-State athletics director, he successfully campaigned with the rest of the conference's ADs to drop Thompson from the broadcast team, since they had the power to recommend to Carl James, the conference commissioner, whom the broadcasters should be.

But Urick says now, a decade and a half later, it's all history for him. "I have no animosity for Gary Thompson, and I really respect how much he's done for Iowa State," he said. "It was just that he and Lou McCullough got crosswise—starting out over basketball and then it carried over into everything else—and I was loyal to Lou. He was my boss."

Indeed, that is how the strain with McCullough started, Thompson says—over the Iowa State basketball program.

Lou McCullough was "a football man," as former Iowa State football coach Donnie Duncan once described him. Former Iowa State men's basketball coach Lynn Nance remembers McCullough as "a throwback, without a doubt. There were a lot of ADs like Lou back then, football guys, tough guys."

Rod Williamson, who was a young staffer in the Iowa State sports information office, recalled that he often was summoned by McCullough to be his driver and occasional breakfast partner. "Lou was the ultimate, fiery, intense competitor, with a flash temper," Williamson said. "As an administrator, he ruled with an iron fist. Gary Thompson may have had just as much of an iron fist at times, but unlike Lou, he kept it in a velvet glove." Even Urick said that while "Lou was great to me," he also "was very opinionated—stubborn in his own way."

McCullough was a native of Alabama, a U.S. Air Force veteran and a four-sport athlete during his undergraduate years at Georgia Military Academy and then

Wofford College in South Carolina. He also had a master's degree from Columbia University in New York City. He had served as an assistant football coach at Iowa State under head coach Clay Stapleton in 1958-'59, and he also coached at Wofford, Wyoming, Indiana and Ohio State under the legendary Woody Hayes before he was hired in 1971 to become athletics director at Iowa State.

On the one hand, during the 11 years McCullough was athletics director, Iowa State may have accomplished more than under any AD before or after him. Consider the *Ames Daily Tribune's* recitation of his record, in its August 28, 1982, story, which reported that McCullough would leave Iowa State by the end of the '82-'83 school year, which was just getting started:

"During his tenure here at Iowa State, McCullough has watched the Cyclones appear in four post-season football bowl games, capture the NCAA wrestling championships and the gymnastic championships three times each, take the national women's cross-country title five times and bring home conference titles in men's track, baseball, swimming, cross-country and women's indoor track, outdoor track, cross-country, gymnastics and softball.

"Also during his time here, Iowa State has dedicated the 14,300-seat Hilton Coliseum, home of Cyclone basketball, wrestling and gymnastics teams, the new 50,000-seat football stadium in 1975, a new athletics administration building, a new nine-lane synthetic surfaced track facility, a softball complex and six new all-weather tennis courts.

"During these years attendance at Iowa State football games has more than doubled, going from 24,000 to 50,000. Also competition with the University of Iowa has been resumed in all sports."

Before McCullough came to Iowa State in 1971, the athletics director for the Cyclones was his mentor Clay Stapleton, the former football coach. The men's basketball program then was in a down spiral under Coach Glen Anderson. However, in late February of '71, Stapleton pulled off a shocker by persuading the revered coach Maurice "Maury" John to leave Drake University in Des Moines to become the Cyclone basketball coach.

John had taken the Drake Bulldogs to the NCAA Final Four in 1969, then the Midwest Regional finals in both 1970 and '71. Right after that '71 regional tournament, John disclosed he was leaving Drake for Iowa State, where more money, bigger challenges and greater opportunities awaited him.

The Cyclones in that '70-'71 season had won only five games. Iowa State fans, including Gary Thompson, were thrilled that John was coming to Ames. "It was the biggest coup," said Thompson, "especially that Clay Stapleton got him without word getting out in the press.

"Clay was my kind of man," Thompson continued. "He was a man who tried to make Iowa State better. In football, for example, he provided his coach John Majors with more support than Clay ever received when he was the football coach, and that tells me something about Clay."

Stapleton's surprise hiring of the Drake legend happened 2 months before another big surprise—Stapleton left Iowa State to become athletics director at Florida State. Presumably, he recommended that his pal McCullough be summoned from a position as assistant football coach at Ohio State to become AD at ISU.

So McCullough started his new duties at Iowa State about the same time Thompson was hired to become the new analyst, or "color commentator," on the Big Eight Conference's basketball games aired twice a week on network TV, beginning with the 1971-'72 season.

As you learned in Chapter 19, Thompson worked his first 2 years with play-by-play broadcaster Merle Harmon, who then moved on to do play-by-play of Big Ten Conference basketball on another network. Harmon was replaced on the Big Eight games by another well-known network broadcaster, Jay Randolph, and he and Thompson worked the next 19 seasons together.

From that fall of 1971, things went well for Thompson, McCullough and Iowa State men's basketball—for three seasons. Coach John led the Cyclones to a 3-year record of 43 victories and 35 losses, which wasn't great but it was a heck of a lot better than Iowa State had been doing in the years before he took over. But during the '73-'74 season, everyone was stunned to learn that John was diagnosed with cancer.

"Iowa State was playing Drake in Des Moines one night," Thompson recalled. "Maury was normally a fiery guy on the bench, but that night, Drake came back against us and took a lead, and Maury just sat there. I was really surprised at that, but the next day I found out that at 11 a.m. the day of the Drake game, he'd been told he had cancer. Then I understood why he'd been so quiet."

John resigned his coaching position in the mid-summer of 1974, when his condition began to rapidly deteriorate. Thompson was among those named to a "search committee" to help McCullough find a new basketball coach. Generally, such search committees have a half-dozen members, including representatives from the faculty, alumni and other Cyclone supporters.

"Early that August, I went to lunch with Maury, to ask him about his assistant coaches" as candidates for the job, Thompson said. "He was really getting weak by then. After lunch, I drove him back to his office at Hilton Coliseum. I drove down the tunnel on the east side of the building.

"As he was getting out of my car, I said, 'I'll go in with you,' but he said he could make it alone. He was too proud a man to have help. He slowly walked to the door, pulled it open, barely could turn around because he was so weak, waved and said, 'Goodbye, Gary.' I'll never forget that. It just tore me up, seeing what cancer could do to an individual who had been so full of life."

On October 15, John died at the age of 55.

Meanwhile, McCullough had hired John's replacement, Ken Trickey, who had been very successful as head coach at Oral Roberts University in Tulsa. But Trickey's Iowa State teams went 13-40 in his 2 years as the Cyclones coach, and he was fired.

Then in 1976, Lynn Nance, who had once been an FBI agent but most recently had been an assistant coach at the University of Kentucky, was hired.

Nance, in four often-stormy seasons directing the Cyclones, had a 44-64 record and resigned before he was going to be fired.

Thompson also served on the search committee when Nance was hired.

"It is important to understand that on these two search committees, it was Lou McCullough who brought in the candidates," Thompson said. "Our job was to interview them and then give our opinions on the selection of the coach."

Thompson remembers that he "was the only member of the committee who did not vote for Nance. I didn't personally know him at that time, but for my own satisfaction, I did call some Kentucky friends close to that program, and they left me feeling uncomfortable about Nance as a choice for Iowa State."

Thompson said one coach who wanted the Iowa State job then in 1976 was Bill Olsen, an assistant to head coach Denny Crum at the University of Louisville.

"I had worked some Louisville TV games and got to know Denny Crum and Bill Olsen pretty well," Thompson said. "They had a terrific program going, and of course, Crum had coached under John Wooden at UCLA, so Olsen was my choice."

Olsen indeed visited Iowa State for an interview during the regular season, when Louisville was playing Drake in Des Moines.

"Lou McCullough had called me to see if I was interested in the Iowa State job and if I'd come for an interview," said Olsen, who is retired in Louisville. "Gary had talked to me about the job, too, and he'd told me he thought it was a real opportunity.

"Maurice John had shown that if you could get some talent in there, you could win in the Big Eight. At that point in my own career, I was happy at Louisville, but I thought I was ready to be a head coach, too. So besides Iowa State, I had looked at Colorado and at Southern Methodist, and I thought Iowa State might be a good spot for me.

"But the way it worked out, we scheduled the interview for when Louisville was playing Drake, and Gary couldn't be there—he was probably off broadcasting another game. I talked to Lou McCullough, of course, but when I was interviewed by the committee, they were mainly academic people from the university, and it was like talking to people who didn't really understand, you know? I guess I didn't impress them, either, because I never heard from them again."

Olsen wound up staying at Louisville, helping Crum guide the Cardinals to the national championship in 1980, and then becoming U of L athletics director for the rest of his career.

Another candidate surfaced as the regular season was ending in that late winter of '76, Gale Catlett, the head coach at the University of Cincinnati. In his six seasons there, his teams were 126-44 and qualified for the NCAA post-season tournament three times and the National Invitational Tournament once.

Thompson was very enthusiastic about the possibility of Catlett coming to Iowa State, and apparently so was McCullough—for a brief period of time. But Catlett and his Cincinnati team qualified for the NCAA tournament just when McCullough was in hot pursuit of him.

Three years later, in a story looking back at that coaching change, the Des Moines Register reported that Catlett had declined to sign an Iowa State contract while his Cincinnati team was still alive in the tournament. In that same story, the Register reported McCullough's explanation to the search committee was that "Catlett wouldn't sign a contract, and that Iowa State could not wait for him to make up his mind. Thus, the search continued, and Nance was hired."

But Thompson had learned later that Catlett had said he was "95 percent sure" he would have accepted the Iowa State job had McCullough been willing to wait for the Cincinnati season to end. "Catlett probably would have come to Iowa State if the matter had been handled differently at the time," Thompson told the Register.

Catlett, by the way, stayed at Cincinnati one more season, and then went to his alma mater, the University of West Virginia, where he coached 24 more years and built a powerhouse program that produced 439 victories against 276 defeats, and made it to the NCAA tournaments 11 times and the NIT nine times.

It was during the hiring process of those two Iowa State coaches, Trickey and Nance, that Thompson's real trouble with McCullough took root, although Thompson didn't look on it as serious trouble until considerably later.

Other than Olsen and Catlett, the prospective coaches McCullough was finding were not impressing Thompson.

"When I was on those coach search committees, I'm wondering, 'Geez, are these the best candidates we can get at Iowa State?' " Thompson said. "We were a Big Eight school with great facilities, and it seemed to me like we should be getting better coaches interested in our job.

"That's when the trouble with McCullough began..."

"I knew a lot of coaches around the country, and I was giving our athletics department some names of several that I thought would be good candidates and were coaches we might be able to get. Of course, I felt like our athletics director would do the best he could for our university. Then I was told they (McCullough and his assistants) were talking with these coaches, and just couldn't convince anybody to take the job."

Thompson said he began "wondering whether Lou had actually talked to these people. Some of them were friends of mine, and when I asked one why he turned down the job, he said, 'Gary, I never talked to the guy.' "

The story of how McCullough found Lynn Nance—and Nance's stormy four years as the Cyclones' coach—is an especially intriguing one.

Nance talked about it in 2006 from his horse ranch outside Bolivar, Missouri, where, after retiring from basketball, he has been writing adventure novels, among other pursuits. He recalled "he was only 31 or 32 years old" when he got the Iowa State job in 1976.

"I was an assistant coach then at the University of Kentucky when the Iowa State job opened up," he said. "Basketball at UK was so big that the Kentucky governor's office often played a role in helping out our program. Someone in the Kentucky governor's office knew somebody in the Iowa governor's office, and a call got made for me. That led to Lou McCullough agreeing to meet me in the Chicago airport for an interview."

But it got even more intriguing.

Nance's head coach then at Kentucky was Joe B. Hall, who had taken over the Wildcat program from the basketball icon Adolph Rupp, when Rupp retired.

"Mr. Rupp was getting up there in years then, but he still came into the office every day," Nance said. "I got to know him a little, and he knew I was one of the young assistant coaches, but he'd get a little confused about me. He'd say, 'Now which one of those teams of mine was it you played on?'

Nance had actually started his college playing career at Southwest Baptist Junior College in the same Missouri town, Bolivar, where he lives now. Then he finished as an All-Pac Eight Conference player for the University of Washington. After graduating, he was an assistant at the college level, then joined the FBI, eventually became an investigator for the NCAA, then joined Hall's coaching staff at Kentucky.

All of that led to Adolph Rupp making a phone call to Lou McCullough and recommending Lynn Nance for the Iowa State head coaching position. "Lou later told me that call made an impression," Nance said.

Once at Iowa State, Nance realized it was hardly a dream job.

There was an ice hockey "club team" at the university, he remembers, "and they put down ice in Hilton Coliseum for them to play on." When hockey games were coming up or being held, "they were making me take the basketball team over to old State Gym for practice. I mean, I'm trying to compete with Kansas, Kansas State and Missouri in basketball—and they're making me move our practices so a club team can play ice hockey?"

He said he hadn't been there long "when a problem came up. Someone from the business side came to me and said, 'How in the world could you have spent $50,000 or $60,000 on new tennis shoes?' I said, 'What!' I was always pretty frugal in my spending for equipment, and I knew I hadn't spent any unusual amount for shoes for our basketball team. It turns out they'd bought tennis shoes for the whole football team—that's what they were wearing on Astroturf back then—and they put them on my budget. They made it look like the new guy had gone crazy."

But Nance admits now he created some of his own problems, too.

"I was a young coach, trying to get a program going that had only won a couple of games the year or two before, and I did some things that were controversial," he said. "I wasn't the easiest young guy to be around. I made several moves that, when I look back, were very embarrassing to say the least."

One year at the Big Eight tournament in Kansas City, Nance got a technical foul that wound up giving the opposing team 11 points. "I got thrown out of that game, and I was all over the front pages of the Kansas City papers," Nance recalled. "I wanted to make the point with my players that I was not going to take losses lying down."

Then, back in Ames, after the Cyclones played terribly and lost a game he thought they should have won, Nance berated his players in the locker room. He told them to take off the new uniforms they were wearing "because you don't deserve them!" Then he sent them back out on the floor at Hilton Coliseum "and I made them practice in their jockstraps and shoes. Part of the cleaning crew was still up in the arena, and they were shocked, as you can imagine.

"By the time I got home from that late practice, I already realized how out of line I'd been," he said. "I felt terrible about it."

Nance said that the next morning, he got an early call to report to ISU's President Robert Parks.

"When I went in to see the president, I told him right away, 'I am so sorry!'" Nance said. "You know, Dr. Parks was a great president for me. He realized how young I was, and he gave me a lot of good advice, which unfortunately I didn't listen to all the time. But I learned a lot from him."

You can imagine that Athletics Director McCullough was also unhappy about all that. And Gary Thompson must've been shaking his head about the stories that were filtering out of Hilton Coliseum. But Thompson said he was intentionally staying out of any fusses, at that point.

Nance developed the team well enough that in his second year, 1977-'78, the Cyclones finished in a tie for second place in the Big Eight regular season. McCullough was still very critical of him.

"He thought we were playing too soft a schedule in our non-conference games," Nance said. "And we were. But I really believe that winning is a habit, and we had a lot of young guys who needed to win and get some confidence before we headed into the conference season.

"Eventually Lou called me in and told me he was going to take over my scheduling—I wouldn't be able to sign contracts any more—and that he was going to schedule in non-conference opponents who'd been making the NCAA tournament regularly. He said, 'We'll see how you like that!' I knew right then, I was going to be dead meat at Iowa State."

Nance's marriage was also falling apart. He and his wife later reconciled, and are still together. But in 1978 and '79, he was an embattled young man, to say the least.

It was in the fall of 1978, Thompson said, when McCullough somewhat surprisingly "invited me as a guest on an Iowa State football trip for a game in Oklahoma. He took me out to play golf at the Oak Tree Country Club at Edmond.

"Lou told me he was having trouble with Lynn Nance," Thompson recalled. "He told me Lynn was having marriage problems, and I told him I'd heard a rumor about that and felt bad about it. I said I hoped that it was not true because the head coaching job is too big to be burdened with additional problems. And that was about the whole conversation."

Thompson, as he did for years, was regularly playing noon-hour basketball then at State Gym with several faculty members, other old Cyclones and a couple of Nance's assistant coaches.

"After that conversation I had with Lou in Oklahoma, I noticed that all of a sudden, Nance's assistants Reggie Warford and Rick Samuels were kind of giving me the cold shoulder during our noon-hour games," Thompson said. "I finally asked them what was going on, why they weren't talking to me, and they indicated I'd have to ask Lynn Nance himself. So I hit up Nance, and asked him what was going on. He told me that Lou and others in the athletics department had told him I was spreading rumors around town that Nance was having marital trouble and getting a divorce."

Thompson was shocked—and furious.

"I told Lynn that was just a lie, that I certainly had not been spreading any stories about him, and that I wanted to set up a meeting with the three of us," Thompson said. "I said if somebody is going to lie about me, then they're going to have to do it right across the table from me, looking me in the eye.

"I also told Lynn right up front then that I would support him, but I wanted him to know that I had been the one vote against him on the search committee when he got the job, but that after he was hired, I was supportive of his program. Lynn told me he already knew that, and had appreciated my support."

Thompson said he came away from that conversation with Nance concluding "Lou had been lying to me about the coach searches, and now that he was lying about me to Lynn."

He began making some phone calls to coaches and athletics directors around the country, trying to check on how earnestly McCullough had conducted the past coaching searches, and also checking on how Iowa State's athletics department was being viewed around the conference and across the country.

Of course, it didn't take long for McCullough to hear about Thompson's inquiries. And McCullough immediately took aim at Thompson's position on the Big Eight Conference basketball broadcasting team, beginning a campaign to have Thompson removed as the game analyst.

Word about that got back to Thompson quickly, too. He was pro-active in his response.

"I was working a game at Kansas, and Chuck Neinas (the Big Eight Commissioner) came over to say hello," Thompson said. "I told him then that I was having some problems with the Iowa State athletics director, and that he was probably going to pressure the Big Eight to remove me. Chuck said, 'Well, Gary, no one's going to tell me who I'm going to hire and fire. If the TV producer tells me you're doing a good job, you'll keep the job.'"

McCullough apparently did write letters to other athletics directors around the Big Eight, asking them to support his proposal to drop Thompson.

When word of that got around, "one of the top Big Eight administrators talked to me," Thompson said. "He told me, 'Gary, don't worry about being let go. I hate to tell you this, but the others in the conference don't pay much attention to Lou.' Being an Iowa Stater, that was kind of hard to take, hearing how Iowa State was perceived by others in the conference."

But McCullough did take his idea to Commissioner Neinas.

"Lou told me he wanted to replace Gary Thompson on our television package," Neinas recalled in 2005 from Boulder, Colorado, where he was running his own sports consulting company. "I said, 'Lou, that's not going to happen.' I went on and said that Gary's a great representative of the Big Eight, that he was doing exactly what we asked him to do on the broadcasts, that he was doing a great job and that he'd be staying, as far as I was concerned. But Lou brought it up before the entire group of the Big Eight Conference athletics directors. All the rest of them agreed with me, so it was not a tough sell for me at all that Gary would keep his position."

Meanwhile, McCullough was having other trouble in the athletics department. *The Daily Tribune* in Ames reported that financial audits were "critical of the athletics department's financial dealings from 1976 to 1978."

Rod Williamson, the young fellow in the sports information office then, remembers a lot of strain in the department in that era.

"Lou was a guy who always seemed to have an 'us vs. them' outlook, and he'd point over in the general direction of the campus when he'd say that," said Williamson, who left Iowa State in 1983 to become sports information director at Vanderbilt University and, in 2008, was still athletics media relations director there. "He always told us to write everything down—like whom we were meeting with, when and what the discussion was. It was almost a Watergate kind of mentality."

Stories were rampant—and unconfirmed—in Ames about McCullough and his operations of the athletics department. Thompson certainly heard them.

Max Urick, who by early 1978 was emerging as McCullough's key assistant athletics director, said "my recollection is that Lou was accusing Gary, I think, of going to Dr. Parks about getting Lou fired. I don't know if it was some budget issues that Gary was in disagreement with, or what it was."

Thompson's answer to that, years later?

"Yes, I did in fact visit with Dr. Parks then, and I told him our basketball program was in trouble," Thompson said. "Nance had gone around Lou McCullough, and convinced Dr. Parks to add another year to his contract, and that really upset McCullough. Because of that, McCullough wanted to get Nance fired, so he was going to schedule the non-conference games with teams we could not beat.

"Nance had also told me they cut his recruiting budget, and he didn't have any money to bring in kids to visit. Some of our Iowa State players whom I knew well, told me that Lou and Max were second-guessing Nance's coaching, even saying the team should be playing some other defense or some other offense. It was unreal to me that Lou and Max were willing to sacrifice the Iowa State program just to get Nance fired. None of this was personal to me—it was just a matter of feeling I should be standing up for Iowa State."

President Parks listened, then told Thompson he should meet personally with McCullough, to try to work out their differences, the *Des Moines Register* later reported.

In about March of 1979, that meeting was held—and things erupted.

Thompson said he was startled, shortly before the meeting, when McCullough said that he would be asking Max Urick to sit in with them as "a witness." So Thompson took along his trusted friend Ted Tedesco.

Tedesco, as mentioned in earlier chapters, had a very successful insurance agency in Ames and also served as statistician on the Big Eight Conference TV games that Thompson and Jay Randolph were broadcasting. Eventually, he was elected mayor of Ames and then re-elected, serving from 1998-2006.

So on that day in 1979, the four of them met for an hour or longer in McCullough's office in the northwest corner of the Olsen Building, north of the football stadium.

> *"They moved our practices so the club team could play hockey!"*

Urick said he "had a good relationship with both Gary Thompson and Ted Tedesco up to that point, but I knew things were not good between Lou and Gary. Lou would always talk down about Gary to me, not complimentary at all about Gary. I didn't know why. When the conversation started at that meeting, it was cordial at first but tense. And then it got pretty intense. I don't remember what it was all about, but it seems like it was a lot of who told what to whom and when."

Tedesco, speaking in 2005, said he was shocked at what happened in the meeting, and much of it has never been reported publicly until now.

McCullough immediately "made an accusation" that Thompson and Tedesco were trying to get him fired, Tedesco said. "Then he told us that he kept 'a black book' on people, and he had things written down in there on Gary Thompson and me, and that was how he was going to fight us off."

Tedesco and Thompson both now say they were astonished. Tedesco said McCullough did not show them any "black book," but motioned like it was in his desk. Tedesco said they asked Urick if there actually was such a book, but got no response. "We said to McCullough, 'Well, bring it out—let's see it,'" Tedesco continued. "It never came out."

Thompson said he told McCullough, "You get your black book, because you'll never have anything on me in it, because I don't do the kinds of things that get in black books."

Tedesco said later neither he nor Thompson was intimidated, or even worried what McCullough might have written, if indeed there was a black book somewhere.

"First of all, I know Gary Thompson and I know Ted Tedesco," Tedesco said, "and I know there was nothing improper about either one of us. Quite honestly, you wouldn't find two straighter guys than Gary and me. We've always been loyal to our wives. I've never been a drinker, and Gary's never been a drinker.

"So at that point, we accused Lou of flat-out lying, and we told him if he went public with whatever he had in that black book, if he really had one, it'd be slanderous."

The *Des Moines Register* later reported that "it was during this meeting that McCullough first raised the possibility that Iowa State's athletics department might drop the future use of Phillips 66 credit cards."

Tedesco told the newspaper, "Yes, McCullough brought it up at that meeting, saying he might have to call the Phillips Petroleum Co. and discontinue using their credit cards. And Gary said, 'Lou, I thought you might think of that.' Later McCullough said he wouldn't do anything like that—but then (a short time later) he did."

The meeting ended with nothing resolved. "I left with a feeling of real disappointment that people with that kind of character were running that department at Iowa State," Tedesco said.

Word spread fast around the athletics department, across campus and in certain circles in Ames that there'd been a blow-up, but there was no public confirmation about it until 3 or 4 weeks later, on April 17, 1979.

That's when Buck Turnbull, of the *Des Moines Register*, broke a story on page one of the sports section, reporting that McCullough had directed Jim Overturf, Iowa State's business manager of athletics, to recall all of the Phillips 66 credit cards that the athletics staff were using.

"McCullough denied that the withdrawal of the Phillips 66 credit cards was a personal slap at Thompson," the story reported, noting that Thompson was the oil company's distributor in the Ames area. "But Thompson said, 'Why else would he have done it if he didn't think it would hurt me?'"

Thompson explained in the story that, actually, losing the athletics department's business would have no effect on him personally or financially, "but it might be hard on some of the Phillips 66 dealers in Ames."

McCullough denied he was trying to use economic pressure on Thompson.

"That's not it at all," McCullough told Turnbull. "I have no conflict with Gary Thompson and don't know why he feels that way."

The story went on to mention the recent meeting between Thompson and McCullough, with Thompson explaining he'd been unhappy with the way McCullough conducted the basketball coaching searches, especially not landing Catlett, the Cincinnati coach.

McCullough told Turnbull he was aware that Thompson was making inquiries around the country about McCullough's coaching searches, and about the ISU athletics department. Turnbull asked McCullough if he knew why Thompson might be doing that.

"I have no idea," McCullough told him. "When somebody told me about this, it came as a complete shock and surprise to me. I said I considered Gary Thompson a good friend and that it had to be a mistake. Of all the things that have happened to me in my lifetime, this is my biggest surprise. Gary has gone on trips with us. I have played golf with him, and I have never had one word (of dispute) with him."

Thompson today says he learned later that a McCullough staff member, who was alarmed at McCullough's directive about reclaiming the Phillips 66 credit cards, called the Register about it, prompting Turnbull's story.

And Rod Williamson, who was working in sports information then, remembers that most of the staff members in the athletics department were indeed embarrassed by the order. "Lou just wanted to stick it to Gary," Williamson said. "He had a zest for kind of popping it to Gary."

But within a day, ISU vice-president Carl Hamilton, the right-hand man of President Parks, ordered McCullough to rescind his memorandum.

"That made Lou McCullough look like a jerk," Buck Turnbull said in an interview, as he recalled the incident. "The whole thing had been a really dumb move by McCullough."

Thompson says the credit cards matter "was never an issue with me at all. My loyalty to Iowa State was never tied to whether the athletics department was using Phillips credit cards, or whether they were even doing business at my stations. The issue to me was our coaches and basketball program."

But the "Great Credit Card Caper," as the *Register* headlined it, triggered several consecutive days of coverage, not only in the *Register* but also by other newspapers, radio and TV stations in the state. The coverage was fanned by the fact that in the middle of that week when the story broke, the ISU Athletics Council had its regular monthly meeting.

That council—which served to monitor and advise the athletics department with some limited oversight powers—had 15 members. Those included seven elected from the university faculty, three appointed faculty members, two alumni representatives, two students and McCullough. One of the alumni positions was held by Thompson.

Both McCullough and Thompson attended that April council meeting, and their feud really went public. During a 90-minute portion of the meeting, *The Register* reported "there were several sharp exchanges" between the two over the searches and hiring of the recent basketball coaches.

At one point, council member Dahlia Stockdale, a professor in child development, interrupted the chairperson Rollie Knight, another ISU professor, and said, "Mr. Chairman, isn't there a better procedure by which these grievances can be aired? I am disturbed about the lack of dignity here."

A student member of the council, Denise Sofranko, then a graduate student in journalism from the Iowa small town of Lovilia, said she agreed with Thompson that there was "a lack of communication" between McCullough and the Athletics Council. "Everyone is aware of the situation," Sofranko said. "It needs to be out in the open and clarified. The council is the proper vehicle to deal with it."

That idea may have inspired Bill Kunerth, then an Iowa State journalism professor who was not on the council but was closely observing its deliberations, to ask for an even higher-level inquiry into the situation. After the Athletics Council meeting, Kunerth circulated a petition among his journalism faculty colleagues, and 18 of them signed on, asking that ISU President Parks order an investigation of athletics department operations by a special university committee.

The petition, a *Des Moines Register* story noted, suggested that the special committee "should focus on McCullough's relationships with the Athletics Council and with employees of the varsity athletics program. Several reports have been made of extreme dissatisfaction among employees (of that program). Even more serious have been charges of intimidation of theses employees. Such charges have been heard by members of the Athletics Council, faculty members and media representatives."

> *"If they're going to lie about me, look me in the eye..."*

Kunerth, now retired in Belle Fourche, South Dakota, said in 2006 that he still thinks about that petition.

"There were some profs and I who had become disenchanted with the way Lou operated," Kunerth said. "He was pretty heavy-handed and very hard on his help. Old-timers in the athletics department were treated shabbily. Anyway, we thought the flap (with Thompson) would give the university a legitimate excuse to check into some of the complaints about Lou."

He presented the petitions at the president's office on Friday, April 28, and later the same afternoon, Parks declined to take action on it, other than agreeing to refer it on to the Athletics Council. Parks' explanation to the *Register*: "If an investigation is needed, and I am not convinced it is, the group that will do it is the Athletics Council."

Kunerth now says he also remembers that some former Iowa State athletics staff members asked the NCAA to look into the trouble, but that request also got no response.

None of that satisfied Sofranko, one of the two students who served on the Athletics Council. She wrote a letter to President Parks, and sent copies to all members of the Athletics Council, asking that "a permanent investigative and evaluative committee be formed to review the athletics department annually."

Did her letter have any impact?

Well, it made big news, Sofranko now recalls from her home in Albuquerque, New Mexico. After getting three degrees from Iowa State—undergraduate, a master's in journalism in 1981 and then a doctorate in veterinary medicine in 1985—she now works for the *U.S. Department of Agriculture*. She is a specialist in elephant welfare, and advocates for elephants that are displayed in zoos, circuses and other venues.

"One thing I remember from all that," said Sofranko, "was my mother, back home in Lovilia, reading my name in the paper every day, calling and saying, 'Uh, Denise, do you know what you are doing?' "

So, did she know?

"Yeah, I think did," she said. "I had never been very vocal in those meetings up to that point. Being a student, and not really having a lot of background on everything, I listened a lot. But no one was very vocal. I think everybody kind of regarded the council meetings as being Lou McCullough's show. The man had some good qualities, I'm sure, but he was also really a dictator, and we all knew that. And Rollie Knight, the chairman, always wanted to do whatever he could to avoid any controversy at all."

She said as she read and listened to Thompson's concerns and allegations, "I found that I was on the same side of the fence as he was, basically."

But she said there was something else that rankled her as much or more as the charges Thompson was making about McCullough's handling of the coaching changes and departmental operations.

"One of the main things that was really bothering me was the disrespect that was going on," Sofranko said. "Lou and others totally disrespected Gary. And the disrespect they showed Ralph Olsen—a very big Iowa State supporter and such a nice man—was terrible."

Olsen was the turkey farmer from Ellsworth who was a member of the Athletics Council, and who gave the major donation for construction of what today is Jack Trice Stadium. One of the athletics office buildings just north of the stadium—in fact the building where the Athletics Council met—is named after him.

"Lou got to the point where I felt like he was dismissive of Ralph Olsen," said Sofranko, "and that really bothered me."

She said she was confident that Thompson, Kunerth and others were raising legitimate concerns about the athletics department, "because some of us who were members of the council had people who were working in the department talking to us. They wouldn't talk in their offices, though; we'd meet them in restaurants around Ames. Some were afraid that their offices were bugged, or that their conversations might be overheard by other people in the offices. A lot of those athletics employees were scared of Lou."

After she sent her letter to President Parks, asking for the formation of a standing investigative and evaluative committee, she said he responded in a way that at first stunned her.

"Dr. Parks called me into his office, saying he wanted to talk to me about my letter," Sofranko said. "I was surprised when I met with him, because he really came down on me pretty hard. I took it as a deliberate attempt to intimidate me.

"It was fairly threatening, to the point where he seemed to indicate that if I persisted in this, I might get kicked out of school. You know, it may have been my youth and naiveté right then, but my response to him, in so many words, was 'You're not scaring me.' And I figured if he kicked me out of school because of the letter, well, I'd be telling a few people about it."

All of that was a run-up to the May 16, 1979, meeting of the Athletics Council, at the end of which, the terms of council members Thompson and Sofranko were expiring.

What happened was surprising, to say the least.

Register reporter Buck Turnbull's story about the meeting carried a banner headline across the top of the next morning's sports page: "McCULLOUGH SURVIVES ISU RIFT." A secondary headline reported, "Gets strong faculty support." And here's the top of Turnbull's story:

> AMES, IA.—Lou McCullough scored what appeared to be a clear-cut victory Wednesday at Iowa State's Athletics council meeting, the second half of which was a lively session.
>
> McCullough, Cyclone athletics director since 1971, received strong support from faculty members on the council in a recent dispute that has found him at odds with Gary Thompson, a former Iowa State basketball All-American.
>
> The rift had led to several petitions being circulated on the campus calling for ISU President Robert Parks to appoint a committee to investigate McCullough's administration and his dealings with employees of the athletics department.
>
> Parks declined, saying it was a matter for the Athletics Council to resolve.
>
> Then several weeks ago Denise Sofranko, a student member of the council, sent a letter to President Parks and other members of the council asking that a permanent investigative and evaluative committee be formed to review the athletics department annually.
>
> Thompson and Sofranko both were ending their terms on the council with this last meeting of the school year, but none of the concerns they had voiced was on the agenda and thus had not been discussed when Rollie Knight, the outgoing chairman, called for a motion to adjourn the old council.
>
> The motion had been made and seconded when Sofranko, a graduate student from Lovilia, interrupted to say she wanted to make a comment on old business or new business—whatever it might be called.
>
> Knight sought a vote on the motion to adjourn, but Sofranko persisted by saying:

"If you adjourn the council, then I am no longer a member. I believe it is appropriate that I at least deserve some sort of acknowledgement that the letter I wrote was received by members of the council."

Knight said that he felt it was a matter for the new council members to delve into if they wished, but added: "You will have input, I guarantee you that."

The motion to adjourn was finally passed, with Thompson leaving the room and Sofranko staying to observe the proceedings while Roy Keller, a professor of mathematics, succeeded Knight as the chairman for next year.

Afterward, when she was asked for no further contribution, Sofranko said bitterly:

"I guess they put me in my place. They just told me to shut up and they had no reason to do that."

The new council then had a brief meeting, at the start of which John Mahlstede, a faculty representative, spoke in McCullough's defense and branded the "attacks" on the athletics director as "subversive treatment, innuendo and subtle gossip. We shouldn't allow that from those who claim to be friends of the university."

Thompson was not in the room to hear that, but Sofranko was. She told Turnbull afterward that she "took that as a personal insult. I consider myself a good friend of the university, and I wasn't on any kind of a witch hunt."

Ralph Olsen, whose membership continued on the new council, spoke up for Sofranko. "I am not a vindictive person," Olsen said, "but some questions have been raised here, and when the young lady tried to talk, you were very rude to disregard her. She is very sincere and takes great interest in the program."

Olsen attempted to voice a few criticisms of the athletics department himself, and at one point, McCullough told him, "You are completely out of order," according to Turnbull's story.

"The way this council operates is crazy," Olsen then said. "They say it isn't a one-man operation, but it is."

He told Turnbull after the meeting he might well take a more "active interest" in the athletics department in the future.

In a "Sports Opinion" column three days later in the *Des Moines Sunday Register*, Turnbull wrote that "the members of the council cannot and should not take pride in how they conducted their meeting in Ames last week." He added that "every effort was made to stifle the controversy."

He also reported that Iowa State coaches "have called members of the media in support of McCullough, so the rift may have served to strengthen his position and unify the department."

Sometime soon after all that, Thompson said, he received a phone call from Turnbull, asking if during that heated meeting in March, he had really been profanely dismissive about Oklahoma University Athletics Director

Wade Walker, a close friend of McCullough. Turnbull said he'd been told that by both McCullough and Urick, Thompson said.

"I told Buck that was another complete lie," Thompson said. "I asked him if he would check that out while I was still on the phone. I told him to use his other line to call Ted Tedesco, so that he'd know I wasn't calling him myself first to tell him what to say. I wanted Buck to ask Ted if I had said anything like that. Buck just said, 'Gary, if you tell me you didn't say it, that's good enough for me.' "

Thompson said he asked Turnbull "two or three times" if Urick had confirmed that Thompson had said such things, and was told, yes, Urick had confirmed that.

"That shocked me," Thompson said later. "Supporting your boss is one thing, but not telling the truth is another. That is when I lost all respect for Max Urick."

Thompson said he never challenged McCullough about that quotation, or misquotation, "because I would expect that from Lou."

But he said he did bring it up a few weeks later to Urick, when he encountered him before a basketball game that Thompson was preparing to broadcast at Iowa State.

"I asked him if he had told Buck Turnbull that, and Max started stammering and said, 'Well, that's been a long time ago,' " Thompson said. "I said that's what Buck had told me, and then Max said, 'If Buck says I said it, I might have said it.' Then Max points to me and says, 'And it's guys like you that are bad for our program!' And he walked away."

Urick said in 2005 that he does not recall that specific confrontation.

McCullough did not officially leave Iowa State until after the 1982-'83 school year, which was more than 3 years after all the controversy in the spring of 1979.

Thompson said that during that time period, when he would encounter McCullough at Iowa State games or around Ames, they were both civil enough, although there was naturally some lingering tension, too. "I was just kind of banned from any athletics department activities," Thompson said.

The fact was, the McCullough era at Iowa State actually began winding down during 1979.

Football coach Earle Bruce, whose Cyclones had finished 8-4 in the fall of '78, left to become head coach at Ohio State—and he had been a strong McCullough ally. Donnie Duncan was hired to replace Bruce at ISU. Duncan's first Iowa State team in the fall of '79 went 3-8, and then the Cyclones played about .500 under him the next 3 years. Meanwhile, men's basketball under Lynn Nance was getting real wobbly. And tension seemed to be growing in the athletics department offices.

There was at least one more bright moment for McCullough, however.

After Nance told everybody at mid-season that he would be leaving the basketball coaching job in the spring, McCullough began another search for a new coach—and he did not ask Thompson for any suggestions.

Tony McAndrews, an assistant coach to Lute Olson then at the University of Iowa, was contacted by McCullough. McAndrews in turn called Thompson and asked for his thoughts on the Iowa State job, and Thompson said he encouraged him "but I told him to get things in writing."

Right at that same time, the Iowa Hawkeyes got hot in the tournament and made the Final Four.

"Lou McCullough apparently felt like he was under pressure to find a new coach and announce it right away," Thompson said. "Tony McAndrews wouldn't allow it to be announced until Iowa was done in the tournament, and they kept winning."

McCullough did not want to wait, as his former assistant Urick remembers it.

"Our program did not have a good reputation at that point," said Urick, "and we knew we had to get somebody quick who could get people excited and who could turn things around. We did not have a candidate for the position, so Lou McCullough called Johnny Orr, who was coaching at Michigan then, to ask him about his assistant coach, Bill Frieder."

What McCullough was startled to find out was that Orr himself was dissatisfied at Michigan, where he'd never made more than $33,000 per year, despite leading the Wolverines to the NCAA Final Four and several Big Ten Conference championships. When Iowa State offered him $52,000 per year, Orr took the job.

Gary Thompson, who was at the Final Four to work on the broadcast team doing the third place game, had no idea Orr was even a possibility.

"Before Iowa's game in the semi-finals, after the Hawkeyes' practice, I talked to Tony McAndrews and told him I was looking forward to him coming to Iowa State," Thompson said. "Tony said something like, 'Well, I'm hoping to be there. I was told they're considering somebody else as well, but I don't consider who they were talking to to be any competition.' At that time, Tony didn't know about Johnny Orr being considered. He thought it was another coach from some small school."

Thompson said he first learned about Orr's hiring "about midnight after the Monday night

"I don't do the kind of things that get in black books..."

championship game. I ran into Maury White (sports columnist then for the *Des Moines Register*), and he told me Johnny Orr was going to be named the new Iowa State coach the next morning. I was shocked. It was the first time I had even heard Orr's name mentioned.

"But I thought it was just great," Thompson continued. "So when I got back home, I called up Orr to congratulate him and to tell him I was glad he was coming to Iowa State. He thanked me but then he said, 'Gary, Lou McCullough and Max Urick told me you weren't in favor of me getting the job.'

"I hadn't known anything about it at all until Maury White told me! And I had never talked to McCullough and Urick about Orr, or any other candidate then. So I said, 'John, you'll have to figure out these guys for yourself, I guess, because I sure can't.' "

Orr, who was Iowa State's coach until he retired in 1995, recalled in an interview in 2005 that "what Lou McCullough and the others told me, before I took the Iowa State job, was they all thought that Gary Thompson was trying to get Lou's job. That's what they said.

"So my relationship with Gary, once I got to Ames, wasn't really a strained one, but because of the way it started, it couldn't ever be as close as it probably should have been. We liked a lot of the same things—basketball and golf—and we both wanted Iowa State to win. He emceed some of my TV shows and the Cyclone Club luncheons, and we got along fine, but we were never real close, I guess."

Thompson recalled that Orr asked him to help find sponsors for his coach's show on TV, "and I was glad to do that."

Orr said he did get angry with Thompson years later, in 1995, and with Thompson's friend Richard Stark, of Fort Dodge, another big Cyclone booster. "I was trying to get my assistant Jim Hallihan my job when I was leaving Iowa State, because he'd been with me 12 years and was a heck of a good coach," Orr said.

"I called Gary and asked him for his help, and he said, 'I can't speak to that.' So I called Richard and asked if he could support Jimmy, and he said he didn't think he could do the job. Made me mad. Both of them did. But I got over it. They went on and got Tim Floyd and he did a helluva good job. Timmy's a great college coach."

But back to 1980.

Orr was like a breath of fresh air blowing across Iowa when he arrived, but good as he was, he was not enough to save McCullough's job—for long. Rod Williamson, who was transitioning from being an assistant in sports information to working with the Cyclone Club, said the athletics staff became aware that the university administration was taking a harder look at McCullough.

"I know there was some effort to have some of Lou's out-of-town activities investigated," Williamson said. "A lot of us suspected Lou was traveling a lot, and not exactly on university business like he said. And he became very moody. When he'd come back from trips, we'd all try to hide. We always thought he'd come back with a guilty conscience, and the way he'd deal with it is he'd just go off on us. So we'd try to avoid that.

"I think a fair number of us in the building felt Lou was just a little too crafty in the way he operated, and that he was eventually going to get trapped," Williamson continued. "Things that he preached to us—all this paranoia about 'us vs. them' and documenting everything—wound up tripping him up. His receptionist took him at his word and wrote stuff down—inappropriate remarks—and it got him."

Urick recalled "there was a sexual harassment thing," and top university administrators "encouraged Lou to step aside."

Some now say that McCullough surprised the administration when he called the press conference on August 27, 1982, announced his own resignation and said he'd serve through the school year.

"Lou's resignation was not a surprise to me," Thompson said. "A source in the university told me 2 weeks prior what was in the works. I knew the day, the hour and who was delivering the message to Lou, that he was through at Iowa State."

When Ron Maly, another *Des Moines Register* sportswriter, contacted Gary Thompson for comment about McCullough's sudden announcement, Thompson responded: "With the best interest of Iowa State in mind, I'm extremely happy with his decision."

President Parks soon designated Urick to be the successor to McCullough, to take over on June 1, 1983.

"Actually I didn't want to be AD, had no designs on it at all and I wondered who they'd bring in for the job," said Urick. "Wayne Moore was a vice-president for business at the university then, and he said he'd talk to Dr. Parks about me, that they'd make me the AD designate.

"I told him I didn't want to be the AD, but he said, 'No, you'll do fine.' The president, Wayne Moore and Carl Hamilton, the vice-president for information services, wound up being great mentors for me. They taught me how to become an administrator."

Urick, who had been an outstanding athlete in football, lacrosse and wrestling at Ohio Wesleyan University, had been at Iowa State since 1974, when McCullough had hired him as an assistant athletics director.

"I was 34 years old when I came to Iowa State, and didn't know from straight up," Urick said. "But I had coached on defense in football with Lou at Ohio State from 1963 to '66, and he must've thought I'd be a good assistant on his staff at Iowa State. I was an assistant football coach at Duke then, so in January of 1974, on a day when it was eight degrees below zero, I drove into Ames in a Volkswagen Squareback that was freezing inside with my wife, three kids aged from 3 to 6, and our dog.

"I wasn't all that anxious to get out of coaching, but when the opportunity at Iowa State came up, I thought I'd give it a try. I knew it'd give me a chance to be closer to my wife and kids than coaching would, and we did get to go through the Cub Scouts, Brownies, Little League and all that with the kids."

He said he essentially had on-the-job training at Iowa State from McCullough, assistant ADs Bob Marcum and Dave Cox, ISU vice-president for student affairs Tom Thielen and others.

Urick said he "wasn't aware of Gary Thompson until I got to know him through the Cyclone Club events. I was not close to Gary, but I came to admire him personally and professionally back then, and I appreciated his support of the basketball program. I think he felt a real sense of loss over the struggles we were having in basketball, with losing seasons and our string of coaches who weren't successful."

ISU President Parks told Urick that he would take over as athletics director on June 1, 1983. But in late January, Donnie Duncan resigned as football coach, and the president told Urick he wanted him—not McCullough—to do the hiring of the new football coach.

"I made a bad decision on that one," Urick said. "I hired Jim Criner, who had had a big year at Boise State out West, and it just never worked out for us. I fired him after 2 or 3 years and hired Jim Walden," who was more popular but no more successful in terms of wins and losses.

That got Urick's AD tenure off to a somewhat shaky start. And he wound up going through a painful break-up of his marriage and eventually a divorce that sent shock waves through the athletics program, the university and Iowa State's fan base.

But Urick was very popular with Iowa State's athletes, coaches, supporters and the media during his 10 years in the position. Part of that was he was so much more outgoing and personable than McCullough had been.

He also stabilized the athletics department's finances, adding some fun new income by opening the football stadium for concerts by such major rock 'n' roll superstars as the Rolling Stones and Paul McCartney. And Orr's Cyclone men's basketball teams were having enough success to keep most Iowa State fans happy the rest of the sports year.

Urick and Thompson had no real conflicts in that decade. They would see each other at Cyclone events, visit briefly and cordially, then go their separate ways—Urick as the athletics director of one of the Big Eight conference institutions, Thompson as the basketball analyst on telecasts of Big Eight basketball games and a growing number of NCAA tournament games.

"Johnny Orr was a breath of fresh air across Iowa..."

"I guess it'd be fair to say that Gary and I had no relationship in those years when I was athletics director at Iowa State," Urick said. "We had only minimal dealings, maybe at a golf outing or something like that. We weren't unfriendly. We just never got more involved than that."

Dr. Bob Gitchell, an Ames physician, long-time Cyclone booster and friend of both men, said "Gary was sort of out of the loop, and that was really too bad for Iowa State. My feeling was here was this person in our own community who knows everybody in the sports world, and they all know him. He was a tremendous resource, and Iowa State didn't take advantage of him."

Perhaps that is understandable, given the hard feelings that had grown in the McCullough era.

As AD, Urick also increased the graduation rates for scholarship athletes, although he also had to endure a couple of high profile cases of athletes being involved in criminal activity or embarrassing academic scrapes.

It was a combination of a couple of those cases making big news, plus the

Cyclone teams continuing to have only modest success, that wound up putting Urick on the hot seat in front of new Iowa State President Martin Jischke in the 1992-'93 school year. Robert Parks had retired from the presidency in 1986, was succeeded by Gordon Eaton, who had little to do with the athletics program, and then by Jischke in 1991.

Jischke, who stayed at Iowa State until 2000 when he became president of Purdue University, quickly established three things when he came to ISU: 1) He was very smart and he was as tough as he was smart, 2) he personally would be making the biggest decisions that needed to be made on the campus, and 3) he wanted the Cyclones to win in sports.

He quickly did his homework about who the influential Iowa State alumni were, and that led him to Gary Thompson. What did the president learn about him?

"I learned that he had been an absolutely sensational athlete at Iowa State," Jischke said in 2005. "Many people gave me very detailed accounts of the basketball game in which he outscored Wilt Chamberlain and the Cyclones beat Kansas in 1957. I learned that Gary was a successful businessman, that he was still very loyal to Iowa State and was very interested in everything happening at the university. As I got to know him, I came to enjoy him on a personal level, too."

Suddenly, it seemed, Gary Thompson's counsel was being sought again at ISU, at least in the president's office. Jischke came to rely on him for advice, especially about hiring basketball coaches.

"He's very knowledgeable about intercollegiate athletics, particularly basketball," Jischke said. "He knew all the coaches, and he knew many of the people in the business side of athletics from his broadcasting career. He was very helpful to us in identifying good candidates."

Did the president ever feel Thompson was meddling?

"No, not at all," Jischke said. "To me, he was utterly honest, straight-forward and transparent with his assessments of people and situations. He always made it clear that he was giving me his own opinion. He had his views, and that's how he presented them—not as being the way things had to be. There was never any question who was making the decision—that buck stopped at the president's desk. Gary was always respectful of that."

Thompson said he quickly sensed something very positive in Jischke's outlook on athletics.

"I give Martin a lot of credit," Thompson said. "He made the decision to commit the resources so that Iowa State was finally going to be able to compete."

Not all perceived Jischke that way, however.

"Martin and I never got along," said Urick. "I could tell by his demeanor, I wasn't going to get along with him. He was not the greatest communicator, and he was very confrontational. It was 'in your face,' and I didn't admire him for that or respond well to it."

Buck Turnbull, the retired *Register* sportswriter, said after he observed

Jischke for a time around Cyclone athletics, "I knew it was going to be tough for Max Urick to work for a guy like him. He wasn't going to survive that. I don't know anybody who's got much nice to say about Jischke during his Iowa State years."

Jischke himself recalled that in the early 1990s, "we were at a time of a lot of change in college athletics," especially at Iowa State. Because of its location, and its reputation as a second-tier competitor in most sports, recruiting of athletes and coaches was very difficult. And revenue from advertising and broadcast rights for Cyclone athletics wasn't even close to what Oklahoma, Nebraska and Colorado were getting.

Many thought the answer was a merger of the Big Eight and Southwest Conferences to form what became the Big XII, which would bring more TV access in major markets in Texas and elsewhere. But if competing with Oklahoma, Nebraska, Colorado and the others in the Big Eight had been difficult, competing with such powerhouses as Texas and Texas A&M would require major new investments in talent, programs and facilities for a university like Iowa State.

"We came to a decision we needed new leadership in the athletics department," said Jischke. He said that would eventually include a new athletics director, new football coach if Jim Walden could not quickly produce a winner, and a new men's basketball coach whenever Johnny Orr decided to retire.

"We gave Max Urick plenty of notice that his contract would not be renewed, so that he could pursue other options," Jischke said. "Max clearly was not happy about that, but I felt strongly that we needed to make a change."

Urick said he got that notice in late January, 1993, from Jischke's assistant Reid Crawford, who told him the administration did not plan to make an announcement until March or April. He was also told he would receive no severance package.

He said after talking to his new wife, Lynn, Cyclone broadcaster Pete Taylor and some of the head coaches, he "decided I better look out for ol' Max, and I called a press conference about a week later. I wanted people in intercollegiate athletics to know I was available. I took the high road with the press. I said I'd been told my contract would not be renewed, and that I wanted to thank everybody for my years at Iowa State. I also thanked the administration for giving me the opportunity to work with them. I meant all that, too."

He soon was among the candidates for athletics director positions that were opening at Michigan State and Minnesota, and he was one of four finalists for the job at the University of Houston. But he wound up pursuing and winning the position at Kansas State, where he was very successful for 8 years before his retirement in 2001.

And Gene Smith, a former football player and assistant football coach at Notre Dame, came from serving as athletics director at Eastern Michigan University to take over at Iowa State. He directed the Cyclone programs until

2000, when he became athletics director at Arizona State. In 2005, he moved up again to become AD at Ohio State.

So, in 1993, did Gary Thompson "torpedo" Max Urick as athletics director at Iowa State, or in his bid to become AD at K-State, as Urick suspects?

"No," Thompson said, "and I'll give you examples."

He recalled that Iowa State President Martin Jischke "invited me to have dinner with him at his home The Knoll, just the two of us, and he wanted some thoughts on the athletics director situation. There'd been a conflict between the administration, the athletics department and Max Urick over a football player's eligibility, and there'd been a lot of criticism of Max Urick about it. The president asked me what I thought about it.

"I told him, 'As you know, I lost my respect for Max Urick because he had not told the truth about me previously.' But then I went on and told the president that with the limited information I had on this case, mostly from reading the newspapers, I did not feel the athletics department should be held accountable in this situation. I also told him that I didn't feel Max should be terminated over this issue.

"In that situation, I think President Jischke was looking to me for a negative about Urick, and I didn't give him one.

"And with K-State, I never initiated anything," Thompson continued. "I was in Manhattan, a guest of Kansas State, to play in the Jim Colbert Celebrity Golf Tournament, a fundraiser for their athletics department. I had been invited to several tournaments previously. Ernie Barrett, a former Kansas State player and athletics director, was hosting a cocktail tournament at his home the night before the tournament.

"Soon after I arrived, Ernie came up to me and said, 'Gary, two guys from our athletics director search committee will be here tonight, and they want to talk to you about Max Urick.' I told Ernie, 'I do not want to talk about Max Urick.' But he said that two of their boosters, Max Moss and Jack Vanier, 'will corner you.' Moss was a former K-State basketball player, and Vanier was one of their major contributers. Later on, both did come over and wanted to know what I thought of Max Urick. I told them I didn't want to talk about him, but they kept pushing and pushing and said they'd keep everything confidential.

"I told them I did not worry about something being in confidence, because whatever I said would be the truth. I had always had a great relationship with Kansas State people, and I finally gave in and told them what had happened between Max Urick and me. I repeated what I've always said, 'I have no respect for someone who does not tell the truth about another person,' and that is exactly what I told them. I didn't say anything about whether he'd be a good athletics director, a bad athletics director or anything about him personally. That was it. Those were the only two people I talked to."

Thompson said with all the friends he had then within the conference, "I knew 2 weeks before I visited Manhattan that Max Urick was being considered for the job. If I had wanted to try to 'torpedo' Max, I'd have picked up the phone and called basketball coach Jack Hartman, Ernie Barrett and a few other good friends in the K-State athletics department, but I didn't. I could have cared less whether Max got the job there. I was just happy he was no longer at Iowa State."

So, Thompson said, "in that situation, the people at K-State were looking for positive reinforcement from me about Urick, and I didn't give it to them. I just told them the truth."

Since Kansas State was also in the Big Eight, Urick already knew all the other athletics directors in the conference. They had recently taken over selection and contracting of the TV broadcast team that would do conference basketball games.

When the contracts were being considered for the 1994-'95 season, Urick said he "told the other ADs that I was let-go at Iowa State, and that I was thankful for the opportunities at Kansas State. I told them Gary Thompson and I had had conflicts, and that I believed he recommended against me getting my K-State position. I said if he can do that to me, if he has those kind of feelings toward me, how can he be impartial in reporting on K-State? Then I said, 'I know how I'm voting—I'm voting against Gary Thompson being part of our basketball broadcasting team.'"

"His Norwegian stubbornness wouldn't let him quit..."

Whether there was an actual vote taken or preferences were just stated is unclear, but Urick said "it was 8-0" against Thompson. That means, presumably, that Iowa State's representative also went against Thompson, which seems unlikely.

Joe Castiglione, athletics director at Oklahoma since 1998 and previously in the same position at Missouri from 1993-'98, said he does not recall a formal vote being taken.

"I remember the issue being raised, but I just don't remember a vote," Castiglione said in 2005. Referring to Urick's allegation that Thompson had recommended against him at Kansas State, Castiglione said it "just didn't sound like Gary. It didn't sound like something he would do. I know Gary. I know Max. I like both of them. If they had a disagreement, I can understand that."

There was additional discussion about the matter later among the ADs, Urick said. "We felt it was susceptible to problems having a guy as a commentator who is so strongly identified with one of our schools. We felt it's better now to have somebody a little more neutral."

When the contracts for the 1994-'95 season were issued, Thompson did receive one, but it was to do only three games rather than the normal number of 13 to 15.

"When I found out that the number of games was going to be cut, I went to the Big Eight office and asked who was responsible," Thompson said.

"They told me Max Urick, the Kansas athletics director Bob Frederick and the Colorado athletics director Bill Marolt, as members of the conference's television committee, were responsible. Because of my concern about Max not telling the truth about me at Iowa State, I called several ADs to tell them exactly what I'd told Max Moss and Jack Vanier at K-State about Max Urick. I wanted to be sure they knew the truth.

"When I called Frederick, he would not return my calls. But Marolt returned my call almost immediately. I told him I wanted him to know exactly what I had said about Max and that I did not try to torpedo him on the job. I told him I was asked by Kansas State, and I told him exactly what I'd said. I told him that I didn't think that should be held against me, for telling the truth. I told him that if he were taking this action of reducing my number of games because he thinks I'm not a good basketball analyst, I couldn't fight that, because that would be his opinion.

"But I asked Bill, 'Is this just a case of you and Bob Frederick being Max's friend, and he wants you to do him a favor?' He said, 'Yes.' I told him, 'Bill, I respect you for being honest.' I called some other ADs and they told me they had no part in that decision. Some said they had cast no votes. And some told me, 'You can quote me on that.' "

Thompson said he also called Pete Derzis, the general manager of the television company producing the Big Eight games then, and told him "that I just wanted him to know the truth about what I'd told the Kansas State people" about Urick. "Pete told me, 'Gary, I would like to give you more games, but I'm caught in the middle, because we want to be able to renew the contract again with the Big Eight.' I told him, 'Don't worry about that.' He offered to put me on the Studio Show, but I told him, 'Pete, I'm an analyst,' and that I had no interest in the Studio Show."

Thompson said his own "Norweigan stubbornness was not going to let me quit, because that is exactly what Max Urick wanted me to do."

But he made a last phone call about the matter, this one to Big Eight Commissioner Carl James. "I repeated to him what I'd told Kansas State about Max, so he also knew the truth," Thompson said. "I told him I'd been through this before with Lou McCullough, and that Commissioner Chuck Neinas had supported me at that time.

"I asked Carl for his support, and he said, 'That is now the TV Committee's job.' I said, 'Are you telling me you now have no authority in hiring announcers? Chuck Neinas had authority over hiring announcers. Are you saying you don't?' And I said, 'Can I quote you on that?' He hung up the phone on me. That was when I made my decision to quit."

Thompson said he cooled down and realized he'd "been at it (on the Big Eight broadcasting team) for 23 years, and that was probably enough. So I called Pete Derzis and told him I'd make it easy on everybody, and I'd just quit."

His replacement, ironically, was Jon Sundvold, who had been a great player at Missouri and a pro player. "So much for not having an analyst with ties to any of the conference schools," Thompson said.

Oklahoma's AD Castiglione, looking back on it, says he is "disappointed something like that occurred. I was sorry it caused Gary to say goodbye to the Big Eight. He was an enormous part of the growth of Big Eight basketball. It really took off in the 1980s and became a national draw. Gary Thompson and Jay Randolph were a big part of making that happen."

Thompson went on to do another 11 years of basketball commentary in telecasts of Iowa State games on the Cyclone Television Network, as you will read in the next chapter.

It seems rather amazing how, all those years Thompson was doing Big Eight basketball, most of us thought it was all about sports. Of course, it was. But there sure was a lot of drama tangled up in it, too.

As retired *Des Moines Register* sportswriter Ron Maly said, when we were talking it over, "You know, it's unbelievable all the stuff that's gone on in Ames."

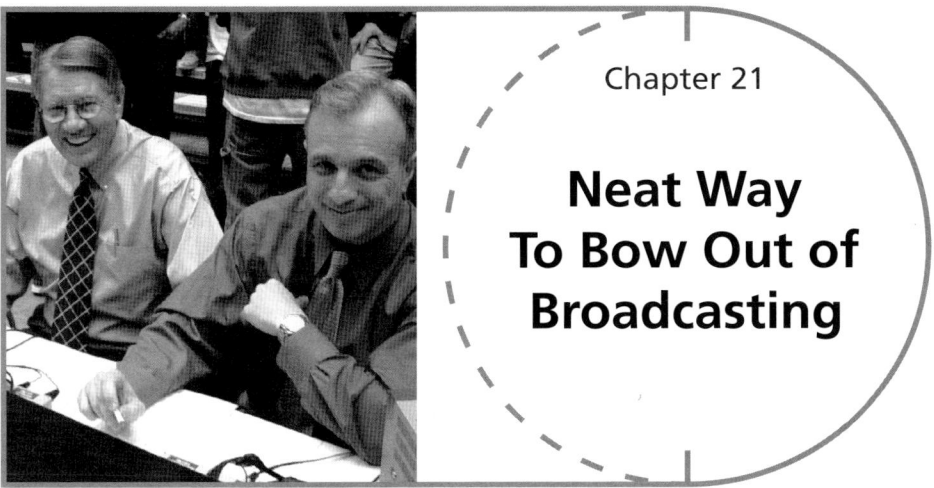

Chapter 21

Neat Way To Bow Out of Broadcasting

WHEN Gary Thompson left the Big Eight Conference TV broadcasting team in 1994, his alma mater Iowa State University quickly snapped him up to serve as the analyst for the telecasts being originated of its own men's basketball games.

It may not have occurred to Cyclone fans at first what they were getting in that deal, since most of them were so accustomed to seeing Thompson around Iowa State. Heck, a high percentage of them knew Thompson personally then, and still do. But it became clear over the next 11 years when Thompson was analyzing Iowa State games, fans were getting to hear one of the most knowledgeable persons anywhere on all things basketball.

He offered commentary in the classic, almost understated Thompson way. He was never a screamer, but at the same time, he was not colorless, and he could laugh right along with his play-by-play partner and the rest of the fans when something crazy happened in a game.

In the Cyclone broadcasts, Thompson drew on his lifelong study of the game of basketball, as well as on his 23 years of television experience doing the Big Eight Conference games, as well as some top regional games and also NCAA tournaments. In that time, he had worked with many of the leading basketball broadcasters of the era.

He brought all of that to his game analysis on Cyclone telecasts, and it was like the fans were receiving authoritative, insightful basketball commentary that they'd never hear anywhere else. And it was delivered up in a way that was neither preachy, nor pretentious—in fact, it was often self-deprecating.

"I'll tell you, the players in my era did not compare well to the size, strength and quickness of these players today," Thompson said over and over in broadcasts. "I think we may have known the fundamentals of the game a little more back then, but with the weight training, speed training and nutritional programs the players have today, they're taking the game to another level."

John Walters, sports director at WOI-TV based in Des Moines and Ames, did play-by-play of Cyclone men's basketball, with Thompson as the analyst, for 6 years, from 1996-2003. In 2003, Walters moved over to the Cyclone Radio Network after the death of legendary Iowa State radio broadcaster Pete Taylor.

"Gary was terrific," Walters said. "When I first started working with him, I didn't have any idea about his accomplishments in TV earlier. I knew all about what he'd done as a player, and I knew he was a real ambassador for Iowa State. But I didn't know he'd worked with the national broadcasters like Dick Enberg and Bob Costas in those NCAA games.

"He was awesome to work with. I always felt like I was getting an education about basketball. Gary could see the little nuances of the game, and explain them to the fans in a way that was informative and interesting without being condescending. I think Iowa State's fans are among the most educated college basketball fans in the nation because they've been listening to Gary Thompson for all those years. They understand basketball a whole lot better than most fans do."

"He even taught broadcast professionals something..."

Youngsters could learn as much about the game as older fans did.

Thompson and I met Jeff Staker, a teacher and coach at Roland-Story Middle School in Thompson's hometown of Roland one day when we were walking through the gym where he first came to stardom. It was during the 2004-'05 season, Thompson's last as a broadcaster. "I tell our kids now that they need to watch Iowa State and listen to what Coach Thompson says," Staker said. "I tell them they can learn a lot about the game of basketball that way."

He also taught a lot to broadcast professionals.

"I learned so much more about basketball from Gary than I ever did going to practices," said Bob Helmers, who served as producer for nearly all the games Thompson did on the Cyclone Television Network through the years. "He elevated that analyst's position to a new level in broadcasting, with his knowledge of the game."

Keith Murphy, now the sports director at WHO-TV in Des Moines, was Walters' predecessor at WOI in Ames, and Murphy did the play-by-play of Cyclone TV games from the early 1990s until 1996. Thompson was his game analyst for a couple of those seasons.

"I was young, and probably in over my head when I started working those Cyclone games," Murphy said. "They paired me up with Gary, a guy 30 years older than me, someone my dad's age. But he made me look better than I had a right to, especially by giving me tips before the game.

"He really taught me a lesson about preparing for the game," Murphy continued. "He always did his homework. When we'd go on a road trip, he'd start preparing a day or two ahead of time, and he'd still be doing research the whole time we were traveling."

The better Murphy became acquainted with Thompson, the more he appreciated him.

"I'd heard of Gary, as a player and a broadcaster, but the first opportunity I had to get to know him was when we worked together," Murphy said. "I realized how good he must've been as a player because we'd show up a couple of hours early for games, and he'd sometimes go out on the floor, shoot a basket or two, and then beat some 20-year-old in a game of 'HORSE.'

"In some ways, he's almost too good to be true. He's the closest thing I've ever known to someone being the classic 'All-American boy.'

"I don't know if I've ever had more respect for the life someone has led than I do for Gary's. He's a two-sport All-American, great family, successful in everything he's done, kind to everybody. I think of him as an old-school All-American."

Murphy said one thing he "picked up from Gary is that he just doesn't curse. Like a lot of guys my age, my language could get pretty rough. After I was around Gary for a while, I realized it's just stupid for me to be swearing like I was. So now, years later, when I'm around my own kids, and if I get frustrated with them, I say, 'Son-of-a-biscuit!' And, of course, I got that from Gary. It's as close as I ever heard Gary come to cussing."

Murphy said he decided to try to emulate Thompson in several aspects of life after a frightening airplane trip back to Ames from Milwaukee, where they had done the telecast of an Iowa State game at Marquette.

"That's the closest I've come to dying in an airplane," he said. "The weather was just terrible, we were bouncing all over in the air and I was scared to death. I looked around the airplane and I saw the other guys on the crew, and they looked scared, too. Then I looked at Gary, and he obviously seemed to be more at peace than the rest of us. I think he knew he had a better ticket to the hereafter than I did. It made me realize it was time for me to start improving my lifestyle."

Dave Armstrong, a broadcaster based in Kansas City, worked as play-by-play man with Thompson 2 years in the early 1990s on the Big Eight Conference telecasts, after Jay Randolph left the crew. In the mid '90s, Armstrong reduced his college basketball schedule for several years while he was doing play-by-play of the Colorado Rockies baseball games in Denver. Then he came back to do many of the Iowa State games with Thompson from 2003 to '05.

"One of the reasons I didn't mind making the 4-hour drive from Kansas City to Ames to do games, besides the monetary reasons, was to have the opportunity to work with Gary," Armstrong said. "He was a joy for a play-by-play guy to work with because, unlike a lot of color commentators, it was never an ego thing for him. He wanted to help make the game more enjoyable for the fans, and he was still really good at that.

"First, he was always so well prepared. Every broadcaster studies the teams to one degree or another, but Gary took it a step further. I never saw him slacking off on that, even when at his age and position, he probably could have and just relied on his knowledge of the game and described whatever he saw.

But he did real research. Second, the thing that really separated him from a lot of other analysts is that he could still see the whole court, probably about like he did as a player 50 years ago. He could see the flow of the game, and how plays were developing, and convey that to the audience."

Thompson would look at the stats on key players, study them and make notes for use during the game.

Armstrong said "one of the biggest things Gary modeled for me, early-on when we were working together, was always to show kindness for people, especially the production crew. He's always been one to go into the production truck, to stop and visit with all the cameramen, taking time for people."

Before one game, I walked with Thompson into the production truck to say hello to producer Helmers. Those tightly-packed trailers, generally parked in the basements of arenas, are a jungle of wiring, gauges, monitors and gizmos. "Man!" said Thompson. "I come in here and see all this, and realize I still don't have any idea how they get the game on the air."

At Cyclone home games, he and his broadcast partners sat courtside in recent years. That meant that fans would walk in the aisle right behind Thompson and the others on press row. Pre-game, halftime and afterward, many of the fans would stop for a quick handshake and chat with Thompson.

Away from the floor, Thompson was almost always welcomed in the teams' dressing rooms, and he was also regarded as one of the regulars in the media rooms.

"Gary fit in well with the rest of us in the media," said Buck Turnbull, retired after a long career as a *Des Moines Register* sportswriter. "He was one of the guys. He had the personality for that. Usually great competitors have great egos, even later in life, but not so much with Gary."

Actually, said Turnbull, "I don't think some of the younger media guys knew just how good Gary was as a player. They've just been used to him being around as a broadcaster."

In his years working on the Cyclone games, Thompson could be more partial to Iowa State, but he never seemed to abuse that and become "just a homer," and that kept his relationship strong with the opposing coaches and players.

But he was also in a position in which he could be more active in his advisory roles around the university. You've read earlier about his serving on committees that were helping hire new coaches, and the occasional calls for advice from top ISU administrators.

He'd also help the players when he could.

"When Tim Floyd was coaching here, he wanted his players to be a little sharper when they were interviewed on TV," Thompson said. "So he had the kids over to his house, and Pete Taylor and I worked with them. We'd ask them questions, like they'd be asked in interviews, and taught them a little about how to be on TV. I'd tell them, 'You have to be ready for an interview, just like for a game. We're not all going to be English majors, of course, but we can sure work at sounding better and looking better.' They were receptive to what Pete and I could show them."

(Continued on page 297)

Gary Thompson's Family, Friends and Business

THOMPSONS TODAY. Above, Gary and Janet Thompson, in their early 70s. "I realize we are in the fourth quarter of life," Gary says. "I'm just hoping for two or three overtimes!" Left, Gary and his brother DeLon Thompson, of Tucson, Arizona, who is still playing baseball in his upper 60s. Below, Gary and Janet with (left to right) son Scott, daughter Kim Wierson and son Rick, all of whom live in the Ames area. (Top and bottom photos by Jacquelyn's Photography, Ames.)

GOT GAME. Gary and Janet Thompson's kids were quite successful in their own sports. Rick, an accomplished golfer, is shown in the 1980s playing famous hole number 12 at Augusta National in Georgia. Kim Thompson (in the Ames jersey) wins the mile run in the Iowa girls' state track meet in 1975, holding off Bridget Seip, of Sigourney. Below, Scott Thompson has been nationally ranked as a water skier.

A VERY CLOSE FAMILY. The extended Thompson family in their Christmas card photos from 2004 and 2005. They all live within 10 miles of each other, and with all the men working together, family gatherings are frequent—and fun! (Top photo in Jack Trice Stadium at Iowa State, by TeKippe Photography, Story City, Iowa. Bottom photo on the steps of Curtiss Hall at Iowa State, by Jacquelyn's Photography, Ames.)

STILL IN THE GAME. Top, Gary Thompson (left) is shown after he'd come out of the 1993-'94 Alumni Game at Iowa State—and he played in another one in 2008 when the Cyclones celebrated 100 years of men's basketball! Above left, during the 2005-'06 basketball season, Janet and Gary Thompson were "guests of honor" of the Iowa State University students who watch basketball games in "Cyclone Alley" at Hilton Coliseum. They took front row seats and joined right in on the cheers and the singing of the Iowa State fight song. Above right, Gary and Janet Thompson are shown together in the year 2000 in Indianapolis after he was inducted into the National High School Sports Hall of Fame by the National Federation of High School Associations.

TEE IT UP. Gary Thompson enjoys getting out on the golf course with his grandsons (left to right) Tyler Wierson, Matthew Wierson and Brandon Thompson. Gary did not play golf until after he had graduated from Iowa State, but despite that late start, he has become one of Iowa's most competitive and successful senior golfers. Golf highlights for him include the 1997 State Seniors Championship. Far more important, he says, are all the interesting people he's met while playing some of the finest golf courses across the nation and around the world.

TRADITIONS. One of Janet Thompson's neat traditions is to have fancy, dress-up tea parties with her granddaughters. Shown here at one in 2003 are (left to right) Erica Thompson, Chelsea Wierson, Rachel Thompson and Emily Thompson. (Photo by Jacquelyn's Photography, Ames.) Below left, Gary is interviewed by Heather Burnside of Des Moines' WHO-TV during the 2008 Alumni Game at Iowa State. Below right, Gary has long been part of a morning coffee group that meets at the Dutch Oven Bakery in Ames. He is seated at the rear center. (Photo by Dale Tryon.)

HIGH HONOR. Above, a replica of Gary Thompson's retired Iowa State jersey No. 20 was hoisted into the rafters in Hilton Coliseum in ceremonies in 1988, with assistant athletics director Elve Everage and coach Johnny Orr joining Gary on the floor. Right, Alan Hoskins, a friend since high school, and Gary attending a Big Twelve basketball tournament, a tradition for the two of them.

MASTERS, INDEED. Left, Gary Thompson's foursome in the 2005 Iowa Masters golf tournament, left to right, Jim Merchant of Iowa City, John Nervig of Ames, Thompson, and Bob Niemann of Webster City. Below left, Gary and Janet Thompson, with Iowa State's Jamie Pollard, when Gary was named to the "All-Century Team" in 2008. Below, as Des Moines Register columnist Ken Fuson wrote in 2005: "Nobody should be allowed to retire who looks like he can still drop 20 points on Kansas."

SPECIAL HERITAGE. Gary Thompson's parents Maurice and Abbie Thompson, of Roland, celebrated their 40th wedding anniversary in the 1960s, so when Janet and Gary celebrated their 40th in 1995, they had their photo taken in a similar pose as his parents had—with the same 40-year "Ruby Anniversary" plate. Gary and Janet celebrated their 50th in 2005 by taking their whole family to Hawaii.

DEVELOPING AN ALL-AMERICAN. Below, Gary Thompson posed with four of his real mentors at his 1997 induction into the ISU Hall of Fame. Left to right, longtime sports information director Harry Burrell, broadcaster Dale Williams who did play-by-play of Cyclone basketball games, Thompson, his high school coach Buck Cheadle and his college basketball coach Bill Strannigan. Right, Janet and Gary Thompson after an Alumni Game during ISU's 2008 celebration of 100 years of men's basketball.

CY'S PALS. Gary and Janet Thompson are about as loyal as Iowa State University supporters could possibly be, and their family saluted that loyalty with a gift of special ISU license plates for the Thompson car. "I love it in Ames—I wouldn't want to live anywhere else," said Janet. And Gary: "We've got our whole family right here, and we've got Iowa State, Big Twelve sports, the arts, music. It's all available to us right here in Ames."

AT HEADQUARTERS. Right, Gary and Janet Thompson's sons and son-in-law are all involved in the management of Gary Thompson Oil Co. Left to right are Scott Thompson, whose CPA firm is in an office at the oil company and does its accounting; son-in-law Tom Wierson, and son Rick Thompson. Above, company headquarters on South Duff Avenue in Ames, and one of their Swift Stop stores.

For Thompson's last broadcast, on March 2, 2005, there were all the special touches you read about in Chapter 1—Jay Randolph coming from St. Louis to do the play-by-play one more time with Thompson at his side, the halftime recognition, and the touching final on-air conversation between Randolph and Thompson.

The veteran producer Helmers said he was in an unusual frame of mind going into that game against Missouri at Hilton Coliseum.

"Really, all I cared about that night was whether Gary had a good time doing the broadcast," Helmers said afterward. "You don't often find me not caring who wins a game, but this time, I really didn't care who won. And frankly, I was really not too worried about whether we even got all the commercials in. I just wanted it all to work well for Gary."

It did. The last image on the screen was video of the Iowa State students hoisting individual letters spelling out, "Thanks, Gary!" Helmers said afterward that "we had run long in the broadcast and needed to get off the air, but I'll tell you, there was no way that was not going to get on."

When the broadcast lights finally dimmed, and everybody on the crew still had their headphones on, Thompson said softly, "Thank you, everybody." He stood up, and as he started to put his suit coat back on, he was suddenly ringed by fans and well-wishers. A few minutes later, Helmers left the production truck, "walked out on the floor and Gary and I hugged each other. That was hard!"

Then the Thompsons, the Randolphs, Iowa State's Athletics Director at the time Bruce Van De Velde, his wife Debbie, Helmers and a few others all went out for a celebration.

"It was like old times," Helmers said. "We were telling old stories. And Jay and Gary couldn't wait to get the scores from around the country fast enough. That's just the way they always were after games."

> *"Great competitors have great egos—not Gary."*

As that last season of broadcasting had been drawing to a close for Thompson, fans would often tell him they hated to see him go. He would remind them, "I'm not going anywhere—I'm just moving to a seat about 15 rows up," at Hilton Coliseum. "And I always said, I wanted to leave while they were still wanting me to continue, rather than waiting for them to ask me if I was going to retire. You want to get out ahead of the broom!"

That seat 15 rows up on the south side of Hilton has been his vantage point for home games since then, from a seat right next to his wife Janet Thompson, and with some of their kids and grandkids in adjacent seats.

"People ask me now if I'm getting itchy not broadcasting," Gary said during the following season. "I tell them that the one thing I notice is I have a lot more trouble with the officiating from my new seat. They don't seem to be nearly as good as when I had my monitor in front of me for instant replays."

Then old Cyclone fan Gary Thompson broke out in a big grin.

Chapter 22

Life Today For Gary and Janet

GARY AND JANET THOMPSON lead a very nice life today in semi-retirement.

They live in a beautiful home they built in 1991 in northwest Ames. They travel extensively. They are the organizers of a lot of family get-togethers as well as reunions of old teams, school classes and other groups they've been parts of through the years. They often have opened their home for receptions benefiting Iowa State. They have a wide circle of friends, both in Ames and Iowa, as well as scattered from coast to coast.

It seems like they are always on the go, either to events or activities they are participating in, or as spectators and fans for their grandchildren.

"Jan says I'm a 'Type-A' person—got to be on the go," Gary said.

"He's very intense," she said. "When his mind is on something, he won't hear anything going on around him. That's funny because if he says one word, I hear it. I hear everything."

"Well, wait a minute," he answered. "Everything?"

"Well, almost," she conceded.

Her point, she then said, is that "his mind is always working. I tell him now that he should just relax, slow it down. And he is sort of slowing down now, I can see that."

"She's got me pegged pretty well," Gary said, as he listened.

"I should after 50 years," she said.

As I listened to this conversation, it hit me again how fortunate the Thompsons have been. They know it. They are humble and grateful about it, too.

We all have close calls with accidents in our lives. Gary Thompson had two that were so serious, either of them could have changed everything.

The first was in early November, 1951, when he was a junior at Roland High School, and he and the three other boys survived the wreck you read about earlier. They rolled a car that was traveling at a high speed, hit an embankment sideways and were lucky enough to come through it with only cuts and broken bones. Thompson says now he easily could have died in that accident, when he was only 16 years old.

But if ever there was a time when Gary had an angel on his shoulder in a moment of extreme danger, it was very early on Sunday morning, August 19, 2001. He was no agile teenager this time. Rather, he was a 66-year-old man. Thank goodness he was also in extraordinary physical condition for a person his age.

First you should know that he has been a lousy sleeper most of his life. It's mostly due to the way excitement, nervousness and/or occasional worry play on his mind, he says. He had a few episodes of sleepwalking as a boy, but never in his adult life until that one fateful night.

Shortly after midnight, he apparently got out of bed and started sleepwalking, without ever really waking up. He came out the door of the Thompsons' main-floor master bedroom, took a partial left turn in the hallway and walked straight into the stairs to the basement. He tumbled down 16 carpeted steps!

"When I fell, I was out of it," Gary said. "I don't remember much of it at all. I felt I was going off a cliff, wondering how long it was going to be until I hit ground. I don't remember thinking that I might die, either during or after I fell, or even thinking that I might be hurt bad."

Janet, awaking from a deep sleep, heard a noise that "sounded like something fell from the wall," she later told reporter Paul Kix of the *Iowa State Daily*.

But when she heard Gary moaning, "Jan, Jan!" she got right up, turned on lights and was shocked at what she found. "I was scared and yet, I somehow had this feeling right away that 'He's going to be O.K., he's going to be O.K., he's going to come through this fine,' " she said.

She ran right down to him, there on the floor at the base of the stairs.

"Oh, I fell—my neck hurts," he said.

"Just lay there," she told him.

She immediately phoned their son Rick Thompson, who lives in the same Ames neighborhood and told him to come immediately.

Then Gary began insisting that Janet "get me up so I can go to the bathroom." She says now she knows it was risky, letting him move right then, but she slowly helped him stand up and shuffle to a basement bathroom. Then, when he insisted, she helped him climb back up the stairs. "Just get me up in bed," he said, "and I know I'll feel O.K. But oh, I'm hurt here," motioning toward his neck.

He got back in bed for a few more minutes, but when he continued complaining of pain, she told him they needed to call for help. "Yeah, I better go to the hospital—I'm hurting," he said. Janet said she would call for an ambulance, but he said he wanted to get in the car and have her drive him. Then Rick Thompson arrived.

"When you get to be 40 years old or so, and you're lucky enough to still have your parents with you, you always wonder if you're going to get a phone call in the night," Rick said. "When that call came, it was like, 'Boom!' All I can remember is Mom saying something like, 'Rick, hurry, your dad has fallen down the stairs, I don't know, I just don't know.'

"I had never heard her voice like that. She was scared, and she got me scared. And I was out the door, on my way to their house. Panic goes through your mind. 'Jeez, is this the call I've dreaded all my life?' "

When Rick rushed into his parents' bedroom, "Dad was in bed, still conscious and able to move a little bit, but he was clammy and cold as can be and his body was shaking," he said. "Mom and I knew we had to call 9-1-1."

When the paramedics arrived, "I think they gave me a shot, and boarded my neck up," Gary said. "I was kind of in and out of consciousness then."

Janet and Rick Thompson called the family's good friend Dr. Bob Gitchell, an orthopedic surgeon, who said he would meet them at Mary Greeley Medical Center in Ames. And they called daughter Kim Wierson and son Scott Thompson.

> *"Gee, could this mean paralysis for me?"*

The *Iowa State Daily's* full story about the accident, written 10 days later, reported that Gitchell had X-rays taken of Thompson, but they showed no damage. However, with Gary in such pain, Gitchell ordered a "CAT scan," in which he could see "fractures along the third, fourth, fifth and sixth vertebrae," the story said. "Gitchell said if the first or second had snapped, it may have led to death."

Gitchell said he wanted Thompson taken to Mercy Medical Center in Des Moines to be seen by noted neurosurgeon Dr. Tom Carlstrom. Gary recalls that "it was in the ambulance on the way to Des Moines, when I heard them say they had a Doc waiting for me, to do surgery. I'm thinking, 'Gee, could this mean paralysis for me?' "

Janet Thompson said she could have predicted that Gary would be an "impatient patient." He's "always been impatient," she said. "So after we got to the Des Moines hospital, he was under medication and kind of drifting in and out of sleep.

"All of a sudden, he said, 'Call that doctor!' Rick and I both told him, 'The doctor's been called and he'll be here soon.' Then Gary said, 'You call him yourself at his home—go and call him.' Finally, I thought I was speaking pretty quietly and I said to Rick, 'Let's just tell him we called the doctor again. He won't know the difference and it will get him off our backs.' "

But Gary wasn't as woozy from medicine as they thought. He looked up and said, "You know, that's not very nice of you, girl!"

Dr. Carlstrom was indeed there soon to see Gary.

"We knew Dad was in good hands," Rick Thompson said. "But still, we couldn't help but think that the worst thing in the world for him, as active as he's been, would be to come out of this laid-up or incapacitated."

Gary remembers that after a thorough examination, "Dr. Carlstrom came in and said, 'Well, I think we can do this with a neck brace or a halo, instead of needing surgery, and you're going to be all right.' Oh, man, what a relief that was!"

He told the *Iowa State Daily* "it was the best news I've ever heard. He said the doctor told him that "since I broke two vertebrae on the left side and two on the right side, that kind of held the spinal column and helped avoid paralysis."

Gary spent 2 more days and nights in the hospital, under observation, and was fitted with the neck brace that he chose to wear during his recovery.

"After 8 weeks in that neck brace, I went back to Dr. Carlstrom," he said. "As he was examining me, I asked him if or when I'd be able to play golf again. He said, 'Well, you can start right now, and you can hit that driver as hard as you can—you can hit it 300 yards if you can.'

"I said, 'Are you serious? If you're not serious, you're telling the wrong guy because I want to get right out there.' He said he was serious. Not long after that, Janet and I went to Mexico, and I took my clubs and started playing again."

Daughter Kim Wierson said she often thinks now how her father "was very fortunate. Seeing him in the hospital, when he couldn't really move and he couldn't feel things, that was really frightening. Then after he was able to come out of it like he has, well, I think it changed him a little bit."

And Scott Thompson said the accident made him reflect on "how you take things for granted in your family, especially when you live so close to each other and work so close with each other. Then something like this happens, and I was scared. I thought about, 'Gosh, I haven't done enough with Dad.' Now it's like we're getting another chance."

Rick Thompson said he still has "this feeling that my folks are going to live forever, even though we all know the reality."

With Gary recovering so fully from the fall, "I just can't think of him as a man in his 70s," Rick said. "Now I'm hoping he gets into his 80s, and that I'm still around then, because maybe I'll finally be able to beat him in golf regularly. But I might be too old myself then." Actually, said Gary, "Rick is already beating me in golf most of the time."

Janet Thompson said she and Gary "talk about what happened now, especially when we see someone in a wheelchair," she said. "Gary will say, 'That could have been me.' It was as close a call as we've ever had, but it turned out alright."

And Gary? You now know why he loves life like he does, and more than ever since that early August morning in 2001.

Now most days at the Thompson house start "at 6:30 or 7 in the morning," Janet said. "I love the mornings, reading the papers, sitting and having coffee together. Then Gary usually goes to coffee with his group of guys every day, and on to the office."

She used to go out with a group like that, too, but now her routine is to stay at home and spend a half-hour on a treadmill, 3 or 4 days per week. "I like doing that," Janet said. "I feel good when I do it. And sometimes I go on walks on the trails in Moore Park near our place."

She is still active in activities at Bethesda Lutheran Church, including Women's Bible Study. She is among the organizers of the church's annual "Scandinavian Coffee" held in October and featuring all kinds of Norwegian delicacies. And she is chairperson of the "service group" that brings food for funerals.

She also volunteers in the "clothing room," which gathers and distributes free clothing to those in need. She was a Sunday School teacher when the kids were small and in the classes, in Bartlesville as well as in Ames. She attends PEO and Theta Chi sorority, plays bridge and earlier was a frequent volunteer in the hospitality shop at Mary Greeley Medical Center in Ames.

Gary has also been involved in church. And he serves on the boards of directors of First American Bank in Ames, the Iowa State Letter Winners and on the Iowa State Hall of Fame Selection Committee.

They enjoy going out for dinner, or late desserts, often with friends but also just the two of them. They divide most of the home chores.

Janet does the cooking, cleaning and gardening, Gary makes the beds. He'll also do the vacuuming if Janet asks him. "When I really want him to do something, I just put it in writing in a list, and hand it to him," she said. "He'll do whatever's there, one thing after another, checking them off. But if I try to just tell him what to do without writing it down, it goes in one ear and out the other."

His response? "I know she means business when she writes it down."

For any home repairs, Janet takes charge and is quick to call in professionals for help. What about Gary? "He's not a 'Mr. Fix It,' I'll tell you that," she said.

He held up his hands, in a sign of surrender, and said, "I haven't got any patience for that stuff. Mechanically, my mind just doesn't work. The sons and son-in-law are better than I am at it. So all I've had to do, as far as repairs around home, is screw in a light bulb now and then. I always say the guys who are good at that stuff, well, they need a job, too. My dad did everything at our house when I was growing up, and I was playing ball all the time, so I never learned how to fix anything."

Gary has learned to yield to Janet on major decorating decisions. "When we were building this house, we were meeting to decide what to do with the family room, which has 20-foot ceilings," she said. "The interior decorator Verna Lou Townsend and I wanted wallpaper in there, but Gary and the architect wanted to paint the walls."

Said Gary: "I was just trying to save a little money." Janet said she finally gave in, saying, "O.K., we'll paint the walls, and I hope I'll be happy."

Gary started thinking about that again the next day, "and I called up the architect and said, 'Wallpaper it. You don't live with her, I do and I want her to be happy!' "

Their home is a great gathering place, and they've hosted events that have had 100 or more people attending.

A particularly memorable reception there was one in 1995 for Christina Hixon, a native of Clarinda in southwest Iowa who had gone on to become trustee of the generously philanthropic Lied Foundation Trust in Las Vegas.

There, she had come to know Sheila Strike Smith, a women's basketball coach at the University of Nevada at Las Vegas, who wound up marrying Gene Smith, who was athletic director at Iowa State. The Smiths had introduced Hixon to Martin Jischke, then ISU's president, and he was able to persuade Hixon to donate $5 million to Iowa State to endow scholarships.

"So, Iowa State asked Janet and me if we'd have a reception at our house for Christina, and we were happy to do that," Gary said. "We had a big crowd that filled up the house, and people were having a great time. I lost track of Christina for a while, and then she came back over to me and said, 'Gary, you need to put a lock on your bathroom door.' I said, 'What? We do have locks on our bathroom doors. What bathroom did you use?'

"It turned out when she wanted to use a restroom, another gal at the party had directed her into our laundry room, where we have a toilet along with the washer and dryer. There is a lock on it, but she hadn't seen it. I couldn't believe it! I said, 'Aren't we great hosts? We have a guest who has given $5 million to our university, and we're having her use the stool in the laundry room!' We had a big laugh about it."

The Thompsons' neighbors are a mix of past and present community leaders in Ames, among them Chuck and Darlene Schmidt. The Thompsons and Schmidts take turns watching each others' houses, and chat regularly about what's happening in their lives.

"They're fantastic people," Chuck Schmidt said of the Thompsons. "They're always interested in how you're doing, what you're doing and what's new in your family. They always seem to take time. What I like even more is that they're great role models for Iowa State athletes and students. They've got high morals and ethics, and they treat everybody with respect."

> *"He's not Mr. Fix-It, that's for sure!"*

Gary and Janet have traveled a good deal in recent years—China with a university group, Mackinac Island, golf in Palm Springs, California and getaway trips to Los Cabos in Mexico. They still use a condominium they own at The Harborage on the north shore of Clear Lake in northern Iowa.

They get to the NCAA Final Four most years—they've only missed three since 1978. They also generally make at least one trip for an Iowa State football game on the road. Gary and Janet have been attending the Big Eight, later Big Twelve, men's basketball tournaments since he played in them in the 1950s.

All of that makes life fun, Janet says, "but family is number one with us."

She has had a great time hosting fancy "Grandma's Tea Parties" for her granddaughters as they've grown up, with all dressing in matching outfits, using the best dishes, enjoying a variety of homemade desserts and teas. One time, she included the grandsons, too, "but they didn't last long. They ate real fast, then turned on the TV and were through with that sitting around the table stuff."

Gary has helped introduce the grandsons to golf. "We think it's really important as grandparents to be around the grandkids," he said.

Gary and Janet also have always hosted the whole family for the big dinners at Thanksgiving, Christmas Eve and Easter. "There are 15 of us in the extended family," Janet said. And they took the whole clan to Hawaii to celebrate their 50th wedding anniversary in 2005.

Birthdays are big. Gary and Janet phone each of the children and grandchildren on their birthdays. And they go out to dinner with the three Thompson siblings and their spouses for each of their birthdays, although that is often a scheduling challenge. And the grandparents try to make a special birthday visit with each grandchild, too.

So there is always a lot happening in their lives. They know how rare it is in extended families nowadays for everybody to live within 10 miles of each other. Though many of their friends spend winters away in second homes, or move to warm weather locations, that idea has never appealed to the Thompsons.

"I love it in Ames," Janet said. "I wouldn't want to live anywhere else. I love the change of seasons here. I even like the winter!"

Gary added that "we've agreed that we don't want a home in Texas or Arizona. We've got our whole family right here, and we've got Iowa State, Big Twelve sports, the arts, music. It's all available to us right here in Ames."

Chapter 23

The Extended Thompson Family Today

GOOD FORTUNE, high honors, great fame and a comfortable lifestyle have all come Gary Thompson's way in his 73 years of life.

So, want to guess what his "happiest moments" are now?

Several times he has told friends that he is genuinely most happy when he and his wife Janet are sitting together with all three of their grown children, their two daughters-in-law and one son-in-law, and their seven grandchildren—all in the same pew for a Christmas Eve candlelight service at Bethesda Lutheran Church in Ames.

And Janet Thompson has often said that family members have all kinds of different talents, and they've celebrated them all, reminding them, "God made us all different!"

Those two vignettes say a lot about why the Thompson family is as good and whole and fun as it is.

It is also an unusual family, by at least one measure of life in America today. How many families now have all members of three generations living in the same community, like the Thompsons and Wiersons do?

Actually, three of the families live a half-mile from each other in the northwest part of Ames. That's Gary and Janet; daughter Kim and Tom Wierson, who have children Matthew, 23, Chelsea, 20, and Tyler, 10; and son Rick and Renee Thompson, who have Rachel, 20, and Erica, 17. Son Scott and Mary Thompson and their children Brandon, 13, and Emily, 10, live 9 miles south on a water skiing lake they're co-developers of near Huxley.

Water skiing Thompsons? Yes, the family has broadened its sports participation well beyond basketball and baseball, the two sports in which Gary made his name. The 43-year-old Scott Thompson for the past 20 years has been among the top water skiers in his age division in the nation.

"I've been water skiing since I was about 10 years old, going back to when

Mom and Dad bought the place in Clear Lake and we started spending a lot of time up there," Scott said. "I think I was in my first skiing competition when I was 15 or 16 years old, and have been at it ever since."

He skied for a time as a member of the old Des Moines Ski Hawks team, then when he was a student at Iowa State University, where he earned his accounting degree, he was the founder of the ISU Water Ski Club. For 20 years or more, he skied five times a week from mid-April through the end of October, sometimes practicing for competitions, or actually competing, sometimes just for recreation.

His best finish ever was a tie for third in the nation in the slalom for 35-to-40-year-olds at the 2002 national competition held in Houston, Texas. Two years later, he tied for fifth. Several times, he has won the regional competition among skiers from 13 or 14 states.

In the mid 1990s, after he left an accounting firm in West Des Moines to start his own practice in Ames, Scott and his wife Mary Thompson partnered with Steve and Sue Tollefson in developing "Dream Lake Estates" on 80 acres of land they purchased just north of Huxley, and just west of Interstate Highway 35. They contracted construction of two 30-acre professional-caliber ski lakes that range from 6 to 9 feet deep, with holes in them as deep as 13 feet. There's plenty of room for 340-horsepower inboard ski boats to operate.

> "Son Scott tied for third in national water skiing competition…"

Then the Thompsons and Tollefsons built their own new homes on the lake, and sold lots to several other families interesting in building there. The families do their own leisure skiing at Dream Lake Estates, but they also allow their lakes to be used for competitions, most notably by the Iowa State Ski Club. In 2006, the ISU club hosted the National Collegiate Water Ski Association All-Stars competition there, featuring150 of the best college skiers in the U.S.

It is a gorgeous setting. In a March, 2006 profile of the development in the national WaterSki Magazine, Scott Thompson said it "truly is an experience like 'Field of Dreams,' " mentioning the famous sports movie filed in Iowa in 1989. "Basically we have the same story, other than replace the baseball field in the middle of the corn with a water-ski lake."

Gary's and Janet's daughter Kim Thompson Wierson, now 50, was a state champion as a high school athlete.

In 1975, she won the mile run in the Iowa Girls High School State Track Meet, holding off the much-longer-legged and defending champion Bridget Seip, of Sigourney. Kim thus became the first state champion in girls' sports for Ames High, which didn't start offering a full slate of girls' athletics until the 1970s.

"I'd always told Kim that in sports, you do your best, and you never quit, because you just don't know how it's going to come out," Gary Thompson said. "Kim led most of the way in the mile run at state, but with 100 yards left, Bridget Seip passed her. Kim was able to stay about a yard behind Bridget, and then in the last 5 yards, Kim made a long stride and beat her.

"Afterward, I told her, 'Kim, winning the state was great, but it was how you did it that is important. If you'd have quit when you fell behind, you'd have never known if you'd have been a state champion. If you'd have quit then, you might have even finished third or fourth.' But she never quit, and because of that, she won that championship."

Kim said still today, she thinks it was her dad's reminder, "Never quit!" that carried her to victory in that race. In 2003 she was inducted into the Ames High School Hall of Fame.

Rick Thompson, at 48, is for now the best golfer in a family of golf fanatics. "He beats me consistently now," said Gary. "I remember several years ago, the first time he got me, I came home and said to Jan, 'Guess what happened today at the golf course?' When she asked what, I said, 'Well, Rick beat me for the first time in golf.' She didn't even hesitate and said, 'Well, good for Rick!'"

Son-in-law Tom Wierson, 52, was a good hurdler in track at Ames High.

The third generation has produced some remarkable athletes, too, and some of the younger ones are still developing. Chelsea Wierson was a good soccer player and swimmer for Ames High School. Her brother Matthew Wierson was the starting point guard for Ames High's basketball team and also played the No. 1 position on the golf team. Rachel Thompson was active in drill team and competitive dance. Her sister Erica Thompson, who is starting her senior year at Ames High in the fall of 2008, plays on the Ames High golf team that played in the state tournament last spring.

The younger grandchildren are all involved in various sports, too, including Emily Thompson in figure skating, her brother Brandon Thompson and cousin Tyler Wierson in all sports. Goodness knows, the whole extended family has seen, and become friends with, many great athletes, because they are all avid Iowa State Cyclone fans and are regulars in attendance at ISU games.

It's hard to imagine an extended family that's more involved in each other's lives. Several of them work together at Gary Thompson Oil Co., as you know. There are also daily phone calls, e-mails, visits in each other's homes and attendance at the grandkids' school and sports activities. Gary and Janet, Kim's family and Rick's family are all Bethesda Lutheran Church members. Scott's family are members at Palestine Lutheran Church, near Huxley, which was Janet Thompson's home church and the place where she and Gary were married.

"It's been really important to me to have my family here in Ames and be close to Mom and Dad," said Kim Wierson, who taught fourth and sixth grades in the nearby Ballard Community Schools for 19 years. "I want to be close to them myself, but I feel like it's even more important for our kids, so they can be this close to their grandparents. Tom and I have always said we hope we can be as good parents as they've been."

Daughter-in-law Renee Thompson, who is married to Rick and works part-time in patient services for McFarland Clinic in Ames, said the solid relationship between Janet and Gary serves as kind of a moral gyroscope for the rest of the family.

"I think their love has just grown stronger over the years, and, wow! It's now more than 50 years!" Renee said. "They're always holding hands. And you can just see it when they look at each other. For younger couples like us, looking up to them and at how they've lived their lives, they're great role models. They may not even know that."

Daughter-in-law Mary Thompson agrees. "Being in a committed relationship to one person as long as Gary and Janet have is close to a miracle in today's world," said Mary, a stay-at-home mother and school volunteer while her kids are young, after earlier working in sales and marketing. "It tells you a lot about the strength of their marriage. It's a love story, that's what it is."

In the family in which Janet Sydnes Thompson grew up, only two other of the seven siblings survive—Sandra Sydnes Wirtz, of their hometown of Huxley, and Linda Sydnes Lantz, of Seattle, Washington. Both are in their 60s. Sandra's husband Garry Wirtz served as mayor of Huxley for a time. (In the family, he is known as "Gary 2 Rs," while Gary Thompson is "Gary 1 R.") Linda's husband Nero Lantz is also a native of Huxley.

The three sisters talk often and get together as frequently as they can.

"Janet comes down to our place at Huxley every fall, we make lefsa, a Norwegian bread, and have the flour flying," said Sandra, "with lots of conversation, of course!" Linda, youngest of the Sydneses, said she always thinks of Janet as "one of my older, prettier sisters."

Two Sydnes brothers died tragically in the 1960s. Paul died at 25 years old in 1963 when, working for a plumbing company on a project at Buchanan Hall on the Iowa State University campus, he was killed in the cave-in of a trench. Carroll died at 38 years old in 1965 from a brain aneurism. Both left behind wives and two young children. The Sydnes sisters have stayed in touch with those women who were their sisters-in-law and with their grown children.

Their oldest sister Helen died of cancer in 2000, and sister Darlene died in the 1955 car accident just days before Janet and Gary Thompson were married, a story told earlier in this book. The Sydnes parents, Tilmer and Carrie, died in 1969 and 1985.

The early deaths of three of their children "was really hard on my dad, and on my mom, too, but I think their faith got them through it," said Linda.

Sandra says they "grew up in a really good family, and it's fun to reminisce back on it. We had some bad times, but we had a lot of good times, and I guess it all goes together, doesn't it?"

Helen Sydnes Kochheiser, incidentally, was the target of one of Gary Thompson's favorite pranks.

"We were always pretty close to Helen and her husband Kenneth, going clear back to when Janet and I were dating," Gary said. "Helen was always a great ice cream eater, and I am, too. She always swore that Schwan's Ice Cream was the best there was, and I'd always argue for Blue Bunny French Vanilla. When they'd be at our house in later years, and I'd serve her a bowl of Blue Bunny ice cream, she'd kid me, 'Why are you giving me this second-rate stuff?'

"So one day I noticed the Schwan's delivery truck going through our neighborhood, and I hailed the driver. I bought a tub of their vanilla, and then I took it home and emptied it out into another container. Then I filled up the Schwan tub with Blue Bunny ice cream. Then the next time Helen and Kenneth stopped by, I said, 'By gum, Helen, just for you—look what I got!' And I got the Schwan tub out of the freezer.

> *"He fooled sister-in-law with Blue Bunny ice cream..."*

"She said, 'Well, it's about time you bought some real ice cream!' And after she ate a bite or two of it, she said, 'Now, this is real ice cream!' So right then I said, 'Well, Helen, I'm glad you like it, because it's Blue Bunny!' I'd always told her she'd never know the difference unless she saw the container, and that time, I proved it!"

Maurice and Abbie Thompson, parents of Gary and his brother DeLon Thompson, died in 1968 and 1989.

DeLon, now 66 and living in Tucson, Arizona, has had a fascinating life that includes professional baseball, management training in major retailing, 3 years traveling the nation with a Christian ministries program doing revivals, 23 years of working in finance and management for large auto dealerships.

And, perhaps most intriguing of all, since the mid-1990s, he has become a professional singer and composer of country music with a wide following in the southwestern United States and in Europe.

DeLon Thompson had a tremendous athletic career at Roland High School, playing as a reserve on the Class B state championship basketball team in 1958; averaging 11 rebounds and 20 points per game in his senior year, and establishing national pitching records in high school baseball, as reported earlier in this book. He also became one of the best singers and instrumentalists in the school.

"I always felt bad for some of the negative stuff DeLon had to put up with in sports because he's my younger brother," Gary Thompson said. "I can remember being home for one of his games in Fernald, like in his freshman year. He made a big play and some Fernald fan yelled at him, 'Who do you think you're trying to be, your brother?' It just killed me to hear that. I just cringed. DeLon was a tremendous athlete in his own right. He could do a lot of things I never could do."

DeLon, after graduating in 1960 at Roland, went on to become a 3-year varsity letterman in baseball at Iowa State. He once was the winning pitcher in both games of a doubleheader against Oklahoma, one as the starting pitcher the other as a reliever.

He signed in 1964 with the Minnesota Twins "for $4,500, and to me, a kid from Roland, Iowa, I suddenly seemed like a millionaire!"

He spent 2 years in the Twins organization, playing with minor league teams in Bismarck, North Dakota, and Wisconsin Rapids. Then, married with his wife expecting their first child, he decided to leave baseball, "mainly because of the lifestyle. It was a pretty lonely life for me because I was not a drinker and would not go out chasing women." Instead, he started into a management training program with Sears in Peoria, Illinois, before being recruited away by the owners of a large local department store.

In the early 1970s, he felt a call to deeper spirituality. While still grieving the 1968 death of his father, DeLon said he felt the call while watching a Billy Graham Crusade on television.

"Gary and I were raised in church, taught by our parents to be honest and have integrity, and I always thought I was a believer," DeLon said. "But when I was watching Billy Graham, I knew I wanted to take the next step. I said out loud right then, 'Lord, I really want to be a Christian—show me how."

That moment wound up putting him and his family on the road for the next 3 years with the Christ Is The Answer Ministries evangelization team, which included about 260 people and 55 vehicles, five of them huge semi-trailer trucks. They presented revivals all over the nation, "usually in a tent we had that was the size of a football field," lasting from a few days to a month or more. DeLon was part of the "street ministry" and the logistics and support team, not involved in the music.

When they wanted to put on a revival on the National Mall in Washington, D.C., at the height of the Watergate scandal, DeLon sought out U.S. Senator Harold Hughes from Iowa. He asked Hughes, himself a "born again" Christian, to help secure permission from the National Park Service to pitch the team's big tent near the Washington Monument, and the senator did that.

Hughes also took DeLon to meet Charles Colson, a former advisor to President Richard Nixon, after Colson had re-started his Christian life while serving a prison term for his Watergate activities. Thompson and Colson have stayed in touch ever since.

The ministries program also took Thompson to Nashville, where he met the great country singer Skeeter Davis, who attended revivals there. She introduced him to her music producer and back-up musicians, and years later, all those people would become important music mentors for him.

In 1976, when his marriage was failing, Thompson returned to Nashville, "just to try to re-group." After "driving an air cargo truck at practically minimum wage" for about a year, he was at a church service when he met a man associated with a major Nashville auto dealership. Thompson was soon hired to work in the finance and accounting end of the business, an area in which he excelled. Over the next 2 decades, his work at the dealership in Nashville wound up leading him to another large dealership in Tucson.

But his time around the burgeoning music business in Nashville had set a new hook in him. He started spending more time on a piano, picking out chords on a guitar and beginning to study country music. The deeper he got into it, the more he liked it. He got back in touch with Skeeter Davis, her producer John Rees and others in the business, and they began working with him as he started performing occasionally and writing his own songs.

Now, since the mid-90s, "DeLon," as he is known professionally, has been able to sustain himself as a full-time professional singer and composer. He has released four albums, performs live frequently in the Tucson and Phoenix areas in Arizona and sometimes beyond, and has built a strong following among American country music fans listening to radio stations in Europe. In fact, he averages 40-45 concerts per year, and has done as many as 73 in one 6-month season. His latest CD is a cross-over country gospel album, which in the fall of 2008 was nominated as "album of the year" in the Dove Awards, which are gospel music's highest honors. He still has a goal of being invited to perform on the Grand Ole Opry in Nashville.

> *"His brother is a professional country singer…"*

And to say DeLon Thompson has kept himself in good physical condition is an understatement. When he was nearly 60 years old, he discovered the Tuscon Old Timers baseball league and again started playing the grand old game. He joined an old timers' team and played three games per week the next several seasons. He also has played on the league's all-star team, which has been in the Old Timers' World Series held in Arizona.

He's generally been the pitcher. One of his catchers has been a fellow in his 80s. Thompson guesses his fastball still reaches somewhere between 72 and 82 miles per hour, only about a 10 mph drop from his prime. And he has been among the league's best hitters, during 1 month having a batting average of over .800!

Gary and DeLon Thompson have a warm relationship, a lot closer in more recent years, when they've been able to carve out time to spend with each other.

"I've told Gary a couple of times, it's almost like we were raised in different households," DeLon said. "Gary is a lot more like Mom, conservative and worried about what other people think. I'm more like Dad, always kind of a free spirit, wanting to do something different."

They are both proud of each other's career accomplishments. DeLon says there "is only one thing I covet in Gary's life—his great relationship with Janet, a stable home life and that he's been able to be around his kids all his life. What a great family!"

DeLon, who married three times, has been single since the early 1990s and has "five wonderful kids who are all doing well in life and have their own families now." He said his unsuccessful marriages made him do plenty of deep soul-searching "and today I know who I am as an individual. I've told my kids that I've found inspiration in reading about the Old West, and in country music. I'm really moved by the spirit of the pioneers. They had so many losses and challenges. They would grieve, they would mourn but they always had a focus and a goal. They never gave up."

DeLon Thompson says his own focus today is his Christian spirituality, sometimes using his music in his testimony. And what did Gary Thompson think of his brother's long-ago "conversion" experience?

"I thought it was great," Gary said. "Anytime I hear of someone being involved in Christian work or becoming more involved in their church, I'm all in favor of it. We need more people like that."

Chapter 24

A Favorite ISU Alum Stays Involved

AS PART of Iowa State University's celebration of its 150th anniversary in 2007-'08, the alumni magazine "Visions" named its list of "Visionaries—150 people who shaped Iowa State."

The honorees came from all areas of college life—digital electronic computer inventor John Vincent Atanasoff; the first African American student and faculty member George Washington Carver; the suffrage leader and Iowa State graduate Carrie Chapman Catt; former student and agronomist Roswell Garst; former U.S. Poet Laureate and graduate Ted Kooser; former U.S. Vice-President and double degree holder Henry A. Wallace; the national columnist and journalism graduate Hugh Sidey, and more.

Gary Thompson was also one of the 150. How did he feel about that?

"That's a little bit of a stretch on someone's part," Thompson told me, "but you can't help but feel honored being mentioned with the other names on that list. With my age, and being here close to the university for so many years, I knew a lot of those people. I feel pretty humble next to them."

The honor came not just because Thompson was an All-American athlete in two sports a long time ago at Iowa State. That was only part of it.

It was much more about his excellent representation of Iowa State in a long career as a college basketball broadcaster, his financial assistance to the university over the years, and his direct involvement as an advisor to presidents and athletic directors in the recruitment of some of the top coaches in Cyclone sports history.

Being among the 150 "Visionaries" is just one of many awards that the university has made to Gary and his wife Janet.

One of those awards that I think is very significant—and likely the most fun one—will probably be forgotten when serious lists of the Thompson honors are compiled. At an Iowa State men's home basketball game against Colorado in February 2006, Gary and Janet Thompson were invited by the 2,500 spirited students in "Cyclone Alley" to be their guests of honor and sit with the group in the seats closest to the court at Hilton Coliseum.

I told Gary Thompson that when you're 70 years old, as he was then, and the student body at your alma mater even knows who you are—let alone cares—you must indeed be someone special.

Gary and Janet, the first non-students ever invited into Cyclone Alley, arrived an hour before the tip-off, pulled the special red T-shirts over their sweaters and started meeting their hosts in the section of seats just beyond the east end of the basketball floor. They even posed for photos like the one on the previous page.

"Hi, I'm Gary Thompson," he said, sticking his hand out to Trevor Kruger, of Grimes, and Tom Danielson, of Johnston, then both freshmen. They had the wackiest Cyclone outfits in the whole coliseum—long basketball shorts, knee socks, wild sports coats, loose neckties, Ivy-style caps—all in the Iowa State colors of cardinal and gold.

"Oh, we know who you are!" said a wide-eyed young Kruger. "We've followed Iowa State stuff long enough that we know all about you."

Later, Danielson told me "you walk in here at Hilton Coliseum all the time, see the banner up in the rafters with Gary's jersey retired there with a few others, and then here he is right with us. You feel like you're in the presence of greatness."

About that time, here came another freshman Mitch Cline, also of Johnston, who asked Gary if they could have their picture taken together. I volunteered to be the shutterbug with Cline's camera. After it flashed and we confirmed we had a good photo of the two of them, Cline gave a thumbs-up and said, "My dad is going to freak out! He's been a Gary Thompson fan all his life!"

The Thompsons, who sat in the front row of Cyclone Alley, made legions of new fans among all those students. They autographed the backs of T-shirts, sang the Iowa State fight song with them (both Gary and Janet know all the words), joined them in waving the 3-foot-long cardinal and gold balloons that were handed out, and obviously were having a ball.

At one point, ISU President Gregory Geoffroy came walking past, stuck out his hand and said to Gary, "Who is this new student here?"

Gary told young Kruger and Danielson that he "really thinks this Cyclone Alley is what college sports should be about," Kruger said. And indeed, it is a fun group, with the students coordinating cheers, chants and other hullabaloo. When Thompsons were with them, Iowa State beat Colorado 96-79.

In another unusual way that Gary Thompson has helped Iowa State, he was asked in 1992 to bring his "famous basketball shot" out of retirement for public display again, to help ISU in its $250 million "Partnership for Prominence" fund drive.

"During the fundraising, they had a special night for 'Order of the Knoll' members—those are some of the university's frequent donors—at Hilton

Coliseum," Thompson recalled. "They set up a portable basket, and asked if I would take five shots from what would have been free throw distance or a little farther, and that the Iowa State Foundation would try to get a promise for a $1,000 donation for every shot I'd make. Dwight Nichols, who'd been the great tailback on the 'Dirty Thirty' football team in 1959, was there that night, and he was doing well in the insurance business in Florida, so he said he'd put up the money, thinking I'd probably only make one basket.

"I said O.K., I'd do it, but I was really feeling the pressure. First, I was dressed in a coat and tie. And the basket was a portable and set back in the corner behind the dinner tables. Without being on a basketball floor and knowing the distance you're shooting, it becomes dicey doing something like that. I asked for them to bring me a basketball, and between the dinner and the dessert, I snuck out behind the curtains and shot a few practice shots up against the wall, by the locker rooms, just so I could kind of get the 'feel' for shooting the ball.

"When the time came to shoot, I had diners all around me, and my back was right up against them. I missed the first shot, but then got the feel for the distance and knocked down four straight! Iowa State got $4,000 and everybody had some fun, but I was almost 60 years old, and it was about as much pressure as I could stand!"

"He canned something like 15 straight threes at 60 years old..."

However, he'd won another very public "shoot-off" in that same time period in downtown Des Moines. A charitable organization staged a noon-hour contest for shooting three-point baskets among Thompson and two former Drake greats—player and broadcaster Dolph Pulliam and former women's basketball coach Carole Baumgarten. The event was held in the atrium of the Kaleidoscope at the Hub.

"That was another portable hoop, naturally," Thompson said, "and I remember the basket only being about 9 feet high, so it took some adjustment on my shot."

He asked for some practice shots, and he wowed the audience. Perry Beeman, a Des Moines Register reporter and Iowa State fan who was in the crowd, said "what I remember is that Gary canned something like 15 straight threes when he was warming up." Thompson won the actual shooting contest, too.

Gary and Janet Thompson have also been involved through the years on many Iowa State-sponsored trips, even helping organize some of them.

In 1971, they were on the ISU Alumni Association chartered airplane to the Cyclones' first football bowl appearance—in the Sun Bowl in El Paso, Texas.

"Our plan was that we'd fly back to Ames right after the game because Iowa State was playing Iowa in basketball at Hilton Coliseum for the first time that night, and I was supposed to be the color analyst on the radio broadcast with Jim Zabel doing the play-by-play," Gary said. "We were bringing Cy the mascot and some of the band back on the same plane. We were getting beat in the football game (Louisiana State won it 33-15), and I was hoping we could leave El Paso a little early, but we didn't.

"There were buses to pick everybody up at the Des Moines airport, but one alum on the plane said he had a car at the airport, and that he could get me to Ames quicker if I'd ride with him. So I jumped in the car with him, expecting we'd go up the Des Moines Freeway and Interstate 35, but he said no, it'd be quicker to go over west through Madrid. I argued a little, but it was his car.

"So, as he was driving, we tuned in the start of the basketball game, and all of a sudden, I heard Zabel say, 'Hey, here comes Cy and the band, back from the Sun Bowl football game!' The bus had made it to Hilton, and I was still on my way in the car! It turned out that Zabel had somebody else sit-in for me on the broadcast, and then I stepped in when I finally got there."

In the fall of 1977, when the first Iowa State vs. Iowa football game in several decades was being played in Iowa City, the Thompsons were on a charter bus from Ames with a load of Cyclone fans.

"We got into Coralville, right outside Iowa City, and we were caught in a huge traffic jam," Gary Thompson said. "I was going crazy on that bus, thinking we were going to miss the kick-off and the start of the game, because of all the traffic. So John Nervig, a friend who worked for the Iowa Department of Transportation, and I jumped off the bus and started running down the railroad tracks from Coralville to right outside Kinnick Stadium in Iowa City. We had to get down one big bank to get to the tracks, and up another big one to get to the stadium. We had sand burs all over our pants, we were sopping wet from sweat, but we made it! And just as we were getting to our seats—in time for the kick-off—in came the rest of the group from our bus!"

Much of Gary and Janet Thompson's most significant involvement with Iowa State has been a lot less public than what you've read here so far.

Gary has introduced several of his former classmates, and others with ISU alliances or interests, to today's university administrators, ISU Foundation executives and athletics department officials. Several of those introductions have resulted in substantial financial contributions.

"For Iowa Staters, Gary Thompson is clearly a symbol of some great success," said Jamie Pollard, current athletics director. "They look to him for leadership, not only in his thinking, but in what he has done through the years for Iowa State. He was on the search committee when I was hired, and he was one of the first persons I went to when I was hiring Greg McDermott as basketball coach. He served as a consultant, but more of a confidante, as I was making that decision. And he also introduced me to two individuals who made the largest gifts to our athletic facilities fund."

ISU President Geoffroy said after he arrived on campus in 2001, "I made a concerted effort in my first year to get to know Gary, because I quickly became aware that he's a big part of this university family. I've worked with him on coaching searches and early on, we had conversations about our athletics program and its future directions. He's a valuable person for me to spend time with, because he's well-networked and plugged-in, both locally and nationally. And Gary is very good at keeping things confidential when they need to be, and as a result, people trust him and will share information with him."

Is Gary Thompson ever a bother with his opinions and insights?

"He's never been a bother at all," Geoffroy said. "When I've wanted advice and input, I've asked him, and he's always been straight and direct. He has never come to me championing some agenda."

Thompson credits Geoffroy "with doing an excellent job of backing the entire Iowa State athletics program, and we've been able to move forward in a lot of areas since he's been here as our president. The same can be said of Jamie Pollard."

There have been five times when Thompson's influence and importance in Iowa State affairs have been most apparent to the public. Two of those were his scrapes with former athletic directors Lou McCullough in 1977-'78 and Max Urick in 1993-'94, and those were covered earlier in this book. The other three were in the hiring of basketball coach Tim Floyd in 1994 to succeed the retiring Johnny Orr, and the hiring and ultimate firing of Floyd's successor Larry Eustachy in 1998 and 2003.

There were some real moments of intensity in each of those. The Tim Floyd hiring was probably the most fun.

After Orr announced he was ending his long, colorful career as the Cyclone coach, then-Iowa State athletics director Gene Smith asked Thompson to help, and the two spent a considerable amount of time with ISU President Martin Jischke on the matter.

Several sources were recommending they interview Floyd, then 40 years old and one of the hottest college coaches in the country. In fact, Thompson had been keeping a file he called "Five Best Young Coaches Coming Up," collecting articles he'd see in various publications, and Floyd was one of those five.

After graduating from Louisiana Tech, he had been an assistant to legendary coach Don Haskins at the University of Texas El Paso for 9 years. Then in 1986, Floyd got his first head coaching job at the University of Idaho. In 2 years there, he gave the program a winning season and a solid base, then departed for the University of New Orleans. In 6 years at New Orleans, his teams were 127-58, averaged 21 victories per year and reached post-season tournaments five times.

Jischke, Smith and Thompson were all very impressed when they talked to Floyd, and made him an attractive salary proposal. Floyd then went back to New Orleans to make his decision.

Meanwhile, Thompson had learned that Floyd's admiration for Texas El Paso's Haskins was so deep "that Tim wouldn't take a job without first talking to 'The Bear,' as Haskins is known." You may remember that Thompson and

Haskins had been friends since they coached against each other from 1965-'67, when Thompson was heading the Phillips 66ers and Haskins was at Texas Western College, as UTEP was called then. "So I was calling Haskins, telling him why Iowa State would be such a good fit for Floyd," Thompson said, "and I was hoping Haskins would talk to Floyd about it."

Haskins, who lived in retirement in El Paso until his death in late summer of 2008, recalled for me in an interview that "Gary called me three or four times while all that was going on. So I called Tim, and he said he'd already just had a press conference," announcing he was going to stay at New Orleans. Haskins said, "He'd always listened to me, so I said, 'Tim, get a pencil and a piece of paper and then get back on the phone.'

"When he got back on with me I said, 'O.K., Tim, now write down $90,000, which is what New Orleans is paying you. Over on the other side of the page, write down the figure Iowa State is offering you.' Was that $400,000? I can't remember for sure now. Then I went on and said, 'O.K., now subtract the one number from the other, and see the difference. Do you see that?' He said he did, so then I said, 'You're not going to coach forever, and you need to be taking care of your family.' And that was about the end of our conversation."

Meanwhile, Iowa State's negotiating team of Jischke, Smith and Thompson felt like they were on a rollercoaster.

"The three of us met at the president's home, The Knoll, one evening, and I called Tim Floyd from there," Thompson said. "Gene Smith had already talked to Floyd, but he hadn't had an answer from him. So I called Floyd from The Knoll and told him all the reasons he should take the job. I said, 'I'm sitting right here with the president, and he can confirm it if you want him to.' Tim said, all right, he would take the job."

Then the next morning, Floyd called Smith back and told him he wasn't going to take the ISU job after all—and that he was on his way to the press conference to announce he was staying at New Orleans.

When Smith notified Jischke and Thompson of that, Thompson asked Smith if he wanted him to make one more phone call to Floyd in New Orleans. Smith asked that Thompson go ahead and make that call, which Thompson made from his company office in Ames.

"I called Floyd's number at home, and got the answering machine, so I left a message," Thompson said. "I can't remember for sure what I even said, but it was something like, 'Tim, Bev, this is Gary Thompson at Iowa State, and I'm calling because I'm concerned you're making a mistake. You know, all of us up here are small town people, just like you are, and I think this would be a perfect fit for you. You'd be in the Big 12 Conference, with major market TV coverage. You've got a school committed to winning. We've had some ups and downs here, but you can win here if you can coach. I think if you want to make it big, this is where you want to be.' And then I told him I hoped he'd give it some more thought and give me a call back."

Beverly Floyd, Tim's wife, was the first to hear "this real emotional message from Gary Thompson," as she called it. "It just stopped me. One thing I remember him saying in it was that he knew Tim had announced he was staying at New Orleans, but then something like, 'There's nothing wrong with admitting a mistake and changing your mind. What would be wrong would be turning your back on such a wonderful opportunity up here. And I just know you're the right person for the job.' I was so moved by it that I tried to call Tim at his office right away, but couldn't reach him there.

"So I called my dad, George Byrnside in Ruston, Louisiana, and played the message for him," Beverly Floyd continued. "After he'd listened to it, I got back on the phone, and Dad said, 'Beverly, I think I'd buy a good coat and move North.' He said, 'I love having you and Tim close to home, but this sounds like the right opportunity for you. It sounds like this fellow is going to take real good care of you.'"

She said she then called Tim again, reached him and asked him what he was doing. "He told me he was writing thank you notes to Gene Smith and President Jischke for how well they had treated us.' So I said, 'Well, Tim, listen to this message.' I played it for him, and he said, 'Oh, wow!' Then I said, 'You know, I really think we ought to go.' He said, 'Do you? Wow, O.K., then let me go so I can call Gary.'"

When Floyd reached Thompson, "he told me if I could get to New Orleans that afternoon and they could get all the papers signed that day, he'd take the Iowa State job," Thompson said. "So I called Gene Smith, and asked him to contact our friend Richard Stark, from Fort Dodge, to see if we could use his jet to fly to New Orleans. As I recall, Janet and I and Gene went on the plane, along with an attorney to do the paperwork."

> "Tim Floyd says, 'Gary's call changed my life.'"

Meanwhile, at Iowa State, the sports information staff began making arrangements for a press conference for the next day to introduce the Cyclones' new men's basketball coach.

"When we got to New Orleans, we started the attorneys talking about the details," Thompson said. "About 4:30 that afternoon, Tim said he didn't have any good clothes at his office that he could take to Ames, and it seems like the Floyds lived about 50 miles from the campus. So in the late afternoon, I told him we better go find a store where we could get him a suit and some dress shoes. We got all that done, then we ate dinner and finally got all the negotiations confirmed and signed.

"It must've been 2:30 in the morning when we finally got back on the jet and left New Orleans. We got to Ames about 5 a.m., so we headed to our house with Tim, Beverly and their daughter Shannon. Janet and I got in bed, to get a couple of hours sleep, but Tim said he wanted to do a little work on his speech. So I left him there in the den. When I got up a few hours later, Tim was still out there, sound asleep in the chair where he'd been working."

He was soon being introduced to the Iowa media and to a gathering of Iowa State faithful as the new Cyclone basketball coach.

Bev Floyd now says that during all those on-again off-again phone calls about the Iowa State job, "Tim just needed that little nudge. He'd been too worried about moving me too far from home. When I told him I thought we should make the move, he said, 'If that's what you want to do, that's what we'll do.' And the way it turned out, going to Iowa State changed our lives.

"If Gary hadn't made that phone call and left the message, we wouldn't have gone to Iowa State. And you know, those were some of the greatest years we ever had coaching, really. I just wish Tim had listened as closely to Gary when he was telling him not to leave a few years later for the NBA!"

The NBA move came in 1998, when Floyd was hired to coach the Chicago Bulls. That team was decimated by the exits of Michael Jordan and other stars, and Floyd got caught in the "lock-out season" of 1998-'99. He never could get the Bulls back on their feet, and resigned in December of 2001 in mid-season. He sat out 2 years, then coached another NBA team, the New Orleans Hornets, for a year, finishing with a .500 record. When he left that job, he told the media that as far as coaching in the NBA, "I wasn't very good at it."

A year later he was hired as head coach at the University of Southern California, where he has turned the program around and put the Trojans back in the NCAA post-season tournaments.

Tim Floyd, in a separate interview, confirmed all the details above about his hiring at Iowa State. And he added, "Iowa State is an incredible university, and when Gary said 'We'll treat you right,' he wasn't kidding. I still have dreams about Iowa State."

He said he'd been aware of Gary Thompson as a commentator on TV coverage of college basketball, but after coming to Iowa State and getting to know him personally, "I figured out that he is as astute about college basketball as anybody in the business. The thing coaches all loved about him, he was so trustworthy, and that gave him access other people couldn't get. His word was his bond. As a result, coaches around the country had tremendous respect for him."

Floyd's 4 years with the Cyclones were great ones, with an 81-49 record and three 20-win seasons.

"From those years, I call Gary Thompson the oldest friend I have," the coach said.

"We always had fun, and I'd always try to give him a jab about something, playing to his competitiveness. The only two guys I allowed to come to practice were Gary and Dr. Bob Gitchell, another great friend. I called them 'OQ' and 'UQ.' Gary was 'OQ' because he was 'Over Qualified' to be there. Bob was 'UQ' because he was 'Under Qualified' to be there.

"So after practice, the assistant coaches would be finishing up with the players, and I'd usually sit down with Gary and Bob and say, 'UQ, what's your assessment today?' and then, 'Now you, OQ, what do you think?' We had so much fun together, I don't think either one of them missed a practice in my 4 years there."

Floyd said from Los Angeles that while his career path after leaving Iowa State was bumpy at first, things have smoothed out at USC, and that he often thinks how he wouldn't be there without his stop first at Iowa State.

"All I can say is that phone call from Gary Thompson is the reason I made the decision to go to Iowa State in '94," he said. "And Bev and I now thank God that Gary took time to make that call."

Larry Eustachy, who was Floyd's successor at Iowa State, says his opportunity with the Cyclones also came about both indirectly and directly because of the work of Thompson.

"I really believe Gary is the biggest reason I got the Iowa State job in '98," Eustachy said from Hattiesburg, Mississippi, where since 2004-'05 he has been head coach at the University of Southern Mississippi. "He was the confidante of Gene Smith, and so when Johnny Orr was retiring, Gene was smart enough to say, 'Gary, you go find me a basketball coach.' He got Tim Floyd. Then when Tim left, Gene said, 'Gary, you did all right on that last coach, so now find me another one.' And that's when Gary came after me."

Eustachy had been an assistant coach to Floyd in 1986-'87 at the University of Idaho. Then Eustachy served 2 years as an assistant at Utah, one year as an assistant at Ball State, and then got his first head coaching job at Idaho in 1990. In three seasons there, his teams were 61-33, then he went to Utah State for 5 years, where his teams were 98-53. By 1998, he was considered a top prospect for a coaching job in a higher-profile conference.

That's when Thompson called about the Iowa State position.

Susan Harman, who was writing a sports column in 1998 for *The Tribune* in Ames, told the story well: "Let's see. You're Gary Thompson. You're 63 years old. You are a successful businessman by any stretch of the imagination. You were a high school legend as a basketball and baseball player and later an All-American in both sports at the nearby university. You have a lovely home and a lovely wife and a grown family. You have nothing to prove to anyone. You could spend your time on the beach. Fly to Paris. But you don't."

Instead, Harman continued, "You fly around the country in search of basketball coaches, and you always get your man. Your university is beholden to you unlike most universities are beholden to their former athletic stars. Sure there are plaques and pictures of your accomplishments, but how many guys are actually still in the arena saving the day for dear old State U?"

She wrote that Floyd's resignation started a frenzy of phone calls from Thompson to coaches around the country who had won NCAA championships, "to check out the potential successors." She continued with her description of what Thompson had done: "…not even 48 hours after the resignation is announced, you are on a chartered jet winging its way to Logan, Utah, to interview the man you think will be the successor. You spend 2 ½ hours interviewing the candidate at the man's home and then climb aboard the jet for another 2-hour flight back to Iowa. You spend your time with your colleagues discussing whether this coach is the guy. You all agree he is the guy."

Harman's conclusion: "People around here take this man (Thompson) for granted. They shouldn't. They should build a statue to him."

Eustachy had a terrific run of success, with the Cyclones going 15-15 his first year, 1998-'99; then 32-5 in 1999-'00, and 25-6 in 2000-'01. His '99-'00 team reached the Elite Eight in the NCAA tournament, and he was named national coach of the year.

The next 2 years, Eustachy's teams didn't do as well, 12-19 and then 17-14. We all learned later, in stories and photos in the *Des Moines Register* and on the Internet, that Eustachy's drinking was out of control. He was photographed drinking with students at two other Big 12 universities after basketball games, and in at least one instance was photographed kissing college women. When the *Register* made the stories and photos public in early May of 2003, Eustachy called a press conference, admitted his drinking problem, said he had been diagnosed as an alcoholic and that he would go into treatment.

Thompson had heard the rumors during the late winter and early spring, but he was still shocked when the story broke.

"The day the photos hit the *Register*, Larry was on his way back to Ames and he called me," Thompson said.

"They should build a statue to this guy..."

"He said I was the third person he was telling this to—that he'd been diagnosed as an alcoholic. He asked me if I thought he could salvage his career. I said, 'Larry, if you're telling me you're an alcoholic, you've got to go get treatment for it, professional treatment, and I'll support you in doing that if you promise to get treatment."

Thompson said that earlier in his career, he had dealt with a couple of his employees who were battling alcoholism, and "we always tried to help them out as long as they were getting treatment, going to Alcoholics Anonymous meetings and bringing us back signed statements that they were attending. Unfortunately, it didn't work out in either one of those situations."

He said as he collected his thoughts about Eustachy's situation, "my concern didn't have anything to do with the basketball program or wins and losses. I was concerned for his health and his family."

Thompson went to President Geoffroy and then-Athletics Director Bruce Van De Velde "and gave them my viewpoint. I thought it was an opportunity for us as a university to come out a winner in two ways. First, we could help a person with a problem. Second, if he was able to turn his life around, we'd all win and retain a proven coach. And, if he wasn't able to turn it around, well, we did give him a chance."

Eustachy said Thompson's stand for him "meant everything to me. He was not only trying to save my job, he was trying to save my life. I realized Gary had been behind me all the way at Iowa State, from the beginning to the bitter end. He and a few other guys were more than supportive of me, but no one moreso than Gary. Of all the schools I've ever been to, I've never had someone support me as completely as Gary did."

But they got whipped. Iowa State decided to fire Eustachy.

"Gary fought hard for me, but we lost the battle for all the right reasons," Eustachy said in an interview 5 years later. "God had to bring me to my knees for me to deal with my alcoholism, and that meant I needed to be fired. I know that now."

Some people who wanted to give Eustachy a second chance are still angry at Iowa State for its handling of the case. Not Thompson.

"You know, I've never been a 'my way or the highway' kind of guy on these things," Thompson said. "I give my opinions, accept the decision and move on. I wasn't mad at Iowa State, and the Iowa State family was probably split 50-50 on Larry Eustachy."

Eustachy said Thompson's reaction "is what everybody should have done. I've encouraged everyone who was behind me to do that. I'm not mad at Iowa State, that's for sure. I'm grateful for all the opportunities I had there, and I'm sorry for the problems I caused."

Meanwhile, with 5 years of sobriety in the spring of 2008, Eustachy looked back on his 4 years at Southern Mississippi, and said he is especially pleased with the 20-11 and 19-14 records his Golden Eagles have had the last two seasons. "We are very close to doing something big here, very close," he said.

Eustachy's marriage ended in divorce, and his children still live in Ames. "When I come back to see the kids, I try to see Gary as often as I can," he said.

However, Eustachy is awful about returning phone calls—from reporters, even from old friends like Gary Thompson. So on a spring morning in 2008, after I told Thompson that Eustachy had just called me, he made an immediate call to Eustachy's cell phone. Here was the message Thompson left on the answering service:

"Larry, I am at Mary Greeley Hospital in Ames, as I just had a heart attack. Chuck told me that he talked to you on the telephone, and I immediately had the heart attack as I was in shock—because you never return or take calls!"

Within minutes, Eustachy "called me back and we had a nice visit," Thompson said.

I think leaving that phone message may well be the most evil thing Gary Thompson has ever done. But then, he and Eustachy have been through a lot together.

Come to think of it, Thompson and Iowa State have been through a lot together.

Chapter 25

Gary's a Real "Grinder" at Golf

GARY THOMPSON'S golf game, even now that he is in his 70s, is a demonstration of some of the best eye-to-hand coordination you'll see from anybody of any age. When he tees off, he is normally 250 yards straight down the fairway. He is good with his irons. He is the picture of confidence out there.

But when he comes to the greens, our All-American can become a quivering mound of self-doubt. "Actually, in earlier years, I was a good putter and saved a lot of pars with my putting," he said. "It's been in the last 3 or 4 years ago that the self-doubt started."

His friend Dr. Bob Gitchell, the retired orthopedic surgeon in Ames, has counseled, coached and cajoled Thompson about his golf jitters during the many rounds they've played together. Here's Gitchell: "I've told him many times, 'Gary, if you'd been as nervous in the way you shot a basketball as in the way you are hitting a golf ball sometimes, you would have been known not as the Roland Rocket—you'd have been known as the Roland Clank!' "

Nevertheless, Thompson has been one of Iowa's better golfers for 40 years, and that's all the more remarkable because of his comparatively late start in the sport. He got his first set of clubs and played his first rounds in 1957, after graduating from college.

In the 1970s and '80s, he played in a lot of 1-day, 27-hole tournaments at golf clubs around Iowa, and recalls winning tournaments in Jefferson, Garner and Jewell. He also played in a lot of two-man tournaments, winning several times.

In the 1990s, when he turned 50 and began competing in "seniors" events, he has often been a contender "or at least in the hunt," he said. He has played in senior tournaments and special events in Arizona, California and on top courses all over the Midwest. In addition, because of his contacts through sports, he has been able to play many of the great golf courses, including Augusta National in Georgia and Cypress Point in California.

About a decade ago, he and three friends—Jim Mitchell and Jim Bianco of Des Moines and Bob Nieman of Webster City—took a golfing pilgrimage to Scotland, and played on 15 major courses there in 10 days. On five of the days, they played 36 holes per day; on the other days, they'd play 18 in the morning, then drive 3 to 5 hours to their next destination course.

A high point in Thompson's golf career: He won the 1997 State Seniors Championship in the Iowa Golf Association tournament held that year at the Mason City Country Club. Thompson shot a 73 on the Sunday of that tourney, to finish at 218, two over par—one stroke ahead of his friend Gitchell. He's also finished second, third and fifth in the State Seniors tournaments.

Thompson also has won the club championship three times in three different decades at his home course, the Ames Golf & Country Club. He also won the Ames City Championship three times in three different decades. "I guess I put my 'A' game together once every 10 years," he said.

His handicap on that course has ranged from a one to a three, "but in the last 2 or 3 years, due to my putting, it has gone from four to six."

And he has "shot his age"—getting an 18-hole score equaling the number of his years—starting at age 65, missing when he was 66 and then matching or beating his age every year through 73. In fact, in his 73rd year, in the summer of 2008, he shot a par 72 in the Iowa Masters. "I am hoping 'shooting my age' gets easier, but age has a way of equaling things out," he said.

His approach to golf? "I love the game, but what I love most about it is the competition," he said. "I always say I'm not really a golfer. I'm an athlete playing golf."

He elaborated on that in an interview with the *Mason City Globe-Gazette's* Tom Thoma after the Iowa Senior championship in '97.

"I'm a late-comer to golf," Thompson told him. "I didn't learn the right way. I should have started with fundamentals. I've just been kind of a trial-and-error golfer in the way I picked up the game. I got by on hand-eye coordination. But I have been playing better as I get older."

Almost no one played golf around the town of Roland when he was a boy. "In those days, people made fun of anybody who played golf," he said. "They'd call it 'cow pasture pool.' Most of people would've thought if you were taking time to play golf, it was time you should have spent working."

Nevertheless, he became intrigued by the game in his Iowa State years, when he heard so many other athletes and coaches talking about it, and learned what an important part of business life it could be. Then he heard that Jack McGuire, the Iowa State swimming coach who would eventually coach Cyclone swimmers in 4 decades, had a set of used Golf Craft clubs for sale. Thompson bought them.

He quickly learned that there was a whole lot more to golf than he'd realized.

"I went out to Homewood Golf Course, one of the public courses in Ames, to play the first few times," Thompson recalled. "I mean, I'm slashing and spraying the balls all over the course. People would recognize me, standing on the first tee with a ball, and they'd say, 'Hi Gary, are you next to tee off?' I'd say, 'No, I'm waiting for somebody else that I'm going to play with. Go ahead.' It'd take me an hour to get off the tee, because I didn't want anybody to see me hit!"

He also bought his wife Janet Thompson a set of golf clubs. "Gary came home one day with a set of clubs, and I'd never even asked for them," Janet said.

Gary recalls he bought those clubs—made specially for women and endorsed by early golfer Hazel Hixon—from his old Roland High School teammate Ralph Johnson, "who got a deal on them." He gave them to Janet, who used them sparingly. "I'm a spectator," she reminded him, when the matter of her golf clubs came up in recent conversation. "But we've still got those Hazel Hixons," Gary said. "They're real antiques now."

> *"He won his first State Senior Championship in 1997…"*

After his first frustrating rounds of golf in that summer of '57, Thompson got busy establishing his basketball and professional careers with the Phillips 66ers and Phillips Petroleum Co. in Bartlesville, Oklahoma. He also spent most of the summer of '58 in military training with the U.S. Army, so by the spring of '59, his golf game was still very rough

The late George Durham, the Phillips 66ers publicity director when Thompson joined the team, said in an interview he was surprised to find out how weak Thompson's golf game was in those years.

"I just figured that as good an athlete as he was, he'd probably be decent in golf, too," Durham said. "At the end of the second basketball season Gary played with us here in Bartlesville, I said to him, 'Hey, how about us going out to Hillcrest Country Club and playing some golf?' He showed up wearing a pair of old basketball sneakers, and he barely knew what end of the club to pick up. It was a miserable time."

Evidently it inspired Thompson to get better.

"Gary went to Des Moines that summer and worked in Phillips' marketing division office there," Durham continued. "That fall when he came back to Bartlesville, he told me he wanted to go out to Hillcrest and play again. So we did, and he came out wearing brand new FootJoy golf shoes. He pulled out his driver and hit the ball 250 yards right down the middle of the fairway. He must have taken lessons over that summer, because he was a different man out on that golf course from what I'd seen in the spring."

And his game kept getting better in the years ahead. From 1962 to '64, when Gary had ended his Phillips 66ers playing years and before he went back to the team as its coach, he played a lot of golf while working in the Cedar Rapids-Iowa City area for Phillips Petroleum.

By the time Thompson's coaching career was completed in 1968 and the family moved to Ames, he started becoming a more competitive golfer.

In the late 1970s, he was putting on the practice green at Ames Golf &

Country Club when a new young man in town came out, introduced himself and asked if Thompson would be interested in playing a round of golf with him.

"My wife Karen and I had just moved to Ames from our hometown of Davenport, to go into business," said Gary Youngberg, who with his wife operates Ames Silversmithing, designing and creating fine jewelry. "I went into the pro shop at the golf club, told them I was new, mentioned I was a decent golfer and said I was looking for somebody to play who'd be pretty competitive. The fellow in the pro shop pointed to the guy putting on the practice green and said, 'There's your man, right out there,' and Gary and I have been friends and golf partners ever since."

They started playing regularly in the Thursday Men's Day events at the country club, joined for several years by Bill Wise and Michael McKinley. About 20 years ago, Wise and McKinley moved out of the foursome, and they were replaced by Dr. Chuck Olson, an Ames radiologist, and Mark Power, a professor of finance at Iowa State University. They're still playing Thursdays together, teeing off at midday and playing through the afternoon.

That's an interesting mix of occupations they have, not that they do any business trade-outs.

"I know I haven't had any free radiological services, or free jewelry and I'm certainly not getting my gasoline free," said Power. "There's been no bartering by the three of them for my financial expertise, either. We're a pretty eclectic group. There's no lack of interest in what each other does, though. We all read a lot, so we stay pretty attuned to what's happening in each other's professional field."

They're not a group to linger over dinner after they play. "We tend to change our shoes in the parking lot, duck in the clubhouse for a soda and then head home," said Power.

It's testimony to Thompson's continuing prowess at golf that he is about 20 years older than Youngberg, Olson and Power. And they are excellent golfers. Youngberg, probably the best of the group, carries a plus-one handicap. They generally all walk the 18 holes, carrying their own clubs, although recently, Thompson has started using one of those handcarts to carry his clubs.

The age difference often starts the kidding in the group. Power said he can provide "detailed analysis of Grandpa Thompson's 'yips,' shanks, muttering and other annoyances on the golf course, especially since he has had his hand in my pocket book for so many years."

Olson said "it used to be that Grandpa would often leave the ball short of the cup on his putts, so we started referring to him having 'The Thompson Shorts.'"

Youngberg notes that Thompson "has gotten better in many ways. He still wants to get better and works at it all the time. But he's had some issues with his game through the years, particularly around the green. He'd get a little 'handsy' with his shots, and he'd shank them. It always amazed me because here's a guy with the best pair of hands you can imagine. They helped make him a great basketball player. And in basketball and baseball, he got used to performing under all kinds of pressure. But put him out on a golf course in a friendly game, and all of a sudden he'd start getting a little 'gitchy' around those greens."

But all three know that, seriously, Thompson "is a phenomenal golfer for his age," as Youngberg put it. "He hits the ball beautifully off the tee, and of course he's just the ultimate competitor, but in a friendly way. He's won the three club championships, and I've won six of them. There've been a lot of years when we've played each other in that tournament, and we've both always gone into those matches saying, 'If not me, then thee.' "

Power said Thompson "is the best golfer I've ever played with who hasn't had formal training in the game. I'm not sure he's ever taken a formal lesson. But he's a great driver and certainly a great competitor. He's got his weakness around the green and with his putting. Still, he's such a competitor that if he's got a money putt, chances are he'll make it."

Olson said the four men occasionally play in twosomes or with other players, if all four can't make it to some golf date.

"One day when the other guys weren't around, Gary and I decided to go out and play," Olson continued. "Gary has a little trouble with vertigo now and then, and as we started that round, it started bothering him. When he'd bend over to put the tee in the ground and the ball on it, he'd be a little unsteady for a second when he straightened back up. I told him we could just quit, or I could put the ball on the tee for him, if that'd help, but he said he'd just play through it. So we decided to play just nine holes, and at the end of those nine, Gary was three under par! I couldn't believe it."

Among other Thompson playing partners through the years are Richard Stark, Dave Sergeant and Phil Joselyn, all of Fort Dodge; Michael Mumma, of Jefferson; George Turner of Des Moines and John Nervig of Ames. Turner and Nervig are legends in Iowa golf, having run the Iowa Masters tournament for decades on the Veenker Golf Course in Ames, and in 2007, Nervig played in his 50th Iowa Masters.

Thompson has played in celebrity golf tournaments with well-known people like the late U.S. astronaut Alan Shepard, who in 1961 was the first American to go to outer space, and former National Football League quarterbacks John Brodie and Fran Tarkenton.

"The time I got to play with Brodie and Tarkenton was when Jay Randolph and I went to a fundraiser tournament in Houston back in the late 1970s," Thompson said. "At that point, Brodie and Tarkenton, were both out of football and were actually the broadcasting team covering a lot of professional golf tournaments.

"I've always remembered that while we were playing, we started talking about what would be the ideal job to have in professional sports. We talked about how much travel was involved in baseball and basketball, the risk of injury in football, and about many other sports. I said my pick would be professional golf because you'd get to play all the great courses and your career would probably be longer.

"Tarkenton said we were all wrong, that the best pro sports job is football. He said that while training camp was rough, once the season started, they'd never 'hit' in practice. They were only playing about 14 games in the regular season then, and half of those would be at home, so you didn't have to travel much. And back then, they didn't train and workout all year long like professional athletes do today. He said when his season was over, he could leave for the off-season and do whatever he wanted.

"That story is one of the things I've always liked most about golf," Thompson continued. "You get to be around a lot of really interesting people, and you're together long enough that you really have some fun conversations."

On winter vacations, Thompson has often played golf in Palm Springs, California, with his old Iowa State classmate Roy Reiman, Ames resident Lin Bundy and former Missouri coach Norm Stewart.

"We have a lot of fun when we play out there," Thompson said. "One time, Roy and Norm were on one team, and Lin and I were on the other. Either Roy or Norm was left with a putt that was 2 or 3 feet away from the hole. They're looking at us, like they're asking if it wasn't a 'gimme.' But neither Lin nor I would answer—wouldn't say a thing. Then as the four of us were walking off the green, Norm said, 'You know, it's really something—we spend $500 million and come up with a treatment for AIDs, but we won't spend anything on lockjaw!' "

But Thompson has been on the other end of not getting a "gimme," too.

On a trip to Los Cabos, Mexico, he went to the Nicklaus Ocean Course to see if he could find somebody to play a round with, and was introduced to Feargal Quinn, founder of a supermarket chain in Ireland and a member of the Irish Senate. "We hit it off really well," Thompson said. "In fact, when it came up in conversation that I'm from Iowa, he asked if I knew Ron Pearson, who was the CEO of the Hy-Vee Stores in Iowa. They'd gotten to know each other through the grocery business.

"So we started playing, and we got to a green, and I left a putt a couple of feet from the hole. I just kind of dragged my putter across the green and kind of swept the ball toward the hole, and said something about it must be a 'gimme.' But Feargal was like a lot of players from Europe—they really are strict about following all the rules. He said, 'You know, Gary, you Americans are just too loose with golf's rules. Like what's this 'gimme'? Ever heard of a 'lemme'?' I said no, and asked him what it is. He said, 'Lemme see you make that little putt!' "

Gitchell, the Ames surgeon who also has played a lot with Thompson, said he'd win most of their matches in earlier years, but that "it's been a pretty even battle" the last 20 years. "When you watch him play, and even at his age now, you can see what an athlete he's been and still is," said Gitchell. "His hand-eye coordination is so incredible, and he has the intensity that we've seen in golf's best athletes—Ben Hogan, Jack Nicklaus, Tiger Woods. I really believe that if Gary had been born with a golf club in his hand and started playing early, he'd have made a lot of money in this sport, but he went a different direction in sports and didn't pick up golf until later."

When you play with Thompson—and maybe even more so when you play against him—"he'll drive you nuts," Gitchell continued. "He fiddle-faddles in his set-up over the ball. He grips and re-grips his club 10 or 12 times. He puts the club down behind the ball, lifts the club back up, puts it down again, lifts it up again. People playing against him the first time, if they get focused on him and his fiddle-faddling instead of on their own game, then he's got an advantage already."

Mark Power, from the Thursday foursome, said when he started playing with Thompson 20 years ago, "everybody warned me that you can grow old waiting for Thompson to hit. He 'milks' the club, grips and re-grips, re-sets his feet. I don't think it's that he's nervous, though. I think it's a matter that he is searching for just the right feel, and he can't find it. He's disciplined enough that he won't hit until he finds the grip that feels right and has himself in the right mental spot."

Thompson said all that gripping and re-gripping is a result of his having "started wrong in golf. When I started playing, I'd grip the club hard and swing fast, which I learned later is just the opposite of what you're supposed to do. But I've never been able to handle grip pressure and tightness in my swing, and that's kept me from being a consistent golfer."

Dr. Gitchell even provided a medical analysis of Thompson's game.

"Older male golfers have a name for the way he fidgets around, especially with the putter—'the yips,' " Gitchell said, referring to a golf term you read earlier here. "The Mayo Clinic has measured it, and it starts in the nerve endings in the muscles. The interesting thing, it only affects the low-handicap golfers, it increases with age and it knows no limits."

For about 10 years, Gitchell and Thompson played as teammates in what were called the Tri-State Tournaments for senior golfers who still wanted to play competitively.

There would be teams of 16 players each, chosen to represent the states of Iowa, Wisconsin and Minnesota, and the annual tournament would move from one state to the next. Twelve of the players on each team would be between 55 and 65 years old, and four would be "super seniors"—over 65 years old. They'd play 54 holes of golf over 3 days. Some took it more seriously than others, of course.

"Gary is such a competitor that I always say he doesn't do things for fun in golf," Gitchell said. "It doesn't matter if he's 10 strokes up or 10 strokes down, if there's something he doesn't think is right about his game, he'll go work on it. Sleeping has always been hard for him. He can get so wound up about things, that he seldom sleeps more than 4 or 5 hours per night.

"So, I can remember traveling with him for those Tri-State Tournaments, and we'd sometimes stay together in motels. If he hadn't had a good day on the course, one of the room lights might go on at 3 a.m., and there'd Gary be standing in front of the mirror with a golf club in his hands, thinking about what he might be doing with his swing or his stroke."

All of Thompson's practice, and his intensity, do make him an extraordinary golfer for his age, Gitchell agrees. "He's an especially long hitter off the tee for a man his age," Gitchell said. "That comes from his strength and his coordination. And his iron play to get to the green is excellent. If golf was just tee to green, Gary would beat everybody on the senior circuit."

Thompson said his putting has been a constant aggravation the last 5 years. When I was walking a round with him in the Iowa Masters tournament in 2005, he erupted in frustration when he missed one putt. "When you get this close to the hole, doesn't it seem like you ought to be able to get the ball in there?" he muttered. He missed a second time, too, then finally got the ball in the cup. "Three-putt! Three-putt!" he said. "That's what just kills you in this game. Son-of-a-biscuit!"

He tried using a "cross-handed" putting style, reversing the way most right-handed golfers position their hands on the putter. In 2008, he started using "a long putter" that has an extended shaft. When he wields it, he almost looks like he's standing up erect and using a closet broom.

"It's helped me to get rid of the yips," Thompson said. "Of course, you've still got to make putts, but now I feel like I've got a chance to make them. And it does seem to have helped me. It's got me back to a three handicap at my club this year."

He said that as he has aged, he does notice "that I'm losing some distance on my drives. I always had drivers with stiff shafts, but now I need to get them with more 'whip' in them, to try to pick up a little more distance."

> *"He's 'shot his age' every year but one over last 8 years..."*

He says, with a touch of pride, actually, that he's no longer always the best golfer in the Thompson family. His son Rick Thompson beats him regularly, and grandson Matthew Wierson, who was Ames High School's top golfer before his graduation in 2003, also has beaten him.

But Gary Thompson still gets after it when he steps on to a golf course.

"I'm a grinder," he said. "If I get off to a bad start after four or five holes, I immediately set a goal for myself to play from one-under to one-over the rest of the round. You don't always succeed with that goal, but it makes me bear down. I always pride myself in never quitting, regardless of whether I shoot a 70 or 90. I've tried my best on every shot. Ten to 12 years ago, when I was playing my best golf, I always thought I had a chance to win. Now, I'm older, I know my chances are slim and none, and slim just left!"

Yet, he still amazes people who see him play. "How does a man over 70 years old play golf like he does?" said his son-in-law Tom Wierson. "I'd take every bad shot he has, and it'd improve my game tremendously."

And when Iowa State University Athletics Director Jamie Pollard was asked if it seems odd that he gets along so well with an older man like Thompson, he asked a question back. "Have you had him out on the golf course?" Pollard said. "He doesn't come across as being 30 years older than I am out there, I'll tell you that."

Chapter 26

Gary and Janet Look Back at Their Lives

SUDDENLY, or so it seems, Gary and Janet Thompson are in their 70s.

"You go through the years, and it's just your life—you don't think a lot about it," Janet said one day when I had asked them to reflect on their lives now. "I never realized what a great life it's been until I started getting older, and now I feel very fortunate."

Gary says he notices that he is "usually a generation behind now." Leadership in most things he's interested in has passed, or is passing, to younger folks. And actually, he says, he enjoys watching that happen.

What about this whole idea of getting older? "I've never had a problem with age," he says. "I just look at it as another step in life. You can be old at 35 if you don't have your health, or you can be young at 85 if you have your health. The key to life is your health. It's way more important than money or anything else."

They have been blessed with extraordinarily good health—but they've worked at it. Their children have grown into solid adults and real contributors in their communities, and are raising fine children themselves. They have been successful in business—with a lot of work there, too. They are at a stage of life now where they giving a lot of their time and attention to their extended family, Bethesda Lutheran Church, Iowa State University and other institutions that mean a lot to them.

Gary is still loyal to his hometown of Roland, too. "I've always tried to come back when they've asked me to participate," he said. "The reality is that most Roland residents today probably don't even know I grew up in Roland.

"I don't get up there as often as I used to, with no family there any more, and when I do go now it can be a little sad because it's usually for a funeral. But when I leave Ames, go north up U.S. 69, and about when I turn east on the road to Roland, great memories start coming back to me. I drive around and see the places where I grew up and others lived, and it makes me grateful all over again for all that Roland people did for me.

"There are a lot of us from Roland who feel that way about the community. I'll never forget the all-school reunion that was held in 1988, right before the Roland-Story Schools were going to tear down the old building and put up a new one. Everybody wanted to get one more look at the old school. So, in a town that only had 750 people or so when we were growing up, more than 1,000 Roland High graduates came back for the reunion. That really tells you something about how important that town was to us all."

There are three real anchors in life for Gary and Janet Thompson today—their deep Lutheran faith, their marriage and their family.

"Church has been real important," Gary says. You don't expect a person who has reached his age and station in life to tell you, when you're heading off on a first visit to his hometown, that a must-see there is "the giant stained glass windows in Salem Lutheran Church. One is the 'Good Shepherd' and the other one is 'Christ Praying in the Garden.' There's nothing more beautiful than sitting in the church with the sunrays bringing out the brilliance of the colored stained glass. I've spent a lot of time looking at those windows. They mean a lot to me."

It's been a life-long thing, for both of them.

"Believing in God has never changed for me," Janet adds. "From when I was a little girl, my faith has always been important. As a girl, I would talk about how I wanted to go to heaven. That was discussed a lot, from my grandparents to my parents to us kids. Our upbringing was very strict—there were a lot of rules—but it wasn't hard for us because we didn't want to do anything wrong. I'm very thankful for that now. However, I wasn't perfect."

They passed their belief in God, and their belief that it helps to actively practice your faith, on to their children.

"We're real proud that our kids all have good marriages—the three couples have been married 29, 22 and 17 years right now—and that they're all involved in churches," Gary said. "We always thought that church life is important to the success of a marriage and a family. We told the kids, as they were getting married, to make sure their kids will be involved in a church, and they decide what the church will be."

But a good marriage isn't built on faith alone. There needs to be passion for your partner, and the Thompsons have still got it for each other.

"When Wilt Chamberlain's autobiography came out, he said in there he'd had sex with 20,000 women," Gary said, and indeed the lifelong bachelor Chamberlain made that claim in his 1991 book "A View from Above."

"That really got my coffee group going," Thompson continued. "They were all kidding me, saying, 'Well, you and Wilt were playing basketball at the same time, and on the All-American team together, so is it like that for you with women, too?' My answer to them was, 'I could compete with Wilt in basketball, all right, but when it comes to women, I'm 19,999 behind him!'"

Gary and Janet Thompson are still going on romantic trips together. For part of their celebration of their 50th wedding anniversary in 2005, they recreated their honeymoon trip to Chicago—even stopping by the old L-Ranko Motel in Toledo, Iowa, where they spent their wedding night, just to see it again, finding it's now a Budget Inn. They drove on to spend several days at the Omni Hotel on Michigan Avenue in downtown Chicago. For the drive, Janet arranged to get a CD of their favorite Elvis Presley hits from the 1950s.

On another trip, to celebrate their 70th birthdays, they went to the elegant old Grand Hotel on Mackinac Island, Michigan, where Gary surprised Janet by having roses, chocolate, wine, cheese and diamond earrings waiting in the room. It's hard not to envy them!

But, like with most marriages, "we've had our ups and down, of course," Janet said. "But I never had a thought that it wasn't going to work. We've always remained committed to each other. When I made a promise to God at the altar, 'till death do us part,' I meant it. And we'd do it all over again."

"When you beat me, I want you to feel you've accomplished something.."

Gary says she "has had the tougher part of the marriage, being alone a lot when I was gone on trips as a player, then coaching and later broadcasting. She had to be a mother and a dad a whole lot of times."

She acknowledges, "It was sometimes difficult."

Gary says Janet "has done so well. In my business, there were so many demands on my time, and a whole lot of travel, so I wound up missing a lot of things I really wanted to be home to do, especially being home with the kids more."

Janet says she "always regarded Gary as the head of the family. That's how we grew up ourselves—dads out working, moms staying home with the kids. I wanted to and loved staying home when the kids came along, and Gary did well enough at work that I could stay home with them. But I've always had my opinions, and I don't hold them in, either."

Gary says they've both been good at airing their differences "and being able to talk through them and agree on what we were going to do." Janet added, "We're both stubborn Norwegians at times."

Both say that with Gary forever being a competitor, his intensity around any kind of competition, can sometimes be bothersome.

"He'll be critiquing players—even in kid sports—and I'll have to remind him, 'Not everybody can do what you did as an athlete,' " Janet said when the three of us were talking. "I think it's hard for you to understand that."

Yes, he said, "but I also believe everybody can give the effort, no matter what their athletic ability is."

She said she would "just cringe when people would come up and say to our sons Rick or Scott, 'Are you going to be an athlete like your dad?' "

Gary says "and that's why I never ask other people's kids that. I didn't push our kids in sports, probably less than I should have. But I've been around so many overbearing parents during my athletic career, that I swore I'd never be that way with my own kids. I wanted them to enjoy whatever sports they tried, and maybe the most important thing, if they started something, I wanted them to finish it, and they have."

A classic story about Gary's competitive fires still burning, sometimes too brightly, comes from a family bowling outing a few years ago.

Janet was "a fairly good bowler, back when I was bowling regularly," she said. "I had a 200 game once, and I carried a 137 average. It's really the only sport other than skating that I was good at."

So the Thompsons went bowling with kids and grandkids one day, and when they formed teams, Gary and Janet wound up opposing each other. "I was doing O.K. until right at the end, and he literally psyched me out," Janet said. "Gary had not bowled for a long time, and I was ahead of him with about three frames to go. He said to me, 'If you don't mess up, you could beat me!' I just lost it, and had a gutter ball or two. I was so mad at him the rest of the day, I had to keep reminding myself that I love him."

Said Gary, "All I did was just put it in her mind, that's all. But the rest of them got on me pretty bad that day. I heard a lot of, 'That isn't fair, Dad!' "

He wouldn't even let-up in ping pong games with the kids, Janet said. "He'd be playing ping pong wth them, and I'd say, 'Why don't you let them beat you? It'd be good for their self-esteem.' "

Gary answers that, actually, he'd "let them beat me when they were little kids and didn't know the difference. But when they got old enough to know I was letting them win, I quit that. If you're going to win, it has to mean something, to know that you'd actually won and I hadn't let you beat me, and those times did come—ping pong, pool and golf alike. But I'll never let someone beat me. I'll spot them 10 points, or something, but I'm going to play hard." He laughs and adds, "When the kids eventually beat me, I wanted them to feel good about winning, knowing it wasn't 'gift-wrapped'!"

Janet said she thinks "other people would be so disgusted with him being so competitive. Yet in golf, they all still want to play with him."

But do not mistake his competitive instinct with any desire to hold on to the fame that life brought Gary Thompson's way. He has handled that—still does—better than any other high profile athlete I've ever known.

"I think my mother was probably the best blessing to me, from that standpoint," he said, "because there was no way she was going to having me behaving in a way that anybody would be able to say, 'He's got the big head.' She told me that was about the worst thing anybody could say about you.

"I always wanted to be the same person. I just played the games to win—that's the way I was taught—and I never thought a lot about the other things that might come with winning and playing well. Along the way, I learned that if you have to tell somebody what you've done, it's not worth as much. Dad always said, 'If you're good, people will know that, and you won't have to tell them.'

"My idea was to be a team guy and play to win. I can only remember one time setting goals for personal achievements as an athlete, and that was when I was starting high school. There were three of them: I wanted to make the varsity squad, I wanted to be in the starting line-up eventually, and I wanted to make the all-county team sometime.

"After that, I never had any other personal goals, just team goals. Of course, I don't think there ever was an athlete who played who didn't like to see his name in print, and I've enjoyed that, too. But I've never ever asked to be interviewed, to be on radio or be on TV. I wouldn't do that."

He said besides his parents, his Iowa State basketball coach Bill Strannigan also cautioned about putting too much stock in sports accomplishments once you move on in life. "He told me one time, 'Gary, remember when you graduate, you're history, and prepare yourself for that,' " Gary said. "He was right, too. I've seen coaches and athletes really struggle with that as they go on in life. You have to make it on your own."

He said when you're a high-profile athlete, eventually you come to an understanding of dealing with the renown. "Athletes get the rewards of being athletes—the limelight, the press," he said. "But they have to remember that once they're getting a lot of recognition and attention, they'll also get the limelight and press if they do bad things. And I've always understood that."

He said one reason he has not tired of it is because "I've always enjoyed visiting with people. It's really a small world out there, and I like seeing what connections there are between people I meet and others I've known."

That may come from him having a lifelong interest in current events.

"I read the newspapers every day, cover to cover, every little thing," Gary said. "Part of the reason I've done that over the years is I get so tired of hearing the phrase 'dumb athletes' and 'dumb jocks.' I didn't want to be that way. I did not want to be a one-dimensional person.

"For example, I'd occasionally see Don Muhm, who was the farm editor of the *Des Moines Register*, at various functions. He always seemed to be surprised when I'd tell him that I was reading all of his articles. But the reason I did, this is a farm state we're living in here. I wanted to be able to go up to a farmer and at least be able to ask halfway intelligent questions about how things were going for him. I wanted to be well enough informed that when I'd be in a social setting, I could ask people about whatever field they're in."

Inevitably, though, Don Muhm or nearly anybody else Thompson has talked to over the years would wind up asking him about sports.

So I did, too. What's the best thing about sports?

"The discipline," Thompson said without hesitation. "When you learn how to be prompt for practice, get ready for games, bring what you're taught to the game and then execute under pressure, be on time, be accountable to your coach, your teammates and yourself—those are valuable lessons that will help you the rest of your life.

"In business, I've seen it over and over—it's the people who are disciplined who have a greater chance to be successful. When you're a salesman, like I was earlier, you have a lot of freedom. You're out on your own. No one would know if you take off work and go golfing or fishing. That's when you've got to have that discipline. You've got a job to do, and you do the appropriate things at the appropriate times. You have to build cohesiveness in a business the same way you do on a team. And sports can teach you how to deal with all kinds of people, and you have to know how to do that in later life, no matter what field you get into."

The worst thing about sports?

"Athletes who begin thinking they're more important than they really are, and think people owe them something, just because they're athletes," he said.

A remarkable thing about Gary Thompson—athlete, coach, broadcaster, businessman—is that the transitions from one phase of his life to the next have never seemed difficult for him.

"Gary has always looked forward so much to whatever the next thing is going to be," said Janet, "and that's made it easier for him to let go of what he'd been doing. He's always been like that. That's how it was when his playing career ended in basketball and he was going into business full-time. He was that way again when he finished coaching and was going into his own business. It seems like he's always been ready when the time comes for him to move on to something else."

> *"I've been happy with my life all the way..."*

Is he happy now? Many successful people I've known struggle with that simple question later in their lives, like they're not sure whether they're as happy as they think they should be.

That's not the case with Gary Thompson.

"I am happy," he said. "But you know, I've been happy with life all the way. I've really enjoyed it in all the different stages, and I've been able to do a lot of different things. At my age now, sometimes I do start thinking, 'Hey, if there's anything I still want to do, I better be picking it up a little here,' because I might be running out of time!

"As we were getting ready for our 55th Roland High class reunion, my classmate Cleone Michaelson Bauer said to me, 'Can you believe we're getting this old?' I told her age doesn't bother me, I'm just trying to keep thinking and acting young. But I realize we are in the fourth quarter of life. I'm just hoping for two or three overtimes!"

Chapter 27

What Others Say About Gary Thompson

ON OPENING DAY of the 2004 Iowa high school boys' state basketball tournament in Des Moines, I arrived late and a big game was underway. I quietly slid into a seat on press row and looked up to find myself sitting next to Gary Thompson.

He introduced himself, which was pretty funny, considering that his name and face were probably more recognizable to most Iowans than the governor's. Gary explained that he was doing his homework on teams he might be talking about later in the week, when he would be doing commentary on the network TV coverage of the championship games. I was mostly loafing, but also taking a few notes for a book on the centennial history of the Iowa High School Athletic Association, which sanctions boys' sports in the state.

As our conversation unfolded there on press row, and later in the media interview room, Thompson told me that "an individual has come to me, wanting to write a book about my life story to raise some money for a charitable organization.

"I know you've done some books," he said. "Would you give me an honest answer on this—do you think my story is even worth doing in a book?"

That was pretty funny, too, although I could tell that he was being Gary Thompson-sincere in asking.

"If your story isn't book-worthy," I assured him, "nobody's in Iowa is." Hopefully you're in agreement with that, now that you've reached this point in Thompson's story.

I've taken you well beyond the basic biography, to experience some of the elements of his story that were especially intriguing to me—the fun of the Roland Rockets' great success; life as a teenager and college student in the 1950s; the dramatic changes in the game of basketball during Thompson's career; life as an entrepreneur and owner of a family business; the opportunities and challenges of his 34 years as a basketball broadcaster; his later involvement in so many ways with his alma mater Iowa State, and his genuine devotion to so many people with whom he's shared life.

Once you know all those angles in the Thompson story, you begin to realize the significant lessons that are part of it.

Donna Hagen Henry, who was a Roland High School classmate of Thompson and now lives in Colo, Iowa, identified one of those lessons. "I think the Gary Thompson story should give young people the example that they can accomplish a lot, too," said Henry. "He started out as a little guy in a little town, and he knew he had to work harder. He did, and look where it's taken him."

Ted Tedesco, the former mayor of Ames, has been observing Gary Thompson at close range for a half-century. He was a year behind Thompson in their student years at Iowa State, "and I can remember watching him walking across campus back then. He was the biggest star Iowa State had, but he was saying hello and visiting with everybody he ran into along the way."

Years later, Tedesco wrote and carried much of the insurance for Gary Thompson Oil Co., and he also served as the statistician on many of the basketball telecasts with Thompson. "Gary never got a star's head, or a big TV head," Tedesco said. "He was always just Gary Thompson, one of our finest Iowans, somebody that everybody felt like they knew."

As a businessman, Thompson "has been outstanding," Tedesco said. "I look on him as very progressive in his business, especially when I think of all the changes in his business that he's been out front on. I admire him even more, though, because he's always been honest and straight-forward. He's never tried to pull any deals behind anybody's back."

All that, said Tedesco, has resulted in Thompson "still being looked on as one of our outstanding citizens in Ames. He's not only supportive of Iowa State, but he's also been very supportive of the city and most of the big projects that have happened here, and he's been very supportive of the Ames schools. And I know he's stayed very supportive of the Roland-Story schools, too."

Imagine the perspective of Bill Hoefle, a professor of small animal orthopedic surgery at the Iowa State University College of Veterinary Medicine. The first 25 years of his life, Hoefle had Gary Thompson as his sports hero. The past 35 years, they've become great friends, traveling together once with their wives to the NCAA Final Four tournament, and also playing occasional rounds of golf.

"In the early 1950s, when Gary started to have the unbelievable success at Roland High School, I became aware of him," Hoefle said. "I was in grade school then in Grand Junction, Iowa, and Gary became kind of my sports idol. After following him a year or so, I wrote him a letter. And he wrote back—very courteous, very encouraging. Over the next several years, as he was going through Iowa State, I continued to correspond with him, and I think he always wrote back.

"My folks took me to a couple of Iowa State basketball games, and I got to meet him afterward. Same in baseball. You know, I look back on that now, and I was nothing but a little brat kid from a farm in rural Iowa. It's kind of neat he'd take time to write a letter back to somebody like me. Ever since then, in my mind, Gary Thompson has seemed to me to be the way athletes used to be, when kids would idolize them."

Hoefle graduated from East Greene High School in 1960, went to Iowa State and became a classmate, baseball teammate and friend of Gary's brother DeLon Thompson. Hoefle then went on to Iowa State's veterinary school, and practiced in Florida for 4 years, before returning to Iowa State in 1970 and joining the veterinary faculty. He reconnected with Gary Thompson soon after that, and they've stayed close ever since.

"After I joined the faculty and got to know Gary as a friend, another thing I've admired about him is his undying loyalty to Iowa State," Hoefle said. "When the university calls on him for help—whether it's recruiting a coach or some other project—his willingness to give of himself and to stay in the background is impressive."

Dr. Bob Gitchell, an Ames physician and another friend via Iowa State sports and golf, said when Thompson goes to work on something for the university, "he wants literally whatever's best for Iowa State. And the reason he's had such credibility with so many different people at the university—and this goes for business, too—is that there is not an ounce of hypocrisy in him. He's a straight shooter, his word is his bond and he never tries to work a deal on you."

Gitchell said after years of observing Thompson, he has his friend analyzed.

"There are three reasons why Gary Thompson has been so successful," Gitchell said. "As an athlete, he has been blessed with incredible hand-eye coordination, so when he sees something in a game, he adjusts and reacts much quicker and better than nearly everybody else does. The second thing about him, he has a level of intensity as a competitor that almost none of the rest of us can match, and what it means for him is that he has never wasted a bit of the talent he's been blessed with. The third thing that has made him successful—and without this one the other two wouldn't have meant much—is he has great character. He is a stand-up person as a husband, father, friend, businessman and golf partner."

> **"Gary's whole life has been a race..."**

Gitchell sometimes shakes his head about his friend's competitiveness.

"Gary's whole life has been a race," Gitchell said. "I mean, if you and he are both going downtown, and you're driving separate cars, he'll figure out a way to beat you there and then point it out to you!"

Richard Stark, a Fort Dodge banker and commodities broker, said Thompson channels that competitive nature well into business. He has Thompson serving on the board of directors of his First American Bank, which has 10 locations across the state.

"Gary plays the game in business just like he did in basketball," said Stark, "all-out and hard, but with the highest ethical standards. And he's been pretty successful in everything he's touched."

Stark continued that "a lot of guys who've made it big in sports have a lot of trouble years later when their fame is faded and they're forgotten as athletes. A lot of them really struggle with that. Gary was an All-American athlete—as big as you can get—and he's never struggled with that at all. In fact, he's used a lot of what he learned in sports to help him become successful later in business and in broadcasting."

Stark and Thompson have been through some controversies together, as key supporters of Iowa State and its athletics programs. They've generally lined up together, and have generally prevailed on whatever the issues are. But Stark said the wounds of those squabbles don't bother him as much as they bother Thompson.

"Gary is a person who almost always does the right thing," Stark said. "So if there's some misunderstanding, or if some other person is struggling with something he thinks Gary has done wrong, it bothers Gary a lot. He's a person whom almost everyone likes, so when the rare person doesn't like him, that bothers him, too."

Stark said it's interesting traveling with Thompson, "in seeing all the people who are yelling at him, waving and walking up to shake hands and say hello. And I'm talking about from some of the biggest celebrities in the sports world to average Joes walking down the street. He takes time for everybody. If you become friends with him, you're his friend regardless of what your personal circumstances are, and he doesn't forget you. That's one of the things I like best about him.

"If there was ever somebody you'd point to as being the kind of person you'd want your kids to grow up like, it'd be Gary Thompson."

So, that's the Gary Thompson story, about as All-American a tale as could ever be told. And that's the true measure of the man.

Epilogue:
A few words from Gary Thompson

"Janet's the director behind the scenes..."

ANYONE involved in athletics, be it coaching, playing, administration or broadcasting, is well aware of the tremendous demands on your time, and the time spent away from home. It takes an understanding, super spouse to be part of that life.

Janet has been a tremendous wife, mother and grandmother. She has sacrificed in many ways because of my involvement in athletics and broadcasting.

She probably has sat on more basketball and baseball bleachers watching me play than anyone I know. She has spent a lot of nights at home alone because of my heavy travel. So many times, it would happen that we would be invited to some party or event that she really wanted to attend, but I was scheduled to be out of town. I would encourage her to go without me—she did a few times—but she never felt comfortable not going as a couple.

She had the big responsibility when the kids were young of really being both mom and dad, because in my playing years with the Phillips 66ers, we were on the road a lot. Jan had to get the kids to school and all their activities. It would have been easy for her to sleep in on a Sunday, but she always had the kids up and dressed for Sunday School and then to church with her.

I am proud of our family, but Jan deserves all the credit for the sacrifices she made to bring up our family in the Christian way. The early years are so important in the children's development, and she was terrific with them then.

She allowed me to be involved in athletics—something I really enjoyed—and it made my life rewarding. If you related our lives to the broadcasting business, you would say I was out front before the camera, and she was the director behind the scenes.

We all know the director is the most important person to the broadcast. Janet has been the most important person to me and our family, and I love her for it.

—*Gary Thompson*

THE BOX SCORE ON

Gary Thompson

ROLAND HIGH SCHOOL (1949-'53)

Basketball

First team All-State three years

Iowa high school single season scoring record: 837 points

Iowa high school career scoring record: 2,043 points

First Iowa high school player to score 2000 points in career

Scoring average 13 points per game as a sophomore, 21.3 ppg game as a junior, 24.6 ppg as a senior

High school team record: 127-8 (5 losses in the state tournaments)

All-Tournament team at state three consecutive years

National High School All-Star Game, Murray, Kentucky, 1953

Jersey No. 24 retired, only Roland athlete so honored

Baseball

Pitched 6 career no-hitters

Lost only three games as pitcher in his last two years, all three in the state tournaments

Pitching records of 4-0 and 7-2 in his sophomore fall and spring seasons, lost only one game in the two seasons of his junior year (records lost), and was 8-1 and 8-1 in his senior seasons

In fall of senior year, pitched 58 innings and had 108 strikeouts, in spring of that year pitched 64 innings and had 134 strikeouts

Career batting average over .450

In his last three seasons, team was 51-7 playing in fall and spring seasons, qualifying for the state tournament four of the six seasons, runners-up in spring 1952 season

Horseshoe

Iowa State Junior Horseshoe Pitching Tournament champion, 1951 & '52 (undefeated each year)

IOWA STATE UNIVERSITY (1953-'57)

Basketball

Associated Press 1st Team All-American, 1957

Look Magazine 1st Team All-American, 1957

MVP of East vs. West College All-Star Game in Kansas City, 1957

Big Seven Conference basketball player of the year, 1957

Big Seven Conference, 1st team All-Conference, 1956 & '57

1st Iowa State player to score over 1,000 career points (1,253)

1st Iowa State player to score 40 points in a game

Scoring average 16.14 points per game as a sophomore, 18.78 ppg game as a junior, 21.14 ppg as a senior

On championship team, Big Seven Conference Holiday tournament, 1955

Iowa State Athlete of the Year, 1956 & '57, first Cyclone to be so honored two consecutive years

Jersey No. 20 retired, first Iowa State basketball player so honored

5th round draft choice of Minneapolis Lakers of NBA, 1957

Baseball

3rd team All-American, shortstop, 1957, becoming Iowa State's 1st two-sport All-American

Helped Iowa State to first appearance in the College Word Series, 1957

Helped team win Big Seven Conference championship, 1957

First Cyclone to start three consecutive seasons at shortstop

Senior year, hit .311 with four home runs, 18 RBI in 27 games

Four Major League Baseball teams offered contracts to Thompson in 1957: Chicago Cubs, New York Yankees, Chicago White Sox, Cleveland Indians

Phillips 66ers playing career (1957-'62)

Amateur Athletic Union (AAU) All-American, 1958, '59 & '62

MVP National AAU Championship game, 1962

On USA Pan American Championship team, 1959 in Chicago

On USA All-Stars team, World Championship Series, 1961 in Manila, Philippines

On USA All-Stars team, touring Soviet Union, 1961

Sixth in career scoring all-time for Phillips 66ers (2,348 points in five seasons)

Head coach, Phillips 66ers (1964-'68)

Four-year record, 159-36 (winning percentage: 81)

Coach, USA World Championship Team, 1963 in Santiago, Chile

Golf

State Senior Champion, 1997

City Champion in Ames, Iowa, three times in three different decades

Club Champion at Ames Golf & Country Club, also three times in three different decades

Champion in amateur tournaments in Jefferson, Jewell and Garner, all in Iowa

Halls of Fame & special honors

Helms Foundation Hall of Fame

National High School Hall of Fame, National Federation of State High School Associations

Iowa Sports Hall of Fame, Des Moines Register

Iowa High School Basketball Hall of Fame

Iowa State University Letterwinners Hall of Fame

NCAA "Silver Anniversary Team," 1982, for career accomplishments after an All-American playing career

Included on "Iowa Walk of Fame," in business district sidewalks in Shenandoah

Inducted into the Iowa Broadcasters Association Hall of Fame for his long career as a basketball game analyst on TV and radio

Honored with life-size bronze statue of him as a basketball player, Iowa Hall of Pride, Des Moines

Named to Iowa State men's basketball "All-Century Team" during the 100th anniversary celebration of the program, 2007-'08

One of "150 people who shaped Iowa State" by the ISU Alumni Association magazine "Visions" during the university's sesquicentennial celebration, 2007-'08

CHUCK OFFENBURGER, the author of "GARY THOMPSON: All-American," is an Iowa writer who has been covering the state for 45 years. After 21 years as a Des Moines Register columnist, he now writes from "Simple Serenity Farm" near Cooper in west central Iowa, where he and his wife Carla operate the Internet news & opinion site *www.Offenburger.com.* Chuck is also a columnist for the Iowa Farm Bureau Federation's "Family Living" feature magazine, and a frequent commentator for KMA Radio in his hometown of Shenandoah, Iowa. The Offenburgers have both taught at several Iowa colleges and universities, and are leading advocates for economic development, recreation trail development and tourism in the state. They're major sports fans, too.

MARK MARTURELLO, who designed the cover of this book, is an artist and graphic designer for the Des Moines Register, where he and Chuck Offenburger became friends and colleagues. Marturello, who took his art and design training at Grand View College in his hometown of Des Moines, joined the Register in 1988 and today is recognized as one of the top newsroom artists working in the U.S. His interest in the Gary Thompson story comes partially because he's long been a fan of college basketball, growing up cheering for the Iowa Hawkeyes, later the Kentucky Wildcats and later yet the Iowa State Cyclones.

ROY J. REIMAN, the book's editor: A close friend of Gary Thompson's since they were classmates at Iowa State, Roy grew up on a rented farm near Auburn, Iowa. After graduating in Agricultural Journalism and spending some time in the military, he became Managing Editor of *Capper's Farmer* in Topeka, Kansas. (Best part of that job, he says, is that's where he met his wife, Bobbi.) He moved to Milwaukee where he eventually started Reiman Publications in the basement of his home. It grew to 14 national magazines, 16-million paid subscribers and 640 employees. After selling the company, he "totally flunked retirement" and launched *Our Iowa* magazine for his home state.

MARIBETH FLEISCHMANN, the book's designer: An Army brat who moved 18 times in her lifetime, Maribeth married her high school sweetheart 14 years ago and has a 7-year-old daughter. She graduated with a Bachelor of Fine Arts degree from Texas State and moved back to Wisconsin to be near family. She is currently a Communication Design Instructor for Milwaukee Institute of Art and Design, and does a variety freelance graphic design from her home, including regular work on *Our Iowa* magazine.